"**Grimya!**" Her mind was floundering and she called the wolf's name aloud, groping for a spar of coherence in the heaving sea that her consciousness had become.

Grimya's mental voice seemed to come from a vast distance. *I can't reach you! They are holding me back! Indigo—*

B__ __ __ __ __ __ __ wolf's __ __ __ __ cut off as though a s__ __ __ __ __ __ he__ __ __ mo__ __ __

Tor books by Louise Cooper

Mirage

INDIGO

THE TIME MASTER TRILOGY

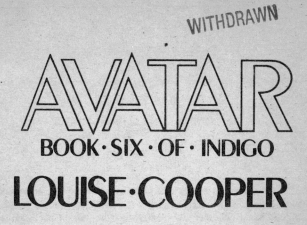

AVATAR

BOOK · SIX · OF · INDIGO

LOUISE · COOPER

TOR
fantasy

A TOM DOHERTY ASSOCIATES BOOK
NEW YORK

This is a work of fiction. All the characters and events portrayed in this book are fictitious, and any resemblance to real people or events is purely coincidental.

AVATAR

A Tor Book
Published by Tom Doherty Associates, Inc.
49 West 24th Street
New York, N.Y. 10010

Cover art by Gary Ruddell

ISBN: 0-812-50802-5

First edition: January 1992

Printed in the United States of America

0 9 8 7 6 5 4 3 2 1

Let them hate, so long as they fear.

—*Lucius Accius, 170–90* BC

For Tim and Dot Oakes
One of these days we *will* have that jam. . . .

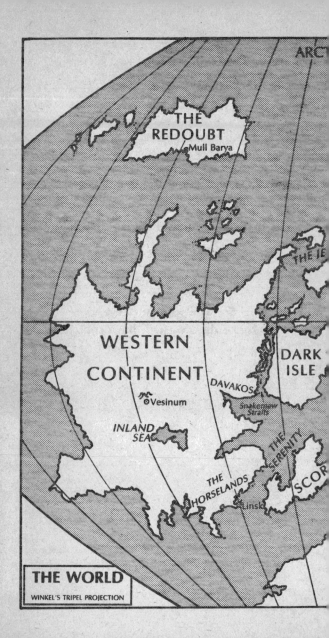

ARCT

THE
REDOUBT
Mull Barya

THE IE

WESTERN

CONTINENT
DAVAKOS

DARK
ISLE

Vesinum

Snakemaw
Straits

INLAND
SEA

THE
SERENITY

THE
HORSELANDS

Linsk

SCOR

THE WORLD
WINKEL'S TRIPEL PROJECTION

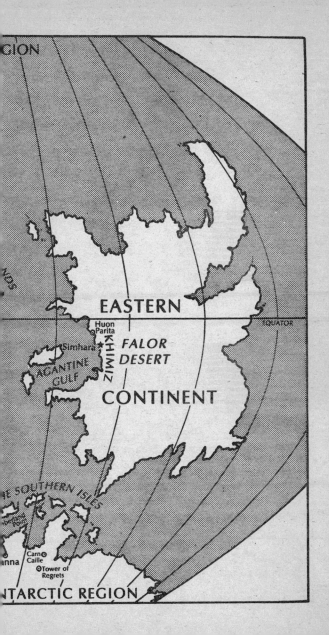

GION

EASTERN

Huon
Parita

Simhara

AGANTINE
GULF

KHIMIZ

FALOR
DESERT

CONTINENT

EQUATOR

SON

E SOUTHERN ISLES

etland
oint

anna

Carn
Caille

Tower of
Regrets

NTARCTIC REGION

·PROLOGUE·

Now, on the rare occasions when she looks in a mirror, she asks herself: *how long has it been?* And the answer sends a shiver through her marrow.

For almost half a century she has roamed the earth, and in all those long years she has aged not one day, since the moment when she left her homeland, far in the south, to begin a journey that, seemingly, has no end. She cannot die, she is immortal; and her name might by now have become a legend, but for the fact that in her fifty summers of wandering, she has taken care that the trappings of fame, or notoriety, or even simple knowledge, should not attach themselves to her. She has good reason to ensure that no one should know the name she was given at her birth, long ago and far away in her father's home at Carn Caille. And the name she uses now—Indigo, which is also the color of mourning in her homeland—is one she hopes that those she meets upon her long road will forget in good time.

Half a century ago, she was a princess. Half a century ago, wild curiosity got the better of her and she broke a taboo that her people had upheld since time immemorial.

Seven evils, pent for centuries past in an ancient and crumbling tower long shunned by mankind. Seven evils, released upon the world by her hand, to wreak havoc. Seven evils, which she alone must find and conquer and destroy, if she—and the world—are ever to know peace again.

Indigo's travels have taken her to strange countries and led her into stranger adventures. She has seen the burning heartlands, where smoke blackens the sky at noon and the thunder of volcanoes shakes the land's very foundations. She has lived among the shimmering, dreamlike palaces of Simhara, fabled city of the East, where Death wore a deceiver's mask. She has danced and sung with the traveling players of Bruhome, where she learned the true meaning of illusion. And she has turned her face to the freezing snows of the polar north, and heard the ominous voice of the Snow Tiger that promised joy and grief in equal measure. She has made dear friends and bitter enemies, she has seen the beginnings and the ends of many other lives; and now four evils, four demons, have been destroyed by her hand. But the price has often been a cruel one, and though from time to time she has rested from her wanderings, she knows that her quest is by no means ended.

For a few years she has known a kind of peace. From the icy northern wastes she traveled south when spring opened the sea-lanes, and in the cheerful, sprawling ports of Davakos, famed for its ships and mariners, she returned to the seagoing ways of her own people, and for a while found something akin to happiness. Now, though, the hiatus is over and she must move on. The lodestone that has guided her in her wanderings is alive again, and this time it is urging her eastward to the Dark Isle, whose peoples and ways are shadowed in mystery. Another demon awaits her; another battle must be joined.

Yet Indigo will not face this newest battle alone. Throughout the years, one friend has remained constantly by her side; a friend who has chosen to share her immortality, and whose loyalty and love have become a touchstone in Indigo's life. The mutant she-wolf Grimya has also known what it is to be an outcast among her own kind, and the bond that has formed between them is one that no power could ever break.

Now Indigo and Grimya have made their last farewells to Davakos, and to the ship that carried them to the Dark Isle's hostile and sweatingly humid shores. Ahead lies an unknown country, with unknown dangers, and they know that at the end of their road, they must face another mystery. They have learned that it is wiser not to speculate about the nature of each new trial. But as the long trek begins, through strange forests and among alien creatures, perhaps they cannot help but wonder, despite their resolution, what their future may hold this time. . . .

·CHAPTER·I·

From the heart of the forest something vast, invisible and decaying exhaled a huge breath. The air shifted, stirring leaves on the branches of the overcrowded trees, lifting dust in sluggish eddies; and a sweet-sick stench of earth and rotting vegetation and mortifying flesh filled the she-wolf Grimya's nostrils as she raised her head, alerted to the sudden change in the atmosphere.

Her long, lean body quivered and the brindled fur along her spine rose, bristling. A growl formed in her throat but died before she could voice it. The rising of the wind presaged rain; she could feel it as surely as she felt the ground under her feet, and she didn't like the omen. By the time the sun touched the treetops, this road would be a river, yet still there was no sign of anyone who might help her.

She turned and looked back along the empty track. The trees crowded in like predators, their branches tangling overhead to form a dank, gloomy tunnel. Only a few stray shafts of sunlight broke through here and there, creating distorted shadows, and the heat under the claustrophobic green blanket was becoming insufferable. Even the background racket of the jungle, which had been beating against her ears in an incessant, inescapable and nerve-racking assault, had ceased utterly: not so much as a bird's cackle broke the oppressive silence.

She couldn't stay here, Grimya thought. Not like this, not with the rainstorm coming. She had to go on. And however hard it might be, whatever persuasions or threats she had to use, she must make her companion go with her.

She turned onto the track once again. No matter how great the urgency, she couldn't run; her body and her instincts rebelled against the rank, suffocating heat and it took all the strength she could muster to plod wearily back to where the track was crossed by a lesser path through the jungle. Here the bushes encroached onto the rough road to provide some cover, if not shelter, and Grimya had hoped that someone might pass by, a logger perhaps, or even an ox-cart bound for one of the outpost settlements in the forest's depths. But the hope had been futile and now she dared not wait any longer.

Indigo was sitting in the midst of the three bags that were the sum total of their belongings. Her shoulders were slumped and her head hanging so that her long, gray-streaked auburn hair obscured her face like a damp curtain; her thin shirt and loose trousers were dark with sweat. Even from a distance, Grimya could see her shoulders heaving convulsively as she breathed, and drawing nearer, she heard the stertorous rattling of air in her friend's throat.

"In-digo!" Grimya's voice broke the stillness harshly. With only the animals and birds of the forest to hear her, she made no attempt to hide her peculiar ability to speak in human tongues, and she ran forward to lick Indigo's hands where they lay passively in her lap. "In-digo, we c . . . can't stay here any longer. There's a rr-*ainstorm* coming. We must find shelter!"

Indigo looked up. Her eyes were red-rimmed and a film of sweat gave her face's pallor a disturbingly unnatural sheen. For a moment she stared at Grimya as though she

were regarding a stranger; then a glimmer of dull comprehension struggled to the surface.

"I feel . . ." She stopped, tried to wipe her mouth, but
seemed unable to coordinate her hand movements and abandoned the attempt. "I feel so *sick*."

Pity swelled Grimya's heart, but fear was stronger. "Indigo, we *must* move on! There is dan-ger here." She looked
quickly along the track in both directions, licking her chops
nervously. "We dare not stay and hope that someone will
come. It is too grrr-eat a risk. Please, In-digo. *Please*."

"My head . . ." Indigo bit her lip and shut her eyes as
an injudicious movement made her wince. "It *hurts* so. I
can't make the pain stop, I can't make it go away . . ."

"But—"

"No." She spoke the word through clenched teeth, so that
it came out as little more than a painful grunt. "No, I—I
understand. We have to go on. Yes. I'll be all right. If I can
just . . ." she started to paw feebly at her baggage ". . . just
gather these. I won't leave them."

Slowly she unfolded her body from its cramped posture,
moving like an arthritic crone. Grimya watched anxiously,
frustrated by her inability to help as Indigo awkwardly
pulled together the three bags and gathered them onto her
back. At last they were in place. Indigo tried to stand up,
staggered, and caught at a low-hanging branch to steady
herself.

"No," she said again before Grimya could speak. "I can
walk. I *can*." Cautiously she released the branch and took
two unsteady paces to the track. Her face and neck flushed
crimson, and sweat broke out anew on her brow, dripping
down into her eyes. "I m-might have to stop. In a while.
If . . ." She shook her head as her tongue refused to obey
and allow her to finish the sentence. For perhaps half a
minute she stood swaying a little; then she blinked and drew
a gulping breath. "The birds," she whispered. "They're
not calling anymore."

"They know what is coming."

Indigo nodded. "Yes. They know, don't they? Shelter. Must find . . . find shelter."

For one awful moment Grimya thought Indigo would collapse where she stood and be unable to rise again, but with a great effort, Indigo got a grip on her reeling senses and started forward. At that same moment, through the deep and long-established telepathic link that they shared, the wolf felt something of the fever burning in her companion's mind, and an involuntary shudder racked her as she realized that the imminent storm was by no means the worst of the dangers that faced them now.

She swallowed back a whine of misery, paused briefly to glance up at the darkening canopy of leaves above their heads, then set off in Indigo's wake.

The storm came with the fall of the swift tropical twilight. The first bolt of lightning lit the forest in a silent, jagged flash, and from deep among the trees something shrieked like a murdered woman in frightened response. There was no thunder and, at first, no rain, but the heat and humidity pressed down harder and the earth below exhaled another great breath of putrefaction. As a second livid spear burst the dusk apart, Grimya looked worriedly over her shoulder to where Indigo stumbled two paces behind her. Indigo seemed oblivious to the lightning; her eyes were open but wide and febrile, as if she were looking into an imaginary nightmare world of her mind's own making, and her lips moved as she murmured to herself. The wolf paused, waiting for her to catch up; then her heart contracted as she heard the first hissing—like a thousand angry snakes—high up in the leaf canopy above their heads. Seconds later, the rain began.

It wasn't like the kindly summer rains of her own homeland far away in another continent and another era. Nor even like the great deluges that swept her native forests in the spring of each year to herald the reawakening of life. This rain didn't carry life, but death. A cataract, a cataclysm, pouring from the sky in a savage torrent that battered the trees and scoured the earth and turned the world to a sweltering, drowning hell from which there was no escape and no relief. This rain was *evil*. Grimya hunched her shoulders against the stinking downpour, looked through her streaming eyes at the swaying, staggering figure behind her and knew that Indigo wouldn't be capable of standing up to the onslaught.

"Indigo!" She cried out as loudly as she could, but the increasing roar of the deluge swept her voice away, and when she tried to reach Indigo by telepathy, she met a hot, blazing wall of fever and sickness that reason couldn't penetrate. Indigo was shuddering as the water poured down on her, her hair was plastered over her skull and shoulders, and she had lost all sense of direction. Already the first rivulets were beginning to race along the sides of the track, spreading out over ground too parched to absorb them. Within a matter of minutes the road would be awash, and though Grimya might escape the water easily enough, Indigo hadn't the energy or, in her fevered state, the wit to find shelter.

Grimya caught hold of the hem of Indigo's shirt and pulled with all her strength. The fabric tore; Indigo spun about, swaying, and staggered toward the undergrowth. More lightning ripped across the heavens, and a titanic crack as the bolt struck the forest made Grimya yelp and leap back in fright. She heard a roar somewhere in the distance as a tree ignited, and then the searing noise of fire and water meeting and joining battle. The forest was alive with flickering, deadly light, branches bending and tossing as though the trees were struggling to tear up their roots and escape.

"Indigo!" the wolf cried again, frantic now. "Indigo, *this* way! *Come on*!" She ran after the stumbling, uncoordinated figure, and this time she was able to get a grip on one strap of Indigo's pack. Teetering on her hind legs, almost overbalancing, she managed to steer her friend back onto the trail and for a few moments almost believed that it would be all right, that Indigo would pull herself together and find the strength to continue. But the hope was short-lived. An-

other lightning flash blasted through the forest, and as its glare hurled Indigo's face into ghastly relief, Grimya saw her eyes roll up in their sockets. The wolf projected a frantic appeal, but Indigo swayed helplessly, keeled forward and fell face-first to the ground. For a few seconds she lay motionless. Then she tried to struggle up, supporting herself on her hands—and doubled over again, vomiting a thin stream of bile and blood.

Panic clutched at Grimya as she realized that Indigo had reached the limit of her endurance. The wolf hadn't the strength to drag her friend to shelter, and she raced around her in a circle, whining and yelping and nosing at her. Indigo, though, was no longer capable of responding; she huddled on the ground, her hands clenching and unclenching spasmodically, an ugly moaning vibrating in her throat.

At length Grimya stopped circling and stared desperately through the rain at the track ahead. She didn't want to leave Indigo's side, but she would do nothing to help her, and every moment spent fruitlessly here would only make matters worse. She needed human aid. She *had* to find someone.

She turned back to Indigo, wanting to explain her reasoning and say that she intended to run for help, but realized at once that any explanation would be meaningless. Whimpering, she swung about and broke into a weary, stiff-legged run, splashing through water that was now becoming a steady and deepening stream, racing, with the little energy she could still muster, away down the path. As she ran, she prayed silently to the great Earth Mother to take pity and help her—to let her meet a hunter or a logger, to let her find a safe shelter, anything, *anything* that would bring succor to Indigo. . . .

Turning a bend in the track, she saw the *kemb*, and she slithered to a halt with a shocked yelp.

For some moments she hardly dared to believe what her eyes told her. The *kemb*—it was one of the few words of the local language she'd so far picked up—was a single-storied, wooden, cabinlike structure, rattan-thatched and built on short but sturdy poles that held it clear of the ground and out of reach of water and snakes. A covered veranda ran the length of its frontage, with wooden steps leading up. From inside, discernible to Grimya's nose even through the stinks of the hot and sodden forest, came the mingled smells of wood smoke and cooking food and human sweat.

The Earth Mother had answered her! Grimya raced for the steps and scrabbled up the short flight, yelping and barking. Startled voices were raised inside the *kemb*, something clattered noisily; then a stocky, swarthy man appeared at the half-open door, with a dumpy woman behind him. His eyes widened as he saw the shuddering, soaking wolf and he uttered a stream of words that sounded angry and frightened together, flapping his arms wildly.

Grimya cringed back, whining, then scrabbled about and barked toward the forest before turning again to fix him with a look of desperate appeal. He frowned, hesitated—the woman said something, shaking her head—and Grimya, bristling with the frustration of being unable to communicate more clearly, tried again to convey what she wanted. Something must have struck a chord, for after a swift exchange of words with the woman, the man called back into the *kemb* and another, younger man emerged. Cautiously they approached Grimya, not coming too close but speaking to her in interrogative tones. She wagged her tail, her tongue lolling; then she ran down the steps, looked back at them and barked urgently.

Both men immediately disappeared inside the cabin and the wolf feared that they hadn't understood. Moments later, however, they reemerged, the younger man carrying a heavy stave and the elder armed with a machete, and both hastened down the steps to join her. Grimya jumped up gratefully to lick the young man's hand—she kept clear of the other's knife, lest her gesture should be misinterpreted—and then set off at a run along the trail. She heard the men volubly cursing the storm, but it seemed they were inured to such conditions, for they followed her swiftly and surefootedly.

At last Grimya saw Indigo's huddled, motionless figure ahead. She was lying on her side now, rivulets of water streaming all around her, and at first, Grimya saw, the men thought she must be dead. They bent over her; then she stirred and her eyelids flickered, opening to reveal a blood-shot, unseeing stare.

The older man uttered a sharp imperative before turning to the wolf, making a placating gesture as he spoke to her slowly and soothingly. The younger man lifted Indigo bodily, heaving her over his shoulder, baggage and all. Then, staggering a little under his burden, he turned about and began to plod back toward the *kemb*.

If anxiety hadn't eclipsed all other considerations, Grimya might have thought that they made a strange procession as the *kemb* came in sight. Certainly their arrival drew attention; the dumpy woman was standing on the veranda, watching for them through the rain, and by the time they reached the steps, she had been joined by several others, all of them talking and exclaiming in astonished voices. Grimya saw another young man, a toothless grand-dame, two young women and a scattering of children among their number. They surrounded her, patting, pulling her across the veranda and in through the rattan door, where she was engulfed by curious hands and faces while her rescuers bore Indigo away. Someone was try-ing to wrap her in a large cloth that stank of wood ash and rancid fat. Grimya struggled, wanting only to follow the men who were taking Indigo away, but there were too many anxious faces and restraining arms and she suddenly felt too exhausted to resist. She began to tremble; then abruptly her legs gave way and she sprawled like a newborn cub. Two of the women made cooing, pitying noises, and a bowl of brackish water was pushed under her nose. She didn't want it but she made herself lap a little so as not to seem ungrateful, while her ministrants clapped their hands in approval.

Then one of the young women knelt beside her and began to dry her fur with the rancid-smelling cloth. Grimya whined, her nostrils flaring as she searched for Indigo's scent. She tried to get to her feet; with a soft laugh, the young woman pushed her down again, and a small child, bolder than its siblings, reached out from the press of faces and bodies to stroke her nose. Grimya didn't have the strength left in her to protest, and she couldn't tell them that her only concern was for her friend, so the whine died to a whimper and then into silence. She was so tired. Her eyelids drooped; the touch of the child's hand was comforting, and others, losing their initial fear, were also reaching out to stroke her while the young woman murmured reassuringly.

Surely, Grimya thought, Indigo would be safe now. These people were generous and kind, they had helped her in her time of need. There was nothing to fear. The Earth Mother had answered her prayers.

Exhausted, and yet comforted, Grimya slept.

When she awoke, the rain had stopped. With its cessation an eerie quiet had descended; outside, the creatures cowed by the storm hadn't yet found the courage to start up their clamor again, and even the small night sounds of the forest were absent. Moonlight filtered thinly down through the leaf canopy and in at the windows, pooling in dim patches on the *kemb*'s floor, and from above her head, Grimya heard furtive rustlings amid the dull drip of water as insects stirred in the sodden thatch.

She got to her feet. The woman had laid her on a rough blanket and had left a dish of meat nearby; hunger gnawed at the wolf's stomach and she couldn't resist snatching a few mouthfuls before she began to explore her unfamiliar surroundings.

This place, it seemed, was a trading house. Since beginning their long trek into the interior of the Dark Isle, she and Indigo had come upon a number of such stations, which provided a vital service for travelers and local tribes and clans alike. Most of them were owned and run by several generations of a single family, for whom the *kemb* was both workplace and communal home, and the large room in which Grimya had slept was, it seemed, the main store. Sacks and crates of provisions were stacked around the walls, baffling the wolf's sensitive nose with a confusion of unfamiliar smells, while jumbled among the assortment was a range of implements, from cooking pots to weapons, essential to life in the forest. In one corner stood an open-topped stove blackened with years of use; this, Grimya surmised, was where her hosts cooked their meals. But where were the other rooms, the private chambers? Where was Indigo?

She put her nose to the floor and started to cast about, but it was impossible to isolate any one scent from the plethora of smells. Nor could her telepathic senses pick up any sense of Indigo's consciousness. Once she thought she detected what might have been the faint trace of a dreaming mind, but it vanished before she could be sure, and with an unhappy whine, the wolf gave up the attempt and resigned herself to finding her friend by other means.

She padded across the floor to the back of the room. Here, in the darkness where the moonlight couldn't reach, she found two doors. One was barred on the far side, but the other shuddered open when she pushed at it with her muzzle, and Grimya slipped through to find herself in a narrow passage that separated the store from another and more private part of the *kemb*. Dim light from a small window at the passage's far end revealed three more doorways, each covered by a curtain, and Grimya moved eagerly to investigate them in turn.

The first and second rooms were dark, but a sense of warmth, the faint sounds of breathing and the unfamiliar human scents told Grimya that they were both occupied, though there was no hint of Indigo's presence. As she pushed her nose through the curtain of the third room, however, Grimya was confronted by the comparatively brilliant light of a small bowl lamp, and behind the lamp a figure rose quickly from its place beside a low bed frame. Thinking it was Indigo, Grimya started forward eagerly, her tail wagging; then the figure flapped its hands urgently at her and hissed anxiously in an unfamiliar voice, and she recognized the young woman who had dried her and ministered to her when they first arrived at the *kemb*. Grimya looked up hopefully, but the woman reached down to grasp the fur at the nape of her neck and tried to push her back out of the room. Though she didn't understand her speech, the wolf sensed agitation in her mind. Then, as the woman moved around to get a better grip on her scruff, Grimya saw Indigo's still figure lying on the bed.

No! Please, let me go to her! Grimya made the telepathic plea instinctively before remembering that she couldn't communicate, that even if she were to speak aloud, the woman wouldn't understand her. She whimpered, resisting, her claws scrabbling on the bare floor, and her head ducked from side to side, craning to see her friend. The woman's tone softened and became sympathetic. She was trying to cajole and explain something at the same time, and she slackened her grip on Grimya long enough to gesture toward the bed and make soothing motions with a flattened palm. Then she put a finger to her lips and pantomimed someone sleeping.

Grimya relented, aware that the woman was only doing what she thought best for Indigo and that she didn't want her to be disturbed. Head and tail drooping now, the wolf allowed herself to be backed out of the room. She sat down dejectedly in the passage, staring at the curtain that had fallen back into place, blocking any view through the door. If only she could make them understand that she merely wanted to sit by Indigo's bed, that she wasn't just a foolish dog and that she knew better than to jump up and lick and whine and make a fuss. She simply wanted—needed—to know how her friend fared and if the fever had left her.

There were sounds from the far side of the curtain, and to Grimya's surprise, the young woman emerged a few seconds later. She shook the creases of long sitting out of her skirt, pressed the heels of her hands into her back as if to ease stiffness, then moved away along the passage, snapping her fingers to the wolf and uttering an encouraging chirrup as she went.

Grimya padded after her, and in the storeroom the woman set about lighting more lamps and riddling ash from the stove. The patterns of silver-gray light had vanished from the room as the moon set, and outside, the forest was beginning to stir with the approach of dawn. The *kemb*'s other inhabitants would be up and about soon, Grimya surmised, and perhaps once the family had set about its business of the day, she would be able to slip away and go to Indigo. Comforted by that thought, she settled back on her makeshift bed and watched the young woman as she went about her work.

Light began to creep into the *kemb*, pushing back the shadows; a few minutes later other human sounds began to impinge on the quiet, and first the young man, then the older woman, then the girl-children came yawning into the room. There was some whispered discussion between the two women, with much muttering and sighing from the elder, but Grimya didn't comprehend the subject of their conversation until the old woman poured something she'd been stirring on the stove into a wooden bowl and the two of them went back through the door toward the inner rooms. A few minutes passed but they didn't return, and suddenly a disquieting intuition made the hairs along Grimya's spine prickle.

The man and the children weren't watching her, so she rose to her feet and slipped out into the passage. Light glimmered under the curtain of the third room, and as she approached, she heard muted, anxious voices and caught the whiff of a pungent herbal smell.

Grimya's intuition swelled into fear and she ran to the curtain and pushed through. The women turned, startled, and for a moment their thoughts and emotions showed nakedly on their faces and confirmed the thing she had dreaded most. They were employing all of their skills, but so far, to no avail. Indigo showed not the smallest sign of improvement . . . and the women were coming close to despair.

·CHAPTER·II·

All the women of the *kemb* tried with signs and gentle
words to reassure Grimya, but the wolf refused to be comforted and at last, relenting, they allowed her to take up a
vigil at Indigo's bedside. She stayed there throughout the
sweltering day, constantly watching her friend's flushed and
feverish face, occasionally reaching out to lick tentatively
at one of her burning hands.

For most of the time, Indigo was unconscious, but now
and again she would stir and her eyes flicker open, staring
with unfocused intensity at the ceiling for a few moments
before she began to thrash and cry out in delirium. Grimya
had never experienced anything like these bouts, and the
wild thoughts that came surging from Indigo's subconscious
like a fire running out of control terrified the wolf. She
would rush to the doorway, barking frantically; someone
would come running, Indigo's face and torso would be
bathed and another herbal nostrum forced between her
clenched teeth. For a while then she'd quieten, but only for
a while before the whole ugly cycle began again.

The women were doing all they could, but by evening it

was obvious to everyone in the *kemb* that Indigo wasn't responding to their treatment. Her fever was worse, the intervals between bouts of delirium growing shorter, and the women's limited healing skills were exhausted. Grimya finally understood that they had given up hope of curing her by normal means when, as night descended on the forest, all the adult females of the family came back into the shuttered and stifling room and gathered around the bed. They lit stubby candles that gave off thick smoke and a smell that made Grimya bare her teeth uneasily, and they began to repeat a peculiar, off-key chant while the old grand-dame shook a carved and tasseled stick over Indigo's head.

Prayers, or spells . . . they had accepted defeat and were trying to help the sick woman by the last resort of an appeal to magic, or to whatever gods or powers they worshiped. Grimya shivered as the monotonous chanting continued. Then, at last, unable to bear it any longer, she slunk away through the curtain to the passage outside, where she lay down with her muzzle on her front paws in abject and helpless misery.

The women continued their vigil until dawn. Sometimes the chanting stopped for a short while and Grimya would raise her head in a mixture of alarm and hope; but then the droning voices picked up the threads once more and the nightmarish ritual went on. Alone in the passage with nothing but her own thoughts for company, Grimya wondered over and again what was to become of Indigo. She believed that the women expected her companion to die, and she couldn't convey the truth to them: that Indigo couldn't die, but was destined to live, as she had done for almost fifty years, without aging and without the threat—or the promise—of death.

Yet though her fate might have made her immortal, it wasn't proof against sickness and disease, and Grimya didn't know what might befall her friend if the fever refused to loose its hold. Would she be trapped in some kind of limbo, reduced to a helpless shell, yet still clinging to physical life? Would her

mind be affected, her body ravaged beyond recovery? Grimya
didn't know the answers, and her speculations frightened her.

She dozed occasionally as the night crawled on, but always there were ugly dreams waiting to pounce and jolt her
shuddering out of her sleep. At last, though, she saw the
first hint of dawn begin to lighten the narrow window at the
end of the passage, and as she stood up, raising her muzzle
to sniff the change in the air, the curtain over Indigo's door
shifted and the women came out. They glanced at the wolf
but said nothing and moved away toward the main room.
Only the young woman who had first befriended Grimya,
and who emerged last of all, paused and looked down.

"*Ussh!*" She put a finger to her lips, then crouched to
stroke Grimya's head, speaking to her in a low, calm, but
sorrowful voice. Grimya was slowly coming to understand
a few snippets of the native language. She knew the words
for *no*, for *quiet* and for *sleep*, and could glean meaning
from a voice's inflection, and she surmised that the woman
was trying to say that Indigo was sleeping and there was no
more to be done for the present. The wolf licked her hand—
it was the only way she knew to show her gratitude for the
family's kindness and persistence—then looked hopefully
toward the doorway and whined an interrogative. The
woman smiled, though sadly, and nodded, lifting the curtain back so that Grimya could enter.

Grimya could hear Indigo's saw-edged breathing as she
approached the bed. She probed tentatively for any sign of
recognition, or even life, from her friend's mind, but there
was nothing. Indigo was deeply unconscious, and clearly
very ill. The flush on her face had flared into two patches
of high, hectic color on her cheeks, her skin was lined and
papery, and her eyes had sunk deep in their sockets, giving
her a chillingly corpselike look. For a long time Grimya
stared at her, her own amber eyes filled with misery. Then,
railing at herself because she knew she must accept that
there was nothing she could do to help Indigo, or even to
communicate with her and try to bring comfort, she lay

down at the foot of the low bed frame to take up the vigil
that the women had abandoned.

That morning seemed endless to Grimya. The sounds of
human activity filtered through the *kemb*'s thin walls from
the storeroom, mingling with the soporific background hum
of the jungle that surrounded the outpost like a soft blanket.
One of the children brought a dish of food and a bowl of
water, but though she drank a little, the wolf had no appetite
and the meat remained untouched.

Indigo was muttering in her unnatural sleep, turning from
side to side as though trying to escape from the private hell
of her fever. Twice she screamed out in the tongue of her
old homeland, calling to her father and mother and brother,
who had been dead for more than half a century, and calling, too, the name of Imyssa, her old nurse. The young
woman came in at the sound of her cries and succeeded in
calming her, but when she was gone, Indigo began to weep
in long, racking, mindless sobs, and her dry lips and swollen tongue whispered another name that Grimya knew all
too well. *Fenran.* The lover Indigo had lost, the man whose
soul and body were held in a world between worlds, and
whom she dreamed of freeing.

The wolf closed her eyes and turned her head away when
the whisper shivered through the stifling room, feeling that
she was intruding on a place where she had no right to
venture, and her tongue lapped at the simmering air as she
tried to cool herself a little and think of other things.

Grimya couldn't judge the hours in this alien latitude, but
she thought that it must be nearing noon when she heard
the clamor of new arrivals at the *kemb*. The sounds of feet
clattering on the wooden steps alerted her; then came exclamations, hastily muted, and new voices—three, perhaps
four—in the storeroom. Grimya raised her head, ears pricking forward to catch the nuances of the unfamiliar sounds.
She had the distinct impression that the newcomers were
people of some importance, for the *kemb* family sounded
deferential and it seemed that some kind of interrogation

was taking place. Then the door at the end of the passage opened with a sharp jerk and four strange women appeared.

Grimya instantly sprang to her feet, goaded by two separate but violent instincts that slammed simultaneously into her mind. These were strangers, an unknown quantity, and therefore potential enemies. And at the same moment, her acute psychic senses had registered an emphatic sense of power.

The group's leader saw Grimya and held up a hand, halting the small procession. She was a woman of middle years, mahogany-skinned, black-haired and squat, with rolls of spare flesh on her bare arms and scantily clothed torso. A leather bag was slung from one shoulder, and in her right hand she held a heavy stave. She stood with her legs braced like small tree trunks, and the intricate bone carvings that hung over her face from a narrow hide band around her head clinked together as she glared at Grimya. Her three companions were younger but no less daunting. Taller and slimmer than their leader, they wore their hair in a complicated system of braids; two of them had painted sigils on their cheeks and chins, and all three carried machetes casually slung in their belts.

Grimya's hackles rose; she bared her teeth, not wanting to show overt aggression but nonetheless indicating that she wasn't to be trifled with. Then the young woman of the *kemb* appeared, easing her way past the group with placatory and apologetic gestures. She spoke respectfully to the fat woman, bowing her head and clasping her hands together, then hastened to Grimya and soothed her, demonstrating that the newcomers were not a threat. Grimya subsided, though the aura of power still made her uneasy, and the group walked on, ignoring her, to Indigo's curtained room. Immediately the wolf tried to follow but in great agitation, the young woman pulled her back, emphatically repeating the word that Grimya believed meant *help*.

The four strangers disappeared, and from behind the curtain came rapid, low-pitched muttering. Grimya heard the bed frame creak; then, moments later, the curtain was

pushed back and the fat woman emerged. She looked at
them, her stare sharp and intense, then spoke three emphatic words before turning and striding back into the room.
Grimya's embryonic understanding of these people's speech
wasn't enough for her to be sure of what was said, but a
telepathic inkling of the meaning, and the *kemb* woman's
gasp, which seemed to mingle astonishment and awe, were
enough to confirm her suspicion that the fat woman's words
translated roughly as: *she is the one*.

Grimya didn't know where the four strange women had come
from or who or what they were, but it was clear from the
outset that the *kemb* family held them in awe. More important, it seemed that they believed the newcomers might help
Indigo where their own efforts had failed. No one was allowed to witness what took place in the curtained room,
and whether the skills the women used were medical or
magical, Grimya would never know, but after an hour or
so, their leader returned to the storeroom with a look of
stern satisfaction on her face.
    By the time she made her appearance, the *kemb* had been
transformed. The family, caught unawares by their visitors'
unexpected arrival, had made frantic efforts to prepare every
possible honor and facility for their guests. The children
had been set to sweeping and tidying under the shrill command of one of the young women, and the grand-dame and
the dumpy wife were busy at the stove, while the men had
hung a strange but obviously precious assortment of decorations and fetishes at the storeroom's windows and door.
Bundles of leaves and fleshy, alien-looking flowers had been
hastily brought from the surrounding forest to be woven in
among the decorations and strewn on the floor, and one
rattan chair had been adorned like a makeshift throne.
    The fat woman stopped on the inner threshold and looked
about critically. The entire *kemb* family had gathered def-
erentially at one side of the room, and for perhaps half a
minute no one spoke. Then the fat woman nodded curtly,

uttered a grunt that seemed to imply *very well*, walked to
the bedecked chair and sat down.

The atmosphere palpably eased. Muting a sigh of relief,
the eldest of the men snapped his fingers at the younger
women, and they hastened to the stove and began to fill
wooden bowls from the three pots simmering there. Another man brought out cups and poured some strong-
smelling brew from a stone jar. He handed the first cup to
the grand-dame, who in turn offered it to the fat woman,
and her acceptance was the sign for other cups to be
filled. The grand-dame was then permitted to sit; the others, though, remained standing as the mute, wide-eyed
women set bowls of food on the floor at their guest's feet.
The fat woman selected a morsel from each bowl, chewed,
nodded approval and then turned to address the granddame,
who, it seemed, was the only one present who warranted
being treated as something akin to an equal.

Grimya, who had found herself a place as close as possible to the newcomer without being conspicuous, listened
carefully to the speech she made and to the old woman's
responses. Each time the guest paused, the grand-dame
would nod complaisantly and repeat the same two words,
"Ain, Shalune." *Ain*, Grimy knew, meant *yes*, and she
quickly realized that Shalune must be the fat woman's name
or title. She was, it seemed, either issuing instructions or
stating a series of facts, and as she continued to speak, the
grand-dame's expression and those of her kin changed. They
were excited by something Shalune was telling them; at one
point the *kemb* owner's dumpy wife gave a little exclamation
of delight. When finally Shalune was done, everyone in the
room bowed forward, their palms flat together in gestures
of reverential gratitude.

Grimya, though, felt only alarm. Unlike the *kemb* family
Shalune's mind was psychically active and therefore, at least
on the shallowest level, open to a little telepathic probing,
and the wolf had gleaned something of her thoughts as she
spoke. It seemed that she and her cohorts considered Indigo
important in some way. Grimya didn't know how or why,

but Shalune's meaning was unmistakable—as was her intention. She meant to take Indigo away from the *kemb*, to somewhere—Grimya couldn't understand it clearly—that was especially significant, while the family was to be rewarded or granted some particular privilege for diligence in caring for her before Shalune's arrival. As Shalune's hosts repeated their thanks over and over again, Grimya felt her stomach contract queasily. Where was this place of Shalune's? And why was she planning to take Indigo there? What did the women want with her? If they meant to harm her in any way . . . but no, Grimya reasoned, she'd sensed no harmful intent in Shalune's thoughts; rather, the opposite. Indigo was important to these strangers. But *why*? It made no sense.

Surreptitiously she looked toward the inner door, wondering if she might slip away to see Indigo without being noticed, but then she remembered that Shalune's three companions were still in the curtained room. She must be patient, bide her time, cope with her fears and wait for an opportunity to visit her friend when—if—she was untended for a few minutes. It wouldn't be easy, but, for now at least, it was all she could do. Disconsolately, she settled down to wait.

Grimya's opportunity came later that afternoon. After her meal, Shalune had rejoined her companions in Indigo's room, and it was some time before she returned. When she did, however, Grimya's heart quickened eagerly, for this time all four women entered the storeroom together, leaving Indigo alone.

By now, word of the group's presence had spread. The grand-dame, presumably with Shalune's permission, had dispatched the youngest boys to put the word about to their neighbors, and a small crowd had gathered in respectful silence outside the *kemb*. Most had brought some gift for the women, and after quenching her thirst with another cup of the household's brew, Shalune condescended to step out onto the veranda to look the offerings over. The gifts were apparently the price expected for some small service such

as a medical prescription, a piece of advice, an adjudication
in a dispute.

It was clear now that Shalune and her ilk were the guardians and the instruments of religion or law or both, and their
preoccupation with the incomers gave Grimya the opportunity she had awaited. Taking care that the young *kemb*
woman wasn't watching her, she eased her way around the
edge of the room, then slipped through the door and ran
along the passage to Indigo's room. She pushed at the curtain with her muzzle, wriggled through—and stopped.

Indigo was sitting up in the low-slung bed. Her back had
been carefully bolstered and her skin looked like thin, damp
paper, but she was conscious, and Grimya knew as their
eyes met that the fever was all but gone.

Indigo! The wolf remembered just in time not to shout
her friend's name aloud. She rushed to the bed and leaped
up, her whole body quivering with excitement as she licked
Indigo's face.

"Oh, Grimya!" Indigo hugged her with all the little
strength she had. "Grimya, Grimya!"

Hush! Grimya warned. *I'm not supposed to be here. They
would drive me out if they knew. Indigo, are you all right?
I've been so worried!*

Indigo subsided and her arms fell to her sides. The effort
of embracing the she-wolf had exhausted her, though she
tried not to let Grimya see how weak she was. *I'm mending
fast, my dear*, she communicated silently. *I don't know what
that woman gave me, but it drove the fever out more quickly
than any nostrum I've ever known.* She paused. *How long
was I delirious?*

Some days, Grimya told her, *if you count the time in the
forest before we found this place. Do you remember the
storm?*

Indigo shook her head. *I don't remember anything from
the morning when I woke up and felt the fever coming on.*

*That was five days ago. You were so ill, I didn't know
what to do. At last I asked the Earth Mother for help, and
I believe She answered me and brought us here.*

Indigo looked around at the room. *What is this place, Grimya? I tried to ask the women, but we don't understand each other's tongue.*

As best she could, Grimya told her about the *kemb* and its inhabitants and described the circumstances that had led her to seek help here. *But*, she said when the explanation was done, *there's something else you must know, something that worries me greatly. I don't understand the women's speech either, but I've been able to read some of the thoughts of the fat one—Shalune, I think she is called. Indigo, they mean to take you away!*

Take me away? Indigo frowned. *Where?*

I don't know. To some very special place, I think, but I don't know where it is or why they mean to go there. I believe . . . Grimya hesitated, wondering if her suspicion would sound foolish, then decided that it must be said. *I believe that you are important to them in some way.*

Indigo was both astonished and baffled. *But I'm a complete stranger, an outsider—*

I know. I don't understand it either. But I think there is something religious in this. The one called Shalune, she seems to be some kind of . . . The wolf groped for the right word, and Indigo ventured: *Priestess?*

Yes! Grimya's tongue lolled eagerly.

A priestess. Indigo considered the thought uneasily. She couldn't think clearly; the fever hadn't completely abated and in addition to her physical weakness, she still felt that she might all too easily slip back into delirium. She needed time to recover her strength and her full wits, time to assimilate what Grimya was telling her, and above all, time to consider what she should do. If, that was, the priestesses were willing to give her any say in her own future.

Suddenly there were sounds of feet in the corridor and the low murmur of voices. Grimya turned around with a guilty start, and the curtain swung back to admit Shalune and her three cohorts.

Shalune saw Grimya and her brows knitted quickly. Uttering an angry expletive, she strode forward, clapping her hands imperiously to drive the she-wolf off the bed and out of the room.

"No!" Indigo protested. "Let her stay . . . I want her to stay."

Shalune paused. Grimya had hunched down nervously, and Indigo slipped an arm around her, holding her protectively. She looked the fat woman directly in the eye and repeated, slowly and clearly, "I want her to *stay*."

Indigo was prepared for a confrontation, but it didn't come. Instead, Shalune's expression became chagrined. She made uncertain signs, as though trying to confirm Indigo's meaning, and Indigo nodded vigorously, first pointing to Grimya and then patting the bed's surface with emphasis. Shalune understood. She put the palms of her hands together in an acquiescent gesture and bowed her head submissively, stepping back a pace.

Then, to Indigo's and Grimya's utter astonishment, as though their leader's action had been a prearranged signal, the other three women dropped to one knee in a formal and unambiguously reverent salute.

·CHAPTER·III·

Five more days passed before Shalune judged Indigo fit to travel. It was a peculiar and uncomfortable hiatus, for the presence in the *kemb* of the four priestesses had an inhibiting effect on everyone. The trader family's lives were greatly disrupted; they spared no pains to serve their guests in every way possible, and it was clear that they considered themselves greatly honored by the visit, but with their best sleeping accommodations given over to the strangers, and a good deal of business lost in the hours they spent ministering to their needs, the strain began to tell.

As far as she was able, Grimya kept out of the priestesses' way. She was very wary of Shalune and her companions. The feeling didn't quite extend to dislike or mistrust; it was just an instinct that she couldn't rationally explain. She said nothing to Indigo in their few private moments, not wanting to worry her, but instead took the simple expedient of avoiding the four women's company whenever possible.

To begin with, the she-wolf suffered many lonely hours. Indigo was asleep for much of the time, slowly recovering her strength, and during her short waking periods, Shalune would more often than not detail at least one of her subordinates to sit with her in the close, quiet sickroom. The *kemb* family was too busy to pay Grimya much attention—even the youngest children were allowed no time to play with her—and beyond the ordinary routine of giving her food and water and an occasional kindly word, they left her to her own devices.

Had they been anywhere in the world but the Dark Isle, Grimya thought, she might have spent her time hunting, a pleasure that she greatly enjoyed and that might have enabled her to repay her generous hosts with some fresh meat. But hunting in this dank, heavy forest was a far cry from stalking and chasing through the cool greenery of the Western Continent or over the snows of the Redoubt. Here there were pitfalls at every turn: flowers and leaves that stung like hornets, reptiles that spat poison, crawling things that could bite even through her thick fur to draw blood and raise painful rashes on her skin.

Besides, Grimya didn't know that she'd want to catch, let alone eat, the game animals she had seen lurking among the trees hereabouts, for something about them repelled her. They looked unwholesome, dull and slinking and surly things, living their lives in a world of lush semidarkness and decay, and utterly alien to a wolf born and bred in the clean, bracing cold of the far south. Their uncooked and unspiced flesh, she suspected, would taste as repellent as they themselves looked to her, and—though she knew the comparison was irrational—they reminded her in an obscure way of the warped creatures she'd seen, more years ago than she could count, in the poisoned volcanic mountains of Vesinum.

She wished with all her heart that they'd never come here. The Dark Isle had a reputation throughout the world as an unhealthy, unclean place that was better shunned, and when Indigo had made the decision to leave the city-state of Davakos on the Western Continent and set out once more on her travels, Grimya had tried to persuade her not to cross the great island but to find another route for their journey.

Indigo had refused. They must go northeastward, she had said, and northeastward meant just that. The only other choice was to sail north through the Snakemaw Straits and then bear toward the Jewel Islands and the Eastern Continent beyond, and that was something she didn't want to do. Grimya had understood the reason for her reluctance. Both the Jewel Islands and the Eastern Continent held terrible memories for Indigo: memories of friends who had died a quarter of a century ago during her desperate bid to find and unmask the Serpent-Eater of Khimiz. Memories, too, of friends who had survived that ordeal with her but who had since aged a quarter of a century while Indigo remained unchanged, friends who would now be unrecognizable. Indigo desperately didn't want to risk meeting them again. Worst of all, she didn't want to risk discovering that time had got the better of them and they had died a natural death. She'd already suffered that blow once, when she and Grimya had returned to Davakos after an absence of more than twenty years. They had had an old and dear friend among the Davakotians, a tough little woman called Macce, who had been both shipmate and close confidante when Indigo had crewed on the *Kara Karai* under her command. Indigo had promised Macce that she would return one day. She had kept the promise at last, but its fulfillment came too late and she and Grimya had reached Davakos's shores only to learn that the little sea captain had come to the end of her natural span and gone peacefully to the Earth Mother.

Indigo had grieved deeply. She felt—and nothing Grimya could say would sway her—that she had betrayed her old friend. The wolf didn't understand this complex and peculiarly human reasoning, but she knew Indigo well enough to believe that her decision to travel directly across the Dark Isle and subject herself to its hostilities rather than take the easier route was some kind of self-imposed penance, a way of atoning for her failure by inflicting hardship on herself. Macce, Grimya thought sadly, would never have approved of such foolish behavior.

But, wise or no, the thing was done now and they must make the best of it. At least there was the cheering knowledge that Indigo was improving by the day—indeed, almost by the hour—and whatever her doubts about Shalune and her followers in other ways, for that Grimya was deeply grateful to them.

On the third day of her recovery, Indigo was allowed to leave her bed for the first time, and while she sat on the *kemb* veranda in the comparative cool of late afternoon, she and Grimya had their first chance in some while to talk privately together without interruption. In the last few days, Grimya's telepathic sense had enabled her to pick up a good deal more of their hosts' tongue, and though she had kept her distance from Shalune's cohorts, she had nevertheless overheard snippets of their talk here and there. That, together with the extraordinary scene she had witnessed at Indigo's bedside, had enabled her to piece together at least a partial jigsaw of the women's intentions.

They were talking of omens, she silently told Indigo, after glancing back—illogically—over her shoulder lest someone should be watching them. *I didn't understand much of what I heard, but I think they were led here by something that happened or something that they saw. It has a connection with you, Indigo, I'm sure of it. With what they said before about you being "the one."*

Indigo stared at the still, heavy forest canopy a few yards from the *kemb.* "The one . . ." she mused aloud, then switched back to telepathic speech. *You didn't overhear any more details? Such as in which direction this place of theirs lies?*

No. Grimya paused. *Why? Is that important?*

It might be. Indigo reached into the neck of her shirt and took the small lodestone from its leather pouch that hung constantly around her neck and was one of her oldest possessions. Grimya looked at the stone as it slid into Indigo's palm and said, *Ah. . . .*

I studied it last night before I slept. But the message it gave me wasn't as straightforward as I expected—look, I'll show you. Indigo held the stone out so that Grimya could see its flat surface. Quivering within it was a minute fleck of gold light, and as Grimya felt Indigo's mind focus and concentrate, the tiny pinpoint moved abruptly to one edge of the stone.

Northeastward, just as before, the wolf observed, and glanced at Indigo in puzzlement. *I don't understand.*

Watch, Indigo told her. The point of light continued to flicker at the stone's edge for a few seconds more. Then suddenly it shifted back to the center and began to dart rapidly between the two points like a trapped firefly.

It did the same thing last night, Indigo said as Grimya showed her teeth in surprise. *It's never behaved in such a way before, and I have a suspicion of what it's trying to tell me. Northeastward and yet here at one and the same time, as though it can't decide which is the more accurate message.* She gave Grimya a long, thoughtful look. *Could that mean a connection with Shalune?*

Grimya understood. *With Shalune, and yet also with this place to which she wishes to take you?*

If it lies northeast of here, yes. Indigo looked back into the *kemb*, where the women were preparing the midday meal. Shalune wasn't in evidence, but Indigo had an instinctive feeling that she and her cohorts weren't far away. She turned to Grimya again. *If it does, then I think that we may have found what we were looking for. Or rather, that it's come to find us.*

During that day and the one that followed, Indigo tried by every means available to discover more about Shalune and her intentions. That was no easy task, for although Grimya was slowly learning words and phrases of the Dark Islers' language and tried to teach Indigo what she knew, it wasn't enough to allow, yet, for any communication with the four women. Then, on the fifth morning, Shalune came into Indigo's room, made what had become her customary obeisance and indicated that she wished Indigo to follow her. She seemed pleased about something, and Grimya, picking up the tone if not the gist of her thoughts, warned Indigo that something was afoot. Cautiously, Indigo allowed Shalune to escort her along the passage, through the *kemb*'s main room and out onto the veranda.

She stopped dead when she saw what awaited her. How the women had come by it, she couldn't begin to imagine, but set incongruously on the hard-packed earth before the *kemb* was a litter, made from bamboo and rattan, curtained with multicolored fabric and hung about with grotesque fetishes of wood, bone, stone and feathers. Beside the litter stood the three subordinate women; they, too, made obeisances, and Shalune, smiling with satisfaction, gestured toward the litter and said something in which Indigo caught only the word for *people*.

Grimya stared at the litter. *I think she is telling you that the villagers have made this thing,* she communicated uncertainly. *She also says something about going, but I can't understand any more than that.*

Shalune, still smiling, indicated the litter again, and abruptly Indigo understood. With no preamble and no apparent preparation, the priestesses meant to depart from the *kemb* this morning—and the litter was intended to carry Indigo herself.

She heard movement behind her and turned to see two of the *kemb* women emerge through the door with her packs in their hands. They carried them reverently and a little nervously, as though half afraid to touch them, and at a brusque signal from Shalune, they hastened past Indigo and down the steps to load their burdens into the litter. Indigo stood still, not knowing how to react. She wasn't prepared to simply capitulate to the women's wishes without knowing where they meant to take her or what they meant to do with her, yet how could she make them understand that? How could she voice her protest?

They were waiting for her, and Shalune's heavy brows were starting to knit in the embryo of a frown. Indigo looked at her, into her hard eyes, and said carefully in the Dark Isle's tongue, ''What is this?''

Shalune looked astonished. This was the first time that Indigo had ever addressed her in her own language, and the question caught her completely by surprise. Recovering her composure, she bowed low with a flourish of one hand and spoke rapidly and emphatically.

Grimya, what did she say? Indigo communicated desperately. She hadn't understood; the speech had been too fast and too complex, but she didn't want Shalune to realize how limited her grasp of the tongue as yet was.

I think . . . The wolf struggled to match the words she had recognized with the impressions that her telepathic senses garnered from Shalune's mind. *She is saying you will be carried. She talks of esteem, and of something else—I don't know what it means, but it feels like a good word, a word of praise.*

Shalune was watching Indigo expectantly but warily. Quickly and silently Indigo asked the wolf, *What's the word for "where"? I must find out where they mean to take us!*

Grimya told her, and Indigo repeated the phrase aloud. Again Shalune replied rapidly and at length, and Grimya said, *She talks of water and . . . a place, a building, I think. A special place. Like . . . a temple?*

Indigo nodded. It was what she had suspected, and she met Shalune's gaze steadily.

"Where?" she said again, and this time gestured first to her right and then to her left, her eyebrows raised slightly in a clear interrogative.

Shalune bowed again and turned to indicate the track that ran past the *kemb* and away, farther into the island's depths. "That way," she replied. Indigo knew enough to understand her words this time. "Five days of walking."

Indigo stared past the woman's pointing finger, and her face gave away nothing of the sudden quickening of her pulse. Northeastward. The lodestone's seemingly ambiguous message was explained. For a moment she stood very still as a mixture of emotions and reactions rioted in her mind. Then she realized that above them all, one clear instinct stood out, and it swept away all doubts, all caveats, all other considerations.

She said silently to Grimya: *We must go with them. There's no other choice that makes any sense.* And with a grave nod to Shalune, she walked down the veranda steps toward the litter.

Her hosts heaped gifts upon her before they would allow the procession to depart. Indigo didn't want to accept them; the family might be modestly prosperous by local standards, but it was by no means rich and couldn't easily afford to give away the foodstuffs and utensils and bolts of fine-woven cloth that were piled into the litter at her feet. Her protests went unheeded, and all that her erstwhile hosts wanted—hungered for, it seemed—in return for their generosity was for her to lay both her hands on the heads of each of them in turn, from the old grand-dame to the smallest babe-in-arms.

Indigo felt like a charlatan, but she didn't have the courage to refuse them, and when finally the blessing ceremony was over, and amid noisy farewells, the four women bore the litter away, she sank back behind the colored curtains feeling shamed and guilty. What had Shalune and her co-horts told these trusting people? That she was some special being, imbued with the power to bring them good fortune? Did Shalune herself believe that . . . and if she did, why? What *was* she to these women?

She sighed and pushed back the curtain, which was making the already overheated air inside the litter unbearably stifling. Grimya, who disliked confined spaces and had preferred to run alongside the litter rather than ride with Indigo, looked up as the fabric twitched back. She had read her friend's thoughts and she spoke in Indigo's mind.

It seems to me that we cannot hope to have the answers to those questions for a while yet. We must be patient, and trust in the lodestone.

Indigo smiled affectionately. *You're right, my dear, as always. My only fear is that these women might have mis-*

taken me for someone else. If that's true, then things might not go well for us when they discover their mistake.

Grimya considered this for a few moments. Then she said: *I don't think we need trouble ourselves about that. These are not evil people; I sense that clearly. Besides . . .* She hesitated, then glanced up at Indigo again, her amber eyes peculiarly intense. *I don't know any more than you do what these women think you are. But the lodestone doesn't lie, Indigo—so perhaps they are not mistaken after all.*

Indigo looked sharply at her. *Grimya, what are you saying?*

The wolf turned her head away, her tongue lapping the heavy air. *Only what I think. What I suspect. But I don't know if I'm right.* Another pause; then she met Indigo's eyes again, though a little reluctantly, Indigo thought. *You shouldn't think about it. Thinking won't help, not yet, not until we know more. You should sleep. You haven't regained your full strength, and this journey promises to be tedious. Go to sleep, Indigo.* A cajoling, faintly pleading note crept into her mental voice. *Go to sleep. That's what you need now above all else.*

Against her expectations, Indigo did sleep through much of that long, monotonous day. The four women, it seemed, were tireless; they stopped only once during the daylight hours, to eat a swift meal and drink copious quantities of water, and she suspected that they must be using some herbal drug to enhance their stamina beyond natural boundaries. The steady jogging of the litter, together with the sense of claustrophobia engendered by the stifling air and the muted but incessant sounds of the forest, lulled her into a strange, half-dreaming stupor that now and again almost harked back to the fever.

They halted for the night as dusk began to fall and shadows closed down like a blanket on the forest. There was no sight of any human habitation, and before preparing a makeshift meal, the women made a circuit of their chosen site, chanting and leaving small parcels of food in a wide

circle around the litter. Grimya told Indigo that as far as
she could tell, these were offerings meant to placate ghosts
or demons that might otherwise be tempted to attack the
party, and throughout the night, the forest's susurrations
were augmented by more low-pitched chanting and the staccato sound of rattles being shaken as the priestesses kept
watch turn by turn.

The pattern of that first day continued through the five
days and nights of their journey, broken only by two more
violent rainstorms. They took shelter while these storms
were at their height, huddling with the litter under a swollen-
trunked species of tree with eight-foot leaves as broad as
the span of a man's arms, then trudging on again through
the sweltering humidity when the downpours slackened.
Several times they came upon human settlements, and on
each occasion they were welcomed with awe and delight.
More gifts were heaped upon Indigo, and again the givers
wanted only her blessing in return. Shalune held court, dis-
pensing advice and justice, and then, after perhaps two or
three hours, the litter was lifted once more and they continued on their way.

The fifth morning dawned humid and oppressively still,
with the promise, Grimya said, of another big storm. The
women had pressed on late into the previous night, halting
only when the moon set and the darkness grew too intense
for them to make safe progress, and as soon as the first
glimmer of light touched the forest, they broke camp and
were away again.

There was an air of eager anticipation about Shalune and
her cohorts this morning. The litter-bearers sang as they
walked, a rhythmic walking song with a faintly disturbing
minor harmony, which Grimya—who could understand a
few of the words—said was to warn off any creature, human
or otherwise, that might wish the party ill. It seemed to be
an unnecessary precaution, for they had passed no settlements for a day or more, nor even any sign of human activity, in what appeared to be untouched virgin forest; but as
the morning wore on and the air sweated into a sweltering

hell, the song became more emphatic, more urgent . . . and just before noon, they reached their journey's end.

Indigo was dozing fitfully and uncomfortably behind the litter's closed curtains, but Grimya's telepathic alert woke her with a start. She raised herself on one elbow, pushing the stifling shrouds aside to look out, and her eyes widened with amazement.

The tangle of trees and undergrowth had ended as abruptly as though a giant's scythe had cut a swathe through it, and they stood on the shores of a circular lake that reflected the sky's stone-hard blue like a huge mirror. The sun, almost directly overhead at this latitude, battered down blindingly, bleaching the vista and making Indigo's eyes ache with its intensity. All around the lake's edge the trees crowded thickly, but on the far shore, their gray-green wall was broken by a gigantic bluff of red rock, stepped and flat-topped to form a ziggurat that towered high above the trees. The ziggurat's face was pocked by what looked like unnaturally symmetrical caves, and at the truncated summit, too distant for its source to be discernible, a thin plume of smoke rose into the still air.

The women set the litter down. They were staring eagerly across the lake to the rock bluff, and Indigo made to climb out of the litter and join them. Seeing her, Shalune made a negative gesture, indicating for her to stay put, then rummaged in the bag she carried and brought out a disk of brass-colored metal some ten or twelve inches in diameter. The disk's surface was polished to a brilliant sheen; Shalune squinted up at the sky, then took a few paces toward the lake and held the disk up, angling it back and forth so that it caught the sun's rays. They waited, and seconds later a brilliant pinpoint of light flashed high on the bluff as the signal was answered. Shalune grunted, satisfied, and thrust the disk back into her bag; the women picked up the litter once more and they set off around the lake's perimeter.

They had covered perhaps half the distance to the ziggurat when the quiet was shattered by a cacophonous and brazen fanfare. Grimya yelped a shocked protest, and Indigo, leaning perilously out from the litter, saw a group of brown-skinned people on a ledge near the summit, with long brass horns raised to their lips. Twice and three times more the horns blared out deafeningly, and then there was movement on the bluff and Indigo saw that a procession was coming down to meet them.

Stairs had been cut into the rock, zigzagging down the steep terraces past ledges and cave mouths to a patch of sandy ground that formed an open arena between the bluff and the lake's edge. Moving down the stairs like a slow, bright stream came some dozen women, led by a tall, raw-boned figure dressed in a thin skirt and matching breastband of multicolored fabric· and crowned with a headdress of feathers. They reached the foot of the last flight as Shalune and her party arrived, and Shalune stepped up to the tall woman and spoke a formal greeting. The tall woman inclined her head, said a few clipped words in response, then walked past Shalune to the litter. Grimya, who had crouched down in the litter's shade and was watching the stranger warily, communicated: *I think she is the powerful one here, the ruler. Be careful, Indigo.*

I shall. Indigo had already noticed that the tall woman's attendants were armed with long spears and that some also carried machetes in their leather belts, and she was as wary as Grimya as, slowly, she eased herself out of the litter and stood up.

For a few seconds she and the newcomer stared at one another. Indigo was tall but this woman was a good half-head taller, and the headdress emphasized her height so that Indigo felt dwarfed. Dark, intense eyes in a strong face with a stubborn jaw looked hard at Indigo; then the woman stretched out a long-fingered brown hand and pressed the first two fingers to Indigo's forehead. Indigo caught her breath but didn't move, and after a few moments the hand withdrew. Then, to Indigo's surprise, the woman bowed her head with arms outspread in an unequivocal gesture of respect.

"My name is Uluye," she said in her own tongue, which

by now Indigo knew well enough to understand a few words at least. "I am—" and an unfamiliar word followed. Grimya supplied silently, *She is a priestess, like Shalune. And I was right: she is the ruler here.*

Indigo bowed gravely in the old Southern Isles manner, which even after all these years still came naturally to her. "I am Indigo."

She didn't have the inflection right, she thought, but Uluye seemed to comprehend well enough, for she launched into a speech in which she repeated Indigo's name several times. Grimya, struggling to keep up with and translate the flow of words, told Indigo that it was a speech of welcome and of thanks—thanks not only to Indigo herself, but also to something or someone else, the nature of which she didn't understand.

A deity, perhaps, she said, *but not the Earth Mother, or at least not as we think of Her.* A pause while Uluye continued to speak, then: *She wants us to go with them, up into that cliff.*

Uluye finished her speech and held out an arm to point toward the staircase. Indigo nodded acquiescence and turned to face the climb. The others formed up behind them, Shalune close on Indigo's heels, and the horns blared again as they started up the long zigzag of steps. The climb was tiring, but after five days with no more to do than rest in the litter, Indigo had recovered a good measure of her strength, and although before long her thighs ached fiercely, she knew she could reach the summit without too much difficulty.

The lake, with its fringe of forest, fell away below them; it was, Indigo realized as it took on a new perspective, almost perfectly circular, and from above, the water looked like blue-green glass. She suspected it was very deep, perhaps the site of a long-dead volcano, though there was no high ground other than the bluff itself that might have formed the walls of an ancient crater. But whatever its origin, one thing was certain: this settlement was an ideal and virtually impregnable fortress.

They were clear of the treetops now, and there was no
shelter from the heat that beat down on them like hammers.
Grimya was flagging, her tongue lolling and her eyes dull,
but she refused any help and padded stoically on. Higher
still, and now at each turn of the stairs, ledges led off to
the caves that pocked the wall. Each cave's mouth was covered with a curtain of colored fabric, and as they passed by,
the curtains were lifted aside and people emerged to watch
them. Indigo saw to her surprise that from the eldest to the
youngest, all of them were women. Were there no men here?
she wondered. Or were the men away from the settlement,
or staying out of sight for some unfathomable reason?
Whatever the truth, the women certainly seemed to welcome their arrival, for every face wore a smile and several
voices called out in tones of eager greeting.

Uluye waved acknowledgment but didn't halt, or even
pause, and before long they reached the final ledge, some
twenty feet or so below the ziggurat's summit. Uluye turned
along the ledge, which was broad enough to leaven the effects of its giddying height a little, and led the party to
another cave mouth, larger than its neighbors, surrounded
by carved sigils and covered by a woven curtain. Shalune
stepped forward to lift the curtain aside, but Uluye was
there before her. They exchanged a sharp glance; then Uluye led the way through, and Indigo's eyes widened in
appreciative surprise as she saw what lay beyond.

The cave had been formed into a comfortable and well-
furnished home. Mats covered the level floor, and the walls
were bright with painted murals. There were three rattan
chairs in the traditional boat-shaped style of the Dark Isle,
a low-slung rattan bed, a cooking hearth surrounded by pots
and utensils, and an assortment of other practical objects,
from feather fans with polished wooden handles to a metal
mirror, and even writing implements in the form of papyrus
and a bone stylus. The chamber was lit by clay lamps that
burned with a bluish light and gave off a sweet, syrupy
perfume from their niches high in the walls.

Uluye looked at Indigo; Shalune hovered expectantly be-

hind her. This cave, Indigo realized, was to be her own,
and the women were waiting for her to react. She looked at
them both in turn and smiled hesitantly.

"It is very good," she said in their language. "Very fine.
Thank you."

Shalune showed her teeth in her fearsome grin, and Uluye
relaxed her reserved manner enough to allow a small, prim
smile. "You will eat now," she said. "And then—" But
the rest of the sentence was lost on Indigo and she shook
her head in defeat.

"Permit." It was the only word Indigo yet knew of their
language that came close to an apology. "I . . . am not . . ."
But her small knowledge failed her and she made a helpless
gesture.

Shalune seemed to understand and she spoke rapidly to
Uluye, explaining, Indigo hoped, that their guest wasn't yet
proficient in their tongue. Uluye nodded, said something
that Indigo thought meant "after," and left the cave. Shalune watched her go and then turned back to Indigo. Her
expression, with one eyebrow slightly raised, was more eloquent than any words, and it confirmed Indigo's small but
burgeoning suspicion that there was more than a modicum
of dissent between the two women. Not wanting to take
sides until she was better acquainted with them, Indigo kept
her own expression reservedly neutral, and after a few seconds, Shalune shrugged and turned to the cooking hearth.
The embers of a wood fire were glowing between the stones,
and something simmered in a lidded clay pot to one side of
the embers' glowing heart.

"For you," Shalune said, indicating the food.

Tentatively, Indigo ventured, "You will eat with me?"

Shalune shook her head emphatically. "No, no," she
said, then added a word Indigo didn't comprehend. "I will
return later. Eat, and rest." She pantomimed someone
sleeping in case Indigo hadn't fully understood, then made
a reverent salute and walked out of the cave.

Grimya, her ears pricked forward, waited until she judged
that Shalune was out of earshot, then turned and looked at

Indigo. "She and the other one are not the best of frr . . . iends, I think," she said aloud.

"I agree. I also feel instinctively that I'd trust Shalune before Uluye, which is a pity, because it's obvious that Uluye's word is law here."

"Yess." Grimya shook herself from head to tail. "And we still don't know what they *w-want* of you. That is what trrroubles me most of all."

"Well, their attitude so far is at least reassuring, and that seems to confirm what the lodestone told us." Indigo fingered the leather bag around her neck. "We must just wait and see."

The wolf dipped her head. "I th-ink," she said, "that this is some religious place, as we were led to believe. That smoke at the top of the cliff—a shrine, perhaps?"

"Possibly. Though if it is, then as you said earlier, it's probably not dedicated to the Earth Mother as we know Her."

Grimya laid her ears back. "That, too, trroubles me. If—"

"No." Indigo held up a hand, forestalling what the wolf had been about to say. She knew Grimya was thinking about the next trial that faced them, the next demon that must be found and challenged, and she said gently, "I don't think it would be wise to speculate about it yet. We've been led astray too often in the past to risk assuming that things are necessarily what they seem now. We must be patient, bide our time." Abruptly that struck her as wryly funny and she gave a small, hollow laugh. "Time is the one thing we can be sure of, after all."

·CHAPTER·IV·

Uluye returned as the sun was setting. Indigo had slept for some hours after eating the meal the women had left for her; surprising, as she'd done little else but sleep during the past five days, but the heat and the quiet were soporific and she had drifted off without intending to. Grimya—who had shared the food, although she found it far too spicy for her simpler tastes—was curled up in the coolest corner, and both raised their head with a guilty start as the curtain was lifted aside and the tall woman appeared on the threshold.

Uluye was still wearing the feathered headdress but had changed her robe for a long, sleeveless shift; and a necklace strung with a myriad bones, each carved into the shape of some animal or bird, hung around her neck and clinked with every movement she made.

"We are ready," she said. At least, Indigo believed that was her meaning. "Come."

Indigo frowned. "Come?" She repeated the word queryingly. "Where?"

Uluye pointed upward, then held out something she was carrying. A robe somewhat like her own, but dyed with swirling shades of blue and purple and black. Indigo took it tentatively and pointed to herself. "You want me to wear this?" she asked in her own language.

Uluye didn't reply but watched expectantly, and after a moment's hesitation, Indigo shrugged and began to change. The robe was cool and loose, far more comfortable than her travel-stained shirt and trousers. When she was ready, Uluye nodded approval and led the way toward the cave's exit. Not knowing her intention but willing to cooperate, at least for the time being, Indigo followed, Grimya padding in her wake.

They emerged onto the ledge and Indigo stopped, awed by the view. The sun's edge was just visible as a thin, fiery crescent above the trees, and in its refracted light the world seemed to have caught fire. The lake was a great, still circle of blood red, the sky overhead like polished brass, and between lake and sky and shadow-drowned forest, the sandstone walls of the ziggurat glowed crimson with the last of the evening light. To the east, clouds were gathering, knife-thin streaks presaging the heavier masses moving in behind them. There wasn't a breath of wind.

Uluye led them to the far end of the ledge, where a staircase much smaller and narrower than the great flights criss-crossing the rock face beneath them led up the final flank to the cliff's summit. Looking about, Indigo was surprised to find that there was no one else to be seen either on this level or on any of the ledges below. The smiling, welcoming faces they had seen earlier were gone, and the bluff seemed utterly deserted.

They began to climb, and as they neared the top of the flight, the thin plume of smoke became visible again, rising against the rapidly darkening sky. A scent hung heavy on the air, growing stronger as they approached the summit: spicy, a little acrid, shot through with an echo of something decaying and unwholesome. Then they mounted the last dozen steps, emerged onto the cliff top—and Indigo stared in astonishment at the sight that confronted her.

Four truncated sandstone pillars rose twenty feet from the

ziggurat's table, marking out a near-perfect square. Stone slabs formed a terraced floor between the pillars, and around the square upward of fifty women, of every age from youngest to oldest, stood in silent, intent ranks. A dozen or more were armed with spears, which they held at a stiff, ritualistic angle; all were robed, all were hung about with wood and bone ornaments; all were utterly still.

But it wasn't the watching, waiting crowd that took Indigo's attention, nor the pillars, nor even the great bowl of beaten metal raised on a plinth and from which the smoke of incense rose in a steady, oppressively perfumed stream. It was the chair—throne perhaps would be a better word—that had been placed before the plinth, near the square's center. Cut from sandstone blocks, its arms and back were carved into intricate and terrible shapes that blended human, animal and other, disturbing and unnameable forms. And enthroned on the chair in an awful semblance of majesty, dressed in a flowing cloak of feathers and crowned by a vast and heavy headdress that dwarfed even Uluye's, was a corpse.

She—it—must have been dead for at least fifteen days, and the decay wrought by the tropical heat in that time was horrible. Indigo quickly turned her head away after one look at the maggot-eaten flesh, the empty eye sockets, the insane, fixed grin where the lips had rotted away to reveal crumbling teeth. The sweet-sick smell that she'd thought a part of the heady clouds of incense was, she realized now, the stench from the corpse, and her stomach threatened to heave. What was this creature? What was its significance? And what had it to do with her?

Uluye stepped forward until she stood facing the thing in the chair. Then she turned on her heel, her tall figure dramatically lit by the incense fire in the bowl behind her, raised her arms high and began to speak. Indigo understood only a few words and could glean nothing from them, but Grimya, at her side, flattened her ears suddenly and her hackles rose.

Indigo— But the wolf got no further, for at that moment

Uluye's speech came to an end and a great wailing cry went up from the assembled women, followed seconds later by the discordant blare of the great horns.

Smiling with grim pleasure, Uluye turned about once more and strode toward the sandstone chair. She made a perfunctory ritual obeisance to the enthroned corpse, then reached up and lifted the elaborate crown from its head. Pieces of flesh and clumps of shriveling hair fell away from the skull as the headdress came free. Then Uluye stepped back, turned, and approached Indigo, the crown held aloft. Indigo watched her, still not comprehending, until Grimya's frantic mental voice broke through her bemusement.

Indigo! I heard what she said to them! This—this thing, the body—it was someone sacred to them, some kind of great oracle. Now the oracle is dead . . . and they mean you to take its place!

Indigo felt as though her feet had fused with the stone beneath her. She stared into Uluye's triumphantly smiling face and saw in the tall woman's eyes the truth of Grimya's warning. She opened her mouth, but before she could speak or react, Uluye had stepped one final pace forward, and to the renewed wailing and bellowing of horns, placed the huge and weighty crown on Indigo's head.

"No . . ." Indigo started to back away. "No, oh no. You don't understand, you don't realize, I'm not—" Grimya yipped a warning and Indigo stopped as she found her retreat blocked by four armed women. They didn't threaten her, but their implacable expressions and the mere presence of the spears in their hands negated the need for any word or gesture.

Wildly, Indigo looked for other escape routes. There were none. The stairway behind her was the only way down from the cliff top; and the other spear-carriers had closed in until she was effectively surrounded. They and the other women, the spectators, were gazing at her with an air of expectation.

Indigo took a deep breath to calm herself and laid a restraining hand on Grimya's head as the wolf began to snarl threateningly. *Wait*, she said silently, then aloud: "Uluye, there has been a great mistake," She knew the priestess wouldn't comprehend her, but she had to make some attempt to communicate before matters got completely out of hand. "I don't know what this means, but I am not a goddess or an oracle or whatever it is that you seem to believe I am. Uluye, you must try to understand—" Seeing that Uluye's expression hadn't changed, she switched frantically to telepathy. *Grimya, she hasn't any idea of what I'm saying! Help me, please!*

Racking her mind, Grimya found a word in the Dark Isle tongue that she believed meant *wrong*. Indigo said it repeating it three times in an urgent, pleading tone. Uluye's smile became supercilious and she shook her head.

"Not wrong," she stated emphatically, and held out one hand. "Come."

Grimya—

She won't listen! Even if I knew the right words, she wouldn't heed them. Indigo, this is dangerous! If you don't do as they want, I fear they might turn on us, and there are too many spears for us to fight!

Indigo had reached the same conclusion. It seemed that for now at least, she had no choice but to comply with Uluye's will. She made a gesture of acquiescence, hoping that her nervousness wasn't too palpably obvious, and allowed the tall woman to take hold of her hand and lead her to the stone chair. In the space of just a few minutes, dusk had turned to darkness as the sun vanished altogether, and two priestesses were feeding the great brazier so that its flames suddenly leaped higher, illuminating the cliff top with hot yellow.

The thing in the chair seemed to loom toward Indigo as though it had suddenly and horribly returned to life, and she shrank back with a gasp before realizing that it was only an illusion created by the flickering light. The mingled smells of incense and putrefaction were making her giddy, the weight of the monstrous crown was unbalancing her; she felt unreal, out of control, as though she were in a nightmare, with no one to wake her.

There was a faint glimmering in the sky, and somewhere in the distance, thunder grumbled angrily. Uluye led Indigo to the throne and they stood together beside it. The stench of the dead oracle's body flowed over Indigo and she thought she might vomit, or even faint. With a great effort she managed to stay upright, and then Uluye made an imperious movement with her free hand and two shadowy figures stepped forward. They moved to the chair and lifted the corpse from its resting place. Uluye drew Indigo aside as it was carried down the steps. Then, with great solemnity, they followed the small procession across the terraced floor to the edge of the ziggurat. Indigo looked down but could see nothing beyond a faint, slate-dark glimmer where the lake must be. All else was lost in the intense darkness of the tropical night.

Suddenly lightning flashed again, momentarily turning the night electric blue and throwing the two figures and their gruesome burden into sharp silhouette. The assembled women began to wail again, and the wailing became a steady, rhythmic and ululating chant that was counter-pointed by the horns and by a sound Indigo hadn't heard before: the thud and rumble of heavy drums beating out from far below, hidden in the darkness.

The two women on the cliff's edge—one of them, Indigo realized now, was Shalune—uttered a shrill scream that rose above the cacophony. They swung their arms back, feet braced, and with a second howling cry, they hurled the body of the old oracle up and out and away over the bluff. Indigo glimpsed it turning and spinning like a rag doll against the sky. Then a fork of brilliant lightning flashed out almost directly overhead, and the roar of thunder drowned all other noise as a phosphorescent glitter far be-low showed that the lake had taken the offering cast down to it.

The chanting ceased and the horns and drums fell silent as the thunder's echoes faded away, and for perhaps ten seconds, the atmosphere was oppressively quiet and still. Then, softly at first but quickly rising both in pitch and in strength, the assembled women began a rhythmic, whispering chant. One word, repeated over and over again: *speak; speak; speak*. Indigo didn't understand the significance of it, but the women's voices carried an unpleasantly insistent undertone that sent a chill through her. Then suddenly Uluye, who alone had not joined in the chant, raised her arms high again and cried out in a powerful voice that rang across the lake and the forest.

"Speak!" Uluye swung around to face her, and the eager, almost fanatical gleam in her eyes as she and the assembled women fiercely chanted shocked Indigo to the marrow as she suddenly comprehended what they meant.

"Speak! Speak! Speak!" It was a litany now, a litany and a demand that Indigo knew she couldn't fulfill. She tried to protest, tried again to make Uluye see that she was not and could never be their oracle, but the women were crowding around her, propelling her willy-nilly toward the stone chair, and her denials were lost in the chant and in a new bawl of thunder that shook the cliff. The chair loomed before her, hands were pushing her to the high seat and turning her around; she shuddered as she felt the touch of unyielding stone at her back and beneath her thighs. Then the women fell back like a wave ebbing, and Indigo sat alone on the oracle's throne.

She felt giddy with the smell of incense, which mingled now with the sharp scent of approaching rain. She couldn't see Grimya among the crowd below the plinth, and she'd lost mental contact, her mind too shocked and confused to allow her to think clearly.

Uluye stood beside her, and from somewhere she had produced a wooden bowl filled with water, which she held to Indigo's lips. Indigo drank gratefully and deeply before realizing that there was more than water in the vessel: herbs, half-dissolved powders, tastes she didn't recognize. She shuddered as the drink went down, but at least it was cooling, easing her parched throat and dry lips. The crown weighed down on her; her head was beginning to ache and she felt fierily hot, as though the fever had returned and was running in her veins once more.

The women's chanting swelled and faded, swelled and faded, and Indigo thought they were forming now into a procession that filed before the stone chair, each individual, from the youngest to the oldest, pausing to bow reverently to her in passing. She saw Shalune's heavy features and long, swinging plaits. She saw an ancient woman who mumbled and could barely clasp her arthritic hands together. She saw a solemn girl who looked like Uluye but was twenty years too young. She saw a toddler, crowing and kicking chubby legs as she dangled from her mother's arms. Dark faces in the gloom, eyes glowing like lamps in the firelight, the shuffle of bare feet, the incessant chanting: *speak, speak, speak*!

"Grimya!" Her mind was floundering and she called the wolf's name aloud, groping for a spar of coherence in the heaving sea that her consciousness had become.

Grimya's mental voice seemed to come from a vast distance. *I can't reach you! They are holding me back! Indigo—*

But suddenly the wolf's call and the chanting and the flickering, feverish scene were cut off as though a solid wall had crashed down between Indigo and her senses. A jolt shot through her body, a moment of excruciating pain gripped her; then clarity returned and she seemed to be hovering, disembodied, amid calm and dark and silence. And someone was addressing her.

She didn't hear the words, but she felt them, and felt behind them the presence that pervaded the darkness around her. Cool, quiet, secret . . . and deeply powerful. There was something menacing about it, yet Indigo didn't feel afraid. It was as if she knew—or *almost* knew—the nature of this power, as if she had encountered it at some time in the past, though the memory now eluded her. As the presence spoke, she knew too that her unconscious mind was absorbing its message and yet that on a conscious level, she was unaware of the message's content or meaning. But it didn't seem to matter. She was calm; she felt at peace. She was content to let this hiatus continue for as long as the presence willed it.

She didn't know how much time had passed—if time was relevant in this dreamlike state—before she became aware that the insistent, toneless murmuring had ceased. The presence began to withdraw, and suddenly Indigo felt a sense of cold as bitter as a polar winter rush through her. She tried to open her mouth to cry out a protest, but she had no body, no physical presence, no means by which to express her shock. She felt herself being pulled away, swept from the darkness's quiet heart toward a clashing outer world of light and noise, and though she wanted to struggle against the pull, she was helpless. The dark was receding faster, faster— Then, just before she was thrown back into the physical world, Indigo saw two eyes staring at her from the vacuum that she had left behind. The eyes were human, but filled with terrible knowledge that transcended human limitations. They burned black, like dark stars, and around each iris was a glimmering corona of silver.

The dark world ejected Indigo, and she shouted in pain and shock as her mind and her body fused into one again and she found herself rigid in the sandstone chair under a thunderous sky alive with lightning. Dark figures were surging toward her; she tried to rise but had lost control of her limbs, and she would have fallen from the chair were it not for the hands that reached out to catch and hold her. Something was hissing in the distance like snakes; she heard Grimya barking but couldn't see her. Then a thunderbolt crashed blindingly overhead, and the background hissing swelled suddenly to a roar as the heavens opened and the deluge began.

Indigo gasped and staggered under the downpour's bombardment. Her foot slid on the wet stone and she slipped, grazing one leg painfully on the chair as her knees buckled under her. Shrill voices rang in her ears; as the women tried to help her upright, she gagged and a thin stream of fluid choked up from her throat to spill on the stone floor. Suddenly she couldn't fight anymore. She felt too ill and too weak to resist the hands—there seemed to be *hundreds* of hands—that touched and pulled and guided. She didn't care anymore. Let them do what they liked. She wanted only to get away.

She let out a soft, sighing breath and went limp in their arms.

The women carried her back down the stairs, treacherously slippery now with the rain pelting down on them, and took her to her cave quarters. Grimya, who had been forcibly restrained by two of the strongest priestesses all the way down the flight, finally broke free, ran at Shalune and bit her as she crouched down to spread a blanket over Indigo's weakly stirring form. Shalune cursed roundly but wouldn't permit the priestesses to hit Grimya in retaliation. Instead, with astonishing strength, she held the furious wolf by the scruff of her neck until Grimya calmed enough to understand that no one was trying to harm Indigo, then released her and peremptorily ordered the other women out of the cave.

Indigo was aware of the fracas but felt too exhausted to even open her eyes and see what was afoot. She heard the women withdraw, then heard voices that she thought were those of Shalune and Uluye arguing near the cave's mouth. After some sharp exchange, Uluye left, but before the argument ended, the word for *fever*, which Indigo knew well, came several times to her ears. Had her fever come back? She feared so, for she felt hot and cold together, and she couldn't shake off the illusion that she was floating in midair and that her fingers had swollen to five times their proper size.

Someone at some time had taken away the heavy headdress. She was glad to be rid of it, glad that she wasn't still sitting in the stone chair, the flesh of her face eaten away and her hair falling out in clumps, and . . . no, she mustn't let her thoughts go down that road. She wasn't the dead oracle; she was . . . someone else. Someone else.

Soft footfalls impinged on her wandering mind, and a square, hard hand, wet with rain, was placed firmly on her forehead. Shalune grunted as though some private opinion had been vindicated, then looked hard at Grimya, who crouched defensively beside Indigo on the cave floor.

"Stay here," she said firmly. Her manner told Grimya that she had no doubt the wolf would understand her. "Indigo needs to rest. Guard her."

Against what? Grimya wondered, but she couldn't ask and Shalune didn't elaborate. The noise of the storm was muted in the cave, though an occasional flash of lightning lit the interior starkly. Shalune prodded the hearth fire into some semblance of life, checked the clay lamps to ensure they didn't need refilling, then walked to the curtained doorway. Looking back, she said something else, in which Grimya caught the words "sleep," "fever" and "in the morning," then pushed the curtain aside and ducked out into the teeming rain.

Grimya stared at the curtain for a long time after Shalune had gone; then at last she rose and padded to the cave's entrance. The storm was cooling the night a little, but the increased humidity brought by the rain made the world oppressive. A dark, earthy smell from the sodden forest far below mingled with the electric scent of ozone. Lightning flickered again, but it was far away now and the following thunder no more than a faint grumble in the distance. Grimya looked up, staring at the steps that led up the bluff's face to the summit. No smell of incense, no sign of smoke or reflected glow from the brazier fire. The women had gone to their quarters; the night was undisturbed.

She withdrew her head and crept back across the cave to lie down at Indigo's side. Indigo seemed to be asleep, which was a blessing. Grimya prayed she wouldn't wake for a good many hours. She didn't want to have to face her and try to answer the questions that her friend must inevitably ask, for she didn't know how she was going to explain what she had seen and heard on the cliff top when Indigo had taken her place on the stone chair.

She thought the word for what had happened was "trance," but she couldn't be sure. All she *did* know was that something strange and frightening had happened to Indigo up there on the summit tonight, and that Indigo was as yet unaware of it. Something, and Grimya didn't know what it was or what it might portend, had taken her friend's place in that chair, and for a few horrifying minutes, Indigo had not been herself, but someone else. Someone who carried the reek of death like an aura.

Uluye and her cohorts had cast down their old oracle tonight and placed a new one in its stead. Indigo believed that they had made a terrible mistake. After tonight's events, though, Grimya was beginning to wonder if it was Indigo, and not the priestesses, who was mistaken.

·CHAPTER·V·

On Shalune's strict orders, Indigo was made to rest for three nights and the two days between. It seemed the fever had returned, though mildly, and Shalune clearly felt that her patient should not have been subjected to the rigors of the cliff-top ceremony so soon after her arrival. She and Uluye had further sharp words on that subject. To Grimya, who witnessed the scene, their discussion seemed to end in a grudging stalemate, but Shalune had her way and Indigo was left to recuperate undisturbed.

Grimya and Shalune had meanwhile reached a tacit and cautious understanding, based if not on trust, then at least on mutual respect. Seeing Shalune appear with a bandaged wrist on the morning following the ceremony, Grimya had felt thoroughly ashamed of her own behavior, but Shalune bore no grudge and, indeed, seemed to admire the staunch loyalty that had made Grimya attack when she thought Indigo might be in danger. She brought the wolf a special dish of unspiced meat, which Grimya suspected was a peace offering, and from then on, a wary rapport existed between them.

In fact, much to her surprise, Grimya found that she held an honored place in the citadel. Even Uluye, though reluctant to unbend from her air of rigid authority, treated her with courtesy, and the attitude of some of the lower-ranking women bordered on reverence. Grimya had complete freedom to roam at will through the settlement, and wherever she went, she found people greeting her, bringing her small gifts of food or bowls of water, even gently touching her fur as though they believed she would bring them good fortune. Grimya rapidly realized that as Indigo's chosen companion, she was looked upon almost as an avatar of Indigo herself, and until Indigo recovered from her relapse and could come among them again, Grimya would be her proxy in these women's eyes.

Under other circumstances, Grimya would have thoroughly enjoyed the attention being paid to her, but her pleasure was negated by dark and troubling thoughts. From their behavior, and from the offerings that were heaped outside the cave's entrance each day, it was obvious that Indigo was deeply revered by the priestesses, so much so that her status in the citadel seemed only one step removed from that of a goddess.

Yet beneath the surface, there was an undercurrent of something the wolf could sense but not pinpoint, like a scent on a changeable wind. She couldn't forget what had happened at the climax of the ceremony on the cliff top, and she couldn't forget the rapt and avid look on the priestesses' faces—and particularly on the face of Uluye—when the eerie thing had occurred. Although the knowledge had been submerged during the last few days by more immediate events, Grimya hadn't forgotten that the lodestone had led them here to find a demon. But what manner of demon might it be?

Worried by her speculations, she resolved to put her freedom to move about the settlement to good use. Aided by her telepathic abilities, which sometimes enabled her to glean the gist of unspoken intentions from unguarded minds, she first applied herself to learning more of the Dark Isle's tongue. She followed groups of women when they gathered to wash clothes in the lake and listened to their talk, committing as many unfamiliar words as she could to memory. She played with the children, whose constant repetition of favorite games made them excellent, if unwitting, teachers. She sat in the high cave while Shalune tended Indigo and fed her with a strong-smelling broth, and listened to the ritual healing chants the woman murmured as she worked. And by listening, watching, memorizing, Grimya quickly learned a great deal about her new surroundings.

She discovered early on that the inhabitants of the citadel within the cliff were indeed exclusively female. Men—of any age—were forbidden to enter the citadel, and the taboo, it appeared, was strictly adhered to by the local population. Like the trading family at the *kemb*, the people of the villages and settlements hereabouts held the priestesses in awe. They were not only the undisputed guardians and interpreters of all spiritual matters, but also lawmakers, judges, healers and advisers. Supplicants came frequently to the citadel, and as word of the new oracle's presence spread, their numbers rapidly grew.

On her first morning, Grimya saw several parties and individuals arrive at the lakeside, including a procession of some eight or nine nervous-looking people pushing a handcart laden with provisions. The convoy halted beside a tree whose lower branches were hung about with scarves and wooden fetishes, and there they waited until two robed priestesses walked haughtily from the bluff to meet them. The contents of the cart were inspected and, presumably, found acceptable; two more women came to carry the offerings away, and the visitors sat down by the lake's edge to parley with the priestesses. They talked for a little over an hour; then the now-empty cart was returned and the villagers departed with the priestesses' blessings and a bag of herbal medicines. As they came back to the citadel, the two women passed Grimya where she sat on a flat rock on the sandy arena between the bluff and the lake; they smiled at her, made a sign of greeting and walked on. And listening to their conversation as they moved away, Grimya heard the name of the Ancestral Lady for the first time.

The words haunted her. Who or what the Ancestral Lady was, she didn't know, but she suspected that there was a connection with whatever power or deity these women worshiped. She heard the name several more times during the morning, and her inability to understand its significance frustrated her. There was a link between the Ancestral Lady and Indigo, she was sure of it. But what was it?

It wasn't long before she learned more. As her comprehension of the Dark Islers' speech grew, she discovered that the priestesses' cult was concerned above all else with death. Death was a powerful and constant presence in this feverish and disease-ridden climate, and the borders between the dead and the living worlds were narrow and often uncertain. The greatest gateway to the realm of the dead, so people believed, was the lake itself—and beneath the lake's waters lay the Ancestral Lady's domain.

If the Ancestral Lady was a goddess, Grimya decided soberly, she was a far cry indeed from the great Earth Mother worshiped in other parts of the world. The Ancestral Lady was undisputed Mistress of the Dead, meting out reward or punishment to the souls of the departed who entered her underworld realm and became, willing or not, her subjects. And it seemed that her subjects, even in death, were unwilling to relinquish entirely their hold on the world they'd left behind.

When she witnessed the evening ceremony for the first time, Grimya didn't immediately understand its significance. As the sun began to set, a group of women left the citadel and walked around the lake's edge. They carried blazing torches, and long staves with which they beat the ground ferociously, and as they walked, they uttered wild shrieks and bloodcurdling howls that mingled with the thud of the drums from the citadel's lower levels. The wolf, sitting on what had become her favorite rock near the water's edge, where the air was a little cooler, watched in fascination, until her sharp ears caught the sound of a soft footfall behind her. She turned her head and saw Shalune approaching.

"Our rituals puzzle you, eh, Grimya?" Shalune grinned at her, then turned to watch the procession, which now had reached the far side of the lake. She clearly didn't expect a response from the wolf, but was merely talking as she would to any animal, and though Grimya longed to answer, she didn't dare reveal that she could speak, or even understand.

"We must circle the lake every night," Shalune went on. "Otherwise, the dead ones might come up from the Ancestral Lady's realm below the lake to trouble us."

Grimya's ears pricked forward and she stared at the woman, astonished. What manner of deity would send dead slaves to plague her own followers? She whined, and Shalune laughed.

"There's nothing to be afraid of. The shouting, and the sticks and drums, will frighten the zombies and spirits away. They won't come tormenting us now. Besides," she added with a trace of pride, "when the Ancestral Lady spoke to us last night, she promised us no plagues this season, as a reward for following the signs she sent us and finding her new oracle. She is pleased with us."

She brushed Grimya's fur lightly, almost as though it were a touchstone, and walked away, leaving the wolf gazing after her in consternation as she realized that her suspicion of the previous night had been confirmed. The arrival of Shalune and her cohorts at the traders' *kemb* had been no coincidence. Some power, some prophecy, had *led* them to Indigo; and that, added to the lodestone's emphatic message, turned Grimya's early suspicion into certainty. The next demon was here, she was in no doubt of it now. And she believed she knew the form it had taken.

The sun had vanished behind the trees, and the blood-red reflections were fading from the lake as its surface dulled to pewter gray. The ritual was coming to an end; the drums fell silent as the priestesses' cries ceased and the returning procession made its way toward the ziggurat. Grimya watched them pass, and shivered. *Indigo*, she thought, *you*

must get well again quickly! There is so much I have to tell
you . . . and I don't think it would be wise to wait much
longer.

On their third morning in the citadel, Shalune at last pronounced her patient fully fit. Grimya was deeply relieved,
for the healer had kept Indigo sedated and therefore un-
reachable throughout her relapse, and this was the first time
since the ceremony on the cliff top that the wolf had been
able to talk to her.

Grimya was dismayed to discover that Indigo recalled almost nothing of what had happened at the ceremony. At
first she wondered if the aftereffects of Shalune's herbal
drugs were clouding her friend's memory, but Indigo was
too lucid and too clearheaded for such a theory to be possible. She simply didn't remember; and when she heard
what Grimya had to tell her, she was deeply disturbed.

"You say that I *changed*?" They were alone in the cave
while Shalune was about other business, but Indigo suspected that they wouldn't have their privacy for long.

"Not in the way you l-ooked," Grimya told her. "But I
sensed someone—or something—else where your mind
should have been. And I did not l-like it. Then, when you
began to speak, I knew that that, too, was not you."

"What did I say?"

"I don't know. I did not under-stand the words. But the
women grew very excited, and there was r-rejoicing."
(What had Shalune said as they watched the lakeside ceremony the next evening? "The Ancestral Lady is pleased
with us . . . .") Grimya hesitated, then: "Indigo, have you
st-udied the lodestone since you woke? For I fear that . . ."
She stopped as she saw her friend's expression, and Indigo
nodded gravely.

"Yes, Grimya, I've studied it, and it confirmed what we
both suspected. The demon's here in the citadel. And you
believe we've found it, don't you?"

"Yess," Grimya growled softly. "I believe it takes the
form of this cr-reature they call the An-cestral Lady." She

showed her teeth in an uneasy gesture. "I also think she
was the one who came into your mind when you sat in the
stone chair. I smelled death, like rr-otten meat, and she is
very closely con-cerned with death."

The thought that such a being might have gained control
of her mind, however briefly, made Indigo shudder. "By
the Mother, this is some kind of insanity," she said, softly
but with feeling. "I'm not an oracle!"

"The women here think that you are." Grimya hesitated,
then added ominously, "It would seem that the An-cestral
Lady thinks so, too."

Suddenly, unbidden, an image of dark eyes fringed with
silver flicked momentarily through Indigo's mind. She was
startled by it, and Grimya's head came up sharply as she
caught the momentary disturbance in her mind. "Indigo?
What is wrr-ong?"

"I don't know." The image had gone, and Indigo shook
her head. "I thought for a moment that some memory from
that night was coming back to me, but I must have been
mistaken." She glanced toward the cave's entrance. "I wish
I could talk to Uluye. If only I could speak her language, I
might make her understand that I am not what she thinks
me."

Grimya remembered the spear-wielding priestesses who
had subtly but emphatically reinforced Uluye's will during
the ceremony. "I am not s-sure if that would be wise," she
said. "Uluye has great power here—worldly power, that is;
I don't know about any other kind. If you tell her that you
don't want to be her oracle, she will not l-like it. She would
make a dangerous enemy. It would be safer to do what she
wants, at least for now. Besides," she added, "there might
be other rreasons for saying nothing. If this Ancestral Lady
is the demon, what does that make Uluye herself?"

Indigo looked at her in chagrin. "I hadn't considered
that—I hadn't even thought of it!"

"I'm not s-saying that Uluye is evil. I am saying that we
do not kn . . . *know.*"

"And until we do, we'd be very foolish to risk telling her

anything like the truth. Besides, even if Uluye isn't directly connected with the demon, I doubt that reasoning with her would achieve anything.''

Indigo looked around at the well-furnished cave, at the growing heap of gifts and offerings brought by the citadel's inhabitants during the past two days. "These women may fete us and bestow every luxury on us, but that doesn't change the harsh fact that we're prisoners here; and that effectively means Uluye's prisoners. The priestesses may revere their supposed oracle, but whether they know it or not, their first loyalty is to Uluye herself. The oracle speaks, but Uluye interprets and acts, and as the oracle's mouth-piece, she has absolute power over everyone." She smiled grimly and without humor. "When she proclaimed me as the new oracle, I became the cornerstone of that power. She won't let any dissension from me jeopardize her posi-tion, and she has enough warriors at her beck and call to ensure that I don't dissent. So it seems, doesn't it, that I've little choice but to bow to her will.''

Grimya dipped her head. "That might not be such a bad thing though, m-might it? If we are rright about the demon, then as the oracle, you at least have found a way to come close to it.''

"True; but in many ways that troubles me more than anything else. Remember the Bray curse and what came of it? I wouldn't want to risk opening myself to a power like that a second time." A small, sharp frown knitted her brows. "I don't think I could bear to go through something like that again.''

Grimya whined softly. "I am sorry. I didn't mean to bring back painful memories.''

"No, no; you were right to say what you did. It's just that . . .'' She sighed. "Don't mistake me, dear Grimya. I know how loyal you are and how strong you are, and that means more to me than I can ever say. But even with your love and your help to support me, I still wish I had another ally here. If there were someone in the citadel whom I could trust to help me in what I have to do, I'd feel less vulnerable.''

Grimya was silent for a few moments. Then she said: "Perhaps you should talk with Sha-lune.''

"Shalune?'' Indigo looked at her in surprise.

"Yess. I don't wish to be rrr-ash, but . . . since you fell ill again, I think I have begun to like her. Also, my instinct tells me that all is not well between her and Uluye. I think they disagree about many things, and that Sha-lune would like to be leader here in Uluye's place. I don't know the proper word for it, but I think she is . . . a better person.''

Accompanying that statement came a mental image that combined rationality, common sense and a willingness to reason without dogma. Indigo, who had thought that choosing between the two priestesses was a matter of deciding the lesser of two evils, was both surprised and intrigued. She'd surmised that Shalune was second only to Uluye in the cult hierarchy; if, as Grimya implied, Shalune was dissatisfied with Uluye's leadership, then it was indeed possible that she might prove to be the ally they needed. Indigo didn't want to become embroiled in a power struggle between the two women; it would involve too many complications, perhaps even too many risks. But if she could win Shalune's trust, while keeping herself apart from any quarrels that might be brewing between the woman and her leader, at least the worst of the risks might be avoided.

"I would not say that you should trrr-ust her,'' Grimya said. "Not yet. But I think she might be ready to be our frriend, and my instinct tells me that would be a good beginning.''

"Your instinct's rarely wrong, Grimya, and I'm inclined to rely on it. Shalune's as unlikely an ally as anyone might think to find, but I'll try to befriend her.'' Indigo glanced again toward the cave's entrance. "It may be only a small step. But if the Ancestral Lady is the demon we're seeking, it could be a vital step.''

·CHAPTER·VI·

Indigo watched as Shalune deftly hooked a pot from the fireside and began to ladle the contents into two clay bowls.

"This is the first time I've been able to tell you how grateful I am to you, Shalune," she said in the Dark Isle tongue. "I should have expressed it before now, but I didn't know how to say it properly in your language."

Shalune looked up and grinned at her. "There's nothing to be grateful for. I only did what the Ancestral Lady told me; anyone else would have done the same."

Indigo listened while Grimya silently translated unfamiliar words and phrases. These were few now; they had been in the citadel for fifteen days, and with the wolf's help, she had made very rapid progress in learning the Dark Islers' speech. She returned Shalune's smile, wondering if she might venture to ask her some questions that Uluye, it seemed, wasn't prepared to answer in any detail.

To begin with, she hadn't yet been called upon to perform the oracle's duties a second time. She wouldn't deny for a moment that she was glad of that, but she also found it strange. However, when she had tried tentatively to ask Uluye about it, Uluye's only response had been to shrug and say that that was in the Ancestral Lady's hands.

Shalune, though, might be more forthcoming, and so Indigo said: "Shalune, may I ask you a question?"

"Ask." Then Shalune chuckled. "Though it should be me asking you, eh? You're the oracle, after all!"

"So everyone says. But since that first night, I've not been expected to speak again." She paused. "I've been wondering when the next occasion will come."

"We can't predict that," Shalune told her. "It's for the Ancestral Lady to choose the time and the place for her next revelation, not us. She will speak through you again when she has something to say, and not before. But don't worry," she added, again giving Indigo her startling, ferocious grin. "When the time comes, you'll know of it before anyone else!"

Encouraged by the woman's good humor and her willingness to speak freely, Indigo asked, "But what if the time doesn't come? What if you're wrong, and I'm not an oracle after all?"

Shalune looked blank. "That's not possible. You are."

"How can you be certain?"

"Because the signs were clear, of course. Uluye surely told you about the signs?"

Indigo shook her head. "No. I tried to ask, but . . . well . . ."

Shalune hesitated for a moment, as though not sure of how frank she dared be, then shrugged. "Uluye maybe had her reasons for not saying. But I haven't got any reasons. The Ancestral Lady's last words to us through her old oracle were that we should travel southwestward on our search and we would find the chosen one taking shelter from a great storm. The chosen one, the oracle said, would have an animal for her companion, and our first test would be the saving of her life with our healing and our magic." She shrugged again. "How could the two we searched for have been anyone but you and Grimya? Unless you were a *hushu*

trying to trick us, and we'd have found that out by now!"
She chuckled throatily.

Indigo stared at her. "A what?"

"You don't know about *hushu*?" Shalune paused with
her ladle in midair and a peculiar expression on her face.

Grimya, too, was nonplussed, and Indigo shook her head.
"I've never heard the word."

"Ah. Well, better maybe that it stays that way; save you
from a few bad dreams. Anyway, you don't need to worry
about *hushu* now that you're safe here." She showed her
teeth again. "I'm proud that I was the one to find you. The
Ancestral Lady is pleased with me, and that gives me plenty
of *ches*."

Grimya supplied silently: *I have heard that word. It means
that she is more greatly respected than before by the other
women.* Sagely, she added, *Uluye is not pleased about that,
I think.*

Uluye wouldn't be. . . . Indigo suppressed a smile.

Unaware of the exchange between them, Shalune set a
bowl in front of Indigo and another on the floor before
Grimya. "Enough questions for now," she said firmly.
"Eat, or there'll be no time to enjoy your meal before we
must start to prepare for tonight's ceremony."

She rose to leave, and Indigo said, "Shalune—one last
question. What will be expected of me tonight? I know
nothing about the ceremony, or even why it's taking place."
Hoping she didn't sound glib, she added, "I don't want to
make any mistakes and let you down."

Shalune frowned and her mouth quirked briefly in a small
moue of irritation. "Uluye didn't tell you that either? *Ach*
. . . well, I suppose it doesn't matter. This is Ancestors
Night, the night of the full moon. A lot of people from the
villages hereabouts will come to the lake to take part. All
you must do is go to the lakeside and be seen. Nothing else.
Don't talk, just look, and let the people we bring to you
touch your robe for good luck, the way they did on our
journey here."

"I understand." Indigo was relieved, though still deeply

curious about the ceremony's nature and meaning. "Thank you."

Shalune grinned. "Eat now. We will be back soon."

The curtain fell behind her, and Indigo turned her attention to her meal. It was one of the many odd quirks of this cult that no one was permitted to dine with the oracle, or even to watch the oracle dining. Indigo's food was prepared for her—she wasn't, as she had discovered early on, allowed to do more than the absolute minimum for herself—but to witness her eating her meal was taboo.

Other taboos included stepping over the threshold of her cave quarters if she were not present or were seen to be asleep, speaking the names of any of her predecessors in her presence, and touching her, in however small a way, without the express permission of a high-ranking priestess. High rank, Indigo had learned, was reserved for a very exclusive few, who included Uluye, Shalune and a bare two or three others—among them, Uluye's own daughter.

When Yima had been introduced to her ten days ago, Indigo had been astonished, first by the extraordinary physical resemblance she bore to her mother, and second, by the revelation that the High Priestess should have a daughter in the first place. It surprised her that while the women of the cult disdained all but the minimum of contact with men, there was no taboo among their ranks against the bearing of children. Grimya, after a little judicious eavesdropping, had found out more. It seemed that if they wished to, the women were permitted to leave the citadel and to take and live with a mate for a short while. Any daughters of the union were welcomed into the cult when their mothers chose to return; sons, however, were fostered to families grateful for such a privilege, and thereafter forgotten.

It was hard to imagine that Uluye had ever borne a child for the sake of love, or for even a passing passion, but easy enough to see another and more pragmatic motive. Yima was sixteen years old and destined to be the image of her mother in more than the physical sense, for she was training to become, one day in the future, Uluye's successor as head of the cult. A little to Indigo's surprise, Uluye's intention seemed to have the approval of all the priestesses, even Shalune's. The only one who apparently had not been consulted was Yima herself, but that, it seemed, was an irrelevance. Yima would obey her mother in this as in everything else, and when the time came, she would take up her role without demur.

Despite the fact that she was Uluye's child and Uluye's puppet, Indigo took an immediate and intuitive liking to Yima. Though she had inherited her mother's physical qualities of lean, rangy frame and strong-boned features, two more different temperaments would have been hard to find. Where Uluye was quick-tempered, authoritarian, and suspicious of all around her, Yima was quiet, modest, and trusting almost to the point of naivety. It was a pity, Indigo thought, that her life both now and in the future should be so circumscribed by her mother's rigid demands, for she had a suspicion that Yima was not cut out to be a natural leader. She also suspected that Shalune privately shared her view, though the fat woman never broached the subject. But it was not Shalune's place—as Uluye had made quite clear—to question the decisions of the High Priestess, or even to express an opinion of her own.

Not questioning Uluye's decisions was a matter that Indigo suspected would become a bone of contention between herself and the High Priestess before long. Uluye demanded absolute obedience from all the women about her—and that included the oracle, whom she theoretically served. So while in most respects Uluye accorded Indigo all the reverence given the oracle by the other priestesses, she nevertheless expected her every command to be instantly obeyed, reinforcing Indigo's feeling that despite her outward pretense, Uluye looked upon her as little more than a tool with which to implement her own will. Indigo disliked that intensely, but bearing Grimya's earlier caution in mind, she kept her resentment to herself as far as was possible. Only to Shalune, and even then with great diplomacy, did she occasionally hint that she was not satisfied with a situation that suited Uluye's will to the exclusion of all else.

Her relationship with Shalune had changed a great deal in the past few days. Now that they were able to communicate, Indigo found herself liking the fat woman more and more; as Grimya had predicted, they were becoming friends. There were still barriers of caution and uncertainty, complicated further by the gulf of Indigo's status in the cult, but Shalune was both a realist and a pragmatist; Indigo behaved toward her as an equal, she therefore responded in kind and without awe. Why should even a goddess's avatar not have friends if she so desired?

There was, of course, a degree of self-interest involved, for to be the oracle's confidante earned Shalune still more *ches* among her peers, and it also ensured that Indigo did not fall too far under Uluye's influence. As her language skills improved, Indigo realized that there were indeed areas of major disagreement between Uluye and Shalune and that, as Grimya suspected, Shalune would have liked to be head of the cult in Uluye's stead. Observing the two women together and separately, she came to the conclusion that Shalune would have been the better choice, at least where secular matters were concerned, for she would have tempered Uluye's rigid adherence to law with a modicum of common sense and compassion, qualities that Uluye either did not possess or was unwilling to show.

Under other circumstances, Indigo might have felt some sympathy for Uluye, for she had an intuition that the High Priestess's unbending attitude sprang from the insecurity and loneliness to which absolute rulers so often fell prey. But however hard she tried, she couldn't bring herself to like the tall woman. Shalune, for all that her friendship might have an ulterior motive, at least presented a human face to the world.

Grimya had already finished her food, licking the bowl to savor the last drops of liquid. Indigo had eaten enough—Shalune's portions were more than generous—and she set her own bowl on the floor, urging the wolf to finish it. As she poured herself a cup of water from an ewer, she asked, "What did Shalune say was the name of this full moon ceremony, Grimya? Ancestors Night?"

Grimya licked her muzzle. "Yess. But I don't know what that means."

"Some rite of remembrance, perhaps, to honor the dead." Indigo spoke casually, but at the same time, she repressed a small inward shiver. What kind of underworld, or otherworld, was the Ancestral Lady's realm? Did she truly have dominion over the souls of the departed? The priestesses had explained very little of their religion to her, but she knew that they believed the Ancestral Lady had the power to grant joy or torment in the afterlife. Joy or torment . . . an old, old memory stirred in Indigo's mind, and with it came a dull, aching grief that over the years had become as familiar to her as her own features in a looking glass. A name in her thoughts, a face before her inner vision. Fenran. . . .

Grimya, sensing something amiss, looked up. "Indigo? What's wrong?"

Indigo made to dissemble, not wanting to share her thoughts—not even with Grimya—at this moment, but before she could speak, they heard footfalls outside the cave and the sounds of several voices. Grateful for the interruption, Indigo called out that she was ready to receive visitors, and as the curtain was moved aside, she saw Uluye on the threshold, with Shalune, Yima and two other women behind her.

Indigo inclined her head formally to the High Priestess. Two, she had decided, could play Uluye's game; if she would not unbend, then Indigo would follow her example. "I've finished my meal," she said. "You may all enter."

Uluye stalked into the cave. At her curt order, the two lower-ranking women gathered Indigo's and Grimya's empty dishes and took them away to be washed. When they had departed, Uluye said, "I understand that Shalune has told you what is expected of you at tonight's ceremony."

"She has." Indigo was tempted to add: *which is more than you would condescend to do*, but she stilled her tongue.

"Very well." Did a swift, unfriendly glance flick between Uluye and Shalune then? Impossible to be sure. . . . "You will be carried to the lakeside at sunset. Please speak to no one, and allow only those we bring before you to touch you."

"Thank you," Indigo said with a faint edge to her voice. "Shalune has already given me that instruction."

This time there was an unmistakable exchange; anger from Uluye and smug satisfaction from Shalune. Yima, who stood between the two, quickly cast her gaze down and concentrated on her feet.

Then Uluye's upper lip twitched and she addressed Indigo again. "I have brought your ceremonial robe. Please dress. We haven't long before the rite begins."

Grimya, who disliked Uluye even more than Indigo did, was keeping her thoughts carefully neutral. Hiding a smile, Indigo took the garment that Uluye held out. "Thank you," she said again, more gently this time, and began to dress.

The drums that for two hours had been throbbing out their summons to the faithful of the villages fell silent at last, and a fanfare from the great horns announced the appearance of the ceremonial procession on the staircase. As they emerged into the fiery light of sunset, Indigo was astonished to see how many had answered the drums' call, for the waterside was ringed with people, thronging in a circle that stretched all the way around the lake, from one side of the citadel to the other. At an order from Uluye, the warrior-priestesses at the head of the procession lit torches; fire flared on the staircase, and a huge shout went up from many massed throats as the crowd below saw the signal. They moved forward, the warriors leading, Uluye in full ritual garb following, and Indigo, precariously and nerverackingly carried on an open litter, behind her. She shut her eyes as the descent began, horrified by the litter's swaying and by the effect of the great headdress on her sense of balance, and heard Grimya's mental voice from where the wolf walked between Shalune and Yima in the litter's wake.

It's all right, Indigo, it's safe. The stairs are wide enough, and the women must have done this many times before.

Indigo tried to concentrate on that reassurance and make herself believe it as their progress continued. Halfway down, the drums began again, thundering out an insistent rhythm, and she thought she could hear, mingling with their din, voices crying out and calling encouragement. Then at last they were on the final flight, a broad sweep that took them down onto the arena of bare red sand between the cliff wall and the lake. A flat, squared-off rock four or five feet high stood in the center of this plateau, and the litter-bearers set their burden on the rock, so that Indigo was enthroned above the heads of the crowd, where she could look down upon the entire proceedings.

It was, she thought as she drew in a sharp breath, an awesome scene. The sun had blazed down behind the trees, and the tropical night was falling with its uncanny rapidity. Before her in a line stood the priestesses, and Uluye alone before them, her crowned figure nightmarish in the torches' jumping glare. Around the lakeside, the congregation watched and waited. A few, granted a privileged position on the edge of the arena, were lit by the torch glow, and Indigo saw strain and fear in their faces.

Suddenly the horns blared out another short fanfare, and the drums ceased. A bird shrieked from somewhere in the forest's depths, and then as the last echoes died away, there was silence.

Uluye stepped forward. Arms crossed over her breasts, she walked with dignity to the lake and without a pause, waded into the water. An eager murmur went up from the watchers; a child wailed and was quickly hushed. Uluye kept moving, advancing down the sloping bank. The water rose to her thighs, to her waist, to her shoulders. Then she stopped, uttered a high-pitched cry and ducked under the water so that only the crown of her elaborate headdress showed above the surface.

The watchers gasped again. Two of the warrior-priestesses set down their spears and moved with silent efficiency to take up stances at the water's edge. Every eye was on Uluye's headdress, and Indigo found herself counting the passing seconds. They stretched on and on, and her pulse quickened. Surely no one could stay underwater for so long without coming up to breathe. She exchanged an uneasy glance with Grimya, kept counting. . . .

Abruptly there was a great churning in the lake, and Uluye rose. Water streamed from her hair and clothing, and the rattling groan as she sucked air into her lungs echoed across the lake. The warriors splashed into the water and caught her arms as she seemed about to fall; she was rigid in their grip, head thrown back, eyes wild as though possessed, and her mouth stretched wide in an agonized but triumphant smile. Her helpers pulled her back toward the edge, until they all stood knee-deep in the water. Then, as though suddenly regaining her strength and her wits together, Uluye shook off their guiding hands and raised her arms high.

"The Ancestral Lady favors us!" she cried. "I have stepped into her realm and returned unscathed, and I am strong in her eyes!"

A howl of approach went up—mingled, Indigo thought, with more than a little relief. Nodding gracious acknowledgment, Uluye left the water and stalked toward the rock where the litter was set. As she approached, her gaze met Indigo's briefly, and Indigo saw the truth behind her proud demeanor. Uluye's immersion in the lake for minutes on end without drowning had not been magic, though to her simple and superstitious audience it surely had all the trappings of something supernatural. It had been a self-imposed test of endurance, proof to herself, as much as to anyone else, that she could triumph where others would fail. Proof of her faith in her own will and her own strength. Was that, then, the crux of Uluye's religion, and was the Ancestral Lady nothing more to her than a means to an end, as Indigo

was? Did Uluye even believe in the goddess she professed
to worship?

Grimya, catching the thought, looked up from where she
sat by Indigo's feet. *She may not believe*, the wolf communicated silently, *but the people do, and that is all she
needs*.

Uluye stood now before the rock and turned to face the
lake once more. On the cliff side, more torches were being
lit, turning the ziggurat into a strange and shimmering wall
of dancing flames that illuminated the arena below as
brightly as day. Indigo smelled incense, saw clouds of
smoke rising from braziers set around the dusty square and
tended by the younger priestesses. Uluye gazed on the scene
with taut satisfaction, then raised her arms again, her fingers
clawing toward the sky.

"Come!" she cried in a fierce, stentorian voice. "Come
to us, you who are bereaved. Come to us, you who have
cause to fear the departed. Come to us, you who would
dispute with the dead. I, Uluye, will partake of your offerings! I, Uluye, will intercede for you! I, Uluye, in the Ancestral Lady's name, will put wrong to right and see justice
done. Come to us, and let the rites of Ancestors Night begin!"

From somewhere away to the left of the arena, where the
trees crowded thickly, a woman's voice screamed out. "Oh,
my husband! Oh, my husband!"

Uluye's head turned sharply; she snapped her fingers and
two priestesses hastened toward the source of the cry. Moments later they returned with the woman—hardly more than
a girl, Indigo saw now—and brought her before Uluye,
where she collapsed sobbing in the dust at the High Priestess's feet.

Uluye stared down dispassionately at her. "Your husband
serves the Ancestral Lady now. Would you try to deny him
that privilege?"

The girl struggled to bring her emotions under control.
"I would see him, Uluye. Just once. Just once more,
please. . . ."

"What gift do you bring to honor him?"

The girl fumbled with a small sack slung under one arm. "I bring the soul bread . . ." her voice quavered, almost broke ". . . baked with my own hands, that he may eat. I bring the sap of the *paya* tree, sweetened with honey, that he may drink. . . ."

She reached out, holding a leaf-wrapped package and a small water skin. Uluye gazed thoughtfully at the offerings for a moment, then took them. She unwrapped the soul bread—a flat, unleavened loaf—and ate a corner of it. Then she drank a mouthful of liquid from the skin. The girl covered her face with her hands, trembling with relief, and Indigo heard her whisper over and over again, "Thank you, Uluye! Thank you, Uluye!"

Her two escorts led her away to stand at one side of the arena. As a second supplicant shuffled forward into the torchlight, a figure, fire and shadow in the shifting glare, moved close to the rock where Indigo sat, and Indigo looked down to see Yima at her side.

She leaned down and whispered to the girl, "What's happening, Yima? Who is that woman, do you know?"

"Yes, I know her," Yima replied softly. "Her husband died of a fever three full moons ago. She has been grieving for him ever since, but has only now found the courage to ask to meet him again. It's very sad. He was only twenty-two years old."

There was compassion in her tone. Indigo frowned. "How can she meet him again?" she whispered back. "Surely Uluye won't—" She checked herself, amended hastily: "The girl doesn't mean to *die*?"

Yima turned wide, surprised eyes up to the litter. "Of course not," she said. "He will come to her. From the lake."

Shalune, who stood a few paces away beside another young girl whom Indigo didn't recognize, heard the whispering and gave Yima a warning frown, at the same time nodding expressively in Uluye's direction. Yima flushed, made an apologetic gesture to Indigo and moved away. In-

digo stared after her, alarmed by what she had said. The
dead rising from the lake? Surely that couldn't be literally
true. She tried to catch Shalune's attention, wanting to
whisper an urgent question, but Shalune either didn't see or
felt it prudent to ignore the signal.

Grimya was still staring at Uluye, who now was repeating
the question-and-answer ritual with a spindle-shanked old
man, and Indigo asked silently: *Grimya, did you hear what
Yima said?*

I heard. But I don't know what she can have meant. The
wolf darted Indigo a quick, troubled look. *You don't think
that it could be true? That the dead will really return?*

I don't know. I truly don't know.

The old man had been dismissed to stand with the still-
weeping girl; two more people were coming forward. The
clouds of incense were thickening with no breeze to carry
them away; the smell was acrid in Indigo's nostrils and becoming unpleasant as it mingled with the tarry stink of the
torches. She already felt a little disoriented—there *was* a
narcotic in the incense, she was sure—and the scene and
the atmosphere were beginning to take on a dreamlike tinge.
At all costs, Indigo thought, she must keep her wits. She
had to discover the truth about this rite; whether it was a
simple trick to soothe the bereaved and frighten the trou-
blesome, or something more sinister.

Six supplicants had now brought their offerings to Uluye,
and a seventh was led before her. The sound of Uluye's
voice raised suddenly in anger alerted Indigo, and she
looked up to see a scrawny woman cowering on her knees
in the red dust with three other grim-faced people, two
women and a man, behind her.

Uluye loomed over the groveling woman like an avenging
angel. "Justice?" she roared, her voice carrying across the
lake. "Justice, for a murderer of children?"

"I didn't do it!" the woman whined. "He did it, *he* was
the one! He said we could feed no more mouths, that seven
was too many, that three must die! What could I do? I tried
to stop him, but he beat me . . . look, Uluye, see, here are

the marks. I am only a poor, weak woman and he is so much stronger than I—''

Uluye interrupted chillingly. "Where is your man now? Why is he not here to speak for himself?''

"He ran away, Uluye. He ran away because he is guilty and he knew that you would punish him. He killed three of my children and he took the other four, and he has left me to mourn my little ones alone and uncomforted. See, see the marks he made on me, the scars—''

Uluye's voice cut across her babbling. "Where are your offerings?''

The woman scrabbled in a bag she carried and brought out a parcel and a water skin, but she held them close to her breast, clearly reluctant to proffer them to the priestess. "I have brought them. Food and drink. Look, I have them. But they have cost me dearly; I must go hungry now, for my murdering husband has left me with nothing. Have pity on me, Uluye; have pity on me!''

Uluye stared at her for a long moment. Then, very slowly and deliberately, she reached out and plucked the offerings from the woman's hands. She unwrapped the bread, unstoppered the skin. She ate. She drank.

The supplicant's face crumpled into an ugly, childlike expression. She didn't try to argue, but as her three companions—or perhaps, Indigo suspected, "guards" was a more apt word—took her to join the other postulants, her hands and feet began to twitch in mute but uncontrollable terror.

Uluye's stare raked the gathering and she said with deceptive mildness, "Who is next?''

As the eighth candidate came forward, Indigo darted a glance at Shalune. The fat woman was watching her whilst appearing not to; Indigo signaled surreptitiously and Shalune edged away from her companion and sidled toward the litter, until she was just within murmuring distance.

"You should not talk.'' The pitch of her voice reminded Indigo of the Southern Isles hunters' whisper; Shalune had learned the knack of suppressing any sibilance in her voice. Indigo smiled thinly and answered in a similar tone.

"I know. But there's so much I don't understand. Who was that woman?"

"Her? Child slayer. Poisoned three of her brood and claims her husband did the deed. He's disappeared; it's likely she killed him, too, though his body hasn't been found yet. Her whole village knows she's guilty, but they haven't any proof. So they forced her to come here, to find out the truth."

"How *can* they find out?"

Shalune looked straight at her, faintly surprised. "From the children, of course. They'll know their own murderer."

"But—" Unthinkingly, Indigo had raised her voice, and Uluye snapped a venomous glare over her shoulder. Swiftly Indigo turned the exclamation into a cough, but when Uluye looked away again, Shalune made a quieting gesture.

"No more talk," she whispered. "Wait and watch. You don't need to do anything more." She pulled a face at Uluye's back and sidestepped to rejoin her young companion.

Indigo sat back in her chair, stunned as Shalune's careless remark reverberated in her mind. *From the children, of course.* She still couldn't bring herself to believe that it was possible. She didn't *want* to believe it, for if it were true, if tonight the spirits of the dead were to rise and walk again in the world of the living, then—then—

"Nnn—" The sound came involuntarily from her throat; she couldn't silence her tongue in time. Uluye turned again swiftly, but this time in anticipation rather than in anger, as though expecting to see some change in her.

Indigo shut her eyes against the priestess's intense stare, thinking: *No, Uluye, this isn't the oracle, this is me, me!* Something flicked across her inner vision: eyes, silver-fringed, but they were gone so quickly that they didn't take root in her memory. *Control yourself*, she told herself savagely. *Get a grip on your wits.*

It was the incense affecting her . . . this sudden light-headedness that seemed to come from nowhere, as though she were rising from the litter and floating above it. Narcotic smoke in the air. She was starting to hallucinate; she thought that mist was rising from the lake and clouding its surface, blurring the reflections of the torchlight, turning the water into a huge, golden mirror. How much longer would this ceremony continue? She wanted it to be over. She was thirsty. Hungry, too. She wanted to go back to the familiar cave retreat, to sleep. . . .

Indigo shook her head, and the miasma cleared. Blinking, she saw that fifteen people were now clustered to one side of the arena and that no new plaintiff stood before Uluye on the red sand. *Fifteen* postulants? Perhaps she had dozed after all. And Grimya had gone. Where was Grimya?

Grimya? She sent out the call and was relieved when the wolf's mental voice answered immediately.

I am here, Indigo. Behind your chair. A pause, then: *I . . . I don't like what I am feeling. I can smell something. I don't recognize it, but it makes me very uneasy.*

The drums began again then. At first the sound was so subtle that Indigo was aware of it only on an unconscious level, but it grew stronger, louder, faster, until it seemed that the air was thick with the throbbing rhythms. Disruptive and unsettling rhythms, crossing and recrossing, clashing one with another, making Indigo shudder, she felt, to her bones. She looked at the lake and saw that the mist had returned, not a hallucination this time, but real, rising in silent, smokelike curls from the water and forming a pall like steam over the surface. The priestesses had begun to chant with the drums' impossible beat; yodeling, shrilling, ululating noises like a cacophony of mad birds.

Shalune had gone, Yima had gone; they were with the others, a line of stamping, shouting women advancing down toward the lake's edge, and with them went the supplicants, stumbling, crying out in joy or terror. Indigo heard the bereaved girl calling her dead husband's name, heard the murderess's shrill protest as she was dragged across the sand by two machete-wielding women, and for one terrible moment she felt that she had become both those unhappy creatures.

The bereaved and the guilty. Weeping for her lost loved ones, yet carrying the knowledge that she was a slayer and that for her, there could be no redemption.

Indigo! Grimya's telepathic cry rang in her head as she pushed herself to her feet, but she didn't heed it. She was standing now, unsteady, the oracle's heavy crown making her sway like a tree in a gale. Something was trying to force its way out of her soul, through her heart, through her ribs, through her flesh. A word, a name, was trying to form on her lips, trying to compel her to say it, shout it, scream it aloud. The drums were inside her and a part of her, her own pulse, her own chaotic heartbeat. The women's voices dinned in her ears . . . and something was forming in the mist over the lake. The surface waters were moving, agitating, broad ripples spreading to the banks and lapping there in tiny waves.

"Fe—" Then something choked the word off in her throat before she could utter it. The chanting stopped, the drums stopped. So suddenly that Indigo could barely comprehend what had happened, there was silence. No, not quite silence. She could hear the gentle slap of water on the lakeshore, licking at the red dust. And a moan, abruptly curtailed. She knew who that was: the murderess; it could only be she. Indigo blinked, looked again at the lake and saw what had loomed out of the mist and now waded through the shallows toward dry land.

A solitary woman came first. She was old, and smiling the awful smile of incurable madness. Her eyes burned like cold, dead stars in her skull, and she reached out clawing hands toward two young men who huddled together on the bank, her expression filled with ineffable but utterly insane love. Indigo heard their heartbroken cries of *"Mother! Mother!"* and had to look away as they took her corpse's hands and kissed them over and over again.

Next came a young man, naked. Indigo looked at his face, at the sores twisting what had been a handsome mouth into a festering parody, at the blackly swollen tongue, at the film that dulled his staring eyes. His body shone slickly with the sweat of fever, and he trembled, trembled even as his distraught wife rushed forward and flung herself down in the shallows to clasp and embrace his ankles.

Indigo was beginning to understand. As they had died, so they returned: mad, diseased, fever-ridden, as they had been in the last moments of their earthly life. Even as she realized this, the third revenant emerged, and this time she had to look away, for what stalked from the water was a man who held his own severed head cradled in his arms. She heard the cries of his brothers, who sought to avenge him, but she couldn't bring herself to watch their reunion, and only when the gruesome figure was lost in the melee, did she dare to raise her eyes again.

She was in time to see the children. They came out of the lake hand in hand, and their small bodies were stained crimson with the blood that had flowed from their cut throats. Their mother began to scream, and her screams redoubled as, one after another, the children raised their hands and pointed at her in clear accusation. They didn't speak; their windpipes had been severed with their jugular veins, and they had no voices now. But their hands, and their looks, were more eloquent than any words.

After the children there were many others, though none quite so ghastly. Inured by now, Indigo watched them with detached and dispassionate fascination, as though a part of herself refused to accept the reality of what she was seeing and had dubbed it a dream. At last, though, there were no more. The wailing and the crying and the exhortations and the protests had dulled to a murmur, like the soporific drone of bees in a drowsing garden; she was aware of it and yet not aware; her surroundings were remote, a little unreal.

Then, over the lake, the mist swirled suddenly and the waters were stirred once more.

Grimya whimpered, and the sound so close by startled Indigo out of her stupor. She looked at the lake, and then she saw the last revenant of all. His skin was deadly pale, shocking contrast to those who had come before. His long black hair was matted, sweat-soaked. He moved like an old man racked with arthritis—or a young man bound by chains that his soul could hardly bear—and as he limped toward the shore, Indigo saw the network of lacerations that scarred his skin: arms, legs, face, every part of him, the searing and savage work of a hundred thousand poisoned thorns.

She knew she had cried out aloud. On another level, another plane, from another world, she saw shocked faces turn toward her in the torchlight, saw Uluye's fanatical delight as Indigo—or something beyond Indigo—uttered a howl without words. The pale, hunched figure at the lake's edge paused. Then he reached out toward her, across the red sand, across the physical gulf that separated them, and he called to her by the name that she had been compelled to renounce so many years ago when the Tower of Regrets had been breached, when she had brought evil on her home and family and loved ones, when the demons had entered her world. Her true name. The name by which he had known her in the happy days before she was Indigo.

"Anghara. . . ."

The thing that had been trying to burst from Indigo's soul shattered and imploded within her, and she flung her head back and screamed with all the strength she possessed.

"Fenran!"

The world vanished.

·CHAPTER·VII·

"**I** can't see you. Fenran, I can't see you! Where are you?"

Darkness; silence. She could feel her body, though it didn't seem to have its familiar physical dimensions. The blackness was so intense that her inner vision invented colors, striving to create some sense of orientation out of the bewildering dark.

Then a voice said "I am here."

"Where?" She had spun around before she realized that it was not Fenran's voice, but that of a stranger, and that it had not spoken aloud, but in her head.

"Here. Behind you. Before you. To your left and to your right. Above and below. Look, Indigo. Look, and you will find me."

Someone was breathing close by. She heard the steady *hush-hush*, not in her mind this time, but real, tangible. The claustrophobic air shifted momentarily as though something had disturbed it, and a faint smell impinged on Indigo's nostrils. What was it Grimya had said in describing what had happened in the cliff-top temple? *I smelled death, like rotten meat.* Yes, this too had the whiff of decay, of putrefaction. . . .

She drew just enough breath to speak. "You are not Fenran."

"Fenran?" There was faint, chilly amusement in the query that seeped through her mind. Indigo felt a peculiar blend of anger and fear begin to form within her.

"Yes, Fenran. I saw him. I saw him coming out of the lake."

"Ah. The lake has many secrets, which it does not easily give up. People have many dreams by the lakeside, and dreams are not always reliable."

The smell was changing, sweetening, taking on a quality redolent of the incense the priestesses burned at their ceremonies. Indigo inhaled and felt smoke fill her throat and lungs.

"I don't believe I was dreaming, or that I'm dreaming now." She paused, trying to take mental hold of her anger to bolster her confidence, but suddenly it was too tenuous to grasp and it slipped out of reach, eluding her and leaving only a renewed sense of disorientation.

The voice in her head laughed softly. "No, you are not dreaming now. I am here. You do not imagine me."

"Then I did not imagine Fenran."

"Perhaps not. That is up to you to decide."

Indigo's gaze flicked about, but still she could see nothing; the darkness was absolute. "Who are you?"

"You know who I am."

Yes, she believed she did. . . . Indigo's teeth clenched and the muscles of her throat contracted as the smoke, sickly sweet now, stifled her. "Where is Fenran? Where has he gone; *where you have sent him?*"

"You will not find him here. You will find only me, and those whom I choose as my servants, as I have chosen you."

Indigo frowned, though for some reason she found it a tremendous effort. "I am not your servant. I acknowledge only one mistress: the Earth Mother herself."

"Do you, Indigo? I think not. I think that although you

may not yet allow yourself to believe it, you are ruled by another.''

Indigo's anger rose again; again she tried to grasp it, and again the essence of it eluded her. Even so, her voice was knife-sharp as she retorted, "Not by *you*, madam!"

A throaty chuckle echoed ghostlike in her mind. "We shall see, in good time. Now, Indigo, I shall speak and you shall be my mouthpiece as before.''

"No." Indigo shook her head. "I will not be your marionette a second time.''

"You will. You are my oracle. I have chosen you, and you have no choice but to obey me.''

Indigo started to say, "I have every—'' but suddenly she found that she had no voice. Her tongue had frozen, locked to the roof of her mouth, and neither her physical strength nor all her willpower could move it. Again the soft laughter filled her head.

"You see? You *are* my servant, Indigo. Now, listen well to me and carry my words back to my people. They are waiting for you.''

Far away, like the distant roaring of the sea, Indigo heard the sound of many voices. At first their noise was no more than a blur, but swiftly it resolved into a single, rhythmic word, repeated again and again.

"Speak! Speak! Speak!" They were calling her, calling the oracle. They had seen the signs and knew that the Ancestral Lady was among them. Indigo tried to fight against their exhortation, but with a huge surge, the disorientation came back and her senses deserted her. She couldn't see, couldn't touch; she had lost all awareness of her body and seemed to exist only as a mind without a physical shell.

Listen, Indigo. Listen and speak.

She had no choice. The words were filling her. She was becoming the words; she knew nothing but the words. On the lakeshore, amid the sea of upturned faces, the oracle opened her mouth and a wail of anticipation went up. In another world, in darkness and nothingness, Indigo tried to scream. There was a violent jolt; a blast of arctic cold went through her, and then she felt her mind tumbling helplessly into a vortex as the physical world wrenched her back to blackness and fire under the cold stare of the rising moon.

The drums were sounding again. Urgent, insistent, their rhythm thrummed in her bones, and the torchlight flared against her eyes, making her wince and turn her head away. Shadow shapes moved in the torchlight; the priestesses were moving about the sandy arena in a shuffling dance, their voices counterpointing the drums' beat as they chanted shrilly. Then there was a new shadow at the base of the rock where Indigo's litter was set; a figure clambered up and a strong, square hand held a cup to her lips. Indigo drank gratefully, recognizing Shalune's low-pitched voice as the figure said, "Quietly, now. This will restore you."

Grimya? Her mind still floundering, Indigo searched mentally for the she-wolf's reassuring presence. There was no response.

Grimya? Uncertainty became alarm, and Indigo jerked forward in her chair. *Grimya!*

"Quietly!" Shalune pressed her back, her whisper sibilant. "It's all right."

Indigo pushed the cup aside as it was proffered again, and hissed agitatedly, "I can't find Grimya!"

"She isn't here. She went back to your quarters. I sent her there—she was frightened. Drink again now."

"Frightened?" Nonplussed, Indigo was caught off guard and had swallowed another mouthful of the cordial before she realized it. The liquor had a sweet and powerful taste; some fermented fruit she guessed, and doubtless quite alcoholic. Already her body was beginning to relax, though her mind still whirled. What had Grimya been afraid of? She tried to think back to what had happened, and with a shock realized that she had no recollection of it whatever.

"Shalune!" Her voice was a sharp hiss. "What happened? Did I speak? I can't remember anything!"

Shalune grinned her terrible grin. "You spoke." She was clearly pleased. "Quiet, now. Let the drink do its work and

bring back your strength.'' She dropped to a crouch beside
the litter, effectively cutting off any further exchange.

Indigo sat back, staring in confusion at the lake and the
torches and the dancing, chanting women. She was beginning to feel giddy from the mixture of incense in the air
and alcohol in her body, but a single thought had lodged in
her brain and was harrying her, refusing to be quelled.
Something was wrong. Surely, before the trance overtook
her, the scene had been different? The memory of it still
refused to come back to her, and the cordial was dulling
her brain even as it relieved the tension of aftershock; but
surely there had been others here, and something strange
and unnerving had happened. Or was she deceiving
herself? No, for if she were, what could have so frightened
Grimya that she had been ready to flee back to the caves?

Indigo stared beyond the torchlights' glare to the lake.
The lake. . . . For a few moments her hazy brain absorbed
nothing but the sight of the dark water, the crowd at its
edge, the ceremony, the drums. Then abruptly a sliver of
revelation sprang up from her subconscious mind and
slipped into place.

At once she sat sharply upright and scanned the crowd.
With the first barrier breached, memory of what she had
seen before the trance overcame her was starting to return
in full, like an artist's portrait slowly taking form. Out of
the lake . . . they had come out of the lake, she had *seen*
them. Ghosts, spirits, whatever they were, they had emerged
from the heavy mist that shrouded the water and come to
be reunited with the living souls they had left behind. Children—there had been three children, holding hands, blood-
stained, accusing. A headless man, a fever-ridden youth, a
mad old woman; many, many others. She had seen them
all. And—the last and most painful shock struck her hard
and sharply—*she had seen Fenran!*

Indigo's hands clamped convulsively on the arms of her
chair, and wildly she looked about again. But there were
no apparitions now. The mist had faded away and the lake
was an unruffled black mirror, reflecting only the torches

and the bland, round face of the moon. The revenants were gone. But *where*? Had they merged back into the water that had disgorged them, or were they here still, invisible, the dead mingling with the living and moving among them?

Indigo reached down and grabbed Shalune's shoulder. "Shalune!" she hissed. "Where are—"

"Shh!" Shalune pinched her arm hard in warning. "Not now!"

The priestess pulled away, and with a violent movement, Indigo tried to catch hold of her again. She rose halfway from her seat, then fell back, her head swimming as her limbs refused to obey her command. The cordial had been more powerful than she'd realized, its effect so strong that it had robbed her of strength and coordination.

Gasping for breath and seething with frustrated confusion, she tried to get a grip on her rioting thoughts and force herself to reason more coherently. Fenran wasn't here. He *couldn't* be. The incense and the chanting and the tense, dreamlike atmosphere of the ceremony had opened the floodgates of her imagination, and that last solitary figure wading from the lake, with its ashen face and stooping, painful gait, must have been a hallucination. She had seen him because she had wanted to see him—perhaps she had even expected it, for this bizarre ceremony under the full moon was a death rite, and where else might she hope to find Fenran but among the shades of the dead?

The old, leaden weight that she knew so well settled on Indigo's heart and she turned her head aside, not wanting Shalune to see the tears that glinted suddenly on her eyelashes. For one single moment she had felt something close to hope, but cold reason had dashed it. She had dreamed or hallucinated—she didn't know which, and it didn't matter. All that did matter was the painful knowledge that her lost love had not been among those who had returned tonight, however briefly, to rejoin the loved ones they had left behind.

Suddenly the drums fell silent. Lost in her unhappy thoughts, Indigo started up in surprise as the last echoes

died away and were absorbed by the crowding trees. She
blinked rapidly, trying, though her mind railed against it,
to drag herself back to reality and the present moment. Was
the ceremony over? It seemed not, for the crowd was tense
with anticipation, and the priestesses who tended the brazier
were heaping on more incense. Then, shattering the hiatus
of silence, Uluye's voice rang out.

"The Ancestral Lady has spoken to us!"

The dancers had drawn back and the High Priestess stood
alone in the center of the dusty arena. With a dramatic gesture, she flung out one arm to indicate the rock and the
motionless, enthroned figure of Indigo. "Hear me now!
Hear me, and I will tell you what message she brings!"

Uluye was hoarse, either with excitement or from pro-
longed shouting. The crowd pressed forward, listening avidly, and with a sinuous grace that was both awesome and
faintly repellent, Uluye began to prowl. She moved toward
the throng like a hunting cat, pausing every so often to stare
hard into a frightened face or to make a swift hand movement from which her watchers shrank back. She had a finely
honed sense of the dramatic; the worshipers were enthralled
and as malleable as soft clay in her hands. Then she stopped.

"Tonight we have been doubly blessed," she said, her
voice echoing, eerily out of phase, from the ziggurat wall.
"The Ancestral Lady has granted us not one boon, but two!
She has sent her servants, who now dwell with her below
the lake waters, to commune with us. And more than that,
she has also seen fit to speak to us through her chosen oracle! And the message she imparts to us—" she turned
slowly on one heel, her eyes glittering like faceted jet in the
torchlight "—the message she imparts to us is one of *justice*!"

She began to move again, searching it seemed for one
special face among the many. Even Indigo was mesmerized
by her, and for the first time, she realized that Uluye did
indeed have power, not merely the temporal power of a
secular ruler, but a true occult gift. The air around the High
Priestess was electric, alive. Her congregation—there was

no other word for them, and they *were* hers, hers alone to manipulate as she willed—hung on her every movement, her every word, like children under the sway of a beloved yet terrible mentor.

"*Justice.*" Uluye repeated the word with awe-inspiring sibilance. "Who among you fears the Ancestral Lady's judgment?"

She stopped again and pointed to someone in the throng, then began to turn slowly and deliberately, her outstretched finger finding another target, and another, and another. "Who will have cause to kneel in praise and thanksgiving tonight, and who will have cause for lamentation? The Ancestral Lady sees all! The Ancestral Lady knows all! Through her own oracle she has judged you, and I, Uluye, am charged by the oracle to dispense the right and proper justice of our Lady, who is mistress of your souls."

A female voice rang out, wailing with an emotion that could have been anything from the hysteria of joy to the despair of misery. Uluye spun around, finding the source of the cry with uncanny accuracy.

"*You!* Yes, I see you, and I hear you as the Ancestral Lady has heard you. Come forward, my daughter. Come to me. Don't dare to hold back!"

Slowly, shaking with fear, the young widow whose husband had died of a fever moved out of the press of people. Uluye waited; the girl approached and crumpled to her knees at the High Priestess's feet.

"Daughter," Uluye said, "your man was called from his service to the Ancestral Lady so that you might look again on his face and renew your pledge to him. This you have done, and you are not found wanting. You have been true to his memory and have not deceived him or turned your face to another, and so I will tell you now how the Ancestral Lady has rewarded you. Within the year you will know another good man, and your grieving heart will be healed. You may cleave to this other man without fear of your dead husband's wrath, and you may take him as your own and lie together under one roof in the knowledge that no vengeful shade or hungering *hushu* shall come creeping to your bedside when the night is at its darkest.'' She reached out and laid a hand on the crown of the girl's bowed head. ''Go now, daughter. Make your obeisance, and return to your home without fear.''

Still trembling uncontrollably, the young widow rose to her feet. Across the width of the arena Indigo saw her eyes shining like lamps in the torchglow, and the look on her face of dawning joy, of hope rekindled where before there had been only despair, was like a physical blow. As the girl, ushered by Uluye, began to move hesitantly toward her, Indigo felt as though something deep inside her had turned to ashes. She understood the girl's grief; understood, too, what it was to be granted the hope of a new love when the old seemed lost beyond recall.

In her mind's eye she saw a face, not Fenran this time, but another who once, years ago, she had for a short while believed might taken Fenran's place in her heart. She had been grievously wrong, and the stinging guilt of her folly still haunted her. But perhaps tonight, as the Ancestral Lady's oracle, she had in some small way made amends for that old mistake by being the instrument through which this sad young woman was to be granted a second chance for happiness. It was a cruel irony, for it seemed she had the means to achieve for another the one thing that she herself yearned for above all else but could not reach. No one could grant Indigo the certainty of hope. Not the oracle, not Uluye, not even the Ancestral Lady herself.

The widow came to the rock and stopped. She dared not raise her head to look the oracle in the face, but she dropped to one knee in an awkward curtsy and her uncertain hands touched the hem of Indigo's robe. Over her hunched figure, Uluye's gaze and Indigo's met, and the priestess's eyes narrowed as she glimpsed something that Indigo had not wanted her to see.

''Enough, daughter.'' Uluye touched the girl's shoulder, drew her back. Her expression was speculative and just a little uncertain.

Indigo watched the girl move away, and the worm of envy that had been squirming within her faded. How could she begrudge the young widow her fortune? She didn't know whether the Ancestral Lady's promise would prove true or false, and in some ways it seemed irrelevant. The girl believed, and in belief there was hope and healing. Indigo prayed silently that, for this girl at least, the hope would prove to be real and not an illusion.

One after another they came before Uluye for judgment. It seemed that the Ancestral Lady had been merciful tonight, for almost all of the postulants were granted some measure, however small, of comfort in their unhappiness, or reparation for their loss. The madwoman's sons were told that the Ancestral Lady had taken pity on their mother and would restore her wits in the Afterworld. The brothers of the headless man were promised that within three more full moons, the murderer would meet an untimely end and his possessions would be rightly theirs. Utterly scrupulous, yet coldly detached, like an austere and domineering matriarch, Uluye dispensed justice, and with it, hope—with one exception.

At first Indigo didn't understand when the woman who had killed her children broke free from the two priestesses who held her and flung herself in the dust in front of the rock below her litter, yelling hysterically. Indigo could make no sense of the babble of words, which sounded from their tone as though the woman were cursing her and imploring her by turns, and only when the priestesses pounced on the murderess, pinning her down while Uluye interposed herself between the woman and the oracle's sacred person, did Indigo begin to comprehend. As the woman was hauled away screaming, Uluye turned her head and looked up at the oracle's throne. For the second time that night, their gazes clashed, and Uluye said in a tone that only Indigo could hear, "Don't look so shocked. You spoke the words that condemned her."

Without waiting for a reaction, she stalked off in the wake of the priestesses and their struggling prisoner, and Indigo looked quickly around for Shalune. Shalune, though, had gone. Only Yima stood alone, a few paces from the rock, staring at the small drama with dark, expressionless eyes.

At the lake's edge three more priestesses were maneuvering into position what looked like an upright framework of lashed branches some six feet square. The woman was dragged toward it; as she saw what awaited her, her shrieks redoubled, but the cries were ignored and she was manhandled to the framework and tied to it, spread-eagled and helpless. As the last knots were pulled tight, she seemed to accept her fate, and her cries faded first to whimpering and then to nothing. She was still, hanging from the frame, her head drooping forward in defeat.

The crowding watchers were silent now. Uluye turned to them once more.

"Go," she said. "Go back to your villages and give thanks for the boon we have all been granted tonight. The Ancestral Lady has spoken, and her will and her justice have been done. Turn your faces now, and depart in awe and in gratitude to the rightful mistress of us all."

There was no more ceremony, no drums or horns, nothing. In an eerie atmosphere of anticlimax, and without even the smallest murmur, the crowd began to disperse. On quiet, shuffling feet they melted away into the forest, and within minutes the lakeside was deserted and only Indigo, the priestesses and the bizarre wooden framework with its motionless prisoner remained on the dusty arena before the ziggurat.

At a signal from Uluye, the torch-carriers began to extinguish their brands. One by one the guttering yellow flames were plunged into the sand and went out, and the night's natural darkness closed in like a shroud. The moon stared down at its own distorted reflection in the lake, and the figures of the priestesses became faceless silhouettes. Shalune's heavyset form loomed out of the gloaming with the litter-bearers behind her; she glanced up at Indigo and put a finger to her lips, forestalling anything Indigo might have tried to whisper to her. Silence, it seemed, was the women's watchword now, and in silence the litter was lifted from the rock, and the procession, with Uluye at its head, turned toward the cliff-side stairs.

As she was borne away, Indigo thought she heard a sound from the lake's edge, a whimper of despair and misery and abject fear that carried over the litter's creaking and the soft, muffled hush of the priestesses' bare feet in the sand. She looked over her shoulder, asking herself uneasily what the murderess's ultimate fate would be. Death by starvation, or by broiling in the heat of the sun? Or something still worse? *You spoke the words that condemned her*, Uluye had asserted. Indigo wondered what she had said. What dire punishment had the Ancestral Lady decreed through her lips and tongue?

They reached the foot of the first staircase. Just before the litter carriers turned to begin the ascent, Indigo had one last glimpse of the lakeshore. A column of mist was forming on the water, an oddly isolated patch of moonshot silvergray. Though she couldn't be sure, Indigo thought she saw three small figures forming in the mist, and saw them begin to move, drifting over the surface like wraiths as they slowly converged on the wooden frame and its condemned occupant.

Then her bearers turned, set foot on the first stair, and the high back of her throne obscured the arena from view as she was carried away toward the high caves.

·CHAPTER·VIII·

In the pearl-gray mist of predawn, Indigo woke from a nightmare screaming Fenran's name. Grimya, who had been curled at the foot of the bed, sprang to her feet and ran to her, licking her face and projecting messages of comfort and reassurance until Indigo had struggled through the awful borderland between dream and reality and was fully awake.

For several minutes they sat together, Indigo hugging the wolf close. "I'm sorry," she said over and over again. "I'm sorry, Grimya."

"Wh-at is there to be sorry for? You cannot control your drreams."

"I know, but I thought those nightmares were behind me now. It's been so long since they've haunted me, I thought I might at last be free of them."

Grimya said hesitantly, "You dreamed of . . . *him*?" She was reluctant to speak Fenran's name in Indigo's presence.

Indigo nodded. "I dreamed I was standing on the lakeshore, and he . . . he came out of the water, searching for me. Only when I looked into his face, I realized that he wasn't the Fenran I knew. Something had happened to him, something *terrible*. He was mad, and he didn't know me, and I knew he meant to kill me, so I ran, but whichever way I turned, he was always there in front of me, waiting . . .'' She shuddered. ''Why did I dream of him like that, Grimya? *Why?*''

''I don't know.'' The wolf looked up at her unhappily. ''Perhaps it was because of last night.''

They both fell silent for a few moments. Returning to her quarters after the somber procession back up the great stairways, Indigo had found Grimya in an abject state. The wolf had been desperately ashamed of the fear that had made her run away from the ceremony and hide herself in the cave, but at the same time, as she told Indigo, she couldn't rid herself of the feeling that something very evil was taking place, and she simply hadn't had the courage to face it. The incense smoke had been affecting her head, she said, so that she could barely distinguish reality from illusion, and she had felt so sick and disoriented that when Shalune told her to go, she obeyed immediately and with relief.

Indigo didn't blame her. She too had had a similar feeling, though her senses, less acute than Grimya's, had been dulled rather than painfully sharpened by the narcotic smoke. She still couldn't recall anything that had happened during her trance. Even though the earlier events were now clearer in her mind, there remained a gap in her memory, a void that it seemed she couldn't cross and bring back to consciousness.

She gently pushed Grimya aside and rose to her feet. Thankfully, her scream as she woke hadn't brought anyone running; she couldn't have tolerated the priestesses' anxious solicitude at the moment, and even Shalune's presence would be unwelcome. The cave was making her feel imprisoned and claustrophobic. She wanted to get out in the fresher air, be alone for a while with only Grimya's company and no one else to intrude on them.

''How long before dawn breaks, do you think?'' she asked the wolf.

Grimya considered. "Not ll-ong. It's dark still, but there is a heavy mist, and that means morning must be near."

If they had only half an hour before the citadel started to wake, that would at least be better than nothing. Indigo reached for her clothes. "Let's walk by the lake for a while, before anyone else is about. I feel I need to clear my mind."

Grimya agreed eagerly, and as soon as Indigo was dressed, they left the cave. Outside, the darkness was intense; the moon had set and no starlight could penetrate the mist that folded around them, heavy with the damp smells of the forest. Faint and muted, the myriad small sounds of the jungle impinged on Indigo's ears as its nocturnal inhabitants began to give way to the wakening creatures of the day. Insects chirred, their endless chorus broken now and then by the twitter of a bird stirring to utter its first tentative welcome to the morning. In the distance, something large and unidentifiable grunted hoarsely and there was a brief rustle of undergrowth. Of human activity, though, there was no sound or sign.

Groping her way down the long flights of stairs behind Grimya's more surefooted descent, Indigo began to relax a little. The sting of her nightmare was fading, and the predawn cool and stillness had a primordial feel that she found oddly comforting. They reached the sandy arena, which was scuffed into chaos by crisscrossing footprints, and walked on toward the water's edge. Then suddenly Grimya, several paces ahead of Indigo, stopped with a yelp of consternation.

"Grimya? What's wrong—oh, Goddess!"

She saw it before Grimya could intercept her and turn her aside: the framework of branches at the edge of the lake. She'd forgotten it—perhaps her subconscious had deliberately blotted it from her mind—and so the shock of coming upon it now, looming from mist and darkness, was all the greater. The woman, the murderess, still hung where she had been lashed to the frame, her back to Indigo and her face staring out across the lake. She wasn't moving, and whether or not she was breathing, Indigo couldn't tell.

Slowly, driven by a perverse fascination, she started to approach the frame.

"Indigo." Grimya hung back, her voice unhappy. "Leave it. Don't look."

Indigo paid no heed. She drew level with the skein of branches, some of which had wilted leaves still clinging to them, then stepped around the frame's edge.

Grimya heard her sharp intake of breath, but Indigo didn't speak. She only stared at the frame and what it contained, and after a few moments' indecision, Grimya ran to her side.

The woman was dead. Not from dehydration or from any other natural cause; she had bled to death, killed by a savage slash that had opened her throat and all but severed her head from her shoulders. Blood covered her arms and torso, drying now into a brownish crust like an obscene garment. Her eyes, staring widely even though all traces of life were gone, held an expression of unfettered terror.

Abruptly the spell that had mesmerized Indigo snapped and she jerked her head aside, shutting her eyes in revulsion. She started to turn, stumbling blindly away from the gruesome corpse, but a sudden mental alarm from Grimya halted her.

Indigo! There's someone coming!

Indigo froze and, opening her eyes once more, peered into the mist. She could see nothing, but after a few seconds she heard a new sound. Soft footfalls; someone—or something—was moving stealthily toward them. Images of the horrors she had witnessed last night tumbled into her mind and she felt a flash of panic as a shape, indistinguishable in the darkness, loomed ahead. Grimya growled defensively, hackles rising.

The shape hesitated; then Uluye's voice said, "What are you doing? What do you want here?"

They stared at each other as tension and shock ebbed. Uluye lowered the machete she was holding, and with a great effort, gathered her poise. Her eyes were wary, mistrustful. "You shouldn't be here alone," she said with a hint of aggression.

Her tone nettled Indigo. "I'm not alone, thank you, Uluye," she responded crisply. "Grimya is with me, and she provides all the protection I need."

Uluye flicked the wolf a brief, dismissive glance. "All the same, I would prefer that you return to the citadel. It is not right for the oracle to show herself to any casual gaze by walking about like an ordinary person."

Irritation began to turn to anger, and Indigo retorted, "I hardly think I'm likely to be looked over by anyone when I can barely see my own hand in front of my face!" Then suddenly a new and unpleasant thought occurred to her. Why did Uluye seem so anxious for her to leave? Could it be that there was something she didn't want her oracle to see?

She looked at the machete in Uluye's hand and her suspicion took a tighter hold. "It was *you* . . ." she said softly.

"What?" Uluye frowned. "What was me? What do you mean?"

Oh, she was a good actress, Indigo had seen that for herself. She met the tall woman's arrogant stare directly and unflinchingly, and pointed back to the wooden frame, barely discernible in the mist behind her.

"Tell me the truth, Uluye," she said harshly. "That— that woman—you killed her, didn't you?"

For a moment Uluye looked genuinely puzzled, but then her expression cleared. "Oh," she said. "I understand." She walked past Indigo and Grimya and stopped before the frame. Her eyes took in the corpse with a single critically assessing glance. "So she *is* dead. It was swifter than I'd anticipated." She glanced in the direction of the lake. "The Ancestral Lady has seen fit to be merciful."

"Merciful?" Indigo repeated, appalled.

Uluye looked at her in surprise. "Of course. There are many far less easy ways to die than this. I imagine she must have lost consciousness quite quickly."

Indigo returned her stare, feeling a shudder of revulsion

at the High Priestess's sanguine indifference. "You *imagine*
. . . are you telling me you didn't kill her?"

"I?" This time Uluye's surprise was unmistakably gen-
uine. "Of course not!"

"Then who did?"

"Her victims. Who else? As she slew them, so it is right
that she should be slain by them in turn."

Last night, Indigo remembered, as she was carried to the
stairs, she had seen the mist re-forming, glimpsed the three
shapes moving shoreward. . . . "Sweet Goddess," she said
in an undertone.

A small, cold smile played about Uluye's lips. "As I said
to you at the ceremony, why should you be shocked? She
was condemned to die by the word of the Ancestral Lady,
not by any decree of mine. Indeed, you might as easily look
to yourself as her judge, for you are the oracle through
which the Lady speaks."

"So you tell me," Indigo replied. "But I have only your
word for that, haven't I, Uluye?"

Uluye's expression changed. "What do you mean? I don't
understand you."

The darkness was beginning to lighten perceptibly. Dawn
was close; the mist was already thinning and soon the sun
would rise. Indigo began to walk away from the corpse on
its frame, wanting to remove herself from its vicinity before
daylight forced her to see it in all its stark and grisly detail.
Uluye followed her. She didn't repeat her question, but Indigo sensed that she was holding back only with the greatest
difficulty and through a sense of stubborn pride.

Somehow, without knowing how or why, she had touched
Uluye on a raw nerve. There was something more to this,
and here and now, with no one to overhear them, Indigo
wondered if she might have found a weapon with which to
crack the High Priestess's stone mask and challenge her to
tell the truth. Uluye's cold-bloodedness in the face of another human being's ugly death had made Indigo angry
enough, and thus reckless enough, to try.

She stopped near the rock where her litter had been set

the previous night and turned to look Uluye squarely in the face.

"You may or may not be aware of this, Uluye," she said, "but I have no recollection whatever of anything that happened to me in the trance state. I don't know what I said or what I did. For all I can tell, I might have sat in that chair squealing and grunting in a fair imitation of a pig, while you laughed inwardly at my animal noises and told your congregation whatever you wanted them to hear."

Uluye looked appalled. "That is blasphemy!"

"Not to me. The Ancestral Lady is your goddess, not mine. That is, if you believe she exists at all."

The color drained from the High Priestess's lips and her eyes widened with rage. "Don't *dare* to speak such perversion in my presence! I will not *tolerate* this!"

"You have no choice but to tolerate it, have you?" Indigo retorted. "Not if I am what it suits you to claim I am. Which is it to be, Uluye? Am I your chosen oracle or not? Did I truly speak last night, or did you stage the whole spectacle to inveigle a gullible and superstitious crowd into believing what you wanted it to believe? Tell me the truth!"

Uluye hissed like a snake. "Do you dare to call me a charlatan?"

"Oh, no. You're no charlatan, I know that very well. But when the oracle speaks to the people, at whose behest is she speaking? At the Ancestral Lady's—or at yours?"

Uluye stared at her for a long time. The sun's first rays were touching the treetops now, and in the mist the priestess's tall figure seemed to be haloed in cold fire. Then she spoke.

"You are treading a thin and perilous path, Indigo. I am the chosen servant of the Ancestral Lady, and by impugning me, you also impugn the Lady herself. I warn you, be careful, or you may find that your time in this world will end far sooner than you expect."

Indigo stood very still. "Is that a threat, Uluye?"

"Not a threat; a prophecy. Foresight isn't the province of the oracle alone, and I know the Ancestral Lady's ways far better than you do." She stepped forward, then reached out and took hold of Indigo's arm. "You may be the Lady's chosen oracle, but you are as much her servant as any of us."

Indigo tried to pull her arm away, but Uluye held on. Grimya came forward, a growl forming in her throat; quickly Indigo sent a mental message warning her back. She had broken through Uluye's barrier, albeit in a way she hadn't expected, and she didn't want to lose her advantage now. Uluye wouldn't hurt her; she didn't think the priestess was even angry anymore. If anything, she was afraid.

"I give fealty to only one goddess," Indigo told her with icy calm. "And that goddess is the Earth Mother herself."

"No," Uluye said. "You serve the Ancestral Lady. She has chosen you, and she rules you, as she rules us all."

Suddenly Indigo experienced a terrible sense of *déjà vu*. Her own declaration, Uluye's emphatic reply—she had heard such words before; she had clashed with someone, wrangled in this same way. When, and where? She couldn't remember!

I have chosen you, and you have no choice but to obey me. . . .

Uluye's grip on her arm tightened suddenly. "What? What is it?" For the space of a moment, the scene before Indigo's eyes winked out. Then her senses returned and she found herself staring blearily into the priestess's avid and wide-eyed face.

"Does she speak to you?" Uluye demanded breathlessly. "Tell me—*tell me!*"

Before Indigo could respond or protest, Grimya, snarling, sprang at the priestess and knocked her off balance. Uluye reeled back and the wolf interposed herself between the two women, head down, showing her fangs.

"No, Grimya!" Indigo had recovered her outward composure, though she felt shaken. "She meant no harm."

The wolf relaxed a little, though still bristling, and over her head Uluye met Indigo's gaze uncertainly. "She understands your own tongue . . . ?"

"Yes." Indigo reverted to the Dark Islers' speech. "She won't attack you unless she believes you want to hurt me."

The other woman's eyes narrowed and the frown reappeared on her face. Indigo realized suddenly that Uluye wouldn't *dare* to harm her, for whatever personal animosity she might harbor—and that was an unknown quantity—she believed in her goddess as unshakably as Indigo believed in the Earth Mother, and she also believed that the Ancestral Lady had chosen Indigo as her own avatar.

Uluye said: "She came to you. Only for a moment, but she *came*. I know; I felt her presence." There was a peculiarly defensive note in her voice that Indigo had never heard before; then suddenly her tone changed and the old arrogance was back. "What did she impart to you? I insist that you tell me! I am her High Priestess. I must know!"

Indigo's anger rose afresh. Something had happened, she was well aware of it, but it had come and gone so swiftly that she was left with only the memory of a momentary blackout, nothing more. And Uluye's probing did little but raise her temper. She had had more than enough of this arrogant, imperious tyrant.

"I can't tell you, because I don't know!" She met Uluye's challenging stare with a challenge of her own. "Unless you have the power to delve into my mind and discover the truth for yourself, I can't help you!" And before Uluye could answer, she stalked away across the arena.

"Wait!" Something in Uluye's tone—a pleading note?—made Indigo pause. She looked back. The High Priestess hadn't followed her but stood rigid on the sand. From her expression, Indigo knew immediately that she had no such divinatory power and resented the fact.

"What is it?" Indigo asked, her voice cold.

Uluye approached, but cautiously, keeping a prudent distance. "There is something wrong," she declared harshly. "The Ancestral Lady has spoken to you, and yet you are incapable of telling me what she has said. This has never happened before. You must try to remember. You *must*!"

Indigo's temper boiled over. "Damn you, Uluye, what

manner of retarded child do you take me for? Do you think I'm playing games with you? Do you imagine I take some perverse pleasure in hiding the truth? I assure you, I'm doing no such thing. I don't like this any more than you do; and above all, I don't like the idea that my mind is being taken over and used by something I can't even interpret, let alone control. If anyone is playing games, Uluye, it's your precious Ancestral Lady—so you'd best look to her for your answers, not to me!''

This time when Uluye called after her, Indigo ignored her furious demands to come back. Seething, she strode away so fast that Grimya had to run to catch up with her—until, not looking where she was going, she collided with someone, barely visible in the mist, who cut across her path.

"Your pardon, Indigo!" Yima, Uluye's daughter, made an apologetic obeisance, then stopped, chagrined, as she saw Indigo's face. "Is something amiss? Can I—''

"Yima." Quick, padding footsteps announced Uluye. She stepped in front of Indigo as though to bar her from Yima's sight and stared hard at her daughter. Her voice was clipped as she struggled to suppress her feelings. "You're abroad early. Where have you been?''

Yima blanched a little at the tone and held up a handful of freshly dug roots. "Shalune asked me to gather a supply of *irro*, Mother. She said they should be picked in the hour before dawn.''

She sounded breathless. Uluye continued to scrutinize her face for a few moments, then, apparently satisfied, nodded curtly. "Take them back to the citadel.''

"Yes, Mother.'' Yima seemed relieved to be dismissed and hurried away.

When she had gone, Indigo and Uluye stood motionless on the sand. Yima's unwitting intervention had taken the edge from their clash and both were calmer now, but they were still unsure of each other and as wary as two cats meeting on the borders of their territories. At last, seeing that Indigo wasn't willing to speak first, Uluye broke the hiatus.

"There are matters afoot here that I think neither of us is yet in a position to understand," she said cautiously. "I must think on this, and search for a solution." Then she became aloof once more, distant and coldly formal. "I will consult with my senior priestesses and let you know the outcome of our deliberations."

"As you please," Indigo replied quietly. The explosive moment was past and her anger had subsided; she saw a hint of uncertainty in Uluye's eyes and, for a moment, almost felt sympathy for her.

Uluye nodded. "You'd best return to your quarters now. It's time to eat."

Grimya, behind them, was looking back over her shoulder. Full daylight had arrived, the mist was lifting, and at the lake's edge the wooden frame with the dead woman tied to it was clearly visible. Indigo read what was in the she-wolf's mind and remembered how her clash—or was it a clash? She wasn't so sure now—with Uluye had begun.

"What of . . . her?" she asked, indicating the thing by the water's edge.

Uluye shrugged. "She isn't worthy of being given to the lake; the Ancestral Lady has no use for servants such as her. *Hushu* will come for the body in good time. Tonight, perhaps tomorrow night. There is nothing more we need do." She turned to face Indigo fully and, as Yima had done, made the customary obeisance, though from her the gesture was a formality with little meaning. Then she turned her back, stalked away and began to climb the stairs.

"Wake up. We have matters to discuss."

The imperious voice broke Shalune's pleasant dream, and she opened bleary eyes to see Uluye standing over her. With an effort, the fat woman sat up, saw the early daylight filtering in through the cave's curtain, which Uluye hadn't troubled to close behind her, and grunted irritably.

"It's barely dawn!" Newly awakened and not at her best,

Shalune spoke in a tone that was a good deal less respectful than it should have been. "Why should I be disturbed at such an hour?"

"Because I order it." Uluye's voice took on a venomous edge, and even through the lingering veils of sleepiness, Shalune realized that the High Priestess wasn't in the best of moods. Aware that she'd overstepped the mark, she swallowed a yawn and made a gesture that conveyed both apology and acquiescence.

"Forgive me, Uluye. You took me unaware."

"So I see." Uluye hadn't missed the resentful glint in her subordinate's eyes, but she ignored it, instead bestowing a sweeping, scathing glance on the untidy quarters. "You live like a pig. Have a novice clear this mess, or do it yourself."

Shalune didn't answer but climbed from her rattan bed and shuffled to the hearth, where she blew on the embers of the fire and began to prepare food and drink to offer her unexpected and unwanted visitor. Uluye paced the length of the room a few times, then swept a pile of Shalune's clothing from one of the boat-shaped chairs and sat down, swinging one long leg across the other in a clear indication of her irritable mood. Without preamble, she said, "I want to talk to you about Indigo."

"Indigo?" Shalune paused and looked up at her in surprise. "Yes. What's wrong with her? I wasn't aware that anything was wrong."

"Then you're a fool." Uluye stood up and began to pace again. "There's a flaw in her, Shalune, and I don't like it. The Ancestral Lady speaks through her, and yet afterward Indigo remembers nothing of what happened."

Shalune frowned "I know she had a lapse of memory during her enthronement in the temple. But that was only to be expected; she was exhausted, she hadn't fully recovered from the fever. I told you at the time that you were expecting too much of her too soon." Her dark eyes flashed. "With the greatest respect."

They exchanged a look of mutual dislike, and Uluye's lip

curled. "I'm not talking about the enthronement ceremony. I'm talking about last night. And again this morning."

That took Shalune by surprise. "This morning?" she echoed. "What happened this morning?"

Under other circumstances Uluye would have privately relished revealing knowledge to which Shalune wasn't already privy; however, at the moment she was too preoccupied to even notice the fat woman's chagrin. "At dawn," she said, "while you were still snoring, I went to the lakeside and I found Indigo walking there. While we were speaking together, the Ancestral Lady came to her."

Shalune uttered a soft oath. "What did she say?"

"That's just it. She said nothing. Or at least, nothing that Indigo was willing to tell me."

Shalune looked at her sharply. "Do you mean that she kept the Ancestral Lady's word from you?"

"No, I do not! She wouldn't dare do such a thing. I mean that she didn't even know what had happened to her. The Ancestral Lady entered her mind for only a few moments, and afterward Indigo was unaware that anything had taken place."

Shalune stirred her pot, which was beginning to simmer. "She couldn't have been dissembling? If the message she had been granted was something she thought you would not want to hear—"

"How could she make such a judgment?" Uluye countered scornfully. "Besides, I would know. I would *know*. There are no two ways about it, Shalune. The Ancestral Lady came to her, but she was incapable of passing on what she had been told. That means—can only mean—that something is very wrong."

Shalune took the cooking-pot from the fire and poured the hot drink into two tall cups. Uluye took one without thanks and clasped it in both hands, inhaling the fragrant steam as she stared thoughtfully at the cave entrance.

Shalune asked at last: "She has no memory? Not the smallest recollection?"

"Not even the smallest. That, as I'm sure I don't need to

remind you, is unprecedented. And I believe that something within Indigo is blocking her memory and preventing her from knowing what she does." She took a sip of her drink and started to pace once more. "I suppose we must assume that you didn't make some foolish mistake and bring back the wrong candidate."

Shalune bristled angrily. "I followed the signs, Uluye, as you well know. The Ancestral Lady made it quite clear that—"

"Very well, very well; I'm not casting doubts on your much-vaunted efficiency. So, then: we accept that she is our chosen oracle and that the Ancestral Lady has entered her soul. But what else is within her? What is blocking the gateway in her mind between this world and the world of spirits? It may be that the Ancestral Lady has seen fit to set a flaw in her, as a test of our skills in finding and righting it, but somehow I don't think so. The flaw stems from Indigo herself; from her own will. She's trying to fight the Lady's power, and that is a blasphemy that can't be tolerated!"

Shalune was shocked. "Uluye, I can't believe that Indigo is *evil*!"

"Evil?" Abruptly Uluye turned on her heel and looked hard at the other woman. "I didn't say she is evil. But the flaw in her must be found, for until it is, she will continue to fail in her duty to the Lady." She pointed a long finger at Shalune. "You are our senior healer as well as my deputy. You must help me to find it, and eradicate it."

Shalune looked up from under heavy, knitted brows. "That will be easier said than done, Uluye. *If* you're right," the emphasis was subtle but clear, "and there is something within her striving to block the Lady's influence, I can't begin to imagine what its nature might be."

"Then you'll have to search for it all the more diligently." Uluye finished her drink, set the empty cup down and gave her subordinate a hard look. "She seems to look upon you as a friend of sorts, so I suggest that you make the most of her trust. I charge you to keep watch on her, and to report anything untoward to me immediately.''

Shalune shrugged her agreement. "And if I discover nothing?''

Uluye pursed her lips tightly. "If you discover nothing, I will be obliged to consider other measures. If all else fails, there is one further option—to put the matter before the Ancestral Lady in person.''

Shalune's head came up sharply. "You mean, send her—''

"Yes.''

"But how? Such a thing can be done only when there is an essential reason, or we risk incurring the Lady's wrath on us all.''

"There is an essential reason; or there will be. Yima's initiation trial.''

Shalune was aghast. "*Yima?* She's but sixteen—she's too young!''

"I was little older when I underwent the same test.'' Then Uluye smiled unpleasantly. "Ah, but I forgot—you were originally an outsider, weren't you? My trial took place before you came to us.''

Shalune flushed, as though Uluye had touched a sore point. "Whatever your circumstances might have been, Yima's only a child.''

"She's *my* child. That makes the difference, as it made the difference to my mother before me.'' Uluye looked at the fat woman shrewdly. "Why should you object to her initiation taking place earlier than originally planned? Do you think her unsuitable to succeed me when I am called to the Ancestral Lady's greater service?''

Shalune glowered at her. "Certainly not. I've always fully approved of Yima as our next High Priestess, as you well know. I'm simply worried that she may not yet be ready to face the ordeal of initiation.''

"That,'' Uluye said with asperity, "is not your concern, but mine. I will decide the time of the initiation, and Yima will be ready.''

Shalune made an acquiescent gesture, though she clearly didn't like it. "It is as you wish, of course."

"Quite. And, as is traditional, the oracle will accompany her on her journey." Her dark eyes glinted. "Then we shall see an end to the flaw within Indigo, for the Lady will drive it out and destroy it!" She moved toward the entrance. "I shall leave you now; I have other matters to attend to. Remember what I said, Shalune—watch her, investigate every clue, and keep me informed."

"Yes, Uluye."

At the curtain, Uluye paused and looked back. "Oh, one other thing—did you ask Yima to collect some fresh *irro* root from the forest?"

"*Irro?* Yes—yes, I believe I did. Our stocks are running low." The fat woman hesitated. "Is anything amiss?"

"No, no. She has the new supplies; I'll see that they're delivered to you." She nodded once by way of farewell and left the cave.

Shalune sat back on her haunches as the curtain fell into place once more. The encounter had raised a number of questions that were beginning to link together in a way that made her uneasy. She didn't have the authority to argue with the High Priestess—besides, argument would have cut no ice with Uluye, especially in her present mood—but she suspected some ulterior motive behind this morning's visit. Did Uluye truly believe that there was something wrong with Indigo, and if so, was she right? Shalune doubted it; after all, if anything was amiss, then she as a healer would surely have gleaned some hint of it.

No, there was something else behind this, something more personal. It involved Indigo, it involved Yima, and above all, it involved Uluye herself. As she had so pointedly remarked, Uluye had been born into the cult rather than entering its hallowed precincts from outside, and her mother—whom Shalune remembered as a terrifying old woman with a thoroughgoing sadistic streak—had been High Priestess before her. Uluye had long been determined to continue the dynasty that her mother had begun, and it had

been established and accepted for years among the priestesses that Yima would follow her as leader. No one had
questioned it, no one had dissented.

Yet it seemed that Uluye was now using her supposed
worries about Indigo as a lever to force the matter to prom-
inence at least two years earlier than might otherwise have
been the case. It was as if Indigo's flaw—if indeed she had
a flaw—was nothing more than an excuse for Uluye to bring
the date of the ceremony forward. Why, Shalune wondered,
had the question of Yima's final initiation suddenly become
so urgent to the High Priestess?

She suspected that she knew the answer to that question,
at least in essence. She had read it in Uluye's eyes just now,
seen it in the twitch of her mouth and the unnaturally tense
set of her shoulders. Uluye was worried. Worried that some
new and unforeseen factor might threaten her plans, under-
mine her authority and weaken her—and that factor was
Indigo herself.

With a grunting effort, Shalune got to her feet and, still
in her night robe, shuffled across the floor to the curtained
entrance. Cooking smells were beginning to waft upward
as the citadel came to life, and the air was already baking
as the sun climbed above the trees. What had Uluye sensed
in Indigo that she herself had missed? Was there something
there, some power, some disruptive force, or was Uluye
starting to lose her grip on reality and see *hushu* at every
turn? Whatever the truth of it, seeds were being sown, and
the harvest threatened to bode ill for someone.

Footfalls sounded on the ledge outside her cave, and
Shalune peered round the curtain to see Yima approaching.
The girl saw her, stopped and made an obeisance. "Shalune
. . . my mother told me to bring you the *irro*."

"Ah, yes; the *irro*." There was faint irony in Shalune's
voice as she took the herb and weighed it in her hands.
There were only a few roots; not much for half a night's
gleaning. "Thank you, Yima."

Yima paused, then her face flushed deeply and she whispered, "*I* should be thanking *you*. And I do—I do, from the depths of my heart!"

Shalune eyed her shrewdly. "It may not be so easy the next time. But I'll do what I can. Best go now; your mother will doubtless have tasks for you."

Yima nodded and hurried away, and Shalune stared after her departing figure. Yima's visit had served to remind her that there was yet another complication to be considered, and one to which she must give a good deal of thought. She hoped the child wouldn't make a mistake, let something slip to the wrong ear or be seen at the wrong time. Uluye had already asked one cryptic question, and any arousal of her suspicions could lead to disaster.

Shalune withdrew into the cave once more. Care, she thought; care must be her watchword now. Or, in the light of Uluye's new preoccupation, her own plans could be in jeopardy. . . .

·CHAPTER·IX·

Over the next two days, Shalune did as Uluye had bidden her. Unaware of what had been mooted, Indigo was surprised and a little irked by the fact that, unless eating or sleeping, she rarely seemed to be out of Shalune's sight, but she hid her irritation, for she was growing to like Shalune more and more, and believed that her motives sprang only from kindness and an eagerness to further their growing friendship.

If Uluye had expected her subordinate to report back to her quickly, she was disappointed. Shalune saw nothing untoward; there were no more unexpected trances, no lapses of memory, nothing worthy of further investigation; and this only served to reinforce the fat woman's suspicion that the question of a flaw was a deliberately misleading ploy, and that Uluye was orchestrating something more devious than she had yet guessed.

During the moon's waning the citadel was customarily quiet; fewer spirits and dark things were abroad at this time and fewer people came to the bluff with offerings and petitions, so that apart from their nightly ritual of patrolling the

lakeshore, the priestesses had little to do but tend to their
domestic affairs. The hiatus was a relief to Indigo, as it
enabled her to immerse herself in mundane matters and put
from her mind the horrors she had seen on Ancestors Night
and its aftermath. She suffered no more nightmares; but,
on the second night following the full-moon ceremony,
something occurred that shattered her new-found peace of
mind.

The hour was late, and Shalune was preparing to leave
Indigo's quarters after spending a productive evening in-
structing her in some of the finer points of the Dark Isle
tongue. Lifting back the curtain to usher her guest out, Indigo paused as she glimpsed movement on the lake shore
below. The sky was stippled with clouds so that the moon's
light filtered down through a faint haze, but two hunched
figures were discernible by the water's edge, making their
way from the forest toward the sandy arena at the foot of
the ziggurat. At the lakeside the murderess's corpse still
hung on its wooden frame, and Indigo wondered if these
stealthy visitors were perhaps relatives of the dead woman,
come to take her body away and grant her the small con-
solation of a decent interment. But then Grimya growled
suddenly, and Shalune reached out and gripped Indigo's
arm.

"Come back inside the cave." She was staring intently
down at the arena and her whisper was throatily urgent.
"Quickly and quietly."

"Why?" Indigo was baffled. "Who are they?"

"*Hushu.* Hurry—if they see us it'll be a bad omen."
Grimya, bristling, had already ducked into the cave, and
firmly Shalune propelled Indigo back behind the curtain.
As the patterned fabric fell into place Indigo looked at the
fat woman and saw that her face was rigid with tension.
Sweat had broken out on her forehead and glinted in tiny
beads on her upper lip.

"Shalune, why are you so afraid?" she asked. "These
hushu—what *are* they? Ghosts, spirits?"

Shalune grimaced. "Not spirits. If they were spirits—if

they *had* spirits—we'd have nothing to fear." Her dark gaze shifted toward the curtain. "*Hushu* are dead ones whose souls have also died or been devoured. The Ancestral Lady has cast them out of her realm and so they wander in the forests and feed on the living when they can."

"Feed on the *living*?" Indigo was horrified. Shalune smiled, though the smile was a pale and humorless shadow of her usual grin. "Oh, yes. *Hushu* hate living people; living people have souls and that's what *hushu* want above all else. They want to die, because that's the only way they can be released from their half-existence. But without souls," she shrugged expressively, "they can't be truly dead, just as they can't be truly alive. They must stay forever in limbo, and they know that, and so they take revenge wherever they can on others who are luckier than they were."

Indigo looked quickly toward the curtain again. "The woman out there. Will they . . . feed on her?"

Shalune's expression grew somber. "No. They don't eat dead flesh. They have come to welcome her and take her with them." She met Indigo's stare, a little reluctantly. "She has no soul now, you see. Her victims ate her soul when they killed her, so she too will become *hushu*." She shrugged again. "It's what the Ancestral Lady has decreed."

Indigo said nothing for a few moments. Then, abruptly, she reached out to the curtain and started to pull it back.

Shalune and Grimya protested together, Grimya whining as she projected a silent warning and Shalune more vociferous. "Indigo! What do you think you're doing?"

"Douse the lamps." Indigo's voice was hard. "I want to see them for myself."

"It's dangerous! If they should set eyes on you—"

"They won't look up here if there's no light to attract them. Please, Shalune, do as I ask. Douse the lamps."

Shalune hissed softly between her teeth. She padded across the floor, and there was a soft, sputtering hiss as the two lamps dimmed and went out. Indigo waited until her eyes had adjusted to the darkness, then drew the curtain back far enough to allow her to look out and down over the bluff.

The two *hushu* had reached the wooden frame and were working at it, striving to untie the cords that held the corpse fast. Their movements were stiff and oddly erratic; every so often one or the other would pause and stand motionless for a second or two, as though the decaying brain inside the mummified skull were struggling to recall what should be done next.

Indigo continued to watch them, repelled and yet mesmerized, until, amid a sudden flurry of movement, the last cords parted. The murderess's body slumped to the ground and at once the *hushu* pounced upon it. Grimya, who had refused to look at the scene for herself but was picking up telepathic images from Indigo, whimpered and shrank farther back into the cave, her tail between her legs. Shalune darted the wolf a darkly sympathetic look and said, "Grimya knows best. She knows we shouldn't be looking at this thing."

Indigo ignored her. One *hushu* had taken hold of the woman's arms, while the other gripped her legs; between them they spread-eagled her on the sand, then crouched over her with an obscene air of eagerness. Indigo couldn't see clearly, but she thought that one had put its face close to the corpse's and was blowing into the sagging mouth. At her side, Shalune hissed again and muttered a charm against evil. Then Indigo's skin crawled as slowly, jerkily, the murderess's limbs moved of their own accord and she began to sit up. Her head turned, teetering and flopping on the hacked and ruined pillar of its neck, and the two *hushu* capered delightedly as they grabbed the dead woman's arms and hauled her to her feet. She swayed and staggered like a drunkard between them, but they pulled her this way and that, tugging her, walking her in circles until her limbs had gained some semblance of coordination and she was able to stand unaided. Once she looked toward the lake and raised one arm, the hand clawing as though to reach for the water. At this the *hushu* shook her violently and struck her with sharp, staccato movements until, learning obedience, she turned away reluctantly and at last the three twisted figures moved off toward the forest.

Shalune let out a pent breath and stepped back. She would have relit the lamps, but Indigo, hearing her movements, said: "No. Leave them, Shalune. I can see well enough by moonlight."

Shalune paused, looking at her uneasily. "You're sure? Light would be comforting."

"I'm sure."

The three shambling undead had reached the trees now and were merging with the darkness. For a minute or so longer, Indigo remained gazing out into the night; then at last she let the curtain fall and turned around.

"That . . ." Her voice quavered; she collected herself, then began again. "That fate . . . is what the Ancestral Lady *decreed* for her?"

Again Shalune gave her little shrug and nodded.

Indigo stared at her. She wanted to release what was in her mind, wanted to throw the words down like a gauntlet and say, "How can you possibly claim that such an obscene and disgusting end is the will of a goddess? What manner of monster is your deity?" But as she looked into Shalune's eyes, the impulse to challenge her faded. She'd get no answer that made any sense. Like Uluye—like all of them— Shalune accepted the Ancestral Lady's word as immutable law, and no argument would sway her. Why should it? The priestesses had been carrying out the Ancestral Lady's will for generation upon generation, and to think that a newcomer could hope to make them question that will was supreme and foolish arrogance. Goddess or demon, whatever the Ancestral Lady might be, they were in her thrall.

Shalune was beginning to feel uneasy under Indigo's thoughtful but silent scrutiny. There was something in that gaze that she couldn't interpret and that made her uncomfortable; she felt suddenly that it would be tactful to leave now.

"I should go," she said. "The hour's late."

Indigo's eyes refocused. Her shoulders sagged a little in a way that might have implied simple relaxation or a sense of defeat. "Of course," she said evenly. "I'm sorry to have detained you for so long."

Awkward now, Shalune began to move toward the entrance.

"Shalune . . . one question."

Shalune looked up. "Ask."

"You must know that I've been unable to remember anything that's taken place during my trances. Was that true of your former oracle, too?"

Shalune hesitated. This was the one factor that made her doubt her own skepticism about Uluye and her machinations. She wished that Indigo hadn't asked the question, but she felt obliged to be honest with her—and, she reflected wryly, with herself. "Well . . . no," she said. "She always remembered every detail." Her lips twitched in a quick, pallid smile. "As did all the oracles who have gone before. You're a conundrum among us, Indigo. But I wouldn't let it trouble you. After all, it isn't for us to question the Ancestral Lady's ways."

Indigo watched Shalune walk away toward her own quarters on a lower level of the cave system, then let the curtain fall and crossed the floor to sit down in a chair. She didn't speak, but Grimya could sense turmoil in her mind. At last, troubled by the continuing silence, the she-wolf spoke.

"Indigo, what are you thinking? What is it that trroubles you?"

Indigo raised her head like one emerging from a dream. A little diffidently, Grimya approached and pushed her muzzle against Indigo's hand. "Tell me," she cajoled.

Indigo let out a slow breath. "I don't know, Grimya. Maybe it's not important, but . . . I can't understand why I'm unable to remember any detail of my trances. You heard what Shalune said: every previous oracle recalled her experiences perfectly. But I'm different. I remember nothing." She hunched her shoulders. "It makes me feel that something's using me without my knowledge, let alone my consent, and I don't like that; it's threatening, and I don't like being threatened.''

Grimya showed her teeth. ''I don't think that Uluye likes it, either. When we saw her on the lakeshore the other morning, I sensed that she is afraid of you.''

''I know; I felt it too. But it isn't really me she fears, Grimya. It's the link that I form—or that she believes I form—with the Ancestral Lady. That's what really frightens her.''

She rose and moved to a shelf above the hearth. Whilst to see the oracle eating was taboo among the women, to drink with her was not, and Shalune's contribution to the evening had been a pitcher of mildly alcoholic fermented fruit juice. There was still a little left; Indigo poured it into her cup and took a sip.

''That morning, by the lake,'' she said, ''I accused Uluye of using me as a means to dupe her people into accepting anything she saw fit to tell them. I also wondered if she'd somehow engineered my forgetfulness; it wouldn't have surprised me if she'd had the power to do it. But I was wrong. I saw that from her reaction.''

''She called you a . . . blas-*phemer*,'' Grimya said, re- membering.

''Yes, and that was what made me realize that my accu- sation was unjust. Uluye wasn't simply afraid then; she was *terrified*. Terrified that the Ancestral Lady might strike me down for my heresy, and strike her, too, for permitting it to be spoken.'' Indigo took another sip from her cup and smiled wryly at the wolf. ''We may dislike her, Grimya, but I don't think we can deny that she's sincere in her own strange way. So with any trickery on Uluye's part ruled out, I ask myself this: who or what else could have a vested interest in my not remembering my trances?''

''Ah,'' Grimya said somberly. ''The demon. Of c . . . *ourse*.''

Indigo returned to her chair and sat down again. Her brow furrowed with concentration as she delved into her memory.

"In past times," she said, "the demons we've encountered have never challenged us directly. They've always waited until we have made the first moves—sought them out, in fact—before they've been willing to reveal themselves. This time, though, I'm beginning to wonder if our adversary means to preempt us."

Grimya dipped her head. "I don't un-derstand that word, pre . . . pre . . ." She shook her head, abandoning the attempt. "But if you mean what I think you do, then I agree with you." She looked up searchingly at Indigo's face. "Things change. There have been many changes in you since we began j . . . *ourneying* together. So why should there not be changes in the demons, too?"

Indigo knew from long experience that for all her simplicity, Grimya was an acute observer and could often see what lay at the heart of a question or conundrum with far greater clarity than she herself. All the same, there seemed to be a flaw in the wolf's reasoning.

"Why should this demon want to make the first move?" she asked. "What can it hope to gain by exposing its presence so blatantly? It's as though it's throwing down the gauntlet to us. Surely it would prefer to stay hidden for as long as possible."

"I don't think that is true," Grimya replied. "In the volcano mountains, when we were with Jas-ker, and then through all our years in Ss . . . Sim*hara*, we conquered the demons only with the help of the Earth Mother. But when we went to Bruhome, it was different. In Bruhome you found the power within yourself to defeat the thing we met there. And it was the same in the Redoubt. *You* defeated it. You didn't need to ask the Earth Mother to aid you." She paused. "I don't know what powers you have now. But I sense—I *feel*, like feeling sun and rain on my fur—that you are much strr-*onger* than you were in those days." She licked her lips, then glanced a little furtively over her shoulder toward the cave's entrance. "The demon knows this, and it thinks it would be wiser to become the hunter instead of the prey. So it uses your trrrances to work upon you, trying to weaken you before you can gather your strength to attack it, and it makes you forget afterward what it has done.'' She paused. ''I may be wrong, though.''

''No,'' Indigo said softly. ''I suspect you're right, Grimya.'' She looked with sudden intensity at the wolf. ''You said I've changed, that I'm stronger now. What did you mean?''

''I d . . . on't know if I can explain it properly. It isn't in the or-dinary ways; you're still the same Indigo, you still think and feel as you have always done. *That* hasn't changed at all. But underneath, something is different.'' Grimya hesitated, then: ''Can you remember how long it has been since you last changed yourself into a wolf?''

The question came as a shock, for Indigo had entirely forgotten the extraordinary shape-shifting ability that she had once possessed. She'd discovered the latent power during her early days with Grimya in the forests of the Horselands, and three times it had proved a vital weapon in her battle against the horrors she had faced. Yet she couldn't now count the years since she had last used it. Even amid the snows of the Redoubt, where it would surely have been invaluable to her, it hadn't once occurred to her to summon up the power within her. Since then, in all the journeying that had finally brought her here to the Dark Isle, she hadn't so much as remembered the power's existence.

Grimya asked, very diffidently, ''If you tried now, do you think you could become wolf again?''

Could she? Even the means she had used to bring the power surging up from her subconscious was little more than a hazy memory. Doubtless it would come back to her with an effort of concentration; but would it still work?

She believed she knew the answer to that question, and Grimya saw it in her eyes as they looked at each other.

''I th-ink,'' the she-wolf said wisely, ''that maybe you have outgrown it, just as a cub outgrows its noisy games when it no longer needs them for learning. Becoming wolf helped you at first; and especially it helped you when you needed to run away, to flee from danger. Now, though, you have different weapons, greater and better weapons, and there's no need for you to run. So what use is it to you to become wolf?''

Indigo didn't reply immediately but rose again and walked to the entrance, feeling stifled and in need of fresh air. The night outside was quiet, the lake wreathed in mist. There was no breeze now. She swallowed as her throat seemed to constrict. Grimya was right, she felt it instinctively. Those old days were gone, and the old power with them. But what, she asked herself, had taken its place? "Greater and better weapons" Grimya had said. Yet what value had they to her if she didn't know how to use them?

Reading her thoughts, Grimya said gently, "Maybe they are already proving their worth, Indigo. For instance, have you thought to wonder why, since we came here, we haven't en-countered any sign of Nemesis?''

Indigo turned quickly, feeling a familiar chill stab deep inside her, as though an icicle had pierced her heart when Grimya spoke the name she loathed more than any other in the world. Nemesis. She might well call that silver-eyed, silver-tongued creature her personal demon, for it had been created from her own psyche, the embodiment of the dark side of her soul.

Nemesis had walked in her footsteps since the day she had first left her homeland half a century ago, and its one aim—indeed, the sole reason for its existence—was to thwart her in her quest. Wherever Indigo went, in every place and at every turn, Nemesis had waited to trick her, mislead her, lure her into failure and disaster; and as she drew close to each demon in its turn, Nemesis had mockingly flaunted its presence through the one sure sign by which she could always recognize it: the color silver.

Until now. . . .

Again Grimya was right, Indigo realized. She had found the hiding place of her next demon, and for the first time since her quest had begun, Nemesis had not made itself known to her.

"I th-ink," Grimya said, "that Nemesis might be afraid of you now."

Indigo hesitated, then turned once more to look out into the still, clammy night. For a bare moment Grimya's words had kindled an eager spark, but it had died stillborn. She knew Nemesis too well.

She smiled sadly, not letting the wolf see her expression. "If that were only true, Grimya," she said gently, "I would sleep more easily in my bed tonight."

Later, with the lamps doused and only diffused moonlight filtering through the curtain to lighten the dark's totality, Indigo listened to Grimya's even breathing on the floor at her feet and was thankful that their talk had ended where it had. She had almost voiced the other thing, the small, nagging thing that plagued her like a worm lurking deep in her consciousness, but at the last had decided it was better left unsaid. Yet her silence hadn't banished the thought of it, and now as she drifted toward the borders of sleep, it crept back, quietly, gently, insinuatingly.

The Ancestral Lady. Queen of the Dead. Did she truly exist? Uluye and her priestesses believed in her; even down-to-earth Shalune believed in her. Queen of the Dead. Tonight she had seen the *hushu*, the soulless ones, come to claim a new convert to their numbers. The *hushu*, so Shalune had told her, were cast out from the Ancestral Lady's realm—but what of the others, those whose souls the Ancestral Lady was said to take as her own? She had seen them, too, on Ancestors Night, emerging from the lake to be reunited for a brief hour with their loved ones. And just before she fell into the oracle's trance, she had seen Fenran among their number. . . .

Indigo turned over, hiding her face in the crook of one arm. She tried to fight the thought away, but it was too strong now for her to resist: Fenran, among the dead who dwelled in the Ancestral Lady's realm. But he *wasn't* dead. He was in limbo. She believed that; she had always believed it, for without that belief, there could be no hope of finding him again, and without hope, there could be no purpose, no goal, *nothing*. Yet she had seen him. Walking with the dead, moving among them . . . it couldn't be true. It *mustn't* be true.

She bit her knuckles as tears started to trickle uncontrollably from her eyes. Deep down, she knew, her faith was unshaken, and she still believed that what she had seen by the lake was a cruel illusion, perhaps a gauntlet thrown down to challenge her and to lure her, a demon's evil joke. But the tiny seeds of doubt had been sown, and there was only one way in which they could be stopped from taking root. She must find the portal between the worlds of life and death; she must open the gateway and face its guardian, whether goddess or demon, and learn the truth for herself.

And she was afraid, so very, very afraid, of what she might find.

·CHAPTER·X·

Grimya woke early the following morning, when the first predawn light was just beginning to touch the easterly sky. Indigo was still sleeping, and rather than wait for her to wake, the wolf decided to go out for a while before the sun rose and the simmering heat became intolerable.

She wriggled under the curtain and padded down the zig-zagging stairs toward the foot of the bluff. Nearing the sandy arena, she paused as she remembered the *hushu* who had come to the lakeshore last night, but she reasoned that such horrors were unlikely to approach the citadel at this hour. Besides, what threat could they possibly pose to her? She had nothing to fear from them.

All the same, she gave a wide berth to the wooden frame that now lay abandoned and empty on the sand and set off around the lake in the opposite direction to that which the departing *hushu* and their new disciple had taken. Settling into a loping jog—a pace that she could keep up for hours at a time, if necessary—she opened her physical and mental senses to the sounds and scents of the awakening forest, her nose wrinkling and her tongue lapping at the damp, cool atmosphere. Shadows and silhouettes were beginning to take shape out of the darkness, and the lakeside track was a discernible pale ribbon ahead of her; she felt her muscles relaxing with the pleasure of exercise, and her tail wagged with enjoyment as she continued on around the lake.

She had completed half a circuit, and the ziggurat was a dim outline looming on the far side of the water, when something moved in the trees alongside the path. Grimya stopped instantly, her ears pricking forward as she swung to face the source of the disturbance. A forest animal, she thought, and a large one. . . . Then suddenly the faint breeze veered and her nostrils caught the unmistakable tang of human scent.

Instantly, memories of the *hushu* flooded into Grimya's mind, and the fur along her spine bristled fiercely. Then it occurred to her that though she'd never, thankfully, been close enough to a *hushu* to pick up its scent, surely it wouldn't smell like a *living* human. Besides, her keen nose had caught a hint of something familiar in this, a suggestion that it was the scent of someone she knew.

A voice impinged on the quiet, a quick, urgent whisper, and the undergrowth rustled again, closer to the track this time. Prudently Grimya backed off a few paces and crouched down where the curled fronds of a clump of ferns would conceal her. She heard more whispering. Then light flickered faintly between the branches, and moments later two figures emerged from the trees onto the path.

The first carried a lantern, and though the wick was turned low, it cast enough illumination for Grimya to see his face. He was a young man, a stranger, dressed in loose knee-length trousers of multicolored fabric and a broad leather belt from which hung a machete and a long knife sheath. Another strip of leather was bound around his forehead, and the number of wood and bone carvings that decorated it marked him as well-to-do—the son, perhaps, of some comfortably off trader or logger.

Reaching the path, the young man held out a hand as though to assist someone, and the second figure emerged from the forest. From her hiding place, Grimya stared in astonishment as she recognized Uluye's daughter, Yima. In the lamplight, as the young man drew her close to him, Yima's face was flushed with excitement, and her eyes glowed like a cat's in the gloom.

The young man set the lantern down and they embraced tightly. When at last Yima reluctantly drew away, Grimya heard her companion whisper something; she couldn't make out the words, but Yima's reply was clear and emphatic.

"No—it's too great a risk. Go now. Please." She raised a hand to touch his face gently, almost tentatively, then leaned forward to kiss him lingeringly one last time. Feeling that she was intruding on a very private moment, the wolf tried to shrink farther into the undergrowth, turning her head away. She heard more whispering, heard Yima say again, "No, my dear, no," then the rustling of leaves as the young man moved off.

The faint light of the lantern faded, and when Grimya raised her head again, she saw Yima alone on the track. For perhaps a minute the girl stood motionless, staring after him into the forest; then, with a small shiver, she turned and began to run on light feet toward the citadel.

Grimya waited until she was some twenty yards ahead, then followed. At the edge of the sand arena, Yima halted, peered up at the bluff for any telltale sign of movement, then veered toward the lake. She reached the water's edge; creeping closer, the wolf saw her crouch down and splash her face and hands before quickly and furtively unbinding her long braids and soaking her hair in the water. Grimya moved closer still, curious, and was only a few paces from the girl when a pebble slid and clicked under one of her paws.

Yima shot to her feet as though a firebrand had been thrust at her. For an instant her face registered horror. Then she relaxed with a gasp as relief took the place of shock.

"*Grimya!* Oh, but you frightened me!"

Grimya blinked and licked her muzzle, then wagged her tail by way of apology. Yima dropped back to a crouch, holding out a hand toward her. "What are you doing out at such an early hour?" Her face clouded uneasily. "You didn't follow me, did you?" Grimya licked her hand and she laughed, though nervously. "No, I don't think so; and anyway, you wouldn't betray me, would you? You wouldn't tell them, even if you could." Reaching up now, she began to wring out her wet hair. "I have to do this, you see. Now if anyone questions my being out, I can say I went early to the lake to wash myself, and my mother won't suspect anything amiss."

She was talking, Grimya realized, out of sheer desperation, out of a need to release the emotions within her. Grimya was a safe confidante, for Yima believed the wolf didn't understand the words that craved an outlet. Now the girl sat back on her heels, hugging herself as though trying to recapture the memory of her lover's embrace.

"Oh, Grimya, I do love him," she whispered, looking up at the lightening sky. "I *do*." There was such sadness in her voice that Grimya whined in sympathy, and quickly Yima looked at her again. "I could almost believe that you know what I'm saying. But you don't, do you?" Gently now she stretched out one hand and stroked the wolf's head. "No one knows about us . . . well, only one person, and I don't think even she really *understands*." She rose. "The sun's coming up. They'll all be waking soon. I must go back and become the dutiful priestess and daughter again." She smiled at Grimya, though it was a sorrowful little smile. "Keep my secret, eh?"

Grimya watched the girl run toward the stairs. She was astonished by what she had witnessed. Dutiful Yima, the obedient and unquestioning child. For how long had she been meeting her lover in such secrecy, the wolf wondered; and how had she contrived to hide the liaison from her mother's sharp eyes and ears? Grimya knew what Uluye planned for her daughter and could well imagine the ferocity of her wrath if she should discover what was afoot.

Yima must have great courage beneath her meek exterior, Grimya thought. And someone in the citadel was helping her. Grimya suspected she knew who that someone might be, and she resolved to tell Indigo as soon as she could. Perhaps they too could help her somehow? She hoped so, for she liked Yima, and now that she knew the truth, she felt sorry for her. Why should the girl not be free to choose the pattern of her own life? Why should Uluye control her, as she seemed to control everyone and everything in this place? Though Grimya knew the thought was unworthy, it gave her pleasure to think of the High Priestess being bested, in however small a way, for the wolf strongly resented her enforced influence on Indigo. It would be, she thought, a redressing of the balance.

Yima had disappeared now. Looking down, Grimya saw her own elongated shadow stretching out before her on the sand as the sun rose, and the buzz and drone of waking insects impinged on the quiet. Already it was growing hot, and the ziggurat wall wavered in haze. She was hungry, and Indigo should be waking soon.

Sparing one last glance for the still, brazen mirror of the lake, she trotted toward the stairs.

Indigo! Grimya projected the telepathic call as she approached the curtained entrance to their cave. She had felt Indigo's mind stirring and was eager to reach her and tell her the story before anyone came to disturb them. *Indigo, are you awake?*

There was no answer, and suddenly the wolf slowed her pace as she sensed something untoward. Indigo was awake, but the link with her consciousness was distorted. What could be wrong?

Cautious now, laying her ears back, she called again. Something flickered on the edge of her mental perception but vanished too quickly for her to interpret it, and abruptly Grimya felt alarm. She broke into a run, covering the last few yards to the cave, and dove under the curtain.

Indigo was in her bed. She was lying flat, the thin covering flung aside, but her eyes stared blindly at the ceiling and her mouth was working soundlessly.

"Indigo!" Forgetting caution, Grimya barked her name aloud and ran to her, jumping up. "Indigo, what is it? What's wrong?"

A spasm shot through Indigo's frame; then her body went rigid as though in a death rictus. Horrified, Grimya thrust hard against her torso in an effort to stir her, but she was as immovable as rock. Her throat swelled and contracted in a rapid, jerky rhythm; she seemed to be trying to speak, but her voice collapsed into choking chaos before she could form words. It was as though some powerful, but invisible, hand had cut off her supply of air and was slowly strangling her.

Grimya spun around on her haunches and raced back to the entrance. All thoughts of Yima had fled; she had to get help for Indigo. Writhing through the curtain again, she looked down frantically at the citadel's lower levels; then, seeing no one, she raised her head and gave vent to a full-throated howl. The chilling sound echoed from the bluff and was flung out over the lake. Almost immediately there was a response from below: voices raised in consternation, the slap of running feet. Shocked faces appeared from other cave quarters, and several women, seeing the wolf poised on the high ledge, began to run toward the stairs. One of the running figures, Grimya saw to her intense relief, was Shalune, with Yima only a pace behind her.

Shouldering others out of her way, the fat woman took the last flight of stairs two at a time and pounded along the ledge to where Grimya waited.

"What is it, Grimya?" Shalune was breathless, her muscular diaphragm heaving alarmingly. Grimya ducked back into the cave; Shalune followed, then stopped as she saw Indigo.

"By all my ancestors!"

"Shalune, what's happening?" Yima pushed in behind her.

"She's in a trance." Shalune's head snapped around as she heard others approaching. "Send them back, Yima; tell them to return to their own quarters. I'll deal with this."

"Should I fetch my mother?"

"No. She'll hear of it soon enough, and I'll need your help here."

Yima hurried to relay Shalune's message to the anxious crowd now gathering outside. As they started to move away, Shalune hastened to Indigo's bed, tried to pull her into a sitting position, then swore. "Yima! She's as rigid as a tree, and she's choking. Quickly now, help me to turn her on her side!" She was thrusting expert fingers between Indigo's resisting lips and into her mouth. "Got to . . . stop her swallowing her . . . tongue. . . ."

Yima ran to assist her and they rolled Indigo over. Grimya jumped up, yelping; Shalune pushed her aside.

"Go away, Grimya—we're helping her, not harming her. Keep back!"

Whining Grimya retreated, and Shalune balled her fist and thumped Indigo soundly between the shoulder blades.

"She isn't breathing," Yima said.

"I know; it's as though there's something blocking her throat . . . *ah!*" Shalune thumped again and heard a hoarse rattle of expelled air. "That's it! Lift her back now. We'll get her sitting up if we can."

"She's like stone! I've never seen anything like this!"

"Neither have I," Shalune replied grimly. "Try to move her arms. If we can just—" and she jerked back with a cry of surprise as suddenly Indigo's body went limp and she slumped back onto the bed.

"*Eyes of the Lady!*" Yima stared, stunned. "What *happened*, Shalune?"

"I don't know, but we'd best make the most of it before she has another spasm. Bring some more cushions, Yima, and prop them behind her. I don't want to risk letting her lie flat."

Experimentally, Shalune raised Indigo's right arm and let it drop. Moments ago it had been as rigid as granite; now it felt utterly boneless, and the priestess shook her head in bewilderment.

As Yima carried an armful of cushions from the hearth,

Grimya heard someone approaching. She lowered her head, defensively alert. Then the curtain was flung back, and Uluye stood on the threshold.

"What's going on?" Her stare raked the tableau of Shalune, Yima and the unconscious Indigo.

Shalune glanced back over her shoulder, naked dislike in her eyes. "She went into trance, but something's gone wrong," she told Uluye curtly.

"Into *trance*?" Uluye stiffened. "How did it happen?"

"I've no idea how it happened. I only knew about it when Grimya howled fit to bring the Ancestral Lady's servants from the lake!" Shalune snapped. "I came up here and found her in the trance state and choking to death at the same time."

Uluye strode across the floor and leaned over the bed, peering at Indigo's face. "She's breathing now?"

"Yes, thanks be, but she's unconscious."

"What did she say?" Uluye looked hard at her subordinate, and even from a distance, Grimya saw the familiar, fanatical glint return to her eyes. "Tell me."

"What are you talking about?"

The High Priestess's mouth set in a thin, ugly line. "Don't dissemble with me, Shalune. I won't tolerate it. What was the Ancestral Lady's message?"

"Damn it, there was no message," Shalune said furiously. "I told you, she was *choking*!"

Uluye continued to glare at her suspiciously for a moment, then looked at Indigo once more. "Now you say she's unconscious?"

"You can see that for yourself," Shalune snapped.

Uluye ignored the tone. "Could she still be in trance?"

Shalune stared at her with something approaching disbelief. "Is that all that matters to you? For the last time, Uluye, Indigo might have *died* just now! Isn't that just a little more important than whether or not she's still in the trance state?"

Uluye opened her mouth to retaliate but suddenly became aware of Yima, who stood at the far side of the bed, staring at them both, wide-eyed. The High Priestess raised her head.

"Leave us, Yima."

"Let her be," Shalune said. "I might need—"

Uluye cut across her. "Now, Yima."

Yima's face was scarlet. "Yes, Mother." She didn't look at Shalune but hurried out of the cave.

"Now," Uluye said scathingly when Yima had gone, "I mean to make one thing very clear to you, Shalune. When I ask you a question, I anticipate—" She stopped, and both women looked quickly at the bed.

Indigo had uttered a sound. Not quite a word but a long, exhaled syllable. She might have been trying to say: "You . . ." or "You will. . . ." To the High Priestess's vivid imagination, she might have said, "Uluye."

"Oracle!" Uluye pounced, dropping to a predatory crouch beside the bed and taking hold of Indigo's limp arm. "Speak, oracle! I am here, I am listening. What does the Ancestral Lady want of me?"

Shalune said angrily, "She's not fit. Leave her." She moved forward, meaning to pull Uluye away.

Indigo's eyes snapped open.

"Come to me." It wasn't her voice, though it had her inflection and her accent. Her blue-violet stare met and locked with Uluye's wild gaze, and it seemed to Uluye that Indigo's pupils were surrounded by a shimmering silver corona. *"Come to me. Do you dare? Then come to me."*

Shalune recoiled, uttering a soft oath, and collided with Grimya, who had rushed forward as Indigo spoke. Shalune gripped the she-wolf's scruff, restraining her as Uluye leaned farther over the bed.

"Lady, I hear you! I hear you, but I don't understand!"

The terrible, alien eyes continued to hold her gaze. *"Soon,"* Indigo said. *"Oh yes, very soon. You will dare. I know you will dare."*

Like the swift drop of a curtain, the silver corona vanished. A small frown creased Indigo's brow as she tried and failed to focus on Uluye's face, looming over her. She turned her head a fraction, said in a puzzled but perfectly natural voice, "Grimya . . . ?" Then her eyelids closed and she began to breathe lightly and evenly.

Slowly Shalune approached the bed and looked down at her. "She's asleep," she said incredulously.

Uluye rose to her feet. Her gaze was still fixed on Indigo's face. *"Asleep?"* She sounded dazed.

"Yes. Look at her. She's as peaceful as a newly fed infant."

Uluye seemed reluctant to be convinced, but at last she relented and stepped back from the bed. For a few moments there was silence. Then: "Fetch someone to sit with her," Uluye said. "I want to talk to you in my quarters."

Shalune had expected this, and nodded. "I'll set Inuss to guard her. But if she wakes, I'll want to see her immediately."

"Yes, yes," Uluye agreed with an impatient wave of one hand. "Don't waste time."

Without so much as glancing at Grimya, she strode out of the cave, leaving Shalune to follow. As the fat woman moved toward the entrance, Grimya whimpered. Shalune stopped and looked back.

"She's all right now, Grimya," she said kindly. "Inuss is a good healer. She'll know if I'm needed and she'll send for me."

Grimya swallowed back a whine and Shalune smiled, thinking—not for the first time—that the wolf seemed to have an uncanny understanding. Then she too was gone, leaving Grimya alone with Indigo.

Grimya padded to the bed and stared at her friend for a long time. Indigo seemed, as Shalune had said, to be sleeping naturally and peacefully, but the wolf was deeply troubled. She had seen Indigo's eyes in the moment when they had snapped open, before Uluye leaned over her and obscured her from view. She had seen the glitter of silver. And silver, as Grimya knew all too well, was the sign of Nemesis.

Footsteps sounded outside, and the curtain parted once

more to admit Inuss, a young priestess whom Shalune was training in the healing arts. Inuss saw Grimya and smiled faintly.

"Ussh now, what are you doing there?" She had a pleasant, husky voice that Grimya found both soothing and reassuring. "Your mistress is asleep now. You should go to sleep too, eh?"

Resignedly the wolf padded to the far side of the cave, where she slumped down with her muzzle on her forepaws. Inuss looked briefly at Indigo to satisfy herself that all was well, then settled in a chair. She had brought her sistrum; she laid it across her lap and began to murmur what Grimya thought were prayers, every so often shaking the sistrum gently. The muted drone of her voice was soporific; the wolf blinked, yawned, shifted to a more comfortable position.

Before long, she too slept.

·CHAPTER·XI·

Uluye's quarters were located on the citadel's second level. As befitted the dwelling of the cult's High Priestess, the cave that housed her was larger than any other save for the oracle's own, and signs and sigils had been carved over the entrance. Shalune glanced at these decorations as she approached the cave, and read the familiar messages that, like the oracle's cave on the level above, proclaimed these quarters and their occupant sacrosanct and entrance forbidden to any unauthorized person. Her lip curled in a faint sneer at Uluye's arrogance in placing herself on a par with the oracle, and ignoring the protocol that obliged her to call out meekly and await a summons, she thrust the curtain aside and walked in.

Uluye was sitting in an ornate chair, waiting for her—and behind her, face muscles rigid and eyes miserable, was Yima. Shalune knew instantly what her presence implied, and her heart sank. She avoided the imploring gaze that Yima directed toward her behind her mother's back, and made a cursory formal bow.

"How is she?" Uluye's eyes glinted in the cave's relative gloom.

"Sleeping, as before. I don't think she'll wake for some time yet, but I've told Inuss to alert me if there's any change." Uluye hadn't offered her a seat; Shalune took one anyway.

Uluye folded her hands with a slow and deliberate movement. "I have told Yima of the message that the Ancestral Lady imparted to us," she said and met Shalune's eyes intently. "You, I presume, also heard the oracle's words?"

Again Shalune took great care not to look at Yima. "Yes," she replied. "I heard."

"There can be no doubt of the Ancestral Lady's meaning," Uluye went on. "So we must waste no time, Shalune. Yima's initiation trial must take place as soon as possible."

Shalune stared down at her hands where they rested on her knees. "I see," she said, then looked up. "You *are* sure, Uluye? Sure, I mean, that Yima's ready?" Now she did venture a glance at the girl, but it was brief and gave nothing away.

Uluye smiled with utter confidence. "Even if I were uncertain—and I presume to think I know my own daughter well enough—the Ancestral Lady herself clearly is not. Can you possibly doubt her message?"

"No." Shalune had to admit it; she might wish that the oracle's words hadn't been uttered, but she couldn't deny their validity or place any other interpretation on them. "No, I can't."

"Then I take it you have no objections?" Uluye's tone suggested that any dissent would not be well received.

Shalune couldn't dissemble without arousing suspicion, and that was something she dared not risk. She said, keeping her voice even, "None whatever."

"I'm glad to hear it. Now; the moon is waning, and of course that isn't auspicious. However, the coming new moon will coincide with a favorable seasonal augury. I will perform the necessary divinations, and if all's well, the rite will take place on the first night after dark moon."

Fortunately, Uluye was too preoccupied to hear Yima's sharply truncated intake of breath. Shalune flicked the girl a rapid warning glare and said cautiously, "The first night after dark moon? That's very short notice, Uluye."

"Are you telling me you're not able to make the preparations in time?"

"No, no. That isn't a problem. I was thinking of Indigo. Yima may be ready, but will Indigo?"

"Her only duty will be to act as Yima's escort; she need do nothing more. Besides," a small, surreptitious gesture conveyed a clear warning to Shalune to speak guardedly in Yima's presence, "I'm sure I don't need to remind you of our recent discussion, especially in the light of this morning's events."

So she *had* decided to put Indigo to the test. Shalune wasn't surprised, though she didn't like the prospect at all. She licked her lips. "I'm not happy about it, Uluye; not so soon. We've hardly had time to make any judgment—"

"That's no longer relevant. The Ancestral Lady has made her wishes known to us, and it's our duty to obey her. *She* will be Indigo's judge. It is her will; that is quite clear."

Abruptly Uluye rose to her feet. It was a signal, Shalune realized, that she had issued her instructions and therefore considered any further debate irrelevant. "A full gathering will be called this evening and I'll tell the citadel of my decision then. In the meantime, I leave it to you to inform Indigo and to instruct her in what she'll be required to do. If she wishes to ask me any questions, I shall be available."

It was a dismissal, and there was nothing Shalune could say. She made her farewells, bowed and left the cave. Emerging into the full, searing heat and brilliance of the sun, she started along the ledge, then paused and looked up to the highest level of the cave system. She wanted to run up the staircase to Indigo's cave, find Inuss and speak to her immediately, but a deeper instinct warned her against rashness. She should take time to think clearly and rationally before making any move, for her entire strategy must now change, and that meant a need for detailed and very careful planning. She'd take an hour to collect her wits and marshal her thoughts. *Then* she would speak to Inuss; not before. It was safer that way.

She walked to the end of the ledge and onto the next downward flight of stairs. She was almost at the bottom when, from somewhere overhead, a voice hissed her name. Shalune looked up and saw Yima on the ledge above her. The girl gestured urgently; the fat woman glanced down, then along the ledge at her own level. There was no one else about. Looking up again, she nodded quickly and beckoned.

They moved into the shade of one of the rough-hewn pillars at the staircase junction. It was cooler here and, more pertinent, anyone traversing the levels above or below would be unlikely to see them. Yima took hold of Shalune's hand and clutched it, gasping to regain the breath drained from her by running in the heat. "Shalune—oh, Shalune, what am I going to *do*?'

"Quiet, now." Shalune extricated her fingers and laid a gentling hand on Yima's shoulder to stem her trembling. "It'll do no good to get hysterical. We have to think before we act."

"But there's so little *time*! Dark moon's only nine or ten days away, and we'll never persuade Mother to grant me longer. You know how she is—once something's fixed in her mind, she won't be swayed.

"I know, child, I know." Shalune was frowning, thinking hard.

"Once the ceremony takes place, I'll be lost!" Yima continued, on the verge of tears now. "I can't let it happen, Shalune, I *can't*! I'll have to run away, I'll have to flee the citadel—"

Shalune interrupted her emphatically. "That's out of the question. Your mother would miss you immediately and she'd order a hunt. She wouldn't rest until you were found. There must be a better solution than that."

"But *what*?" Yima shut her eyes tightly for a few moments, then quickly opened them again. "I could feign illness. Better still, I could *become* ill. You're our finest healer, Shalune; surely you could give me a potion that would bring on a fever and force the initiation to be postponed?''

"That's possible," Shalune conceded cautiously. "But it's an option I'd rather not take unless all else fails."

"It would at least give us more time."

"True, but I'm not anxious to risk your safety. The fever herbs aren't to be trifled with, and something could easily go wrong." Shalune held up a hand to silence Yima, as she seemed about to protest. "No, listen to me. I'll speak to Inuss. It may be that we can make ready in time to fall in with your mother's plan, and if that's possible, it's our best solution."

Yima wasn't happy with that. "It's dangerous, Shalune. You'll be putting yourself at risk, and I don't want you to do that for me."

"I have a selfish reason, too, Yima. Don't ever forget that. It's for all our sakes, not yours alone. Now, you'd best go before your mother sends for you again. You'll have little time to call your own from now on."

"But what shall I do about Tiam? I must see him, Shalune. I have to tell him what's happened!"

Shalune shook her head firmly. "No, child, you can't see Tiam again for the time being. Your mother will be watching you too closely. I'll see to it that he knows what's happened here . . . and if there are arrangements to be made, I'll make them. Trust me."

Yima acquiesced, though reluctantly. "I do trust you, Shalune. I'll do as you say."

"Good girl. I'll see Inuss, and I'll speak to you again later if I can. Go now." She patted Yima's arm. "And try not to fret."

She watched the girl hurry away. Her mind was clearer now, and she believed she knew what must be done. A lot depended on Inuss, but Shalune was prepared to gamble that her protégée would be willing and ready to act now. Whether she would prove able was another matter, but that was a perennial risk, and the date set for the ceremony could make no difference.

Running footsteps on the ledge above alerted Shalune suddenly, and she looked up to see Inuss herself at the top of the stairway.

"Shalune?" If Inuss was puzzled to see her mentor lurking inexplicably by the pillar, she didn't show it. "Indigo's awake."

"Awake?" Shalune started instantly toward the steps. "How does she seem?"

"Well enough, though I think she's a little confused. I left Grimya guarding her."

"I'll go to her right away." Shalune ran up the flight as fast as her weight and the heat would allow. As she stepped onto the ledge, she caught hold of Inuss's arm and added in an undertone, "Then I want to talk to you, Inuss. Privately."

The slight tensing of Inuss's muscles showed that she understood. However, she asked no questions but simply said, "Yes, Shalune," and stood back to let the senior priestess pass. She watched as Shalune headed toward the upper levels of the bluff, and though her expression was inscrutable, her eyes and the sudden quickening of her breath betrayed her excitement.

As Inuss had reported, Shalune found that apart from some lingering disorientation, Indigo seemed to have suffered no ill effects from her seizure. With Grimya anxiously watching, Shalune carried out a brisk, efficient examination of her patient, pronounced her fit, then stood back and gave her a long, shrewd look.

"Well," she said. "Do you remember anything this time?"

Indigo sighed. "No." A pause. "Did I speak during the trance? What did I say?"

Shalune opened her mouth to reply, "Nothing of any significance," but then wondered if perhaps it would be better to make Indigo aware of the truth without delay. It also occurred to her that Indigo might be an invaluable ally in the days ahead, and for a moment she wondered if she dared take her into her confidence. But the temptation was eclipsed by innate caution. Unless she could be certain of Indigo—and that was impossible—she should hold her tongue.

She said at last: "I'll tell you exactly what happened, for what help it may be to you." She went on to describe the choking fit, her own intervention, and the emphatic message that Indigo had uttered as Uluye crouched over the bed.

Indigo frowned. " 'Come to me.' What does it signify, Shalune? Do you know?"

"Uluye believes she does, that's for certain," Shalune said a little grimly.

"I don't understand."

"No . . . well, I suppose I'd best tell you, or you'll hear it soon enough from Uluye herself." Shalune sat down. "You know, don't you, that Uluye wants Yima to be her successor in due time?"

"So I understand. She's been trained for the role since childhood, hasn't she?"

"Yes. But there's more to it than mere training. Our High Priestess may nominate her successor, but her choice must meet with the Ancestral Lady's approval. Therefore, before her final initiation and confirmation, the candidate is taken before the Ancestral Lady in person, to be tested."

Indigo looked blank. "In *person*? How?"

Now it was Shalune's turn to seem nonplussed. "Through the Well," she said; then suddenly it dawned on her that no one had explained the Well to Indigo, for until now there had been no need. "Ah, of course; how could you know? The entrance to the Well is under the heartstone of our temple square on the cliff top, and it leads to the Ancestral Lady's own realm."

Indigo stared at her, not sure of what she meant by "the Ancestral Lady's own realm." Was this Well simply a deep shaft or tunnel, leading perhaps to some underground labyrinth beneath the lake; or did the priestesses believe that it was a gateway between dimensions, a gateway that could lead them into the Ancestral Lady's physical presence?

Grimya, reading her thoughts and her confusion, asked silently: *If they do believe that, Indigo, could it be true?*

Could it? Could the door between worlds really be as simple and as accessible as Shalune implied? Choosing her words with great care, Indigo asked aloud, "Do you mean that the candidate . . . actually stands before the Ancestral Lady herself? Sees her face-to-face, as we see each other now?"

"Of course." The depth of Indigo's ignorance quite disconcerted Shalune. "The Well's rarely used, of course. That's why the Ancestral Lady granted us the oracle long ago, to make her will known to us without needing to summon us into her presence. But in the highest matters, we must go directly before her."

"And Yima will be sent down through the Well to be . . . presented to her?"

"Yes. That's what Uluye took your words to mean, Indigo. The Ancestral Lady has decreed that the time for Yima's testing has come."

Again Indigo detected a grim note in Shalune's tone, and she said, "You sound . . ." She hesitated, then decided that she had nothing to lose by being blunt. "The word that comes to me is *dubious*. Do you not agree with Uluye?"

Shalune studied her face, as though she were unsure of how to respond and was looking for some sign that might guide her. Then, after a few moments, she smiled a little stiffly. "You mistake me, Indigo. Of course I agree with her."

Grimya said: *She isn't telling the truth. I see it in her eyes.*

Indigo saw it too but before she could decide whether or not to challenge Shalune, the fat woman spoke again.

"Naturally, I'm concerned for Yima herself; she's very young still, and this is a great responsibility to place on her shoulders at such a tender age. But then, Uluye herself underwent the same trials in her time, so she's aware of what will be required of Yima and knows better than any of us whether she's ready to face it.''

Still, there was something untoward in her voice, and Indigo's conviction that Shalune was hiding the truth—or at least a part of it—grew stronger. Gently probing, she asked, "Have you ever been there, Shalune? To the Ancestral Lady's realm?"

"Oh, no." Shalune shook her head emphatically. "Only our future High Priestess and her sponsors ever make the journey through the Well. In fact, both of Uluye's sponsors are dead now, so she is the only living soul who has ever looked on the Ancestral Lady's face."

"The candidate is accompanied by sponsors?"

"Yes. Two must go with her and formally present her."

Shalune paused. She'd succeeded, to her relief, in diverting Indigo's suspicions about her own doubts—that brief lapse had been a foolish slip, she told herself sternly—but Indigo had now broached another subject, one that Shalune had hoped to approach more gently and perhaps at a later time. Still, now that the door stood open, perhaps she should get it over with.

She steepled her fingers and stared at them. "There is," she said, "something you ought to know now, Indigo. About the candidate's sponsors."

Indigo's eyes narrowed slightly as she caught the sudden tension in Shalune's voice. "What is it?"

Shalune chewed her lower lip, clearly not happy. "As I said, two people must accompany Yima on her journey. One will be chosen by Uluye. The other, by tradition . . . is the oracle."

There was silence. Shalune didn't have the courage to meet Indigo's eyes but continued to stare at her hands. Yet the storm she'd anticipated didn't break. She had expected Indigo to be shocked, alarmed, to make a furious protest; instead, the silence continued, and when at last she did lift her eyes, she saw Indigo still looking at her, her gaze steady and thoughtful.

At last Indigo spoke. "So," she said quietly, "I am to be sent with Yima to the Ancestral Lady's realm."

Shalune nodded.

"When?"

"In a matter of days." Shalune shuffled her feet uneasily. "Normally, a candidate wouldn't face the trial so young. Yima's only sixteen; it should have been another two years at least. But when you spoke—when Uluye heard what you said—"

"She took it as a sign from the Ancestral Lady that the time is right."

"Yes."

"And you agree with her."

Shalune's face became masklike. "Yes. As I said before, I agree with her."

Another long pause. Then Indigo asked, very quietly, "What will be expected of me?"

Shalune blinked. "You have no objections?"

"No. Should I have? You tell me this is traditionally the oracle's task, and there seems to be little doubt in anyone's mind that I am the oracle. Why would I object?"

Logically, Shalune couldn't answer that question, but she still felt thrown out of kilter by Indigo's calm acceptance. To see the Ancestral Lady in person was a rare honor, granted to few living souls, and past oracles had counted themselves greatly privileged to make the journey through the Well and back. Yet Indigo didn't revere the Ancestral Lady as others did. She was an outsider, not even a Dark Isler; she hadn't been brought up and trained in the proper ways. Somehow, without knowing quite why, Shalune had *expected* her to object.

She asked cautiously, "Aren't you afraid?"

"Afraid?" Indigo's look suddenly grew introverted, and a shadow seemed to form behind her eyes. There was a long pause; then, in a quiet, oddly thoughtful voice, she said: "Yes, I'm afraid. But not, perhaps, for the reasons that you might expect of me."

And secretly, her mind closed even to Grimya, Indigo

added to herself: *But my fear must be conquered; it must take second place. Willing or not, I have to face this . . . and I never dreamed that I would find a way to reach this particular demon so easily. . . .*

Uluye announced the date of Yima's initiation trial at a full gathering of the priestesses by the lakeside that evening. The news was received with great surprise, but also with approval. Yima was hugged and kissed, petted and congratulated, while her mother stood by watching with a victor's stern pride, her judgment vindicated.

As the initial excitement began to subside a little, Uluye called for silence, and all eyes focused on her once more. She had, she said, one further announcement to make before the ten-day preparations for the great occasion began, and that was the choice of Yima's sponsors. One, of course, would be their oracle, as was the custom, and she—here Uluye flicked a sharp, sidelong glance at Indigo, who sat as before on her litter throne, a passive observer—was ready and eager to play her part in interceding with the Ancestral Lady. Indigo inclined her head, her expression inscrutable. Uluye frowned faintly and looked away. The second sponsor, she continued, was a matter on which she had both prayed for guidance and conducted intense divinations, and she was now confident that she had made the best, and indeed, the only proper choice.

"To guide my daughter on her journey in the underworld, and to speak for her in the Ancestral Lady's all-seeing presence," Uluye said, "I choose my sister in spirit and valued friend, Shalune."

By sheer chance, Grimya had found herself a place among the gathering not two paces from where Shalune stood, and so the wolf felt clearly the extraordinary mixture of reactions that flickered through the fat woman's mind before she could collect her wits. Bizarrely, Shalune was relieved and horrified in equal measure—both, to Grimya, inexplicable emotions in this circumstance. Curiosity aroused, the wolf tried to see deeper into Shalune's thoughts, but her telepathic senses couldn't probe any farther, and besides, Shalune had already recovered from her confusion and the emotion was buried as she received the congratulations of the other priestesses.

In danger of being trampled as the women crowded around, Grimya withdrew from the throng, puzzled and thoughtful. It seemed from the momentary glimpse she had had into her thoughts that Shalune was torn between wanting—almost *needing*—to be Yima's sponsor and dreading the prospect with a fear that reached down to the depths of her soul. It didn't make sense.

The wolf had no chance, though, to consider her speculations any further, for Uluye was now preparing to lead the assembled women in a celebratory ritual chant, and amid the massed voices and the flurry of swaying bodies and stamping feet, Grimya's only thought was to keep well out of the way. When the chant ended, it seemed that the formalities were completed. As dust settled in the arena, one group of priestesses set off to make the nightly circuit of the lake, while the others gathered around Uluye to ask eager questions about the initiation ceremony and its preparation. The High Priestess was now standing close to Indigo's litter and Grimya couldn't reach her friend, so she moved away, beyond the crowd and out of the circle of torchlight, toward the bluff wall.

She was nearing the foot of the staircase, where she meant to wait until Indigo's litter was borne back to their quarters, when a dark figure moved across her path. Grimya stopped still as she recognized Shalune's outline in the dimness. Then suddenly a second figure darted from the crowd and ran to intercept the fat woman. It was Yima. Shalune hesitated, then turned as the girl caught up with her.

"Shalune! Shalune, did you—"

"Hush!" Shalune put a warning finger to her lips. "Not here—not now!"

"But I must know! *Please*, Shalune—have you spoken to her?"

They were unaware of Grimya's presence a few paces away. The wolf stood motionless, listening.

"Yes," she heard Shalune say, "I've spoken to her, and she's agreed to bring the plan forward. I'm not altogether happy, but . . . we'll do it."

Yima made a sound that could have been either a gasp or a sob. "Oh, thank you! *Thank* you!"

"Hush!" Shalune said again, more vehemently. "We can't talk now."

"But what of Tiam? What shall I do?"

"Leave Tiam to me. I'll tell him. It will be better from me than from you, and easier."

"When will you see him?"

"As soon as I can. Early tomorrow, perhaps; I can always find a good reason for going into the forest. Now—" she turned Yima about "—I'm tired and I want to sleep. Go back to your mother and play your part. When I've found Tiam and talked to him, I'll be sure to tell you."

Yima went, and Shalune walked on toward the stairs, leaving Grimya staring after them both in turn, her mind racing. What was the secret that these two shared, the plan of which they had spoken? Could Tiam be the young man she had seen with Yima by the lakeside, the man Yima loved? And who was the *she* to whom both Yima and Shalune had referred? Not Indigo, as Grimya had at first assumed, for Shalune had said, *She has agreed to bring the plan forward.* Who, then?

The wolf looked back over her shoulder to the torchlit circle. Uluye was still holding court, and it would be a while yet, she surmised, before the litter was carried back up the cliff face and she'd be able to talk to Indigo privately. She decided to return to their cave and wait; and she also wanted to keep watch on the level where Shalune had her quarters. She didn't think that Shalune would leave the citadel tonight, but it would be well to be vigilant. For when she did go to meet this Tiam, whoever he might be, Grimya intended to follow her and try to unravel the mystery once and for all.

·CHAPTER·XII·

When the sun rose the next morning, the preparations for Yima's initiation began in earnest. Indigo had expected an air of celebration and excitement to build up in the citadel, an extension and continuation of the mood generated by Uluye's announcement, but her expectations weren't fulfilled. Instead, the prevailing atmosphere among the priestesses was one of extreme tension—anticipation, certainly, but heavily tainted with a powerful sense of oppression and deep-seated fear. It seemed that the women looked on the initiation not only as a trial for Yima, but also, through her, as a test of the entire cult's standing in the Ancestral Lady's eyes. If Yima should fail, the Ancestral Lady would be angry and all of her servants would suffer her wrath.

It was a terrible responsibility to place on a single pair of young and inexperienced shoulders, and as she began to realize and understand the risks that Yima would be taking, Indigo was plagued by an agonized conscience, for she knew that she herself was largely responsible for the girl's coming ordeal.

It was a matter of simple but devastating misunderstanding. When the oracle had possessed her and she had said, *"Come to me,"* Uluye had interpreted the message as a summons to her daughter and was avidly eager to obey. Uluye, however, was wrong. The creature that had gazed out through Indigo's eyes and spoken with Indigo's voice that morning didn't want Yima; it wanted Indigo herself. The command hadn't been a summons, but a challenge, daring her to pick up the gauntlet and prepare for a confrontation. But Uluye had stepped in and placed her own interpretation on the oracle's pronouncement, and as a result, Yima was to be placed in the path of something potentially lethal.

She should have tried to explain, Indigo told herself. Even if Uluye couldn't accept her explanation—and that was a foregone conclusion—there might at least be some small chance of persuading Shalune that the Ancestral Lady's message had been misunderstood. But the only way Indigo could hope to do that would be by telling Shalune the truth. *All* of the truth, which meant all of her own bitter story. Indigo couldn't do that. Not, or so she told herself, because she couldn't bear the thought of admitting what she was and the nature of her quest, but because to do so would be to tell Shalune that the goddess she and all her fellow priestesses worshiped was not a goddess at all, but a demon. To coin a phrase of Grimya's, that would be akin to wagging her tail in the path of a hunter with a crossbow; she'd be damned as a blasphemer or worse, and would as likely as not find herself condemned to the wooden frame at the lakeside to await her fate at the hands of the *hushu*. She dared not do it. Conscience or no, and Yima's safety notwithstanding, she couldn't take the risk.

Besides, as she admitted to herself in a moment of blunt clarity, to do anything that might delay or impede the initiation would be directly against her own interests. She'd been granted a providential chance to seek out the demon in its own domain—indeed, it seemed that the demon had actively sought *her*, and however strongly she might sympathize with Yima, sympathy wasn't proof against her own more personal needs and desires. She knew that her motive was selfish, but she was honest enough to acknowledge that she was no unbesmirched idealist and never had been. In Indigo's scales of justice, the fate of Yima, who was after all a virtual stranger, must be outweighed by the fate of herself and Grimya.

Grimya, meanwhile, was beset with her own troubles. Since the night of Uluye's announcement, Indigo had been distant and preoccupied, and the she-wolf's efforts to cajole her out of her dark mood had had little effect. Grimya was aware that Indigo had already forced herself to abandon concern over Yima's welfare for the sake of her quest, and with her customary diffidence, the wolf felt unable to add to her friend's burden by revealing the complications of her own small mystery. So, feeling isolated and a little bereft, she resolved to learn what more she could, if for no other reason than to give herself some means of whiling away the long, depressing hours in the citadel.

The task proved to be less easy than she'd hoped. To begin with, Yima now spent almost all of the daylight hours and a good part of each night closeted alone with her mother, while Uluye schooled her intensively for the initiation. There had been no more secretive visits to the forest, and it seemed that Shalune had also been too busy to carry out her promise to meet Tiam. The identity of the third conspirator, the *she* referred to in the brief, surreptitious conversation that Grimya had overheard, was still a mystery, and though she listened to many snatches of talk in and about the citadel, the wolf learned nothing to enlighten her any further. The priestesses' sole topic was the coming ceremony, and the hushed and fearful tones in which it was discussed left Grimya with an unpleasant feeling in the pit of her stomach.

Then, on the third night following the announcement, Shalune slipped away from the citadel.

Grimya was lying on the ledge outside the cave she shared with Indigo. The night was unusually hot and oppressive, even by Dark Isle standards. Indigo was abed, but Grimya had been unable to sleep and had moved to the ledge in the hope that the outside air might be a degree or two cooler than the insufferable interior of the cave.

When she glimpsed the shadowy figure moving quickly and stealthily from the foot of the bluff in the waning moon's light, she sprang to her feet, alert and curious. Then, as the figure showed in clear silhouette against the lake, Grimya recognized it as Shalune.

The wolf stared hard into the darkness. The fat woman was heading toward the forest, clearly in a hurry, and clearly fearful of discovery, for she repeatedly glanced back over her shoulder as though half expecting to be challenged. Keeping low, Grimya padded along the ledge to the stairs, then paused, looking hard again to fix Shalune's position and direction in her mind. Yes, she seemed to be making for the very spot where Yima had held her tryst. Silent as a shadow herself, the wolf dropped onto the stairway and began to descend in pursuit.

But for the sheer fortuity of a stifled cough, Grimya might have missed the clearing altogether. Shalune's wariness and her constant backward glances had obliged the wolf to wait until her quarry had entered the forest before she dared venture across the open arena, and by the time she reached the edge of the trees, Shalune had vanished.

For some minutes Grimya stood still, listening to the susurration of night sounds and testing the air with her muzzle for a trace of Shalune's scent. However, the powerful odors of the forest itself—moist earth and crowding trees and decaying vegetation—swamped any lingering hint that might have remained, and at last the wolf realized that she would have to rely on other means. She cast about, searching for a physical sign of someone moving into the undergrowth, and eventually she found what appeared to be a newly trampled, if faint and uncertain, trail.

Grimya liked this forest at night even less than she liked it by day. Keen-eyed though she was, the trees were haunted after dark by creatures whose eyes were keener still: hunters like herself, but born and bred to this savage region, which gave them a great and dangerous advantage. As she ventured under the canopy of a tree whose branches curved down as though seeking to bury themselves in the ground, something slithered on a bough above her head. Grimya cringed with an involuntary defensive snarl, and a voice answered throatily from the bough. Heart pounding, the wolf backed away quickly and made a detour to avoid the tree altogether—then realized that she had lost Shalune's trail.

She stopped and looked about. Whatever had menaced her from the branches had either moved away or simply lost interest, and the forest was very still. Grimya tested first the air and then the ground, but as before, the scent of Shalune was impossible to pick out and no one sound stood out against the ceaseless background murmur to betray someone moving through the undergrowth.

Angry with herself for letting a moment's cowardice get the better of her, Grimya wondered what she should do. To press on into the forest in the hope of finding Shalune would be foolish. The likelihood of coming on her by sheer chance was remote, and it would be all too easy to lose her own way in this unfamiliar territory. She would have to abandon her plan and return to the citadel.

Then, not far away, someone coughed.

Grimya whirled around, her ears pricking as she sought the direction of the sound. A bird shrieked in alarm, clattering away through the trees' higher branches, and then she pinpointed it: downwind, deeper in the forest and a little to the left of the path she'd been following. The wolf hunched down into the slinking crouch that she used when hunting and began to move stealthily toward the source of the disturbance. Not forty feet on, she found them. They were in a small clearing: two indistinct shapes that even her sharp eyes might have taken for hewn tree stumps, until the shorter of the two moved and Shalune's silhouette showed briefly as the filtered moonlight dappled across it. As she halted on the clearing's edge, only just concealed by a rank-smelling bush, Grimya heard the fat woman's low-pitched voice and a deeper, male answer. Tiam. So she'd been right: Shalune had come to meet Yima's lover, and to bring him a message.

Grimya's ears swiveled forward again, straining to pick out the two humans' soft, urgent conversation from among the sounds of the forest. Many of the words they exchanged escaped her, and Tiam's voice was harder to understand than Shalune's more familiar tones, but she heard him ask a question with the word *Yima* in it, and heard Shalune's reply. "No. No, Tiam, that can't be." She added something more, which Grimya didn't catch, then: "I'm sorry, but you must understand that it's impossible now."

"Please, Shalune!" Tiam pleaded. "I can't simply—" But the sudden chirring of insects made the rest incomprehensible.

Shalune shook her head. "I won't risk it. I'd do a lot for Yima, but not that; not now. It's too late, Tiam. You *must* resign yourself to be—"

Again the insects set up their noise, drowning her words. This time, to Grimya's intense frustration, the shrill chorus went on for a minute or more, and by the time the creatures finally fell silent again, Shalune and Tiam were making their farewells.

Tiam bowed to the priestess and pressed something into her hands: a gift or an offering, Grimya presumed, as payment for her help. Then he said, "You'll tell her that I—"

Shalune interrupted gruffly. "Yes, yes, I'll tell her. She'll know, be assured of it. Now go back to your home. And remember: you must never, *never* dare to risk being seen here again. Never, Tiam—for as long as you live. You understand that, don't you?"

"Yes," he said, his voice taut with emotion. "I understand."

"Then I wish you a long life."

"Good-bye, Shalune. I'll . . . I'll never forget."

"It'll be better for all concerned if you do. Good-bye, Tiam."

Shalune turned so quickly and so unexpectedly toward her that Grimya could only freeze rigid behind the bush and watch, wide-eyed, as the stocky figure strode past her toward the forest's edge. Tiam, too, was leaving, though in the opposite direction, and for a moment Grimya was tempted to follow him back to his home in the hope of learning more. Then the impulse faded as she remembered how easy it would be to lose her bearings, and on the heels of that thought came the realization that she'd be well advised to get back to the citadel ahead of Shalune if she wasn't to risk being seen. Shalune would be sure to take the shorter route around the lake; by cutting diagonally through the trees to the waterside and then running fast in the other direction, Grimya thought she could reach the bluff first. She waited until she was certain that Shalune wouldn't hear her movements, then set off.

As she pushed her way through the undergrowth, Grimya felt sadness well up within her. She believed that she now understood why Shalune and Tiam had met here tonight, and the knowledge had deepened the sympathy she felt for Yima in her plight. This had been Yima's farewell to the man she loved, but delivered by proxy because the sudden change in her circumstances had made it impossible for her to leave the citadel. Yima's every move was now under her mother's close scrutiny; her fate had been set, and she was unable to slip away even for one final, bittersweet tryst.

Now with this final message from Shalune, the young lovers' dreams had been buried forever, and the last exchange between Shalune and the young man echoed poignantly in Grimya's mind. *I'll never forget,* he had said, and: *It'll be better for all concerned if you do,* Shalune had answered. Grimya's heart was easily moved to pity, and had she been human, she would have wept for Yima and Tiam and for the final shattering of their hopes.

The trees had begun to thin out, and the wolf realized that she was nearing the forest's edge. With an effort, she pushed her unhappy thoughts away, then raised her muzzle to peer ahead. She could just glimpse the dark glitter of water through the crowding trunks, and in less than a minute, she emerged onto the sandy track around the lake's perimeter. Shalune was already on the path and walking briskly; Grimya made to turn the other way—then stopped, her hackles rising. There was something on the track ahead of Shalune, between her and the bluff. The woman hadn't yet seen it, but Grimya's keen eyes caught a telltale flicker of movement at the edge of the trees. Another human figure—not Tiam; this shape was too tall. It looked—*Great Mother*, Grimya thought with a jolt, *not Uluye! Not*—

The fearful thought was violently truncated as she realized that it wasn't Uluye, that it moved too strangely, too stiffly, as though unseen hands were manipulating its limbs and taking the place of a brain that could no longer control the body it inhabited. In the same moment, Shalune saw it, too. Her steps wavered; she stumbled, almost lost her footing, righted herself . . . then froze rigid, transfixed as though by a cobra's merciless, glittering stare.

The *hushu* shambled out onto the path and raised one arm. Its movements were dislocated, a series of staccato jerks, but its intention was clear. It reached toward Shalune, and the fingers of its dead hand splayed wide, like a baby's fingers trying to grasp at some desired object. Shalune couldn't move. The monstrosity blocked her path, and she was too paralyzed with terror to even think of turning and running back the way she had come.

Grimya, too, was terrified, but she didn't allow herself the time to let fear get the better of her. A primal instinct, a sense of loathing that was rooted even more deeply in her psyche than her fear of this unholy travesty, surged to the surface, and she launched herself forward, racing down the track and baring her fangs in a savage snarl.

A thin, whistling shriek—whether from the *hushu* or from Shalune, Grimya would never know—set the forest birds squalling and cackling as the wolf's lean, gray shape barreled past Shalune, skidded to a halt in front of her and snarled again in furious challenge. The *hushu* rocked on its heels, its arms flailing, and Grimya saw the half-rotted, half-mummified face, the fleshless jaw revealing black and decaying teeth in shriveled gums, the two white pinpoints of light that flickered deep in the empty eye sockets and betrayed the mindless half-life within the skull. The wolf's flesh seemed to burn, then to turn as cold as a glacier, but she stood her ground, her face twisted into a mask of rage and hatred, her lips drawn back with saliva drooling in ropes between her teeth.

The *hushu*'s jaw dropped open with an audible crack, and a foul stench erupted from its throat. *"Unnnng. . . ."* It couldn't truly speak, for the vital cords and muscles and airways had rotted away; but the abysmal noises the creature made were almost, *almost*, words and gave the hideous impression that it knew what it wanted to say. Again the vile breath swept over the wolf, and the monstrosity croaked: *"Unngri. . . . Unnngggrreeee. . . ."*

Behind Grimya's back, Shalune gagged, the sound almost as ugly as the mouthings of the *hushu*. The thing waved its arm again, the fingers clawing and clenching. *"Eeee . . ."* it grated. *"Hhh . . . hhf . . . hfeee. . . ."* Then suddenly the ghastly voice rose to a wail so dismal that a violent shock coursed through Grimya's entire body. *"Feeee—uh, uhh, feeeeEEED!"*

If she'd paused for one instant to think, Grimya would have turned tail and fled. But there was no time to be rational; instinct, and instinct alone, took over, and she hurled herself at the *hushu* in a flying leap as fear and revulsion and fury combined and goaded her into attack. The *hushu* crashed to the ground under her weight, chittering like a demented bird; Grimya's fangs snapped on air, and a fetid blast like something from an ancient tomb bowled her backward as the *hushu* howled in her face.

Grimya snapped again and again, slavering, nearly hysterical as she tried to bite the warped and screaming skull out of existence. Then hands gripped her scruff and a violent force pulled her back, and she heard Shalune's voice yelling in her ear.

"No, Grimya, no! *Leave* it, let it *go*! Run away! *Run!*"

The *hushu* lay thrashing at the edge of the path. It couldn't rise, couldn't coordinate its limbs; it only kicked and flailed, wagging its misshapen head and uttering gargling noises that sounded both piteous and angry. Grimya stared at it in horror as her own spinning senses came back to earth; then Shalune pulled at her again with renewed strength. "Grimya! Come away. Run!"

She ran, Shalune beside her as together they pelted down the path. Neither had any thought for the risk as they ran across the lakeside arena to the bluff wall, and it was only when they reached the staircase and Shalune collapsed, gasping, onto the bottom step that Grimya thought to look up at the ziggurat towering above them. But there were no flickering torches, no voices, no agitated figures emerging from the network of caves. No one, it seemed, had heard anything untoward.

Shalune was sprawled on the stairs, her face pressed against a stone tread, her torso heaving as she sucked air painfully into her lungs. Grimya looked back beyond the arena to the path and the dark forest. She knew where the *hushu* must be, but a cloud was creeping over the moon now and she could see nothing moving. The forest murmured, as strange and secretive as a distant sea; mingling with its sounds she thought she heard a faint hooting and whistling that was not a night bird, but she couldn't be sure.

Shalune's breathing eased and steadied, and at last the priestess raised her head. Her gaze and Grimya's met, locked briefly; then Shalune rubbed Grimya between the ears and looked away. She was neither curious nor suspicious about the wolf's presence in the forest; she simply assumed that Grimya must have been hunting, and there was nothing unusual in that: she was, after all, simply an animal. But Grimya had seen both gratitude and admiration in the priestess's eyes, silent recognition of the likelihood that the wolf had saved her life. Shalune wouldn't forget that, and her gesture had been a mute but emphatic acknowledgment of her debt.

The fat woman climbed wearily to her feet. Grimya

whined a gentle interrogative, and Shalune looked down at her. She was trying to smile, but her heart wasn't in it. And Grimya saw fear on her face.

Shalune touched a finger to her lips but didn't speak. She looked back at the lake, and a shudder racked her as though an arctic wind had suddenly touched the stifling air. Her lips moved, and Grimya was just able to make out the words she whispered into the stillness.

"Such an omen, such a dire omen! Oh, what have I *done*?"

She turned and, her back bent and her limbs heavy like an old, old woman's, she began to climb the stairs.

·CHAPTER·XIII·

On the night before the initiation ceremony, the citadel and the forest were rocked by a colossal thunderstorm. Grimya had sensed its approach since late afternoon and had been restless and uneasy, and those priestesses who were weather-wise predicted that the storm would be abnormally severe even by Dark Isle standards.

Uluye was grimly delighted by the prediction, pronouncing it an excellent omen, and at sunset, as the clouds gathered and the sky turned from darkly brazen to the purple-black of a fearsome bruise, she gathered a coterie of the senior women and led them down to the arena to chant a hymn of praise to the Ancestral Lady while the nightly circuit of the lake was made.

Grimya, watching nervously from the ledge outside Indigo's quarters, heard their song rising with eerie clarity against a background of total stillness and silence; then she jumped with shock as the first searing triple flash of lightning ripped across the heavens. The following thunder obliterated the women's voices, and as it began to fade, the sky opened and the rain came roaring down. The torches below on the arena guttered wildly for a mere few seconds and then were doused; another lightning flash showed the women pelting back toward the ziggurat, arms clasped over their heads to protect themselves from the battering onslaught as the downpour hit them like a cataract. They scrambled up stairs already treacherous with running water and ran for the shelter of the caves, their hair streaming and their garments plastered to their skin.

Last of all came Uluye, but instead of turning in to her own quarters, she walked on along the ledge toward the final flight of stairs that led to the open temple above the citadel. She passed by Grimya without so much as acknowledging her, and to the wolf it seemed as though she was in a trance. Her eyes stared fiercely ahead, unblinking though the rain was teeming in her face; her mouth was set in a triumphant smile, without the smallest trace of ease or humor, and she walked with an air of absolute purpose, oblivious to anything around her.

The lightning was by now almost continuous, the thunder a constant bawling din vibrating through the bluff. Grimya slunk back inside the cave, wishing that Indigo were here and not spending this last evening, the evening of dark moon, in vigil with Yima and Shalune. Since the night she had followed Shalune to the forest and witnessed her meeting with Tiam, Grimya had wanted to talk to Indigo and tell her what she had seen, but the chance simply hadn't come. In these last few days before the initiation ceremony, it seemed that the oracle's time, like Yima's, was no longer her own.

For several hours each day, Indigo and Shalune took instruction from Uluye in the sponsors' duties; then there were long and tedious rehearsals for the ceremony itself and for the procession that would precede it, and late into each night, small ceremonies at which, Indigo reported, she and Shalune must sit mutely while Uluye prepared her daughter in ritual fashion for her coming ordeal.

The few free hours left to Indigo were only just enough for the basic needs of eating and sleeping, and so yet again

Grimya had felt obliged to restrain her urge to tell her story
and had forced herself not to ask—as she longed to do—if
they might not help Yima in some way. She hoped that there
would still be a chance to make her plea, but the opportunity for that diminished with every new day; besides, she
was forced to admit that she could see no way in which
Yima could be helped now. The die was cast; Indigo
couldn't change matters even if she were willing to try to,
and Yima herself seemed quietly resigned and as obedient
as always. That in itself puzzled Grimya, who had expected
a show of resistance, or at the very least, some sign of bitter
regret, at this eleventh hour. It seemed, though, that Uluye
had imposed her authority so thoroughly on her daughter
that any spark of rebellion in Yima was extinguished beyond
recall.

Grimya spent an unhappy night in the cave. The storm
continued for hour after hour, until it seemed it would never
end, and she slept only fitfully, frequently wakened by the
thunder as it rolled around the bluff. Once, startled out of
an uneasy doze by a double crash directly overhead, she
saw that Indigo had returned and, still fully dressed, was
climbing into her bed, but Indigo was too tired to even greet
her, and disconsolately, the wolf laid her head down once
more and tried to go back to sleep.

With dawn, though, the storm finally abated, and at last
Grimya opened her eyes to see, instead of the ceaseless
flicker of lightning against the black night, the first rays of
the sun rising above the trees. She rose, stretched stiffly and
shook herself from muzzle to tail. Indigo was still asleep,
and the wolf padded to the cave's entrance, pushed through
the curtain and emerged onto the ledge.

The morning was clear, cool and quiet after the storm's
night-long racket. A few isolated puddles shone in the arena
below, but most of the torrential rain had already evapo-
rated under the sun's early rays. The lake was brimming,
its surface choppy in the breeze and glittering in the brilliant
light; two women crouched at its edge, filling pitchers with

water for washing, but most of the citadel's inhabitants weren't yet astir.

It should have been a peaceful, almost idyllic scene; yet as she gazed down from the ledge, Grimya felt something dark and oppressive underlying the apparent tranquility: the sense that a subtle, but inescapable, influence was reaching out to taint everything around it. Brooding; that was the word. Brooding and waiting. She remembered Uluye's strange behavior as the storm broke, and she looked up to where the truncated peak of the ziggurat loomed. The open temple wasn't visible, but a thin trickle of smoke was rising above the towering wall, and intuition told Grimya that the High Priestess was there still, as she had been throughout the night.

Her sharp ears caught a sound behind her, and she turned to see that Indigo was awake and sitting up.

"Grimya . . ." Indigo's voice was heavy with weariness. "Is it already morning?"

"Yess." Grimya ducked back through the curtain and approached the bed. "You can't have had more than a few hours' sleep. You c-came back so late last night."

Indigo smiled tiredly. "I'm all right." She rubbed her eyes with clenched knuckles, forcing herself to full wakefulness. "Has Shalune been here yet?"

"No. Should she have been?"

"She said she'd be early. We're to spend the day with Yima, making the last preparations for tonight."

Grimya's tail drooped. "With Y . . . *ima*? But I thought that today we would be able to be together."

"I know; I'd hoped so too." Indigo reached out and ruffled the wolf's cheek fur. "I'm sorry, my dear. By tomorrow it'll all be over."

Grimya wanted to say, *But it won't!* Then, at the last moment, she stayed her tongue. There was something wrong with Indigo, something the wolf had never encountered before and that she didn't comprehend. Indigo seemed preoccupied, distant. In one sense that was understandable, Grimya thought, for she was overtired and the last few days had doubtless been disorienting; but Grimya couldn't shake off the conviction that her distance was deliberate, that she was concealing some emotion or some intent that she didn't want the wolf to see. And Grimya was certain that whatever might take place at the initiation ceremony, this coming night would not be the end of it.

Indigo was out of bed now and crouching by the hearth-stone, where she poured herself a cup of water from a pitcher. The water was stale and she grimaced at the taste, but drained the cup, set it aside and then poured more water into a bowl and began to splash her face. Grimya watched her uneasily. She thought of Uluye alone in the high temple above them. She thought of Shalune's secretive visit to the forest to meet Tiam. She thought of Yima and of the other, unknown participant—*she;* no other identity, just *she*—in this affair. Something was wrong; she knew it as surely as she knew that the sun rose with each dawn. And, like the scent of hunters on the wind, Grimya sensed danger.

She spoke so suddenly that Indigo started. "Indigo, I have made a decision. When you g-go to the c . . . *eremony* tonight, when you go down into this Well, I am coming with you."

Indigo blinked. "Grimya, you can't. You know that."

"I d . . . o *not* know it. I don't w-want you to go there alone."

"I won't be alone. Shalune and Yima will be with me. There's nothing to fear, truly there isn't."

But there was. Grimya's muzzle quivered. "Indigo, please ll-llisten to me! There is something wrong with this, some-thing bad. I don't kn-know what it is, but I have a terrible feeling about it! Sha-lune—"

"Shalune has no wish to harm me." Misunderstanding what Grimya had been about to say, Indigo interrupted be-fore she could explain. Then, seeing the misery in the wolf's eyes, her voice softened and she turned to face her, taking her muzzle gently in both hands. "Sweet Grimya, it's quite simple. You *can't* come with me. Uluye won't allow it, and I'm not in a position to argue with her. I understand your fears, and I'm touched by your concern, but truly, I don't believe that I'll be in any danger.'' She frowned suddenly, and for a moment her look grew very introverted. "I don't know why I should be so sure of that. It makes no sense in the light of all we've said and all we suspect about the Ancestral Lady. But somehow I *am* sure, Grimya. I *am*.''

This, Grimya realized, was something else entirely. Preoccupied with her own doubts, she'd forgotten what lay at the core of this affair. Not Shalune, not Yima and Tiam, but the Ancestral Lady herself—or whatever dwelt down in the unknown world below the Well and spoke in the Ancestral Lady's name. This, by all standards of reason, was where the danger lay, if danger there was, for this was the demon to which Indigo's lodestone had led them.

Yet Grimya wasn't convinced. Whatever peril the Ancestral Lady might impose, the wolf felt in her bones that Indigo was about to be faced with a far greater threat, and one over which the demon had no influence. But how could she explain such a feeling to Indigo? She had no evidence, no foundation, only her instinct. And in Indigo's present state of mind, that wouldn't be enough.

Indigo was still stroking her muzzle, but absently, her mind elsewhere. Grimya pulled free, backed a pace and made one final effort. "Please, Indigo,'' she said throatily. "I m . . . *ust* tell you what is in my mind. There is something you don't know. Some-thing about Yima herself. She has—''

"Indigo?'' The querying call came from outside the cave. Instantly Grimya fell silent, and Indigo looked up quickly. The curtain parted a fraction, and Shalune's face appeared in the gap.

"Ah, you're awake.'' She made her customary ritual bow, then entered. "That's good. We must make ready. Yima's robes are being prepared now and it'll soon be time to dress her for the vigil.''

Grimya echoed, silently and in dismay, *Vigil?*
I told you: Shalune and I are to stay with her throughout

the day, Indigo communicated. *We must say our good-byes for now.*

"You've eaten nothing?" Shalune asked, before Grimya could reply.

"Nothing," Indigo confirmed. "I drank some water, but I understand that's permissible."

"Yes, yes, of course." Shalune seemed nervous, as though something had either excited or alarmed her. Grimya strove to meet her gaze, but the fat woman's eyes avoided her, whether consciously or not, she couldn't be sure.

Indigo. . . . She tried again to project her thoughts as her mind began to crawl with disquiet. But Indigo either didn't hear or was too distracted by Shalune to answer. Her mind was filled with other matters, mundanities, the small necessities of the day ahead; she slipped her feet into plaited sandals, cast a thin cotton shawl over her shoulders, and followed the fat woman toward the cave's entrance. Only when she reached the threshold did she turn and bend down to rub Grimya's head.

"Be patient, dear one. Inuss will bring you food and see that you're all right, and I'll be back tomorrow."

It had been Shalune's suggestion that Inuss be deputized to take care of the wolf in Indigo's absence. Uluye had agreed to spare the young priestess from the cliff-top ceremony, and Indigo was secretly relieved that someone would be here to prevent Grimya, if necessary, from following her to the temple. Under any other circumstances, she wouldn't have wanted to leave her friend behind, and she knew that she was guilty of deceiving Grimya when she had said that Uluye would never have allowed her to come. Uluye could have been persuaded; even blackmailed if Indigo had had the determination. But Indigo didn't want to persuade her. This time she wanted to face her demon alone.

She kissed the top of the wolf's head. "I'll see you tomorrow morning." And to salve her conscience as well as to reassure Grimya, she added silently, *Don't fret, and don't worry about me. I'll come to no harm.*

Grimya couldn't reply. She didn't have the words to express her fears, and there simply wasn't time to search for another way to explain. She licked Indigo's face, then watched dismally as the two women left the cave. The soft sound of their footsteps diminished along the ledge, and the she-wolf was alone.

The awesome voice of a single horn seared across the night, arousing a cacophony of shrieking and chattering from the forest's denizens. Not this time the brittle, brazen sound of the priestesses' welcoming trumpets, but a single deep and ominous note that set the air throbbing and vibrated through the ziggurat. Grimya, keeping her solitary, unhappy vigil in the oracle's cave, shot to her feet with a yelp of shock, then stood quivering as the horn's echoes slowly faded like thunder dying away in the distance. This was the signal Indigo had told her to expect—the sign that the initiation ceremony was about to begin.

The wolf moved toward the cave's entrance. One part of her didn't want to watch the procession as it went by; another part, though, was drawn helplessly to it, like a leaf in a fast-running stream, and its influence was the stronger of the two. She nosed the curtain aside, took a step out onto the ledge and looked down. There were lights, little more than flickering pinpoints, several levels below her, and rising on the still, humid air came the sound of voices in a dirgelike chorus. Grimya stood still, watching—and at last, as the procession reached her own level and began to move along the ledge toward her, she could see it clearly.

Uluye led the train of women. She was dressed in a dark robe that in the thin starlight looked almost utterly black, and on her head was a tall, bone-white crown that highlighted her face into sharp relief. Behind her walked two torchbearers, and behind them—Grimya cringed in shock as she saw a figure out of nightmare, its head huge and grotesquely distorted; vast, pale eyes staring mindlessly ahead as it walked. Then suddenly rationality slipped back, and she realized that what she was seeing wasn't a true face, but a mask, four or five times the size of a human head and carved to represent a creature that was neither human nor animal nor bird nor fish, but with elements of all those and something more. The mask flowed down over its wearer's shoulders; multicolored ribbons shimmered in the torch-light, forming a bizarre cloak that fell almost to the ground. Glimpses of a plain white robe showed beneath the ribbons, and small bare feet, painted with sigils and adorned with anklets, moved beneath the robe's hem as they followed a little unsteadily in Uluye's wake.

Grimya backed a pace into the cave as the procession drew nearer. Yima—for the hideously masked figure could only be the candidate herself—was followed by her two sponsors, and though their appearance was less grotesque, they were still barely recognizable as Indigo and Shalune. Both wore veils of a fine, translucent material, decorated with a myriad of bone and wood carvings that clinked as they walked. Their robes were dark like Uluye's; their faces, dimly visible beneath the veils, were whitened with wood ash and their eyes ringed with charcoal. After them came two more torchbearers, and then, like the tail of a comet behind its bright nucleus, the whole mass of the cult priest-esses, two by two, their expressions a strange mixture of the solemn and the rapt.

Grimya, her muzzle just protruding through the curtain, watched with wide eyes as the silent file of women went by. No one so much as glanced at her—she doubted that any of the celebrants were even aware of her presence in the shad-ows—and as the last pair passed and walked on toward the final flight of stairs and the temple on the summit, the wolf shuddered as though a cold wind had blown from another dimension to chill her through fur and flesh to the marrow of her bones.

From above her, the great horn sounded again, a darkly triumphant clarion that was shockingly echoed by shrill blasts from the more familiar trumpets. Yima and her at-tendants must have reached the temple. . . .

Grimya slunk back into the cave, her tail between her legs. A whimper bubbled in her throat, but she suppressed it. She didn't want to see any more, didn't want to hear any more; and above all, she didn't want to think about what was happening on the cliff top. All she wanted was for tonight to be over, and for Indigo to return safely to the world.

Smoke rose in a dense column from the great bowl of the brazier, sulphurous yellow in the torches' glare. The drums, which had begun a muted beat as the procession's leaders stepped into the rectangle of the temple, were now rising to the pitch and intensity of distant thunder, and on all sides of the square the massed ranks of women swayed with the hypnotic rhythm. Their bodies glistened with sweat; their skirts swirled in a kaleidoscope of fierce colors, while the flying dark mass of their hair hurled ghastly and almost bestial shadows across their faces.

High above the heads of her followers, beside the brazier and wreathed in its smoke, Uluye stared down like some primitive and savage goddess, her arms outspread as though to encompass and embrace the wild scene about her. Her eyes blazed with joy as she surveyed the heady mayhem of the rite; she was drinking in the energies of the stamping, swaying crowd, feeding on them, drawing power from them and focusing it with the fearsome intensity of a diamond lens.

In the flickering light she looked almost as unhuman as the weird, masked figure of Yima, who stood below her in the center of the sandstone square. Indigo and Shalune flanked the candidate now, each with a hand resting lightly on one of her shoulders to signify that she was in their charge and that they, her sponsors, were also her sworn guardians.

Indigo was giddy with the intoxicating effects of the drums, the sea of movement around her, the dancing torchlight, the clouds of incense that billowed from the brazier and stung her eyes and nostrils. She had vowed that she would remain detached from this, do no more than play her appointed part, but she couldn't control the primal excitement that rose in her as the ritual neared its climax. Civilization had been stripped away; this was raw, unreasoning energy, and she was a part of it; it flowed in her veins, thrummed in her bones, drilled deep into her soul. She felt Yima's skin trembling under her touch, felt her own body quiver as the current of anticipation grew and grew—

Suddenly Uluye flung her arms skyward and let out a shriek that could have awakened the dead. The drums stopped. The echoes of Uluye's voice died away, and for a time that must have been mere moments, yet seemed to Indigo like half of her life, there was silence. Uluye was smiling, that same wild rictus Indigo had seen before, as though a naked grinning skull were about to burst through the flesh of the High Priestess's face.

With a dramatic gesture, Uluye dropped to a crouch before the brazier, and when she rose again, she was holding what looked like a gigantic, stone-headed hammer. An ululating yell went up from the women; the horns blared out in cacophony, and Uluye reared to her full height, swung the hammer above her head, then brought it hurtling down on the dais where the brazier stood. The crash of stone meeting stone dinned in Indigo's ears, and from deep within the cliff itself came an answering rumble. The square beneath her feet shook; then there was a new sound, a grinding, grating sound, the protesting voice of ancient mechanisms creaking into life—and at the foot of the plinth, between the brazier and the oracle's chair, a section of the temple floor moved. As though a huge hand had pushed it from below, one of the stone slabs rose on its end, teetered, then keeled over and fell with a crash that shook the floor afresh and sent a cloud of fine dust flying to merge with the scented smoke.

An awed gasp rippled through the crowd. As the dust cleared, Indigo saw the gaping dark rectangle revealed by the stone, and where the torchlight could just reach, the first few uneven treads of a flight of steps spiraling down into blackness. The Well was open.

Uluye raised her head. The hammer was still balanced in her hands, and though its weight must have been prodigious, she held it as though it were nothing. Again she smiled; again the rictus.

"Go, candidate." Her voice rang richly over the heads of the throng. "Go down from this world and go out from this world, and go you to the domain of the Ancestral Lady. The testing is come and the time is come."

She set the hammer aside, stepped down from the plinth and moved with lithe grace toward the motionless trio at the square's center. Her hand reached out and touched Yima's mask, first on the brow, then on the lips, last at the throat.

"In the Ancestral Lady's name, I set upon you my blessing, and in the Ancestral Lady's name, I set upon you the seal of protection. And I charge these servants to conduct you with faith and with courage to your ordeal. Fear not the dark and fear not the silence: fear not the realm of the dead, for that is our Lady's realm, and our Lady will be your guiding light."

At a gesture from Uluye, two acolytes came forward. Each carried a lit taper; with due solemnity they put them into the hands of Indigo and Shalune. As they backed away, fear and wonder and envy mingling in their eyes, Uluye stepped aside and indicated the Well's black maw.

"Go in hope, my chosen daughter," she said, so softly that only those at the forefront of the throng could hear her. "And return in triumph!"

Shalune moved to stand in front of Yima; Indigo took her place behind. They started forward, and the horns blared out once more, the deep, sonorous booming echoed by shrill fanfares, while the drums rolled a wild crescendo. The noise dinned through Indigo's head; she saw Shalune step down, saw Yima follow, then with a clutching and clenching of fearful excitement that threatened to suffocate the air from her lungs and throat, she took the last pace forward and began to descend into the engulfing dark.

* * *

The sudden renewed clamor of the horns and drums brought Grimya running out to the ledge once more. Craning up, she could see the fringes of a bright glow on the cliff top, and she guessed that the priestesses were reaching the climax of their ceremony. Instinctively, her telepathic senses tried to make contact with Indigo's mind, but what she found was so chaotically tangled with images of the ritual that she could make no sense of it, and she couldn't break through the fragmented blur of color and noise.

The horns and drums continued, a crescendo now, and aware that she could learn nothing from staring uselessly up toward the temple, Grimya made to withdraw back into the cave. What made her pause and glance down before ducking past the curtain, she would never know, but she did pause, and she did look, and what she saw stopped her in her tracks.

Someone had emerged from the bluff and was moving across the sands of the arena. For an instant Grimya thought it was a *hushu*, and her hackles rose as a snarl formed involuntarily in her throat. But then the snarl died stillborn as she realized that the figure's movements were too natural and too controlled to be those of a mindless zombie. One of the children, too young for the rite? No, she was too tall. And there was something familiar in the way she walked. . . .

The figure was quickening its pace, heading not for the lake as Grimya had first thought, but for the path that led around the shore and into the forest. With the moon no more than the thinnest of slivers, only starlight and a dim reflection from the temple illuminated the arena. Grimya's night vision was far more acute than that of any human, but even she could see nothing clearly . . . until, just before reaching the path, the girl paused and looked back. For perhaps the space of two heartbeats, her face was turned up toward the ziggurat—and Grimya's body and mind froze. She tried to tell herself that it was impossible to be sure, that she couldn't make such a judgment from this distance and in this light.

But in her heart she had no doubt. The girl far below her, now turning again and running swiftly, urgently, away in the direction of the forest, was Yima.

·CHAPTER·XIV·

"*There's a light!*"

Shalune's voice hissed so suddenly and unexpectedly that Indigo started and almost lost her footing. The veil she wore blurred her vision, and the glimmer given off by the tapers they carried was feeble and all but useless, but she could just make out Shalune's dim shape ahead and below her, and the figure of Yima, distorted by the mask, between them. Shalune had halted, and one shadowy arm pointed downward.

Since the last glare of torchlight from the outside world had faded behind them—minutes ago? Hours ago?—Indigo had willed herself to concentrate on anything but the mechanics of this bizarre journey. She had tried to ignore the fact that the spiraling stairway had no balustrade, no rail, but was simply a flight of open steps winding around and down the vertical shaft. She had tried to ignore the knowledge that they must by now be far, far below the lowest levels of the citadel, and ignore all speculations about the shaft's depth, refusing to dwell on the fact that when her foot had dislodged a piece of loose stone and sent it plummeting into the darkness, she hadn't heard it strike the bottom. She simply continued on behind Shalune and Yima, step after uneven step, her shoulder pressed against the shaft wall and her gaze fixed unswervingly on the taper in her hand.

Now, though, Shalune's sharp words snapped the mesmeric spell that the climb had begun to impose. Indigo felt momentarily disoriented, as though she'd been abruptly awakened from a sound sleep. Though they weren't forbidden to speak on this journey, no one had found the need for words until now . . . or perhaps, Indigo thought, none of them had quite had the courage to break the silence.

Cautiously she leaned out from the wall to look. There was, indeed, light—faint and colorless, but definite—filtering up from somewhere far below. It created the illusion of a distant, misty pool in the Well's depths, and Indigo quickly leaned back again, suppressing a vertiginous shudder.

The tapers created faint reflections in Shalune's black-ringed eyes as she turned to look back. "There's heat rising from below, too," she said in a whisper. "I believe we must be close to the foot of the shaft."

Indigo was too preoccupied to notice that there was a peculiarly strained note in her voice, and even if it had registered, she would have attributed it to nothing more than justifiable nervousness. They moved on, and she too began to feel the warmth, like a moist breath wafting through the Well. A fetid, decaying smell made her nostrils curl, and as they drew closer to the source of the light and as visibility slowly increased, she saw that the rock wall was gleaming with a faint, wet phosphorescence.

Yima had begun to tremble. The ornaments that hung about her grotesque mask clinked and rattled together, and the colored ribbons of her cloak rippled as her shoulders shook beneath them. Indigo reached forward to lay a hand lightly on her arm, silently trying to reassure her. It wasn't Yima alone who was afraid. Shalune, too, was shivering; she slowed her pace as though suddenly afraid to go on, then abruptly stopped moving altogether. Still touching

Yima's arm, Indigo whispered, "Shalune? Shalune, what is it, what's wrong?"

The fat women shook her head vigorously. "Nothing. I—*uhh!*"

The truncated hiss made Indigo's heart skip painfully; as the shock receded, she looked down and saw what had so startled—or frightened—her companion.

Ten feet below them the shaft ended. And there, where the stairs' final spiral curved away, was a low and narrow door, little more than a hole in the rock face, with utter darkness beyond.

This time when Shalune looked back, the sourceless light made her painted face ghastly beneath its veil, and the fear emanating from her was like a psychic shock wave. Yima whimpered, an ugly, strangled sound, and Indigo gripped the girl's arm more tightly, trying to convey a confidence that suddenly she didn't feel.

"Shalune!" she whispered again. Shalune, however, didn't answer her. She'd forced herself to move on again, but she was muttering, her hands clenching and unclenching with quick and violent movements. She was praying, Indigo realized. And she was terrified almost beyond control.

At last Shalune stumbled down the last three steps, Yima behind her and Indigo in their wake. They stood together on a strangely and unnaturally smooth rock floor on which a thin sheen of water glimmered. The water was warm to their bare feet but felt viscous; more like oil, Indigo thought as her toes curled in faint revulsion. Before them, the dark hole gaped like a silent mouth. It was unmarked, unadorned, but there was no doubt that this was the way they must go. There was no other choice.

Shalune hung back, reluctant even to look, and Indigo asked quietly, "Shall I be first?"

Expression was hard to interpret under the veil and the paint, but she thought that Shalune flicked her a glance of intense gratitude before nodding wordlessly. Indigo drew breath. She still had her taper, and she dropped to a crouch before the hole's maw, thrust her arm into the darkness and peered through.

It wasn't the narrow tunnel that she'd feared. Instead of reflecting closely on rock, the taper's small glow diffused into emptiness, suggesting that there must be a wider space beyond the gap. Beckoning encouragement to her companions, Indigo eased herself into the doorway. She could just get through without dropping to hands and knees, and she emerged into an unlit space that—though it was impossible to be sure—felt large enough for her to at least stand upright. Cautiously, she rose. Her head didn't strike the roof, and when she extended her arms before her and to both sides, she touched nothing. The air was hotter and closer here, the smell stronger.

Indigo turned carefully and called out, "It's all right. I'm through, and there's space enough for us all."

There was some urgent whispering on the far side of the hole, and a long pause. Then at last Yima appeared. The extra height the mask gave her forced her to crawl, and Indigo crouched to help her through as the light of the taper dimly illuminated the girl's struggling figure. Shalune followed, crouching as Indigo had done, and the three of them stood, a little breathless, taking in their new surroundings.

There was little to assimilate. Shalune's taper had been extinguished as she came through the gap, and though Indigo tried to light it again from her own, it refused to glow back into life. The remaining taper gave so little light as to be all but useless; and though they waited, hoping that their eyes might grow accustomed to the dark, the Stygian gloom remained impenetrable.

"Yima, hold my hand," Indigo said at last. Her voice fell away flatly into emptiness. "And Shalune, take Yima's other hand. We daren't risk becoming separated."

Shalune muttered something that sounded like *"Lady, help our souls,"* and Indigo felt Yima's fingers entwine tightly with her own. In the last few minutes it seemed that the emphasis of leadership had shifted; Shalune had lost confidence and courage, and by unspoken agreement, the mantle of seniority now rested on Indigo's shoulders. She wasn't sure that she welcomed the burden, but someone had to take the responsibility or their quest would founder.

She didn't want to speak again, for the timbre of a human voice in this unknown place had a quality that chilled her to the core. All the same, she forced herself to say what must be said.

"We'll move forward, but very slowly. We've no way of knowing what lies ahead. I'll hold the taper at arm's length and pray that it's enough to show us any pitfalls in good time."

Shalune murmured assent; Yima said nothing. Slowly, and with the utmost caution, Indigo slid her foot forward. The floor, like the floor of the shaft itself, seemed level, and the taper gave some little light, but the veil hampered her and she would have thrown it back but for the memory of Uluye's warning that to venture into the Ancestral Lady's realm with their faces uncovered would bring disaster. Only the dead, Uluye had told her, might enter in such a way, and whatever her feelings toward Uluye, Indigo wasn't about to risk flouting the stricture.

At a snail's pace they moved on. After perhaps five yards or so, they came to realize that they were in a tunnel, high-roofed and wide enough to allow them to stand side by side. By contrast to the oddly smooth floor, the walls were rough and unfinished, and embedded with small, sharp-edged fragments that Indigo guessed might be quartz. Shalune, who was feeling her way along the wall to maintain some sense of orientation, swore suddenly and nursed a cut finger; Indigo held the taper to look at the wound, and Shalune said with feeling: "Great Lady, if we only had *more light!*"

"Little chance of that." Indigo examined the finger closely. "It's bleeding slightly, but it's only a graze. I think you should—" and she stopped, staring at the wall beyond.

Shalune frowned and started to say, "What—?" but Indigo had turned from her and was holding the taper close to the wall's surface. Then Shalune saw what Indigo had seen, and she choked her exclamation back to a throaty gasp.

Embedded in the wall was a human skull. Its cavities were almost filled with sand and rubble, but enough of it protruded to make the thing unmistakably recognizable. Beneath the sockets of eyes and nose, a row of rotting teeth grinned maniacally at them, and on the broken and ragged hinge of the jaw, a small, bright-scarlet smear showed where Shalune had cut herself.

"Great Mother . . ." Indigo stared in horrified fascination. As she moved the taper from side to side, she saw that there were more bones: the long, smooth outlines of a femur, a symmetrical curve of ribs, the delicate but crumbling imprint of hands—dozens of bones, *hundreds* of them, all human, all jumbled together in a macabre confusion, fused into the tunnel's wall. A child's cranium leered emptily at her feet. A desiccated hip joint thrust toward her at eye level. And when she moved forward, there were more, and yet more, and yet more.

Behind her, Shalune made another choking sound. "This is . . ." she said, then gagged, collected herself, tried again. "We're in the Lady's catacombs . . . oh, sweet life, preserve us, *we're in the Lady's catacombs!*"

Indigo took hold of her wrist and squeezed it hard. Perhaps she too should have been frightened by the grim discovery, but somehow such a reaction was beyond her. She felt no trepidation, no terror, only a faint but deep-rooted sense of excitement as she realized that they were indisputably following the right path.

Shalune's arm was quaking in her grasp, and the fat woman had begun to mutter. "All of them . . . they all come here, they all end here, all the dead, all those she doesn't cast out—"

"Shalune!" Indigo's sharp reprimand stopped the priestess's slide toward hysteria and silenced her. They stared at each other in the dimness, and Indigo said, "Shalune, we mustn't lose our nerve. This . . . this catacomb, as you call it, may be a macabre and unpleasant place, but the bones of the dead can't harm us. We must go on, as we pledged. We owe it to Yima.''

Shalune glanced apprehensively in Yima's direction and saw the girl standing rigid beside her. Either Yima was unaffected by their gruesome surroundings or—far more likely, Indigo thought—fear had reduced her to passive helplessness. Shalune licked her lips and nodded.

"Yes," she said. "Yes, we . . . must go on."

"Take hold of Yima's hand again." Indigo released Shalune's wrist and moved to resume her place at the head of the trio. "Don't touch the wall; don't even *think* about what's there. Watch the taper and walk slowly forward."

They resumed their slow, careful progress. Shalune seemed calmer now, but the gruesome find had taken its toll on her courage—and, Indigo was honest enough to acknowledge, on her own as well. It wasn't the nature of what they had found that had shaken her confidence, though that in itself was unpleasant enough; it was the ramifications. The thought that among those myriad fleshless remains there might be, might just be, the bones of the man she loved. . . .

No. She mustn't think about that, mustn't even consider it a possibility. It *wasn't* possible, for Fenran wasn't dead. What she had seen by the lake on Ancestors Night had been an illusion, for the Ancestral Lady was a trickster, nothing more. A player of games, a manipulator of minds. A demon. Indigo had learned much about the ways of demons, and she should know better by now than to be intimidated by the mere trappings of their craft.

Very well, demon, she thought. *If that was your first ploy, it hasn't intimidated me as you might have hoped. What do you have in store now?*

There was no answering voice in her mind, no abrupt shift of consciousness to the trance state in which the Ancestral Lady had made her desires known. There was just the taper's pale glow in the darkness, just the soft sound of their padding feet and the quick susurrus of their breathing against the silence. For now, the Ancestral Lady was keeping her own counsel, and she offered no clue as to what they might find at their journey's end.

But Indigo believed that they wouldn't have much longer to wait. . . .

When the glimmer of light showed ahead, it seemed at first to Indigo that it must be an illusion. Her gaze had been unswervingly fixed on the taper in her hand for so long that her eyes had difficulty in adjusting to the change; afterimages of the taper's pinpoint danced before her when she tried to refocus, and it was only when Yima tugged on her hand and pulled her to a halt that she realized she wasn't deluded.

Ahead of them, the tunnel came to an end. The thin, cold light flowed up from the floor to show a solid wall barring their way, and Yima whimpered and turned aside as she saw the grisly mosaic of human remains illuminated by the glow. Indigo, however, was gazing at the floor. There, where the tunnel ended, was the source of the light: a rectangular trap door set into the floor, which glowed as though it were made of some phosphorescent material. Loosing her hold on Yima's fingers, Indigo walked forward to the strange door. There was a ring set at one side; crouching, she grasped it and pulled. The door opened easily, and by the light reflecting from its underside, she saw a flight of wide, shallow stairs leading downward into blackness.

Softly she called out to Shalune. The fat woman came forward very reluctantly; she stopped two feet from the edge and peered down.

"Ah . . ." she whispered. "Ah, no . . ."

Indigo looked at her in surprise as she moved back hastily. "Shalune, what's wrong? This is no worse than anything we've encountered so far—better, in fact, for at least we'll be away from this tunnel."

Shalune shook her head, her veil ornaments clinking rapidly. "No," she said harshly. "It isn't that."

"What, then?"

"I . . . I can't . . . oh, Lady, help me!" And to Indigo's

astonishment, Shalune flung back her veil. Her face was clear in the light from the trap door, and a hard, bright challenge glittered in her eyes as she looked directly at Indigo.

"It's no use," she said. "I didn't intend to tell you, I meant you to find out only when it was too late to argue, but I see now that that would be madness. You *have* to know before we go any farther, or you may well put us all in danger when we face the Lady. I daren't risk that."

Beside her, Yima started to protest, her voice muffled by the mask, but Shalune snapped, "*No!* Be quiet. Indigo has to be told. And it'll make no difference. It's still right."

An unpleasant suspicion was beginning to crawl to the forefront of Indigo's mind. She asked, "What haven't you told me, Shalune? What's going on?"

Shalune looked speculatively at the hole and the staircase. "I think," she said, and suddenly she sounded peculiarly calm, "that those steps are the last stage of our journey. So it's best that we're shriven now. It's too late to change matters anyway." And she turned to the tense figure at her side. "Take off the mask."

The girl hesitated, and for a few moments it seemed that she might disobey. Then, slowly, she raised both hands to the wooden contraption. There was a faint click as she unfastened it, and then the whole front of the mask swung aside.

And Shalune's young protégée, Inuss, looked out at Indigo with frightened but defiant eyes.

Grimya had lost the trail. Caution had been vital, for her quarry was more nervous than a hunted deer, glancing back every few seconds and stopping time and again to listen for any sound of pursuit. The wolf had hung back as far as she dared, but now she realized that she'd made the mistake of being overcautious, for the forest had swallowed Yima's fleeing figure and suddenly even her scent was lost in the pungent smells of the undergrowth.

But although she railed at her own failure, Grimya knew

that in one sense, her ability—or lack of it—to track the girl hardly mattered anymore. She'd come close enough to identify Yima beyond any doubt, and she knew enough to guess, also beyond doubt, what was afoot.

She'd been a fool, she told herself bitterly. She had seen a little, heard a little, and had presumed that her surmise was the truth. Now she knew better. Now she knew that Shalune hadn't been simply a messenger carrying Yima's last sad farewell to her lover; instead, she'd been an active conniver, perhaps even the prime mover, behind Yima's plan to escape the future her mother had decreed for her, and elope. Snatches of the conversations she had overheard—first between Shalune and Yima, and later between Shalune and the young man Tiam—crowded into Grimya's memory. She could put a very different interpretation on them now, and some missing pieces of the puzzle fell into place. The mysterious *she* was still unidentified, but the wolf was certain now that whoever she was, she had taken Yima's place at the cliff-top ceremony and at this very moment was descending through the Well with Indigo and Shalune, to meet the Ancestral Lady.

Grimya's skin turned cold as she realized what that might mean. Indigo knew nothing of this, and the wolf didn't believe for one moment that Shalune and her unknown accomplice had any intention of telling her the truth. What, then, *did* they intend? Grimya had been afraid for Indigo, afraid of what she might find waiting for her in the Ancestral Lady's realm. But now there was a more immediate and human danger for which Indigo was totally unprepared. She'd suspect nothing—why should she? And she was only one, alone, while they were two. . . .

A shudder ran the length of the wolf's body, and she whimpered, looking back over her shoulder to where the lake gleamed between the trees. Yima and Tiam were forgotten; they meant nothing to her. But Indigo might be in peril.

She thrust into the undergrowth, pushing through the

tangle of vegetation with all her strength, desperate to reach the lakeside by the shortest possible route. Over and over again she told herself that this was her doing, her fault; she should have *insisted* on telling Indigo what she knew, not waited and waited, until it was too late and the deed was done and Indigo had gone unsuspecting into that dark shaft with Shalune and her companion. Now there was nothing she could do. She couldn't reach Indigo's mind; she'd tried already and failed. She couldn't warn her, couldn't help her, couldn't protect her.

Grimya burst out from the trees and stood panting on the path. On the far side of the lake, the ziggurat loomed darkly against the stars, and she could see the ceremonial fire still burning at its summit: an angry, orange-red eye in the darkness.

A disturbance without visible source stirred the lake waters suddenly and ominously, and the ripples spread until they lapped at the path's edge with a faint and unpleasant noise. Grimya stared at the lake, and her hackles rose with a sense of horrible foreboding. Even if—and it was a slender hope—Shalune and her cohort meant Indigo no harm, what of the creature that awaited them down there below the water in that eerie, unknown realm of demons? The Ancestral Lady, too, had been deceived. What would she do, in her power and in her fury, when the truth was revealed?

Grimya made her decision. She didn't like it, she feared its consequences, but there was no other choice open to her. She had already held back for too long. For Indigo's sake, she must conquer her fear and follow the candidate and her sponsors down into the Well.

She set off along the path, running with all the speed she could muster. Something chittered at her from the forest; she ignored it, raced on. As she reached the sandy arena, there was another disturbance in the lake, out toward the center, where the darkness was too intense to see whether the ripples were simply an effect of the night breeze or something more dire. Shuddering, and resisting the impulse

to look, Grimya ran for the stairs and streaked up them,
flight by flight, along the ledges, past the cave mouths, until
at last she was scrabbling the last few feet to the top of the
ziggurat.

Gasping for breath, she slumped down onto the stone of
the temple square, but allowed herself only a brief respite
before staggering up again and hastening toward the plinth
and the great bowl where the votive fire blazed. The Well,
so Shalune had said, lay beneath the largest flagstone of all
and was directly in front of the plinth. Grimya ran forward—then stopped, horrified, as the flames' glaring light
showed her the temple floor smooth and unbroken. The Well
had been closed once more. She was too late.

Whining with fear and frustration, Grimya began to
scratch at the stone. It was a futile gesture; she could no
more move the slab than halt the sun and moon in their
tracks across the sky, but desperation drove out reason and
her paws scrabbled frantically at the thin line between the
flag and its neighbor.

Then, under the bowl of the votive fire, a shadow lurched.

Grimya jumped as though she'd been shot, flying into a
defensive crouch and baring her fangs in a frightened snarl.
Staring at her from the plinth, where she had been sitting
cross-legged in solitary vigil, was Uluye.

They faced each other, both shocked, both wary. The
incense used at the ceremony had burned to ash now, but
its effects lingered and Uluye's eyes looked drugged. She
had been in a soporific semitrance until Grimya's scrabbling
disturbed her, and she still wasn't entirely sure whether the
sight confronting her was real or a delusion. For her part,
Grimya was faced with a terrible dilemma. She disliked and
mistrusted Uluye—it was, after all, the High Priestess's ob-
session with her own power and status that had given birth
to this disaster. Yet, at the same time, she recognized that
Uluye alone could help her now. In this, they must surely
be allies and not enemies. She *must* turn to Uluye. There
was no one else.

The she-wolf's body quivered. She stood upright, and her tail began to wag with the first tentative stirrings of hope. Then, to Uluye's stunned astonishment, her jaws parted and gutturally but clearly, she spoke.

"U-luye . . . I n-need your help. Indigo is in d . . . *anger*. And the girl who went into the Well is n-not Yima!"

·CHAPTER·XV·

"I don't regret what I've done." Shalune's eyes glinted with something like their old fierceness as she faced Indigo. "The Ancestral Lady does not choose her High Priestess; we do. But in this case, the choice was wrong." She jabbed an extended forefinger at her own breast. "*I* know it was wrong; I know Yima better than her own mother does, and I know Inuss, too. Yima has never wanted to be High Priestess. She knew she couldn't live up to the standards Uluye set for her, and she didn't want to try. But Uluye wouldn't listen to anyone; she was determined that her dynasty must be carried on, no matter what the wisdom of it or what the cost. She would never allow Yima to leave—even for a short time to bear a child—because she knows Yima might escape her grasp."

She jerked her head aside as though she were about to spit, then thought better of it. "Uluye's frightened. Frightened of growing old, of losing her power and being overthrown. She thinks I want to take her place, and she's wrong in that, too. I only want what's right for us all, and that means a candidate worthy of the Ancestral Lady, with the ability to rule wisely in the citadel.'' She scowled. ''Uluye isn't wise. Strong, yes; *too* strong for anyone's good at times. And she's dedicated to the Lady's will, I wouldn't deny that for one moment. It's simply her interpretation of the Lady's will that I question.''

Her interpretation of the Lady's will . . . that, Indigo thought, was the crux of it. The story Shalune had told her had confirmed a great many of her own feelings about Uluye, not least her conviction that the High Priestess's tyrannical attitude masked a deep-rooted and acute sense of vulnerability. Her determination that her daughter should also be her successor had, so Shalune said, been Uluye's way of ensuring that her power could never be challenged, and she had systematically crushed any opposition to her plans, including the opposition of Yima herself. Unable to persuade her mother to even consider that she might have some say in her own future, Yima had finally turned to Shalune for help. She knew that Shalune privately favored Inuss as the candidate for the High Priestess's mantle, and Shalune had promised to use all her wiles to persuade or, if necessary, force Uluye to acknowledge that she alone was not the final arbiter. They had had another ally in the cult's oracle, but her death and Indigo's subsequent arrival had, as Shalune put it, cast a snake into the *kemb*.

Then when the Ancestral Lady had spoken through Indigo and said, ''Come to me,'' Uluye had grasped her opportunity, and that had forced Shalune's hand. She hadn't wanted to deceive Indigo, she said; but at the same time, she couldn't bring herself to trust that Indigo wouldn't betray them to Uluye. At the last moment, when the candidate had been left alone for a final meditation, Inuss had taken Yima's place, and masked and heavily robed as she was, not even Uluye had known the difference. It had been that simple.

Indigo glanced at Inuss, who throughout Shalune's diatribe had stood mutely watching her mentor. Then she looked at the fat woman again. Strangely, despite the fact that she couldn't claim to know her well, she didn't doubt

Shalune's sincerity or her claim that she herself had no interest in usurping Uluye's place as High Priestess. Shalune, she suspected, would have been shrewd enough to have found another route to preeminence if that was what she had wanted. All the same, though, something in her assertions didn't quite ring true, and as Indigo looked at the woman and then again at Inuss, her suspicions took form.

She said, no hint of her thoughts in her voice, "And you believe that Inuss will succeed where Yima would have failed?"

"I know it." Shalune's reply was emphatic. "I should. I've been her teacher since she was little more than a toddler."

Indigo thought: *Ah.* . . . "Just her teacher?" she queried gently.

Shalune didn't dissemble. "She's my sister's child," she said. "When my sister died, Inuss was brought to the citadel and I became her guardian. No," she turned her head sharply as Inuss tried to interrupt her, "there's no reason why Indigo shouldn't know the whole truth, Inuss. I've no cause to hide the fact that I want the best for my own flesh and blood. Who wouldn't?" She faced Indigo once more. "And Inuss *is* the best. The Ancestral Lady will know it. She doesn't want an unwilling servant; she'll accept Inuss and sanction her. D'you think I'd let Inuss face the test if I weren't certain of that?"

Indigo allowed herself the faintest of smiles. "No. Knowing you, I don't think you would."

"Well, then." For a moment Shalune seemed embarrassed; then her expression cleared. "I'm not much of a one for sentiment—if you know me as you say, you'll be aware of that, too—but I felt sorry for Yima. I know what it's like to want something so greatly that nothing else in the entire world matters. I felt like that about my own ambitions to serve the Lady. Yima wants Tiam. I don't know how she was able to meet him in the first place, or what manner of disobediences she contrived to go on meeting him; she's never told me and I've never asked. But she loves him, Indigo. Why shouldn't she have her chance, as I had mine?" She paused, watching Indigo carefully, then added: "I suspect that if you'd been in my place, you'd have done just the same."

She would have, Indigo admitted to herself. She had no illusions now about Shalune's motives, for she was well aware that with the priestess's own niece confirmed as the next High Priestess, Shalune would gain enough *ches*—the cult's term for status and respect—to give her a great deal of influence. But would that be a bad thing? Indigo thought not; and in the matter of Uluye's successor, the fact that self-interest had taken precedence over philanthropy surely didn't make Shalune's judgment any less valid. Uluye had been too blind to see that she was forcing Yima along a road down which the girl was fundamentally unwilling to travel. If that wrong could be righted now, and a better candidate presented, who was she, Indigo asked herself, to quarrel with the wisdom of it?

Again she smiled the ghost of a smile. "Uluye won't be pleased when we return."

"Uluye may rant and rave to her heart's content; it'll be too late," Shalune rejoined. "Once Inuss has the Ancestral Lady's blessing, even Uluye won't dare to object."

"And Yima? What will become of her?"

Shalune's expression softened a little. "By now, I trust, she and Tiam are on their way to a new life together. I don't know where they'll go and I don't want to know, for what I haven't heard, I can't tell. I just hope that they have the sense to hide themselves far away from here while Uluye continues to live."

"Surely Uluye isn't so vengeful?"

Shalune snorted. "If you think that, you don't know her. Once she knows of this, there'll be a price on the heads of both Yima and Tiam—yes, I know Yima's her own daughter, but that won't make one whit of difference."

"But what crimes have they committed?" Indigo was appalled.

Shalune shrugged. "Blasphemy. Flouting the will of the

Ancestral Lady—Uluye's will, in other words. That's what she'll say, anyway. So we must pray for their sake that she doesn't find out the truth until they've been gone long enough to make a search pointless."

The thought that Uluye would take vengeance on her own daughter for the sake of wounded pride was monstrous. Somewhere, Indigo thought, at the heart of the web it had woven about the citadel and its inhabitants, the thing that called itself the Ancestral Lady must be chuckling richly at such a joke. A small, dark part of her mind turned cold and black. She would dearly like to see the demon pay a hard price for what it had done.

"Well," Shalune said at length, "there's just one more question to be asked. The Ancestral Lady awaits us, and it won't do to test her patience any further. Will you come with us, Indigo? Will you help me to sponsor Inuss before the Lady?"

Indigo was surprised. "Do I have a choice?"

"Yes, of course. I can't force you against your will, and I wouldn't try to."

Indigo looked at the shimmering trap door, at the dark gap, at the staircase. For a moment she wondered if in all conscience she should be as honest with Shalune as Shalune had been with her; but then harsh reason took over, and she acknowledged that that was impossible. The idea of telling Shalune that the goddess she and her peers worshiped was a demon, and that she and Grimya had set out to destroy it, would have been a monstrous joke even under the easiest of circumstances. Here and now, it was nothing short of insanity. She couldn't do it; conscience simply wasn't part of the equation. But although Shalune didn't know it—and Indigo prayed she never would—her motive for going on was far stronger and more personal than the priestess's could ever be.

"Yes," she said, "I'll come with you."

Shalune smiled, vindicated, then turned to Inuss. "Are you ready, child?"

Inuss hesitated, but only for a moment, before nodding. "Yes, Shalune. I'm ready."

With an uncharacteristically gentle gesture, Shalune closed the two halves of Inuss's mask once more and fastened the catches. Then she lifted her own veil back over her face.

"My conscience is clear," she said. "It's in the Lady's hands now."

She turned toward the stairs.

Torchlight blazed across the arena, lighting the ziggurat's towering face and throwing livid reflections on the lake's surface. The buzz of agitated voices blotted out the more normal sounds of the night as the last stragglers hurried down from the ledges and ran to join the crowd of women gathered on the sand.

Uluye stalked among her priestesses, barking out instructions in a voice to which fury had added an extra, ugly dimension. It was mere minutes since she had come storming from Yima's quarters, but in that short time she had, with fearsome efficiency, mustered every one of her women and told them the news.

There was no doubt that Yima had gone. Her clothes and most treasured personal possessions had vanished from the cave she occupied on the same level as her mother's accommodation, and though she had left no parting message of any kind, Uluye didn't need to order a search of the citadel to convince herself of the truth. Final confirmation had come when she had ascertained that Inuss was not to be found. She had already learned from Grimya that Shalune was involved in the plot, and from there it took only one simple step to establish the identity of the candidate who had taken Yima's place.

Uluye's wrath was like a volcano on the brink of eruption. She burned for revenge. Revenge on her daughter, revenge on Shalune and Inuss—and revenge, too, on Indigo. She didn't believe for one moment that the oracle hadn't been a part of this conspiracy. Despite what the mutant animal had tried to tell her, Indigo *must* have known, and Uluye cursed herself bitterly for a fool. She'd sensed a flaw in Indigo, but she hadn't had the wit to realize where it lay. Indigo was a false oracle; she had been false from the day she came to the citadel. Shalune had been the one to find her and bring her back; Shalune had been glibly ready to become her friend. Doubtless the two of them had been in league all along, and now the poisonous seeds they had sown were bearing fruit. Well, Uluye told herself as the rage seared through her, they hadn't bested her yet. This affair wasn't over by a long way. She would have *vengeance*.

Now, with the priestesses gathered before her on the arena, she had made her intention utterly clear. The fiery torchlight glinted on spears, machetes and knives; it seemed that every one of the citadel's inhabitants, from youngest to eldest, was armed in some way, and the sight gave Uluye a sense of hot satisfaction.

"Remember," she exhorted them, "they must be brought to me *alive*. Don't *dare* to forget that for one instant! If they are maimed, if they are so much as harmed, I will flay the culprit and give her living remains to the *hushu*. Use any means necessary to gain information from the villages, but my blaspheming daughter and her seducer must return unscathed!"

She prowled on, then stopped and turned on her heel to face the entire crowd. "They *must* be found! They *will* be found! For if they are not, I shall call the full power of the Ancestral Lady's wrath upon you all. Do I make myself utterly clear?"

Voices were raised in acknowledgment; Uluye nodded grimly. "Then waste no more time. Do your work—and be sure that you succeed."

The crowd divided as the women set off. Most of them headed toward the forest, in the direction that Yima had taken, while a handful went in the opposite direction, along the path that led around the far side of the lake. They would comb the nearer reaches of the forest and then, if that proved fruitless, move on to the villages, search them and persuade or intimidate the inhabitants to yield any information they might have.

At last the arena was empty but for Uluye. The High Priestess stood for some minutes staring at the torches guttering on their poles and at the chaos of scuffed footmarks in the sand; then she turned and strode back toward the ziggurat.

As she neared the first staircase, a gray shadow detached itself from the darkness and ran toward her. Grimya had stayed back from the arena, unnerved by the frenzy of activity, but now she could keep silent no longer.

"U-luye!" Her cry came out as a bark of desperation. "Wh . . . at of In-digo? What are we to d-do?"

Uluye stopped and stared down at her. She still couldn't quite bring herself to accept the truth about Grimya. The idea that an animal could have human intelligence and powers of speech gave her a shudder of revulsion each time she thought of it; it was alien to her, and because it was alien, she resented it deeply. With Grimya she felt out of her depth, and that was a condition Uluye found hard to tolerate.

She said curtly, "I have more important matters to concern me than your precious friend. Move out of my way."

She would have stalked on, but Grimya barred her path and refused to move. "But we must f . . . ind her!" the wolf protested. "She is in dan-ger. We must open the Well again, follow her—"

"Certainly not!" Uluye's eyes blazed contemptuously. "No one may enter the Well except at the Ancestral Lady's invitation. Now, must I tell you again to move?"

"But Indigo is—"

Uluye erupted. "A curse on Indigo, and a curse on you, you presumptuous mutant! Do you think I care what becomes of her? The Ancestral Lady has been insulted, and Indigo is responsible. The Lady will punish your precious Indigo as she sees fit, and neither I nor you nor anyone else will interfere! *Do you understand me?*"

Before Grimya could protest again, before she could even react, Uluye thrust her aside and strode toward the staircase. Grimya made to follow, meaning to plead with her, or even to threaten and bite her if all else failed, but abruptly she realized that both pleas and threats would be futile. Nothing would sway Uluye. The High Priestess was *glad* to see Indigo in peril; she wanted vengeance on those she thought had betrayed her and her evil goddess, and she steadfastly refused to believe that Indigo, too, had been tricked. By Uluye's twisted logic, Indigo could only be as guilty as Shalune and Yima, and Uluye would relish whatever punishment was meted out to her.

But there was more to it than that. Watching Uluye as she began to climb the stairs, Grimya bitterly regretted the desperate impulse that had made her throw caution aside and reveal her own secret and the truth about Yima's deception. She should have known that the coldhearted priestess would offer her no sympathy and no aid, for Uluye had disliked and mistrusted Indigo from the beginning, and with Grimya's telling of her story, that mistrust had flowered into blind hatred. The wolf had gained nothing; indeed, she'd only made matters far worse, for now Yima, too, was imperiled. Grimya hadn't wanted to betray Yima, but Indigo's safety was paramount in her mind and she'd known that her only hope of gaining Uluye's help was to tell the whole truth. Now her hopes were smashed, and there was nothing she could do.

Uluye was already a distant figure on the stairs, climbing toward the temple, from where she would watch for the searchers' return. For a few moments more, Grimya continued to stare up at her; then, with death in her heart, she turned and slunk away into the shadows.

Descending the staircase was like moving through a dream. The light from the strange trap door had long ago faded behind them, and though they still had the taper, its illumination was too dim to show anything beyond the next step. The silence was so intense that even the padding of their bare feet on the stone sounded loud and intrusive; Indigo listened hard for other telltale sounds, anything that might give some small clue about their surroundings, but there was nothing—until, without warning, the flight of steps came to an end.

They stopped, gazing uncertainly at the last stair. Beyond it, the taper's glimmer reflected on what looked like a smooth rock floor, but no one could tell, or liked to guess, what might lie beyond.

At a cautious nod from Shalune, they moved forward and stepped down onto the floor, then stood huddled together, waiting. The rank, moist smell was stronger here, and the heavy air touched them with warm, damp, shapeless fingers. Inuss shivered; Indigo reached out to take her hand reassuringly. Then, abruptly, Inuss's grip tightened as they realized that the darkness was lifting a little.

The transition was gradual, but within a few seconds the utter blackness had given way to a deep, oppressive gloom, like the twilight before a storm. Shadows began to take dim form, sharpened into relief . . . and then the change was complete, and in the pewter-gray gloaming, Indigo and her companions could see their surroundings for the first time.

The soft, awed breath that Shalune exhaled was answered by a hundred whispering echoes. Behind her, Inuss uttered a little cry, and Indigo could only stare mutely at the scene before them. They stood at the edge of a huge, still lake, its far shore lost in impenetrable darkness. Above and around them curved the walls and roof of a vast cavern, and under the cavern's dome, the lake's surface gleamed like a black mirror. Indigo thought suddenly that it might almost *be* a mirror, reflecting an image of that other lake far above them beside the citadel, but the fancy fled as she realized that no sun, moon or star had ever cast its light down into this bleak place. No fish had ever swum in these waters, and no blade of grass had ever taken root among the barren rocks surrounding them. This was truly a region of the dead.

Then, as they stood in silence, not knowing what to think and still less what to do, a faint sound impinged on the quiet. At first there was no pattern to it, but after a few moments, Indigo began to recognize a distinct and familiar rhythm. It was the sound of a single oar, a sculling oar, cutting through the lake's surface in long, steady strokes, and with it came the unmistakable splashing ripple of a boat making its slow way across the water toward them.

Suddenly Inuss clutched her arm, choking back a squeal of fear. Out on the lake a silhouette was emerging from the darkness. First the high, narrow prow became visible, like some sea creature cautiously moving from its lair. Then the boat itself appeared. It was far smaller than Indigo had expected, broad and shallow, and bizarrely reminiscent of the dinghies carried by Davakotian hunter-escort ships; and it loomed slowly out of the murk, rocking gently as it glided over the lake's surface.

And from the stern, gaunt hands guiding the long oar, hair swinging dark and heavy about high, narrow shoulders, the boat's solitary occupant gazed at them through the twilight gloom with eyes that glared like cold, cold stars.

So slowly that she seemed to be in a trance, Shalune fell to her knees. Inuss sank down beside her, and they bowed their heads until Shalune's brow and Inuss's mask touched the cavern floor. Only Indigo stood motionless, watching the boat as it drew nearer; watching the chill, alien eyes that looked back at her with calm but dreadful intensity. She hadn't anticipated this; she had expected some servant, some lower denizen of this world, sent to meet them and to conduct them on the final stage of their journey to the heart of the realm. But this was no mere servant. She sensed the being's power, saw it glittering from the ice-cold eyes, felt an answering shudder in her own marrow. This was the demon. This was the Ancestral Lady herself.

She was, in a terrible sense, beautiful. Her face, though bloodless and deathly white with an eerie, slatelike cast, nonetheless had a translucent loveliness that highlighted her gaunt, proud features and gave her an air almost of sadness. Her lips were black, full and sensual, her hair a darkly shimmering cascade that seemed to merge with her black robe, in which tiny flecks of silver shone like reflected water.

Silver . . . Indigo's heart contracted. Silver, the color of Nemesis, the clue that couldn't be disguised. But no; surely there could be no connection. She knew Nemesis all too well, and however dark its nature might be, it didn't wield power of *this* order. . . .

The boat stopped. There was no flurry of water, not even a ripple; it simply halted, floating motionless on the lake while Indigo and the Ancestral Lady continued to gaze at each other. With a second painful skip of her heart, Indigo saw now that the Lady's eyes were as black as her lips and her hair, but around the irises was a fringe of silver brilliance, like the eerie corona that glowed about an eclipsed sun.

Then, with a graceful, yet somehow faintly reptilian movement, the Lady turned her head. She looked first at Shalune, then at Inuss, and her black lips parted.

"Rise," she said. Her voice was rich, yet cold and strangely lifeless. Slowly, quaking, the two women rose to their knees. Inuss's face was hidden, but through the priestess's veil Indigo could just make out Shalune's transfixed expression, which combined an extraordinary blend of terror and helpless love. The Lady looked steadily at them.

"You have traveled a long way to find me. What do you bring to my realm?"

Shalune had rehearsed the ritual speech a hundred times under Uluye's fierce direction, but now that the moment had come, her courage deserted her. She struggled to find her voice, faltered, clasped her hands together, faltered again, knelt shivering like a terrified animal, and couldn't utter a word.

"Answer." The Ancestral Lady's tone became a shade impatient.

"Great Lady." Indigo spoke suddenly as she realized that Shalune was beyond help. She knew the prescribed words, or at least their gist; if Shalune couldn't say them, then she must. "We bring to you our chosen candidate to take, in due time, the mantle of your High Priestess. We sponsor her and we sanction her, and we have walked the way between your world and ours to conduct her into your presence, in hope that you will accept her as your own.''

The silver-fringed eyes turned to her again. ''Ah,'' the Lady said distantly. ''My oracle speaks of her own volition. Lift your veil, oracle. I wish to see your face more clearly.''

Aware that Shalune was watching her intently, Indigo raised her hands to the veil and lifted it back. The Lady's lips moved in the thinnest of smiles, though her eyes didn't reflect it. ''They have disguised you with charcoal and ashes, but I see through to what lies beneath,'' she said. ''Do you have a name, oracle?''

''My name, madám, is Indigo.'' Indigo paused for a moment, then added: ''As I believe you know very well.''

Shalune hissed, horrified by such recklessness. Again there was a long silence while Indigo and the Lady regarded each other, and Indigo realized with the first stirrings of disquiet that her initial assessment of this being had been wrong. She'd sensed from the first that the Ancestral Lady had power, but believing that she knew what she truly was, Indigo had assumed that her strength was built on false foundations. She had good reason for her belief: in the past, when dealing with the demons of the Charchad and of Simhara, and later in tangling with the shadowy life-devourer of Bruhome and the monstrous but intangible curse of Earl Bray of the Redoubt, she had learned that demons were never quite what they seemed. Their power was real enough, but at each encounter their limitations had proved to be far greater than she had been led to believe. Tapestries of deceit, spiderwebs of illusion and intrigue . . . yet they had had no more substance than a spiderweb, for their fabric had crumbled when the truth behind their trickeries was revealed.

This demon, though, was different. Why she sensed it and why she believed it, Indigo couldn't tell, but she was growing momently more certain that the power the Ancestral Lady wielded was no mere shade. This creature had substance. She was as real, every bit as real, as Indigo herself—and suddenly Indigo began to feel out of her depth.

At last the Ancestral Lady's dark lips parted once more. "I think that you are beginning to understand, Indigo," she said. "You still have a long way to go, but a beginning is better than nothing. Do you fear me?"

Heat stifled Indigo's throat; she opened her mouth to deny the question but found suddenly that the words she wanted weren't there. The Lady's cold, quirkish smile flickered briefly once more.

"Of course you fear me," she said, answering her own question before Indigo could marshal her thoughts. "Who does not? I have never yet encountered a human soul that has no fear of what awaits it beyond death."

"You are not death . . ."

"No. But death and I are cohorts of long standing, and what death begins, I see through to its conclusion. There are many possible conclusions, oracle. The very few who truly please me in life earn peace in my realm, and the sleep that knows no dreams. Others may be granted another kind of life as one among many of my servants, and that, too, can be a boon. But there are always some who, by their deeds or by their words, blaspheme against me and refuse to accept me as their suzeraine. For them there is only the mindless, ceaseless hunger of the *hushu*, for I devour their souls and I give no sanctuary to their bodies, and thus they can neither live nor die, but may only *exist*." She paused, her eyes like coals within their pale aura. "Which fate would *you* choose, oracle?"

Indigo's pulse was hard, rapid and painful, but she forced herself not to flinch. "I would choose none of these, Lady." she said. "My loyalties—and my beliefs—lie elsewhere."

"Do they?" The Ancestral Lady inclined her head, an odd, birdlike movement. "We shall see, oracle. We shall see."

Then her head turned, and the silver-black gaze fastened on Shalune and Inuss. They shrank back; Inuss was shaking uncontrollably, and Shalune seemed little better. Their courage had crumbled to dust.

"Why do you weep, candidate?" Suddenly the Lady's

voice took on a new, cruel edge. "What hides in your heart
that your tears betray? Is it love? Or is it fear?" She paused,
then: "Take off your mask."

Inuss made a terrible sound, midway between a moan
and a cry of pain. Convulsively she wrenched at the wooden
mask, breaking the catches in her clumsy haste; several of
the bone ornaments fell to the stone floor, and then the
thing was off and her stricken face—slick with perspiration
and ugly with strain—stared at her goddess.

The Ancestral Lady said: "Bring the mask to me, my
child. Place it in my hands."

Inuss didn't want to approach her, but nor did she dare
disobey. She rose unsteadily to her feet, shuffled to the lake's
edge. The boat was too far out for her to reach; implacably
the Lady waited, and at last Inuss stepped down into the
water. Indigo heard her suck in a harsh breath as the water
swirled about her knees, her thighs, her hips. She waded
out, then held up the mask with a despairing, imploring
gesture, bowing her head.

The goddess stretched out one hand, and her long, black-
nailed fingers touched the mask. Her nostrils flared; then
slowly, slowly, she drew her hand back. An awful light,
cold as the aura in her eyes, flared about her frame and
hurled her momentarily into black silhouette, and she spoke
in a voice that sent a shock wave through Indigo's blood.

*"You are not the one who was chosen to serve me. You
have come in the place of another!"*

Inuss howled in terror and covered her face with her
hands. Shalune started to her feet, her arms outstretched
imploringly. "Lady, I beg you—"

"Silence!" Echoes ricocheted around the cavern. "You,
who have connived with a traitor, do you dare to speak? Do
you think me ignorant of your deeds? Ah, Shalune my servant, I had expected better from you."

"No!" Shalune cried. "Lady, we are not traitors! We
want only what's best, what's right—"

"Right?" Novae flared in the depths of the Ancestral
Lady's eyes. "Who are you to judge what is right, Shalune?

You have gone against the will of your High Priestess, who is my chosen servant. You have cheated her—and thus you have cheated me. Answer me, Shalune—who sanctions what you shall do in serving your goddess? Who is your goddess's avatar in the world of mortals?''

Shalune's jaw worked spasmodically. "Ul . . . Uluye . . . is your chosen avatar.''

"And in whose name does Uluye speak? Who judges what is right, Shalune? *Who?*''

"Y . . . you, my Lady. You only.''

"Yes, Shalune; *I* judge. Do you accept my judgment?''

Shalune's face was a study in agonized, adoring tragedy. She truly loved this monstrous being, Indigo realized; and though the love had its roots in terror, it was nonetheless as real as the love of a child for its mother, a woman for her lover, a foolish and helpless dog for a hard master who one day, *one* day, might grant unutterable joy by condescending to be kind.

"I accept your judgment, sweet Lady,'' Shalune said, and her voice broke on the last syllable. "I am yours. *We* are yours. Whatever your will, we shall obey.''

For what seemed like an eternity, there was silence. Indigo wanted to intervene, but she didn't know what she could say or what she could do; a single word at the wrong moment or in the wrong place might only make matters worse. Shalune and Inuss stood motionless. Inuss, pathetic now, still stood waist-deep in the lake, her elaborate robe clinging wetly about her. The Ancestral Lady gazed at them both, her eyes hard and her face unreadable. Then she spoke. Her voice had lost its brief edge of emotion and was cold once more.

"I judge you an unworthy sponsor, Shalune, for you have brought me a postulant who is not of your High Priestess's choosing. You have defied your High Priestess's will, and in so doing, you have defied me.'' She looked down. "As for you, Inuss, you have conspired with your mentor in disobedience and deceit. I do not give my blessing to such as you. You are fit neither to return to your own realm, nor to dwell within mine.''

A pause, during which Indigo saw Shalune's eyes grow round and blank with horror. Then the Ancestral Lady said with dire finality: "You know in your hearts that you are guilty. And you know the penalty for what you have done. Your souls are forfeit to me. And I name you among the lifeless, yet deathless ones. I name you *hushu*.''

·CHAPTER·XVI·

"No! You demon, you evil hellspawn, *you can't do that!*"
Indigo's scream echoed through the huge cavern, sending a shock wave of echoes shouting and clashing in the gloom. The Ancestral Lady's head flicked around; she gave Indigo one disinterested glance—and a tremendous force plucked Indigo off her feet and hurled her backward. She hit the wall and crashed to the floor, pain hammering through her and a scarlet mist flaring blindingly in her brain. Her mouth opened, but she had no breath in her lungs with which to scream again or to even make the smallest sound; all she could do was to sprawl on the hard rock, battling to hold her spinning senses together, and watch as a horror unfolded that she could do nothing to avert.

Inuss was wailing on a high, shrill note. She turned about clumsily and made a frantic bid to flounder back toward the shore, but before she had taken two paces, the Lady tossed the mask aside, and as it hit the water with a hollow splash, she grasped hold of Inuss's hair. The wail became a panic-stricken shriek; Inuss struggled, but she was drawn back inexorably and raised up until her feet cleared the water.

Her eyes, bulging in their sockets now, met the Lady's implacable stare—and suddenly she ceased to fight. In the space of a moment, the will to resist left her, and she simply hung limp from the dark figure's grasp, her mouth slack as her cries died away into silence.

The Lady's eyes flared; she said one word.

"Obey."

There was a moment's stillness; then a slight tremor ran through Inuss's body, and her eyes glazed as intelligence, consciousness and life fled from her. It was simple, swift, devastating. The Ancestral Lady opened her hands and Inuss's corpse dropped into the water. There was a splash, the glitter of fracturing reflections, and for a few moments after the sounds faded, the silence was absolute. Two feet from the boat's side, Inuss floated. Her hair and her ribboned robe swirled around her like many-colored strands of waterweed; ripples spread out in gentle circles from her body, and her eyes stared up calmly at the cave's roof; the expression on her face was, obscenely, utterly peaceful.

The Ancestral Lady didn't spare her so much as a glance. Her eyes had focused on Shalune, and the unhuman gaze held the priestess transfixed.

"Shalune," she said. "Come to me. Come."

From where she still sprawled by the cavern wall, Indigo watched in a state of frozen, silent helplessness. She had witnessed the atrocity of Inuss's murder—there was no other word for it—through a daze of shock and pain, but her mind, still floundering in the aftermath of the Lady's violence toward her, couldn't accept that it had happened. Physically as well as mentally stunned, she had convinced herself that this was some mad dream, and she couldn't unravel the skeins of nightmare from the harsher threads of truth.

Passive, uncomprehending, Indigo watched Shalune start forward across the floor. There was terror in the fat woman's eyes, yet her face was fixed in that same look of awful adoration. She knew what awaited her, but no power on earth could have persuaded her to defy her goddess. She had accepted her fate as right and just, and though she might

not go gladly, she went without question and without a murmur of protest. Somewhere inside, Indigo was silently crying: *Shalune! Shalune, don't! It's a lie, it's a fraud, don't
go to her!* But somehow her protest didn't seem to have any
meaning. To call out with her physical voice, or even to try
to stagger to her feet, would be pointless; the ability was
beyond her. This wasn't happening, it wasn't real. It
couldn't be.

As if sensing what was in Indigo's mind, Shalune turned
to gaze at her. A look of ineffable sadness and sweetness
had transformed her coarse and heavy features, as though
the years had been stripped from her and she had become
a child again, innocent, untrammeled, free of all taint.
There wasn't a spark of intelligence in the blank pits of her
eyes.

Still incapable of comprehending, Indigo watched the fat
woman step into the lake. Shalune waded toward the boat,
ignoring the floating corpse of Inuss, then stopped within
hand's reach of the gunwale. The water lapped at her breasts;
she looked up at the Ancestral Lady but didn't speak.

The Lady gazed down. "Shalune, are you my servant?"

Shalune's voice was barely recognizable; here, too, the
helpless child had taken control. "I am, Lady."

"Have you wronged me?"

A pause. Then: "I . . . have wronged you."

The gaunt figure nodded. "Tell me the punishment for
such transgression, Shalune."

The second pause was longer. Shalune seemed to be
struggling with herself, striving not to speak. But at last the
words came.

"The punishment is . . . death."

The Lady inclined her head. *"Obey,"* she said, gently.
Shalune bowed her head; again there was a moment's stillness, again the faint tremor. Indigo saw Shalune's body slip
into the water with a quiet splash as life fled from her, but
it meant nothing. The lake subsided; silence fell again.

The Ancestral Lady's emotionless voice said, "Do you
understand a little more now, Indigo?"

There in the dark lake beside Inuss, her hands clasped on her breast as though in a gesture of piety, Shalune's body rose and fell, rose and fell, on the water's slight swell. Indigo spoke, her voice sounding peculiarly detached and dreamlike in her own ears. "They look so . . . peaceful."

"Peaceful?" There was thin contempt in the Ancestral Lady's tone, and it made a sudden small breach in the barrier that Indigo's mind had built around itself. "No, I don't think so. They have only the reward they have earned, no more and no less." She turned fractionally and looked back toward the lake's far reaches, invisible in the dark. "They may leave now," she said, and gestured carelessly with one hand.

A new ripple spread to the lake's edge, and the two corpses began to move. Slowly, but surely, with no visible force to propel them, they turned about until they were perfectly aligned together, then started to drift away, past the boat, beyond it, out toward the deeper regions of the lake. An unseen current caught and snared them; they twisted suddenly on an eddy, then gained speed and, side by side, floated away into the blackness and vanished in the direction of the far, invisible shore.

The boat rocked slightly as the Ancestral Lady turned again. She picked up her discarded oar, and her eyes, with their white-hot corona, focused upon Indigo.

"Now," she said, "what is to be done with *you*?"

Indigo blinked, then frowned. For a moment her mind continued to flounder midway between the trancelike state in which it had been locked and the dawning shock of reality. Then the barrier cracked, and crumbled. Dream fled, and the full impact of what had happened hit her like a tidal wave.

"Oh, no . . ." Her voice was soft, but it carried the seeds of the most violent rage she had ever known. "Oh, no. . . . You demon, you murdering *monstrosity*!" Her body began to shake; she couldn't control it, didn't try. And suddenly she screamed with all the shrill fury bursting within her: *"They were innocent of any crime!"*

The Ancestral Lady's dead-white face was implacable. "Who are you, that you count yourself fit to judge innocence?" she asked indifferently. "You are no better than the ones you pretend to champion. You are all my servants, and in the end you must all come to me."

"To a *demon*?" Indigo spat. "I think not, Lady! And I tell you now, I am no servant of yours, and never will be."

The Ancestral Lady smiled an old, weary smile. "So you have said before, Indigo, and you are wrong now, as you were wrong then. Haven't you learned that lesson yet, my oracle?"

The silver-fringed eyes flared momentarily, and as the Lady uttered the word *oracle*, Indigo's mind seemed to twist in on itself. *Darkness and silence, the cloying smell of incense. Someone breathing; a steady hush-hush of sound. A figure moving in the dimness, desperately, horribly familiar. And a voice inside her head said, "I am here. . . ."*

It was the trance dream again, the dream into which she had been plunged at the lakeside ceremony on Ancestors Night. At the time, it had been wiped from her memory, but now it came back with terrible clarity and she remembered all that the voice in the darkness had said to her.

"No!" She shook her head violently, flinging the images away. "I am *not* your oracle!"

"But you are. I made you so; I chose you, and I have spoken through you."

"Not at my behest!" Indigo said searingly.

"Do you think not?" the Ancestral Lady replied. "Then it seems that still you don't know yourself. A pity. I had thought you would learn greater wisdom in all your years of wandering, but it seems that the old flaw is still there."

On the verge of a further furious rebuttal, Indigo suddenly stopped, tensing. "What do you mean?" she demanded. "What flaw?"

"The flaw of self-delusion, among others." The Lady shrugged her narrow shoulders. "You came here to seek a demon, but you haven't the wisdom to know its name or its nature. Now something else has diverted you from your search, and that in its turn has brought you to me. It was inevitable." She looked up. "I wonder, will you recognize your demon when you find it—or perhaps I should say, when it finds you? For if you do not, I think that all your brave words will be of little value to you, for you will be enslaved to me as surely as your luckless companions were enslaved."

"Oh, no." Indigo smiled grimly. "You've made a mistake, Lady. You can't kill me. For good or for ill, I'm not capable of dying—and if you were what you claim to be, you'd know that as well as I do."

"Who speaks of dying?" The Ancestral Lady's dark eyebrows rose faintly. "No one needs to meet death in order to serve me." She paused, her expression suddenly thoughtful. "Though what, I wonder, is the difference between being incapable of dying and being forbidden to die?"

Indigo's lip twisted. "Don't waste your riddles on me, madam! The Earth Mother's power is the only power to which I am bound, and She decrees my fate, not you."

"Ah," the Lady said, "but if you serve the Earth Mother, Indigo, then you also serve me. Don't you yet realize that? Are you so *very* set on following the wrong road that you still can't recognize the truth when it confronts you?"

"I know the truth," Indigo said, savagery in her voice.

"I think not." The Lady turned her head to look down at the lake's black surface, and her gaze traveled slowly to the soft edge of the darkness that had taken Shalune and Inuss.

"I didn't kill your friends," she said. "I merely claimed what they had already forfeited. I do not take life, Indigo; that isn't my way and it holds no interest for me. Their killer was the demon you came here to seek."

Indigo stared at her. Inwardly, she reached for the rage that had driven her—but it was no longer there. Her fury had gone without her knowing it, like a cutpurse slipping away from his victim, and in its place, subtle as yet, but growing stronger with every moment, was a sense of acute uncertainty and consternation.

Suddenly and unaccountably defensive, she said sharply: "Don't try to deceive me with your pretenses. I know what you are."

The Ancestral Lady shook her head and uttered a sound that might have been taken for a sigh. "Still you persist in your mistake . . ." she said wearily; then her terrible eyes focused intently on Indigo's face. "I am not your demon. But I know what your demon is. And I don't think that you are capable of conquering it."

Sweat had broken out on Indigo's forehead, but before her lips could form a protest, the Lady went on.

"The demon has already claimed one victory," she said. "That die was cast when your friends accepted their fate."

Indigo stared back at her. "What do you mean?"

"Only that if you had known the demon's name, it is possible that your companions might not have died." Again the cold little shrug. "It hardly matters. They would have come to me anyway, in time."

"Are you telling me that I might have *saved* them?"

"Perhaps. Perhaps not."

Indigo's teeth clenched. "That is a vile lie! What could I have done? You *murdered* them, and I couldn't stop you."

The Lady sighed. "Think what you please. It is nothing to me." She picked up the long oar and with a gesture that was almost listless, swung it over the boat's stern. Then, without another glance for Indigo, she turned away. Water splashed faintly; the boat began to move.

Indigo's throat felt as though she'd swallowed glass. "Where are you going?"

The Ancestral Lady paused and looked back. "To do my work. To patrol my realm. What more have we to say to each other?"

"You mean to leave me here on this shore?"

"You are free to stay or go as you wish." The boat's movement ceased, and the Lady leaned on the oar, regarding Indigo without a flicker of expression. "Whichever choice you make, I have no doubt that the thing you are seeking will find you in time."

So saying, she turned away, and the heavy mantle of her hair swung as she began to ply the oar once more. The boat had traveled some ten yards or more, and the thick curtain of darkness was beginning to encroach upon it when Indigo called out in a voice sharp with tension.

"Wait!"

The oar stopped sculling; the boat slowed again. Icy pinpoints of light showed in the gloom as the Ancestral Lady looked over her shoulder.

Indigo said: "You claim that my demon will find me in good time, no matter what I do."

A nod, nothing more.

"I have no wish to wait for it. I mean to seek it out. How best might I do that?"

There was a long pause while the Ancestral Lady appeared to be considering this. At last she spoke.

"You could come with me, Indigo. If, that is, you have the courage."

"I think, madam, that I'm courageous enough," Indigo said acidly.

"You may be." The black lips curved with faint languor. "Although what you might find should you choose to journey in my company would, perhaps, try you even beyond your ability to endure."

Though the Lady spoke with the same cold disinterest that tainted all of her words, Indigo knew that she was issuing a clear challenge. She felt an angry instinct to reject it and refuse to be manipulated; but then she paused, remembering the impulse that had prompted her to speak out in the first place. She knew she might well be making a mistake that would cost her dearly. But she had to follow it, and the Ancestral Lady's mockingly cryptic words were an additional goad.

There was more to this than the matter of the demon. There was Fenran, and the doubts that the vision by the lakeside had implanted in her mind. She had to face the question that haunted her. She couldn't leave it unresolved, and the Ancestral Lady alone could provide her with an answer. If she turned away now and retraced her steps back through the catacomb, back through the Well, her journey unfinished and her quest unfulfilled, she would never know a moment's peace from now on. If this coldhearted creature offered to show her the way, she must take it, and meet the challenge.

She said: "Very well, madam, I accept your invitation. Prove your claim, if you can. Take me with you—I'm not afraid."

The Ancestral Lady inclined her head. "As you like. It's of no moment to me."

"It seems that little is of any moment or interest to you," Indigo replied with irony. "So I presume that it'll make no difference to you whether my courage prevails or falters; and if I can't anticipate your help, at least I needn't anticipate your hindrance.".

The Lady shrugged for the third time. "As you say." Her wrists twisted, stirring the oar, and, rocking a little, the boat began to drift back toward the shore. The sound as the prow tapped against the rock seemed preternaturally loud, and the Lady held out one hand. Indigo moved forward, grasped the proffered fingers and stepped over the gunwale. For a moment their eyes met, and the Lady regarded her with cool assessment.

"Well, now," she said. "We shall see. . . ."

She released Indigo's hand, took the oar once more. Slowly the boat went about; then, with barely a disturbance on the surface of the water, it moved off from the empty shore and away into darkness.

On the cliff top, Grimya and Uluye had reached an uneasy truce. For several hours the wolf had roamed the citadel and the lakeside, unable to rest, unable to think of anything but Indigo and the dangers she might be facing. Several times a sudden disturbance in the lake had sent her running to the shore to peer across the water in the starlit darkness. Rationally, she didn't know what she could have expected to see, but hope was a powerful goad. Each time, though, there was nothing, and she returned to her restless pacing, unsatisfied and unhappy, until at last, acknowledging that this could achieve nothing, she climbed the long zigzag of stairs to the top of the bluff.

The great brazier was still alight, its bowl glowing sullenly, and the smell of incense hung heavy on the air. Uluye sat on the oracle's carved throne, her shoulders hunched in a way that gave her the look of a giant preying bird or insect, her eyes moody and smoldering with anger as she stared out across the lake toward the forest. Hearing Grimya's claws on the stone square, she turned her head, and her mouth set in an ugly line. She didn't speak, but she made as though to rise from the chair and clenched her fist in a threatening gesture. Grimya flattened her ears and showed her fangs; Uluye paused.

"I will st . . . ay," Grimya said throatily, the words blurring with a growl deep in her throat. "If you trrry to drive me away, I will bite you!"

Uluye sank back and jerked her body around so that she was facing away from the wolf. "Stay or go as you please," she said coldly. "Though what good it will do you, I neither know nor care."'

Grimya's head dipped, and, fangs still bared, she padded around the temple's perimeter to a place where she could see the slab that covered the Well, whilst keeping as great a distance as possible between herself and the priestess. Trying to ignore the incense's smell, she settled down, muzzle on front paws, the brazier light reflecting in her eyes and turning them a feral red. Uluye resumed her brooding posture, staring out at the forest, and silent, umoving, they waited.

As dawn broke, the babble of agitated voices in the distance stirred Grimya from a restless half-doze, and she jerked her head up in time to see Uluye, too, react with a start. The priestess sprang to her feet and ran to the ziggurat's edge, and hastily Grimya followed.

The light was growing rapidly, and down below, in the early grayness, the wolf saw that a number of people were approaching the bluff along the lakeside path. Suddenly Uluye turned and strode toward the stairs. As she reached the top of the flight, Grimya called out, "What? What is it?" She received no answer, but Uluye paused long enough to glance back, and the wolf had a brief glimpse of her face before she vanished. Her expression was granite-hard and murderous.

Hastily Grimya ran after her and reached the edge in time to see Uluye jump down the last three steps and race away along the ledge to the next flight. The figures below were clearer now, the distant voices resolving into clarity; Grimya heard Uluye's name called, then what might have been a muffled cry of pain.

She glanced back at the great slab that marked the entrance to the Well. There was no point in continuing her vigil. Indigo wouldn't return that way; it wasn't possible. Better to return to the lakeside and see what news the searchers had brought, in the hope that it might give some help to her own dilemma.

Quelling a whimper of unease, uncertainty and fear, Grimya turned back to the stairs and followed in Uluye's wake.

"We found them in Hoto's village." The hard-faced, middle-aged priestess who had led the northward search stared down at her party's two captives with a mixture of pity and disgust.

Tiam lay unconscious on the sand; he'd tried to resist and had been felled by the wooden club that now hung at the priestess's belt; a livid bruise was spreading across one side of his face, and one eye was swollen. Yima sat beside him, her hair in disarray and her robe ripped and stained. She had covered her face with her hands and was rocking back and forth in wild but silent grief.

Uluye looked at her for a few moments, then turned her head away. "Was Hoto sheltering them?" she demanded.

"He says not. He says he didn't know that they were runaways or that Yima had anything to do with us. It's possibly true—certainly the boy isn't from his village—but it's more likely that he was well paid to give them refuge and is now lying to save his own hide."

"Then he and his family will suffer the consequences." Uluye's voice was clinically detached, but there was something in her tone that hinted at vast emotions under ruthless control. "How did you find them?"

"We'd searched the village and were about to leave when a woman approached us without Hoto knowing and told us where they could be found."

Uluye nodded. "I'm thankful to hear that there are still some who know their duty. We shall see to it that she's suitably rewarded for her diligence."

"She has a young daughter, and harbors ambitions for her," the middle-aged woman said. Her look conveyed her opinion that the betrayal had been a matter of self-interest rather than of duty, but Uluye only shrugged.

"The Ancestral Lady will decide what is fitting," she said, then looked at the captives once more. "Now, as to *these*—"

As though the violent intensity of Uluye's stare had penetrated her private misery, Yima suddenly stopped rocking. Her hands fell away from her face and, slowly, she raised her head, revealing red-rimmed eyes and cheeks stained with tears.

"Mother—" There was an agonized plea in her voice, and the second syllable broke into a sob.

"Silence!" Uluye said viciously. "You are no longer fit to address me!"

Yima started to climb unsteadily to her feet. "But Mother, please, if you'll only let me—"

"I said, *silence!*" Uluye's arm swung out and down so fast that the girl had no chance to evade the blow, and she sprawled back onto the sand, where she lay sobbing bitterly. Uluye stared down at her, her eyes wild, almost mad.

"I have no daughter!" she said through tightly clenched teeth. The veins and muscles in her neck worked violently. "The treacherous blasphemer I see before me is no child of mine!"

Abruptly she turned on her heel, and those priestesses closest to her flinched at the sight of her face. "Take them into the citadel and set a guard over them," she snapped. "Give them no water and no food. I shall return to the temple and conduct the proper ceremonies to ask the Ancestral Lady to make her will known to me. She will decree their fate; they have offended against her, and *she* will decide what punishment will be exacted."

Obedient to her order, two of the priestesses moved to drag Yima to her feet, while two more bent to gather up the unconscious form of Tiam. But before they could take hold of their charges, there was a sudden sound of water bubbling and churning in the lake. The women straightened with startled exclamations; Uluye, who had begun to walk away, swung around in consternation, and they saw the disturbance near the lake's center. The water heaved, glittering in the pale morning light; great ripples spread rapidly in a circle, creating waves. And suddenly a shape emerged from the turbulence and drifted toward the shore as though the lake had disgorged it.

Two of the priestesses ran toward the lake's edge. Several others followed them, but Uluye stood motionless, staring at the approaching object, her face rigid. The shape reached the shore and beached gently, rolling in the shallows where the sand sloped down to meet the water. One of the women dropped to a crouch—and her scream of horror tore the air apart as she reeled back, covering her face with her hands.

In a single surge, the remaining women ran to the shore, and the uproar as they too saw for themselves seemed to snap Uluye out of her paralysis. She reached the water's edge in seven long strides, and the women's cries and exhortations fell away as she shouldered past them and looked down.

Arms entwined and hair tangled together, Shalune and Inuss lay on the sandy slope in three inches of water. Inuss's mask was gone and her upturned face was stark; Shalune's countenance was a grotesque piebald where the ashes and charcoal with which she had been painted had been smeared by the water. Their eyes, open but unseeing, stared back at their High Priestess like the mindless gape of dead fish.

One of the women had begun to weep, grief and horror and fear mingling in her wailing voice. Slowly, Uluye backed away, the others moving hastily aside to clear an aisle for her. Someone shook the weeping woman's shoulder, and the sobs subsided into ugly hiccups. No other sound broke the silence.

Five paces from the shore and the lake's grisly gift, Uluye's eyes suddenly flickered back into focus.

"Sound the summoning drums," she said in a deathly cold voice. "I want every inhabitant of every village within reach to be here by sunrise."

Even in the throes of her shock, the hard-faced priestess seemed taken aback by the order. "What do you mean to do, Uluye?" she asked uneasily.

Uluye's terrible expression didn't change. "The Ancestral Lady has made her will known," she said. "She has cast out Shalune and Inuss from her realm and sent them back to us to become *hushu*. Therefore she has decreed the fitting punishment for all who blaspheme against her name and seek to defy her."

Uluye turned her back on the lake, and her next words were spoken with ritualistic formality. "The people must be summoned to witness the proper rites. We will begin the ceremonies of purification. We will make offerings to the Ancestral Lady, and we will propitiate her spirit servants in the time-honored ways. At sunset the sinner Yima and her paramour will die—and we will call upon those spirits who have not won the favor of the Ancestral Lady to carry away their bodies and devour their souls, so that they too will become *hushu* in their turn."

Yima had been crouching over Tiam, striving in vain to wake him, but as Uluye uttered her grim pronouncement, the girl froze. Slowly, so slowly, she raised her head, and her eyes focused on her mother's rigid figure in stunned disbelief.

"Mother . . . Mother, *no* . . ."

Uluye looked back over her shoulder. She didn't speak.

"You can't . . ." Yima started to get to her feet. She was shaking violently, and shock seemed to have drained the life from her face. "Mother—Mother, *please*, I'm your *daughter*, you can't—"

"Silence that child," Uluye said coldly, "and if she will not be silenced, cut out her tongue. I have nothing more to say. The Lady has commanded me, and in her name justice will be done." She jerked a hand toward the ziggurat in an imperious gesture. "Sound the drums and begin the preparations."

"No!" Yima screamed. "Mother, no, *no*!"

But Uluye was already stalking away across the arena toward the stairs. Her women stared after her, some in sorrow, some in admiration, but all of them shocked by the depth of their leader's implacability.

Only Grimya, who had witnessed the scene from the shadow of a rock near the foot of the bluff, saw the High Priestess's face as she went by; saw the granite-hard set of her features, the bitter blaze of fury in her eyes—and the tears that streamed helplessly down her cheeks like cold diamonds.

·CHAPTER·XVII·

Time, it seemed, had no place in the realm of the dead. They might have been sailing for an hour, a day or a year, with nothing to mark the passage of the journey but the quiet rhythm of the sculling oar and the gentle slap of water under the boat's keel. Darkness hung about them like black velvet, blurring sight, muffling sound. A tiny witchlight, no brighter than the dim, blue-green shimmer of a glowworm, burned at the prow but gave almost no illumination; when Indigo held up her hand before her, it was gray and insubstantial, the hand of a ghost.

Neither of them had spoken since the voyage began. The boat had sailed out into the lake until the faint glimmer of rock warned Indigo that they were approaching the far shore, and there ahead, the mouth of a tunnel had become faintly visible, gaping like the maw of some blind beast. As they sailed under its arch, the timbre of the water's sound changed subtly and the rhythm of the oar took on a hollow echo, and now, though she sensed their presence, Indigo could barely glimpse the endless walls slipping past them in the dark.

She felt keyed up, nervous, and was oddly reluctant to even turn her head and look at the gaunt figure in the stern behind her. She had an irrational fear that if she did dare to glance back, she would see not the dead-white face in its cowl of black hair, but something else. Something that, though she couldn't predict its nature, would be far, far worse.

She forced the thought away, but still the crawling unease remained, for she couldn't banish the fear that lurked at the back of her mind. Where would this bizarre journey lead, and what would she find at its end? For fifty years she had clung to the belief that Fenran was alive, and both in her dreams and in strange and short-lived moments of reality, she had seen her love and spoken to him across the appalling gulf that separated them. Fenran had no place in this realm where death reigned unchallenged and life was an alien intruder, and yet in cryptic ways and through subtle mind-play, the Ancestral Lady had planted the doubt in her mind, the fear that, perhaps, death had truly claimed him and he now dwelt here with the Lady, her servant and her prisoner for eternity.

Indigo still believed—and wanted to go on believing—that it was a lie. The demons she had faced in her years of wandering had been masters of illusion, and this creature, this enigmatic being, goddess or monster or something in between, was surely yet another such manipulator. But something the Lady had said to her, one careless sentence, haunted her. *"What you might find should you choose to journey in my company would, perhaps, try you even beyond your ability to endure."* What those words meant, what they implied, Indigo didn't know; but the memory of them was like a spear of ice in her heart.

The boat sailed on, swathed in quiet darkness, and Indigo sat fighting with her churning, contradictory thoughts. She couldn't choose between the twin pulls of hope and fear, for whichever way she turned, there was always the specter of doubt to cloud her choice, doubt that was embodied in the creature in whose hands she had placed herself.

She thought again of Shalune and Inuss, and the appalling fate to which the Ancestral Lady had condemned them. Cast out from the underworld to become *hushu*. She shuddered as, unbidden, her imagination conjured an image of their bodies floating across the dark lake in an obscene parody of peace. Perhaps even now they were drifting along this river, close by . . . or had they already returned to the mortal world, and at this very moment were their dead eyes opening to a new and terrible existence as hungering zombies?

"I do not take life," the Lady had said. *"I merely claimed what they had already forfeited."* How had they forfeited their lives? What immutable law decreed that they must accept—even *look* for—death, and an afterlife far worse than death, as the punishment for what they had tried to do? Blind belief, and blind acceptance. *What is the difference between being incapable of dying and being forbidden to die?* Could that be what the Lady had meant? Had Indigo's two companions died because they couldn't, or wouldn't, see beyond the rigid mind-set of their cult, and was that the difference: will eclipsed by obligation?

Or by terror. . . .

Suddenly, her earlier reluctance forgotten, Indigo's head whipped around.

"You tricked them!" she hissed accusingly. "You led them to believe that they had no choice but to die!"

The Ancestral Lady still stood impassively in the boat's stern. She hadn't metamorphosed into something monstrous and grotesque; only a faint nacre seemed to shine from her white skin, a luminescence tinted nightmarishly by the witchlight.

"Your hapless friends?" she said calmly. "No. I had no interest in tricking them. The deception—if there was a deception—stemmed from a less obvious source."

"What do you mean?"

"Nothing of any import. It was merely an observation." Her hair stirred, though there was no breeze; then the silver corona about her eyes flared momentarily. "You should look to your own trials now, not to theirs."

As she spoke, Indigo felt a hand clamp on her arm.

She gasped and whirled back. There was nothing there. Yet she could still feel the pressure, and in the dim light, the faint indentation of fingers showed clearly on her flesh.

Then, slowly, like a baleful star coming out as the sun set, a face formed in the air, hanging disembodied beyond the boat's prow and just beyond reach. A girl's face, young, but haggard with the ravages of misery and disease. Her skin was as white as the Ancestral Lady's own, and it had shriveled on her bones as the flesh beneath desiccated. Her eyes, little more than pinpoint pupils in a sea of bloodshot white, stared at Indigo and through her into an unimaginable world of nightmare, and what once had been a cloud of soft and pretty hair was now falling from her scalp like rain.

Indigo wanted to wrench her own gaze away, but she couldn't. The vision transfixed her, and from the deepest sink of her mind, from a place that for more than forty years she had striven to keep shut away from the light of consciousness, memory surged like a foul, polluted tide.

The phantom's raddled lips parted, showing a blackened tongue, and a voice that spoke from far beyond the grave said: "Take my brooch, *saia* Indigo. I know you will keep it safe. Take my brooch, and send me to Ranaya's breast."

A young widow, bereaved, sick beyond redemption, her only hope now the chill shadow of death . . . but what was her name? In her mind, echoing, Indigo heard the sound of a crossbow bolt sliding into place, almost felt the hard contours of the weapon's physical presence in her hand. Sweet Mother, *what was that poor child's name*?

She drew breath, struggling to force air into her lungs. "Send it away! Banish it! *It isn't real!*"

"It is real," the Ancestral Lady said indifferently. "But she is only one among many of my servants." And the ruined face drifted aside, slipped astern and was lost in darkness as the boat sailed on.

Indigo was shivering and couldn't make herself stop. All the horror and grief and madness from so long ago—she'd forgotten them, healed the wound, only now to have it torn open once more and made to bleed afresh. . . .

Suddenly a shimmer of bright laughter flitted through the tunnel, past the boat and away into the distance. The voices of people celebrating the beginning of the hunting season . . . and Indigo heard, blending with them, the distant, ethereal strains of a harp. The music and the laughter were gone so quickly that she had no chance to react, let alone to call out the names that came to her lips, names from a happier time and a happier place. She was tensed, half risen from the narrow bench seat and straining in an effort to catch the last faint echoes, when from somewhere ahead, another voice, a new voice, sang her name.

"Indigo . . ."

Indigo dropped back onto the seat, her legs nerveless. She knew that voice.

"Indigo . . ."

She stared into the dark, but nothing moved there. Yet the voice was so *familiar*.

"Indigo." And then, in a tongue that was neither her language nor that of the Dark Isle, "Don't you remember me, Indigo?"

Anguished, she looked at the Ancestral Lady, serene and unmoved in the stern. "Who is it? In the Mother's name, tell me, *who is it*?"

The black lips smiled, but without feeling. "Look and see."

Indigo turned. Ahead, a cold, white light had appeared, slanting onto the water like a moonbeam shining through a window. It spilled onto the surrounding rock, and she hissed, feeling an icy shudder go through her as she saw that the tunnel's wall, like the walls of the terrible catacomb through which she had walked with Shalune and Inuss, was filled with the bones of a hundred, a thousand, a million dead. But even their grisly, empty-eyed skulls, their clawing hands, their twisted, fused skeletons, weren't enough to stop her stunned gaze from focusing on what lay at the heart of the shining glow.

The light emanated from a niche in the wall. The niche was arched, and large enough to accommodate, if not a man, then at least a child. As the boat inexorably drew closer, Indigo saw that there was indeed a child standing there: a girl perhaps ten or eleven years old, golden-haired, honey-skinned, smiling and holding out rounded, smooth-skinned arms.

"Dear Indigo." Oh, but she knew that sweet voice now; she would never, ever forget it. "Don't you remember your *beba-mi*?"

Jessamin. The Takhan's daughter, darling of the great city of Simhara, the child bride of Augon Hunnamek—

"No!" Indigo turned her head away violently. "No, I won't look at—at *that*!"

Behind the figure of Jessamin another voice began to scream, and a sinuous shape writhed in the nacreous light, like something dimly seen through water. Still smiling, still reaching out, the small and lovely figure fell behind, and as the screaming faded away, the Ancestral Lady spoke.

"What are you afraid of, Indigo?"

Afraid? No, it wasn't fear; it was revulsion, the revulsion of seeing those old, dead memories restored to a parody of life. But it seemed that the memories weren't done with her yet, for another light had appeared ahead now, another window in the black wall. This radiance was fainter and warmer, like the glow of a dimmed and shaded lamp, and the silent, frozen skulls that crowded about the arch were nothing more than a half-glimpsed fancy. But in the niche there was a tableau that made a cry of pain catch in Indigo's throat. Four people—two men, a woman and a boy—stood grouped around a bed in attitudes of sorrow, while in the bed another man lay white-faced and unmoving. He was dead—Indigo knew he was dead, she *knew* it, she had seen his corpse—but she knew the others, too. Dead; all dead. How could they have come to life again, to grieve for their kinsman. *How?*

One of the mourners, a man older than his companions, raised his head. As though he had heard the gentle sound of the boat passing by, he looked around, looked directly at Indigo. No glimmer of recognition showed in his sad face, but then the girl at his side also looked up, also saw. As her gaze and Indigo's met, she smiled a small, knowing and triumphant smile of sweet hatred. Then, shockingly, her eyes turned a vivid sapphire blue—and, echoing through the tunnel, shuddering through Indigo's marrow, the challenging roar of a snow tiger rang faintly on the murky air and was gone.

The boat glided onward. This time Indigo didn't hide her face but stared at the receding tableau until it was lost from sight. Only then did she look up at the shadowed figure of the Ancestral Lady.

"Why are you showing me these things?" she demanded hoarsely.

The white arms continued their smooth movement, the oar rustled in the water. Then: "I am showing you nothing. You see only what anyone might see within my realm . . . or within their own mind."

"But it isn't the truth! That . . . that *travesty*," she gestured back toward the now invisible tableau, "is a lie. It didn't happen, not in that way!"

The Ancestral Lady didn't trouble to reply to this, and, seething with frustration, Indigo turned her back once more, peering into the darkness but able to see nothing beyond the witchlight's feeble glow. For a while nothing more happened, and the silence became oppressive; she could feel the tunnel closing about her, closing in, claustrophobic and suffocating. Inside her, a small voice asked over and again, *What next?* and though she tried to silence it, knowing it was insidious and dangerous, it persisted. What next? Whose ghost would come out of the dark to haunt her now? *Whose?*

Then suddenly she was all but flung from the seat as something huge and invisible buffeted through the tunnel, struck her and went whirling away astern. As it passed, she heard a cry of agony, a man's voice, and blending with it, a woman's dying shriek.

She knew them—

"No! Father, Mother—"

Something laughed in the blackness ahead, and acrid smoke caught in her throat and lungs. *Burning*—the shadow of a great building burning was flung across the walls, and behind the shadow she could see the flames like serpents rising high above crumbling towers, hear the roar and crackle of stone and wood collapsing into the inferno. Then the illusion was gone, though the afterimage still danced before her eyes, and instead, another bright window opened in the wall and she saw a sad procession, three biers draped with indigo cloths and crowned with wreaths of leaves; not the lush, brash greenery of the Dark Isle, but the sage and lovat and crimson and mellow gold that clothed the trees of a southern autumn. At the head of the biers walked an old man with blind eyes, and a harp held in his arms; he was playing and singing, but Indigo could hear no sound save the bitter moan of a polar wind.

The soundless, moving images fell behind. And then a new voice called out of the dark, and at the sound of it, the last dregs of color drained from Indigo's face. Her hands gripped the gunwale, so hard that a sliver of wood splintered away and gouged her palm. Unaware of it, unconscious of the pain as blood trickled over her fingers, her muscles locked and a cry burst uncontrollably from her throat.

"No! No, please! Don't show me, don't let me see her! *I don't want to see her!*"

"Anghara! My poppet, my sweeting, my little princess!" The voice, so familiar, so dearly loved, trembled with grief and confusion as it cried out Indigo's old name, her true name, which she had abandoned so long ago. "Where are you, Anghara? I can't find you!"

The Ancestral Lady said remotely: "She is searching for you, Indigo. Are you too afraid to call to her?"

"Where is my sweeting?" the voice wailed, breaking with

emotion. "Come to me, dear one; come you to me, I beg you! Oh, Great Mother; bring her back. Bring her back to her loving Imyssa, and I will never let her go again."

"Imyssa!" Indigo could bear it no longer; loyalties and longings that she had learned to silence for half a century overwhelmed her, and she screamed her old nurse's name into the darkness. As the tunnel hurled her voice back in a shattering volley of echoes, a bright halo sprang to life above the water, and a figure took form within its ring of light.

Imyssa, her nurse and her protector and her mentor, held out withered arms, and the small eyes, as bright and as dark as a robin's, shone like stars.

"My poppet! My sweeting princess, my own, my little one! Oh, where are you?"

Indigo got to her feet, careless of the boat's sudden, wild rocking. "I'm here, Imyssa. I'm here. I live!"

The old eyes darted, their gaze flicking this way and that. "Only let me see her once before I go to the Mother. Only tell me that she didn't die! Only tell me—"

"Imyssa!"

Sick horror flooded through Indigo as she realized that the nurse could neither see nor hear her, and she turned furiously on the Ancestral Lady. "In the Mother's name, have you no compassion? Why do you torment her—and why do you torment me?"

The dark figure shook its head solemnly. "Mortals create their own torment, Indigo; I do not inflict it on them."

The Lady looked at the bright halo. The boat was approaching it, close now, and her expression took on a hint of reflective, but still utterly detached, interest. "She lost her mind before she came to me. Grief and remorse are powerful forces, and she never ceased to believe that she might have saved you. At the end, that brought about the final breakdown of her sanity."

The phantom of Imyssa was sobbing now, wringing her hands, and as the ring of light drew nearer, Indigo saw with shock how dreadfully the old nurse had changed before death claimed her. Age had taken its toll, yes; but the depth

of the lines on her face, the darkness of the shadows beneath
her eyes, spoke of ravages far worse than simply those of
the passing years. If only, Indigo thought despairingly, if
only she could reach Imyssa, make her see, make her
understand—

"Imyssa!" She was still on her feet in the prow, and now
she stretched outward and upward to the phantom, trying to
reach the clenching, twisting hands within their bright halo.
"Imyssa, hear me. See me. *I am alive!*"

The boat entered the oval of light. Radiance spilled across
Indigo's face and hands, across the Ancestral Lady's impas-
sive figure. Indigo felt the slightest of tingling sensations as
for one moment she almost—but not quite—touched the
nurse's gnarled fingers, and then the phantom of Imyssa
floated through her, past her, and, still sorrowing, was gone.

Indigo began to tremble. Her limbs shook as though she
had a palsy; her body quivered with a desire to weep or
scream or rage—she didn't know which, but it hardly mattered, for she couldn't express what she felt; she hadn't the
power to give it release. She sagged down onto the bench
once more, trying to regain her self-control. But that too
was impossible, for her mind was keyed up like a cat in a
trap, waiting for the next vision to swim out of the dark
ahead, and dreading what it might be.

The boat sailed on, and there was silence but for the
steady rhythm of its progress. Indigo's senses were strained
to a painful pitch, and the tension grew worse, until she was
almost aching with anticipation of what might come. At last
she could bear it no longer. She turned about, her eyes filled
with anger and pain, and looked at the Ancestral Lady.

"Was that the sum of your challenge, madam?" she asked
savagely. "Am I to presume that you have done your
worst?"

The Lady's calm expression didn't alter. "No. I have done
nothing. You've simply seen a little of your own past, Indigo, and that is gone now and so has no relevance. The
demon lies ahead of you . . . if you can find it. Are you
still prepared to continue with your search by this route?"

Indigo's shaking and shivering was receding now; with no further apparitions to haunt her, she was beginning to regain her self-control. "Yes," she said through tightly clamped teeth.

There was a rustle, like old silk stirring, and the rhythm of the sculling oar altered fractionally. "Very well," the Ancestral Lady said emotionlessly. "Then what must be done shall be done. And when it is over and you have admitted defeat, I trust you will remember that the consequences were of your own choosing."

Suddenly she dug the oar deep. The boat slued violently, changing tack, and Indigo was thrown sharply to one side. She struggled upright, an oath on her lips—then froze as she saw a shape darker than the water loom out of the gloom ahead. A tongue of land, whether a small island or a peninsula of some larger mass, she couldn't tell. A translucent white shimmer showed where the current eddied against a small shale beach, and the underworld river divided to flow past the low-lying mass in two narrow channels.

The boat nosed toward the beach and grounded. Indigo stared past the dim witchlight at the prow. The land ahead rose a mere few feet above the water. It was bare, barren, not so much as a blade of grass to be seen. Nothing moved there, and Indigo looked back at the Lady once more.

"You want me to alight?"

A veil of shadow passed across the dead-white face as the Lady inclined her head. "Yes. We can travel no farther together on the water."

Indigo rose and stepped over the boat's side. The shale was sharp and cold beneath her feet; she advanced five paces or so up the beach before the sound of water shifting made her turn.

The Ancestral Lady had used her long oar to push the boat free, and it was slowly drifting clear of the beach. The Lady stood in the stern, looking back.

"It is time for me to leave you," she said. "From now on, you must face your trials alone."

Indigo glanced over her shoulder at the dark land. "How long am I to remain here?"

The black lips curled in a thin, mocking smile. "Oh, your journey is ended. What comes now will come to you without your needing to seek it. And when it comes, and when you have named it, then you will call out to me and I shall answer."

Her tall figure leaned toward the boat's prow and plucked the tiny witchlight from its anchoring place. "My parting gift," the Lady said, and she cast the witchlight toward Indigo, where it fell in the shale at her feet. "Take good care of it, for it won't last long. Good-bye, my oracle—for the present. I hope you are ready for what faces you now."

As Indigo crouched down to retrieve the light, the boat began to move away. The oar dipped rhythmically and the sound of its sculling in the water echoed with a flat, dreary sound. Then the darkness engulfed it, and Indigo was alone.

·CHAPTER·XVIII·

The sound of the drums that sent Uluye's message to the villages was like nothing Grimya had ever heard before. The wolf had watched uneasily as the great wooden frames with their ancient, taut-stretched skins were brought out and maneuvered into place in the arena and as the message beaters, two women to each drum, took up their huge staves. At a sign from a senior priestess, the staves came down—and it was as though a thunderstorm had broken overhead when the drums' booming, rumbling voices bellowed out and shattered the quiet of the morning. The beaters swung their arms like warriors wielding broadswords, battering a complex, urgent and ominous rhythm that must have been audible for miles. From the forest, all but lost in the din, the shrieks of animals and birds rose in fear or protest, but the noise thundered on, the women sweating now, grim-faced as they attacked the drums with all their strength.

Down at the lakeshore, further activity was in progress. Nine more priestesses had come out from the citadel, each carrying a torch and each with her face hastily painted with grotesque sigils. They were hung about with amulets and fetishes, and their leader carried four long stakes. These were driven into the soft ground on the far edge of the arena to form a square, and, chanting shrilly, the women began to lay further amulets in a ritualistic pattern around the square's perimeter. Four of the torches were fixed to the stakes, where their flames flickered like pale, tattered rags in the harsh sunlight, and when that was done, the women took quantities of black sand and small, dark pebbles from their belt pouches and marked out a narrow path from the square, across the lakeside track, to the forest's edge.

Then, seemingly satisfied with their work, they turned as one and walked slowly and with clear reluctance to where the corpses of Shalune and Inuss still lay at the water's edge. No one had dared to touch the bodies; damned and cast out, they were the rightful prey of the *hushu* now. But the crimes of the two women had been such that the *hushu* would send no ordinary ghouls to reanimate their corpses. The horrors that came to claim blasphemers were the most powerful among all the legions of the demonic and the undead, and so must be placated with offerings and prevented from breaking free to terrorize the living. The path and square would mark the way these gruesome visitors would take, and the amulets and other things of power would control them.

The drummers still worked with grim, frenetic energy; they kept their heads averted as four of the square-makers bent to lift up Shalune and Inuss. The remaining women set up a wailing cacophony, shaking sistrums at the corpses and throwing more handfuls of sand over them, and the two were borne quickly to the square and laid at its center, their bodies crossing each other at right angles. Then, with the chanting and rattling still at fever pitch, the four bearers ran to the lake and flung themselves into the shallows while their companions threw water over them to help cleanse away the taint of the unholy things they had touched.

Grimya witnessed the scene from where she huddled in the shadows at the foot of the lowest staircase. Her heart was pounding with fear and distress, and she couldn't stop trembling; she would have given a great deal just to be able to shut out the sound of the drums, but there was nowhere to hide from their din, nowhere to find the quiet she needed so she could think clearly.

She had been watching for Uluye; the High Priestess hadn't yet reemerged from the citadel, and when the wolf had tried to climb the stairs to find her, the way had been blocked by two guards who menaced her with their spears and refused to let her pass. She realized that she, too, had now become a pariah in the women's eyes. They believed that Indigo had betrayed them, so Grimya, as Indigo's friend, must share in her guilt. It was madness—and the women's hostility made it all the harder for Grimya to find an answer to the question that burned in her mind, the dire and urgent question: *where was Indigo?*

Grimya was sure of only one thing, and though the comfort it gave her was little enough, it was at least better than nothing. Whatever else might have befallen her, Indigo must still be alive. Even a demon like the Ancestral Lady couldn't kill an immortal, and that certainty kept Grimya from despair. But what had become of her friend? Was she trapped, captive, injured? Was she capable of returning to the outside world, and if so, how and where might she emerge? Uluye, the wolf felt sure, could help her, if only she were willing. She had to speak to the High Priestess again, whatever the difficulty. Uluye owed her a debt; she *must* be persuaded to repay it.

Suddenly Grimya heard the sound of voices above her and, moments later, the thud of several pairs of feet on the stairs. She ran out from her shelter, looked up—and saw that the High Priestess was returning.

Uluye was dressed from head to foot in red: a deep, hard crimson that the sunlight turned gory. Her head was bare, and her long black hair hung unbound; it had been oiled, and it swung like heavy, tarred ropes about her torso. Grotesquely, her face was painted to represent an inhuman mask: eyes horribly exaggerated, lips a bloody slash, jagged lines of different colors radiating out from her nose and across her cheeks.

Three masked women hurried behind her, holding an assortment of implements whose purpose Grimya couldn't begin to guess: a flail with vicious barbs, a sistrum with black feathers interwoven in it, a knife too dull to be made of metal, a stained and corroded chalice. They were chanting; not the ululating shrieks of their sisters at the lakeside, but hissing whispers that bore an undertone of chill menace.

The nightmarish procession reached the foot of the steps, and Uluye stepped out onto the arena.

"U-luye!" Grimya sprang from the shadows into the High Priestess's path, and abandoning all caution, cried aloud. "U-luye, I m-must speak with you!"

Uluye stopped dead, and behind her, the hissing chant ceased abruptly as her three companions stared in shock at the wolf. Then, so fast that Grimya was taken completely unaware, Uluye spun around and snatched the barbed flail from her attendant's hand.

"Sorcery!" She spat the word like a curse or a battle cry, and the lash of the flail came whipping down. With a yelp, Grimya sprang back, and the High Priestess came after her, thrashing the flail from side to side and hurling up dust with every strike.

"U-luye—" Grimya tried to call out again, but Uluye gave her no chance to make herself heard.

"Devilry and evil!" she snarled, and the flail came cracking down yet again, missing the wolf's flank by a hairbreadth. "The blasphemers are sending illusions to deceive us even now! Take that animal—take it and bind it and silence it, or the evil will be set loose!"

Her attendants recovered their wits, and all four of them advanced on Grimya. The wolf was cornered, her back to the face of the ziggurat now; she hunched down, ears flat and fur bristling, and as one of the women came at her, she reacted in blind panic, lunging and snapping. There was a scream, the taste of blood in Grimya's mouth; she lowered her head and snarled savagely, and through the snarl her guttural voice panted: "I am not evil! Listen, you *m-must* listen! Indigo is—"

She got no further. Uluye had gathered the flail once more, and she brought the carved handle smashing down on the wolf's skull. Grimya howled and reeled. Light and darkness danced in a mad carousel before her eyes; sickness surged in her stomach; her legs staggered, crossed, gave way beneath her as disorientation hit her like a second physical blow, and she collapsed stunned and whimpering on the sand.

Uluye stared down at her panting, twitching form. "Bind the creature's legs and muzzle its jaw," she snapped. Her breath was coming in short, sharp spasms.

"Should we not kill it, Uluye?" one of the attendants asked.

"Not yet. It is our false oracle's familiar; the Ancestral Lady may wish it to be sacrificed in the proper way. But see that it can make no sound."

The attendant shuddered. "An animal that *speaks* . . . it's unnatural. An ill omen."

Uluye turned furiously on her. "I'll hear no talk of omens! Obey me, and don't think to question my will!"

Grimya was conscious but too dazed to resist as the women fetched strong fiber ropes and bound her fore and hind legs. A third rope was tied about her muzzle so that although able to breathe without difficulty, she could make no noise other than a whimper or a faint growl. When it was done, Uluye sent her three attendants on ahead—she had, it seemed, no concern for the woman whose arm Grimya had bitten—and when they were out of earshot, she crouched down at the helpless wolf's side.

"I will hear no more of your precious Indigo!" she hissed, putting her mouth close to Grimya's ear. "The Ancestral Lady has her now, and she will deal with her in her own way." Her hideously painted mouth stretched in a ghastly rictus. "You've shown me the truth, mutant. You've shown me that our oracle is a false oracle, a demon sent to deceive me and to connive with blasphemers against my

law. Know this now—the Ancestral Lady is not to be trifled
with, nor is her High Priestess and faithful servant. I have
unmasked you and your demon mistress. You have *failed*!''

She jerked upright, turned on her heel and strode away
across the arena. Unable to move or to show any reaction,
Grimya stared after her. Her eyes were filmy, and she was
still dizzy and in pain from the blow, but Uluye's words had
gone home; for the first time, she realized, she truly understood what lay behind the High Priestess's bitter antip-
athy.

Uluye could have ordered her death, but she'd not done
so. The priestess's one urgent desire had been to silence
Grimya, to prevent her from revealing to anyone else not
only her ability to speak human tongues, but also the story
she had told. And Uluye's motive in both cases had been
the same: fear. Grimya had seen it in her face, despite the
grotesque paint, as the High Priestess bent over her to whisper her savage warning. She was afraid of Grimya, because
Grimya was Indigo's companion, and Indigo was a threat to
her power and supremacy.

Yet, at the same time, that fear had made Uluye stay her
hand rather than risk ordering Grimya to be killed. That
proved what Grimya had begun to suspect: Uluye's confidence in the infallibility of her judgment was crumbling.
That, the she-wolf knew, made her unpredictable . . . and
doubly dangerous.

Uluye stalked toward the flat-topped rock in the center of
the arena. The women who had dealt with Shalune and Inuss's corpses had gone back into the citadel; only the drummers remained, still hammering out their inexorable
message. At the rock she turned and looked at her attendants.

''Withdraw.'' Her command wasn't audible above the
drums' noise, but the savagely dismissive gesture that accompanied it was clear enough. They moved away, and Uluye climbed up onto the rock, from where, ignoring the
sweating drummers, she stared out at the lake.

For the first time in her life, she was starting to doubt

her ability to interpret her goddess's will; and that, for Uluye, was a terrifying prospect. What did the Ancestral Lady
want of her? Some things were clear enough: Shalune and
Inuss's treachery had been exposed, and the goddess had
imparted a clear command as to their final fate when she
had sent their sodden corpses up from the lake's depths.
And . . . Yima? No, Uluye thought as fury and pain and
confusion stabbed through her, she wouldn't allow herself
to dwell on that. There could *be* no doubts about Yima's
fate—*none*; and she would prove her faith to the Lady beyond any shadow.

But would that be enough? Uluye felt herself beset by
uncertainty and contradiction. Dominating her feelings was
a deep-rooted terror that the Ancestral Lady was testing, or
punishing, her by surrounding her with conflicting signs.
And at the heart of it all was Indigo.

Uluye had truly believed that the Lady had sanctioned
Indigo's enthronement as the cult's new oracle. All the signs
had been right, all the omens true; there had been no reason
to doubt for one moment that Indigo was the goddess's own
chosen avatar, and though she'd racked her mind for an
answer, Uluye couldn't imagine how Shalune could have
faked the signs and deceived her. Even that creature Grimya
had provided further proof. An animal that spoke in human
tongues . . . she shuddered involuntarily. Such monstrosities existed in legend: evil things, demons, *hushu*. Yet the
Ancestral Lady had known of Grimya, for she had told her
followers that the new oracle would be accompanied by an
animal companion. Again, it seemed that Indigo was the
chosen one . . . and yet she had betrayed them.

Or had she? The question made Uluye's gut clench with
something far deeper than mere fear, as it brought back the
one terrible thought she had been trying to suppress. Had
Indigo betrayed the cult—or could she be innocent, as the
mutant wolf claimed? Or worse, far worse, was it possible
that the Ancestral Lady had turned against her own High
Priestess, and that Indigo was her instrument?

Despite the day's close, muggy heat, Uluye shivered. How

could she have offended the Lady? How might she have blasphemed? Could it be that she had sinned by choosing her own daughter as her successor? No, she thought, *no*. The Lady had *shown* her that Yima was an acceptable candidate; she had *told* her to perform the initiation ceremony. Uluye had heard the goddess's voice with her own ears, and in this at least, nothing would persuade her to believe that Indigo could have tricked her. No one had power of that order—and no one, *no one*, would dare to impersonate the goddess.

Then what else might Uluye have done to arouse the Lady's displeasure? Or could this be a test of her worth, of her fitness to rule . . . of her power? Shalune had wanted to usurp that power and set her own kinswoman in the candidate's place; but now Shalune and her accomplice were dead and the Ancestral Lady had damned them to become *hushu*. Yima had wanted to flout her, too, and had tried to flee with her lover; now she too was condemned to die and to join the soulless ones. Sharp, sick excitement filled Uluye suddenly. Was *that* the nature of the trial the Ancestral Lady had decreed for her? Yes, she thought, *yes*. Now she understood the Lady's plan. She had failed to unmask the deceivers. Surely then it was only right, only fitting, that she should expiate the mistakes she had made and exonerate herself in the goddess's eyes. And she would do it. No matter the cost, she would *do* it, and gladly, for she loved her goddess more than her own life, more than the life of her daughter—

An extraordinary, ugly sound broke involuntarily from her throat. Her attendants, who were waiting a few feet from the rock, didn't hear; even a full-throated scream would have been drowned by the thunder of the summoning drums. But Uluye's self-control was back within an instant, and mercilessly she crushed the feelings within her, choking back the sob, killing it, and killing the wave of utter misery that for one brief moment had threatened to overtake her.

She could have no doubts. The Ancestral Lady's will

would be done, and she would prove her fidelity, her love
and her obedience. Her own hand would wield the blade
that spilled Yima's blood, and she herself would perform
the ceremony that prepared Yima's corpse for the *hushu* and
summoned the soulless ghouls of the night to take her for
their own. She would not falter, and she would not flinch.
She had no daughter now. She had only a goddess, her
mistress and her mother, and she would pass this final test
and win back her Lady's favor. She, Uluye, High Priestess,
would prove her worth. She would do what must be done,
and would never regret her choice. Never, she told herself
ferociously. *Never*.

Movement on the periphery of her vision suddenly
snapped her back to the moment. Her head jerked around
and she saw that one of her attendants had come up to the
rock and was trying tentatively to attract her attention. Uluye's eyebrows rose in a sharp interrogative, and the priestess pointed toward the forest.

There was movement there, the stirring of leaves, flickers
of shadowy figures among the trees. Then a small group of
people emerged. They stood uncertainly on the track, looking toward the arena and the ziggurat beyond.

Uluye smiled coldly. From this distance, she didn't recognize the newcomers, but she knew that they must be from
the nearest village. Swiftly and roughly she counted their
number. Well and good; they'd answered the call in force,
it seemed, and that showed a proper respect for and fear of
the Lady's priestesses. More would soon follow.

She signed toward the drummers. Instantly the thundering beat ceased. The silence was shocking by contrast, and
almost as deafening in its way as the drums' rumbling had
been. As the last echoes died, Uluye heard an answering
beat from far in the distance, in the forest's depths. Good,
she thought; *good*. Village elders were passing the summons on; it would go out far and wide, and the gathering
should be as great as she had demanded.

Now it was time for the first ceremonies to begin. . . .

·CHAPTER·XIX·

Fifteen paces. Indigo had counted them so many times, checking and checking again, that it seemed the number was engraved in her mind. Fifteen paces from one end of this miserable spit of rock to the other, and a bare seven from side to side—and within those small confines not a hummock, not a crevice, not the smallest feature to be found.

Now she sat on the shale slope with her knees hunched up under her chin and the water lapping only inches from her feet. She had thought of testing the river's depth, but had balked at the idea. The water was so dark, so silent and oily; it had the look of corruption, and she was unwilling to even touch it. So, with no direction in which she could go, there was nothing to do but wait and try to control the helpless, futile, but savage, anger that was boiling inside her.

Fifty times now she had cursed herself for a fool. She'd allowed the Ancestral Lady to lead her a grim dance through this labyrinth, convinced that at the end would lie enlightenment, but instead, her guide had abandoned her here in this . . . this . . . Indigo shook her head violently as words loathsome enough to describe this place eluded her. She still couldn't begin to guess what the Ancestral Lady's purpose had been in bringing her here, but she was growing more certain by the minute that she had been tricked. *"What comes now will come without your needing to seek it,"* the Lady had said. How much time had already passed? An hour? Two? More? Yet still there was nothing but the murky darkness, and the silence, and the sense that nothing would happen here, for nothing *could* happen here.

"happen . . ."

Indigo started at the tiny echo that seemed to whisper from behind her. She hadn't realized that she'd spoken aloud, and she shivered, disliking the mean, dead quality that the dark tunnel gave to her voice. As the shiver subsided, she glanced down by her side, where the witchlight lay wedged in the shingle. Its feeble, glowworm illumination still spilled over the stones, but Indigo fancied it was dimmer than it had been a few minutes ago. The Lady had warned her, mockingly, that the witchlight wouldn't last indefinitely, and she wondered how much longer it might continue to glow. The thought of being in utter blackness without even this tiny scrap of comfort was daunting, and carefully Indigo picked up the light and held it in the palm of one hand. It was like nothing she had ever seen before; simply a sphere of what looked like greenish crystal no more than an inch across, smooth and cold to the touch. Its light had no visible source, and nothing seemed to affect it for better or for worse.

The crystal flickered suddenly, like a candle guttering in a draft, and hastily Indigo set it down once more. She watched it closely for some while, but it didn't flicker again, and at last she sighed and turned back to staring at the dark water. Surely, *surely*, she wouldn't be forced to stay here indefinitely? The idea was insane. There must be *some* way of getting off this thrice-damned rock—

"rock."

This time she jumped violently, for the echoing whisper

had seemed much closer. Sweet Goddess, she thought, she must be starting to lose her wits if she was speaking aloud without even knowing it.

"knowing it."

"Ahhh . . ." It was an exhalation and a protest together, and Indigo scrambled to her feet, her heart pounding violently. She *hadn't* spoken aloud that time; she knew it, she was *certain* of it. But something had answered her . . .

"answered."

She swore aloud and spun around, peering into the dark. Dimly she could make out the gentle hump of the islet and the faintly phosphorescent glimmer of the river's surface beyond. Nothing moved on the rock. There *was* nothing there.

Indigo licked her lips. Her instinct was to call out, challenge the voice, but she was held back by an unpleasant conviction that to do so might invite a response for which she wasn't prepared. She wished that her knife was in her hand, rather than left behind with her other belongings in the oracle's cave at the citadel. Better still, her crossbow and a good supply of bolts . . . though how she might defend herself against an invisible assailant was a question she didn't care to answer.

For a minute, perhaps two, she stood still, scanning the rock, her ears alert for any sound. Still nothing; and she began to wonder if perhaps she'd imagined it. Maybe if she took up the witchlight, explored the rock again—

"rock again."

"Who are you?" Indigo yelled. "Show yourself!"

The echoes of her voice shouted back tumultuously from the tunnel walls, then faded away. There was no answer.

"Damn you . . ." Indigo dropped to a crouch and snatched up the witchlight, holding it out before her at arm's length. For a moment a splash of cold light from the tiny sphere illuminated her hand—and then the witchlight flickered, dimmed, flickered again and went out, plunging her into total blackness.

She bit the sides of her mouth against the scream that

wanted to break from her. It was the momentary shock, nothing more; there was nothing to be afraid of . . .

"afraid. us."

It came from behind her; she whirled. All she could see was the water's faint nacre.

"us. Indigo."

Her breath quickened until it was a harsh sawing in her throat, but this time her voice was under her control. "What are you? I tell you again: show yourself!"

"us. help us."

It was such a *small* voice, she realized with a sudden inward frisson. Toneless, lifeless . . . and sad. And it said *us*. Not *me*; *us*.

She sucked dank air into her lungs, and her fist closed around the dead witchlight. "I can't see you. I hear you, but I can't see you."

The voice answered, behind her again, on the islet's bare rock. *"Indigo. home. us, Indigo. want. help us. want."*

Indigo shut her eyes tightly and hissed a prayer through clamped teeth. "Great Mother, if you hear me, if you pity me, help me now! Show me what to do!"

If the Earth Mother heard, She did not answer. And the dull little voice spoke again, now from another direction.

"us home. Indigo. want home. help us."

There was a new sound, a peculiar, faint rustling and clicking, and it seemed to emanate from all around her. Indigo blinked in a desperate effort to force her eyes to penetrate the darkness, but it was futile. There *was* no light, there was nothing.

"but us. home. us home. Indigo. we want. we want."

The rustling grew louder. Then there was movement in the black: a slow, blind sense of something stirring to each side of her, beyond the islet, beyond the gliding river.

And Indigo remembered what lay buried in the walls of this tunnel.

Suddenly, with no warning, the witchlight in her hand flared back into life. She cried out as a livid white glare burst between her fingers, and reflex made her fling the crystal sphere away. It bounced on the rock, rolled, and came to rest at the top of the shale slope, not a dim glow-worm now, but a tiny, brilliant star that hurled spears of light and shadow across the islet.

The tunnel's walls were moving. Their entire surface seemed to have come to life, shifting and seething. Lumps of clay, shaken loose by the upheaval, fell into the water like tiny avalanches, and in the pocks and scars they left behind there was a stirring and a writhing and a dull shimmering of brown bone, moist and dimly phosphorescent. In the witchlight's cold glare, Indigo saw naked skulls emerging from the walls that had imprisoned them, and deep in their eye sockets was a glow like sullen coals, and the first flicker of a hollow and dreadful intelligence.

Horrified, and feeling her gorge rise, Indigo started instinctively to back away before she realized with an icy shock that there was nowhere to which she could retreat. The moving, shifting dead were all about her; she was trapped between their ranks, and even the river, had she dared to brave it, offered no escape, for they were there too, in the walls to either side; and if she took to the river and they came out of the walls and they fell to the water, they would be there, with her and—

"No, oh *no*!" She pressed her hands to her skull, twisting from side to side in frantic denial and trying to shut out the sound of the terrible rustling that now seemed to fill the tunnel, punctuated by sly splashes as more clay crumbled into the river. She wanted to shut her eyes too, not to have to see this horror, but the thought of not seeing, not knowing what was happening, was more terrifying still.

"Go back, go *back*!" Her voice cracked hysterically. "*Please*—in the Mother's name, *stop*!"

"*afraid. Indigo. afraid.*" Through the awful clicking and slithering, the answer came small and sad and dead. The voices were beginning again.

"No—"

"*us. afraid, Indigo. us. don't.*"

Forcing back nausea, Indigo tried to snatch up the witch-

light, her one bastion against the horrors crawling all about
her. But when her hand closed round it, she jumped back
with a cry of pain, for the tiny sphere was burning hot.
Gasping, she wrung her scorched fingers; then, as breath
came back and the agony receded to a hard, stinging throb,
she realized that the small incident had saved her from a
collapse into complete and helpless panic. The mundane
shock of hurting herself had diverted her senses momentarily, and her mind had snatched at the chance to reassert
a measure of self-control.

Crouching on the shale, the witchlight glaring beside her
and her painful hand clenched, she stared quickly from side
to side, holding down the terror, holding down the sickness
of revulsion.

"I am not afraid." She spoke the words like a litany. "I
am not afraid."

The voices answered her. *"afraid. no. Indigo."*

Sweet Goddess, she could see those shattered jaws
moving. . . .

"I am *not* afraid. You can do nothing to me."

"nothing. don't, Indigo. fear. us." A pause, a momentary silence; then, as though the voices were slowly learning—or relearning—a clearer mode of speech, there came a
soft, sibilant chorus that shocked her to the marrow. *"don't
fear us, Indigo. help us, Indigo. take us, Indigo. home.
home. don't be afraid."*

Indigo's stomach contracted, and she had to struggle to
breathe. For the first time, she comprehended the depth of
sheer misery in that tiny choir of voices, and her terror was
suddenly eclipsed by horrified pity. Very slowly she rose to
her feet, her pulse pounding fearsomely, and looked wildly
about.

"What is it that you want?" she called. "What is it you
think I can do?"

The answer came with an awful, hollow eagerness and
longing. *"free. free, Indigo. us. free us."*

"I can't free you. I haven't that power."

"yes. free. us. power. free us."

"I *can't*! I'm not a goddess."

"*no. no. no. no. no. no . . .*" There was sudden agitation in the replies, and she didn't know whether the voices were endorsing or denying what she had said. Then, as the chorus died away, one lone whisper floated across the dark water.

"*afraid. we, Indigo. we. we are afraid . . .*"

Two tiny, bright stars flared in the gloom beyond the witchlight's reach. Indigo's skin crawled.

"Afraid?" Her voice was uncertain, almost shaking. "What are you afraid of? What have *you* to fear?"

There was a hissing, as though a thousand snakes had come to life in the tunnel. At first Indigo thought it was just a mindless sound, but then she realized that the voices were repeating a word, one word, over and over again.

"*she. she. she. she. she. afraid. she, Indigo. she is afraid. we are afraid. we are her. she is us. she is afraid. we are afraid. help her, Indigo. help us, Indigo.*"

Indigo's heart was now thundering against her ribs. She believed she was beginning to understand what the voices implied, and suddenly some of the cryptic and seemingly emotionless words of the Ancestral Lady began to weave into a pattern and form the first hint of a picture. "*We are her, she is us. she is afraid, we are afraid.*" Oh yes, Indigo thought; oh yes. . . .

She called out to the shifting, rustling dead in their prison within the walls. "What do you fear? Tell me its name and its nature."

Instantly all sound ceased. Silence closed in like a shroud; even the river no longer made its small lapping noises. Indigo shifted one foot on the shale, and the hiatus broke; but still the voices didn't respond.

"Tell me," she said again. There was something stirring within her, new strength from a source she couldn't name but that filled her with sudden confidence. Power, she thought. The power to overcome a demon. . . .

Her voice rang through the tunnel in an echoing peal. "I

command you, and you cannot gainsay me! *Tell me the name of your fear!*''

A high, thin, bubbling wail spread up into the dark, fell away to a whimpering moan. Then, at last, a solitary whisper, a solitary word.

''death . . .''

Indigo dropped her gaze to the beach beneath her feet and stood very still as the whisper faded and silence crept down once more. For a long time she stayed motionless, and an air of tension began to build, like the stifling, noiseless hour of waiting before the breaking of a storm. Then, without looking, without even raising her head, Indigo spoke.

''I know the truth now, madam. Show yourself.''

There was a rippling splash somewhere beyond the witchlight's reach, the creak of an oar moving in its rowlock and stirring the water. The boat emerged slowly from the dark, and the Ancestral Lady was a silhouette in the stern. Only the silver corona of her eyes glowed cold and nacreous.

And the boat carried three passengers.

Indigo sensed them even before she looked up, and when she did raise her head, there was no shock, no stab of fear. In the boat's prow, a wolf with brindled fur and her own indigo eyes sat looking steadily at her. She met its stare for a moment; then her gaze slid past it to the two human figures who had ranged themselves on the seat between it and the Ancestral Lady. The child with the silver hair and the silver eyes smiled, showing the small, sharp teeth of a cat; its look was evil. At its side, the statuesque being with hair the color of warm earth and a cloak of green and russet smiled too; sweetly and sadly, and with an air of certain knowledge.

Animal and demon and avatar. But she herself, Indigo thought, she herself was more. . . .

She looked past them, into the Ancestral Lady's glittering eyes, and said: ''No, madam. I am not afraid of them or of what they signify. But I believe that *you* are.''

The Ancestral Lady tensed. ''Ah. So you have learned

something from your sojourn.'' But her voice didn't carry conviction; there was unease in her tone.

"Yes,'' Indigo said. "And these . . . guests . . . you bring to show me aren't yours to control. They are mine.''

She pointed at Nemesis. There was a momentary twisting of her perceptions, a looping of time and space, and for an instant she saw in her inner vision a tower cracking and burning, and heard in her memory the shrieking triumph of a monstrous child's laugh. Then Nemesis vanished. Indigo pointed again. A cold and empty room in Carn Caille, and a girl racked with the agonies of grief, looking up at the bright being who claimed to speak in the Earth Mother's name and stood before her in judgment. When she looked at the boat again, only the indigo-eyed wolf remained.

Wolf, Indigo, wolf! The shock and the thrill of transformation, feeling herself running, racing, low to the ground. The taste of blood in her mouth, the instincts she shared with her wolf companion Grimya, the chill but ineffably beautiful sound of a howl rising on the air of a winter night.

Then the wolf, too, disappeared, and the Ancestral Lady stood alone in the boat.

"They have no power over me,'' Indigo said. "Rather, I have power over them. And that's what you dread above all else, isn't it? Power that may prove to be greater than your own. That's why you have succumbed to the very demon you have striven to use for your own ends. You have wielded it as a weapon, yet it has fed upon you and grown strong from your weakness.''

From the boat came quiet but harsh laughter. "You know *nothing* of me!''

"Oh, but I do.'' Again Indigo had heard the uncertainty underlying the Ancestral Lady's retaliation, and she smiled, not pleasantly. "I know more of you than you dream, madam. I know that you have created this world of the dead about you as a shield, a shell within which you can hide. I know that you have fashioned all the horrors that haunt the nightmares of your worshipers, and that you send them to prowl the living world so that your people will run to appease you and make offerings to you in the hope of averting your wrath. You hold their lives in your hands, and through your oracles, you make them dance and sing and weep and grovel—and you make them *die*!''

Another faint laugh echoed in the tunnel and was answered by a renewed rustling and scraping from the walls. ''But I do not take life, Indigo. That is something you already know.''

Indigo smiled again. ''I didn't claim that you take life, Lady. I said that *you make them die*. There is a very great difference.''

The Ancestral Lady didn't reply, and after a few moments, Indigo spoke again.

''Did they create you? Is that the truth of it? Are you nothing more than an invention of your own human worshipers?''

''*No!*'' The silver-fringed eyes flared savagely. ''I am older and greater than anything their puny civilization can conjure. I am Mistress of the Dead, Guardian of the Portal. And they worship me because they know that in the fullness of time, they must all come to me and serve me in death as they did in life!''

Yes, Indigo thought; that much was true. This creature was far more than a cipher, more than a shell created by the power of human will. She *was* the avatar she claimed to be. Yet perhaps, in the long centuries of her existence, she had forgotten the true meaning of her origins.

''*We are her. She is us.*'' And her servants, these servants whose bones formed the walls of her domain—these and all the countless others whose souls had joined with her down the ages, until there was no difference between them— dreaded death above all else. It seemed on the surface an insane paradox, but death could take many forms. Death of the body, death of the mind or heart—or the death of life itself. And there lay the crux.

Indigo said: ''Shall I tell you the demon's name, madam? Shall I tell you the name of the thing I came here to destroy, and to which you are in thrall?''

The boat rocked violently, and the Ancestral Lady's voice snapped out. "You do not know the demon's name!"

"But I do. Its name is *fear*. One of the greatest and most powerful demons of all . . . and you are enslaved to it!"

"No!" the Ancestral Lady hissed. "You lie, oracle! What have I to fear?"

Indigo glanced to left and right. The bones were still now, the tiny voices silent. *"We are her. She is us."*

"I believe that you fear the very power in whose name you rule," she said softly. "You fear death."

There was a sharp pause. Then a laugh so violent and so sudden that it sounded like the bark of a dog rang through the tunnel.

"I, fear death? Ah, my foolish oracle! How can *I* fear such a thing?" Water lapped on the shale near Indigo's feet as the Ancestral Lady swung her oar suddenly, and the boat began to move toward the beach. "Answer me that, if you can."

Indigo shook her head. "You fear it, madam, because death, for you, would be to lose the hold you have upon your worshipers."

The boat surged nearer; she moved back quickly as it touched the shore, and shingle ground under the keel. The Ancestral Lady took a pace forward, stepping over the seat.

"I will never lose my hold on them!"

"But if you did, what then? If they turned from you, turned their backs to favor another deity, or none at all, what would you become?"

The dark figure was climbing over the prow now, and Indigo retreated again, though she was aware that she couldn't back away much farther. This was the most dangerous moment. If she miscalculated, if she made one mistake, the embryonic plan that had been forming in her mind would be wrecked.

"You rule them by fear, because fear is what drives you. Fear that they will abandon you unless they are too afraid to do so. You want their love—"

"I have their love!"

Indigo remembered the dreadful look in Shalune's eyes in the moments before she died. "Perhaps you have," she said contemptuously, "but that love is warped and made worthless by the cruelty and terror you inflict to keep your followers yoked to your side. Shalune and Inuss died because they believed it was a just punishment for what they had done. It was not. What crime had they committed, save to defy the will of the madwoman who calls herself your High Priestess? Yet you let them die, you *encouraged* them to die, and then you turned them into *hushu* as an example to the rest and to strike even greater dread of you into their hearts!"

She glanced quickly over her shoulder. She was almost at the highest, central point of the islet now; behind her, the rising rock blocked the bright glow from the witchlight, and she could see only intense blackness. She dared not move back any farther.

The Ancestral Lady, however, was not following her, but had stopped on the shale beach. Her dead-white face was ghastly where the witchlight fell on it; her eyes were as black as ink and, for the moment, their silver corona had faded to a dangerous glimmer.

"Do you know," Indigo said in a low but savage voice, "what Shalune was trying to do? She was trying to bring you a fit candidate to be your next avatar in the mortal world. She was trying to replace a priestess who would not have had the dedication to uphold your worship and revere your name with one who would."

The Ancestral Lady hissed like an angry cat. "She disobeyed my will!"

"No, she disobeyed *Uluye's* will. Uluye is like you, Lady—she too has succumbed to the demon called fear, and it has fed like a leech on her until it has all but eaten her away. But who is the mistress and who the servant? Whose fear is the greater? Her fear that if she does not rule with harshness and cruelty, she will incur your wrath? Or your fear that if you do not keep your people under a thrall of terror and dread, they will one day forget you, and thus you might cease to exist?''

Slowly, so slowly, the Ancestral Lady raised one hand. The sleeve of her robe fell back, exposing an arm as thin and as deadly white as the arm of a bloodless corpse. Her black lips parted and she hissed again; not a cat this time, but a snake, lethal and merciless. Taking one step forward, she stamped upon the witchlight and it shattered with a tiny, shrill noise, plunging the scene into darkness. Then a new light began to glow: an aura, colorless and cold, that shimmered around the Lady's gaunt frame. It grew brighter, until she stood haloed in a brilliance that made her own dark form awesome by contrast. Her face seemed to float like the face of a specter within the black frame of hair and robe; her eyes were black windows onto annihilation.

She said softly, and the words were caught up and echoed a thousand times within the crushing dark: "Oh, yes, Indigo. They fear me; and their terror keeps my name alive in their hearts and my will paramount in their minds. Even now my servant Uluye is preparing the ceremonies that will send her child to me for judgment, and I shall judge her *hushu.*''

Indigo was stunned. *Sweet Mother, they have Yima!*

The Ancestral Lady saw her consternation and smiled a grim smile. "Yes, they have Yima; and Uluye's hand will wield the knife that ends her time in the mortal world, for Uluye is my faithful servant and her love for me is even greater than her love for her own child.'' She took another step toward Indigo. "I do not need to teach Uluye the meaning of fear. But *you* have not yet learned the lesson she knows so well. I shall teach you now, Indigo. I shall teach you the meaning of fear, and I shall show you what true terror is and what it can do to the human soul!''

The white hand was coming closer as the Mistress of the Dead advanced up the slope. Deep within herself, Indigo felt her most primal instincts responding: the pounding of the heart, the roiling of the stomach, the sweating, suffocating surge of panic; fear of entrapment, fear of defeat, fear of demons and deities and powers; above all, the unimaginably ancient human dread of death and of what lay beyond—

No, not that! That was her one great weapon; the knife that ripped the demon open, the crossbow that shot a bolt to its heart! She drew breath, and suddenly the words came.

"I don't fear you, Lady, for I know now that I have nothing to fear from you. You see, you have made one great mistake in the means you used to try to cow me. You showed me the dead; people from my own past, my own life, who now serve you in your realm. But among all their number, one was missing. One who, alone, might have provided you with a weapon against which I would have been defenseless. But he did not come, did he? You couldn't use him against me, because he doesn't dwell among your legions. That was my one terror, madam; terror that I would find my Fenran here. But he isn't here. He isn't dead. You have no power over him, and therefore you have no power over me. So do whatever you will—I defy you!"

The Ancestral Lady froze. And suddenly from the walls all about them came a rustling and a clicking and a glimmering of bone, and a cry, a whisper, a plethora of tiny voices.

"us, Indigo. us, Indigo. afraid. afraid. death. home. afraid. help us. help us. help ME. . . ."

The Ancestral Lady flung her head back and shrieked like a banshee. The next instant, the world erupted. The river rose, a turbulent tide of foul black water; the tunnel walls groaned and caved in and down, shattering with a roar like an avalanche as they crashed toward Indigo. Howling lights flashed past her eyes as she fell back, and monstrous shapes tumbled through the air at her: bone and flesh and hair and fur and—

A final, massive implosion flung her into a dimension that seemed to crush her and tear her apart at the same moment. She fell from nowhere into nothing, twisting over and over, screaming without sound, aware only of blackness and blindness and a blaze of pain, a dinning in her ears. There

was a wall rushing toward her; she felt it coming, though
her senses were battered out of existence; closer, closer.
"help us, help ME." Then the wall slammed into her from
all directions at once, and she was back in a physical body
that flailed and thrashed, and something was streaming past
her eyes in huge, dark rushes, and her nose and her throat
and her lungs were burning, and she opened her mouth and
air surged out in a bubbling stream around her head—

Water! She was underwater, breathing it in, swallowing
it, losing the last dregs of her precious air! In an instant,
Indigo knew what the Ancestral Lady had done, and panic
gripped her. *The lake!* She'd drown; she'd never reach the
surface in time—

No! She shut her mouth against the water's onslaught as
the panic gave way to reason. Her own last words to the
Lady—she couldn't die! There was a way up, back to the
light, back to sanity, back to where they were waiting for
her, *waiting* for her! She must reach them. *She must!*

Indigo clamped her arms tightly to her sides and kicked
out. She felt the sudden buoyancy, the instinct of the swim-
mer drawing her toward light and air, and she streaked upward from the lake's depths, cleaving through the black
water like a fish outrunning a deadly pursuer.

·CHAPTER·XX·

There was a storm coming. Grimya had sensed it in the air long before the first haze began to taint the sky, and now the sun, which had passed the meridian and begun to decline, hung like a dim, beaten-copper disk in a dense and colorless sky that was rapidly darkening in the west.

At the lakeside, the grim ceremonies had begun, preparations for the uglier rites that would take place at sunset. More and more people continued to arrive from the outlying villages and were gathering around the arena and at the forest's edge. They would have no part to play in what was to happen; their role was simply to witness the events and to take warning from them. The crowd was silent, and even from where she lay by the stairs, Grimya could smell their fear.

Earlier, the wolf had managed to writhe to a position from where she could see a section of the gathering, and she had shuddered inwardly at sight of the ranks of stony faces, their expressions ranging from morbid curiosity to outright dread. Many had brought offerings, though whether they were intended to placate the spirits and demons, or

Uluye and her women, Grimya couldn't tell. In these people's minds, there seemed to be little difference.

On the shore, the priestesses were constructing the wooden frames on which Yima and Tiam were to die. Remembering the horrors of Ancestors Night and the fate of the woman who had murdered her children, Grimya hadn't wanted to watch the frames' familiar shape taking form, and so she had wriggled painfully back into the shelter of the stairwell, hidden from the view of everyone, and now she lay staring miserably at the ziggurat wall.

She wondered how Yima and her lover were faring. They were still inside the citadel, and Grimya dreaded the moment when they must be brought down and would pass only a few paces from her on their way to execution. The guilt that racked the wolf was second only to her fear for Indigo's safety, and though she knew it was futile, she wished again and again that she could find a way, even at this eleventh hour, to right the wrong she had done the young couple.

The sky grew darker and more oppressive. From the shore came intermittent sounds of chanting, the rattle of sistrums and the sharp *thwack* of small hand drums. The heat and humidity were worse than ever, and Grimya felt giddy and ill. With her muzzle bound, she was unable to pant in an effort to cool herself, and no one had thought—or troubled—to bring her water.

In a feverish state halfway between waking and dreaming, she was beginning to wonder if Uluye's intention was to let her die through neglect, when she sensed a presence close by. With an effort, she opened her eyes and saw that one of the priestesses had approached the stairwell and was bending over her.

"There, now." The girl was very young; younger, Grimya surmised, even than Yima. Her face looked tired and strained, and sweat beaded her brow, nose and jaw. "There. I'm to give you some water, look." She brandished a dish and a small amphora. "Look, here it is."

So Uluye wasn't trying to kill her this way after all. Grimya tried to struggle into a more upright position, but the

bonds on her legs made it impossible. The girl frowned at
the ropes, and for a moment the wolf wondered if she might
untie them; but then she clearly thought better of the idea,
for she turned her attention instead to the knot at Grimya's
muzzle. As the rope came free, Grimya whimpered with
gratitude and her tongue lapped and lapped at the sizzling
air in desperate relief.

"Here." The girl had filled the water dish and pushed it
under her nose. As she did so, a huge, silent flash split the
sky in two and lit the entire ziggurat as though it had caught
fire from within. The girl jumped and cried out, almost
upsetting the bowl. For a few seconds, she stayed still, listening tensely, but there was no answering roar of thunder,
and at last she forced her muscles to relax and returned her
attention to the water. Her movements, Grimya saw, were
nervous and darting. The onset of the storm had clearly
unsettled her . . . but there was more to her fright than that,
and the wolf thought in surprise: *she is afraid of me.* . . .

For a minute, as she drank the first bowlful of water and
whined hopefully for another, Grimya was too preoccupied
to consider the implications, but then, as the girl refilled the
bowl and cautiously pushed it toward her a second time, an
idea came to her. There was a slender chance that it would
work, but if it did, if she succeeded, it might be her one
chance to get free.

The water was reviving her; she drank a third bowl and
then licked her muzzle and turned her head away to show
that she had had enough. The girl picked up the rope and
held it uncertainly.

"Uluye says I must tie you again." Her dark eyes were
wary and she spoke in an artificially soothing tone, clearly
unaware that Grimya could understand her, but simply talking to boost her own confidence. Suddenly another lightning flash turned the sky momentarily to a livid blue-white.
This time it was followed by a distant roll of thunder, and
briefly a capricious breeze sprang up, bringing the scent of
rain. The girl shut her eyes momentarily and muttered a
protective charm under her breath; then, with an effort, she

collected herself and gingerly approached the wolf again, the rope held out. "Come on, now. Come on. I won't hurt you."

Grimya showed her teeth, and a warning growl rumbled in her throat. The girl jerked back with a sharp intake of breath, then licked her lips nervously and tried once more, though moving very slowly now.

"Come . . . *please*. Be good. I promise I won't—"

Grimya snarled. At the same instant, lightning flashed again, and as it lit the sky, her amber eyes seemed to catch fire. The girl screamed, scrambling to her feet and stumbling backward; echoing her cry came a huge bellow of thunder, and then the distant but fast-increasing hiss of the rain sweeping in. As the first drops hit the ground like tiny arrows, Grimya snarled again with renewed savagery and, straining at her bonds, lunged in the girl's direction, her teeth snapping.

It was enough. Her seniors' instructions forgotten, the girl fled from the twin terrors of the storm and the furious wolf. In another lightning flash, Grimya saw her scrambling up the stairs into the citadel, and heard her sobbing in the instant before thunder drowned all other sound. Under other circumstances, the wolf would have pitied her, but there was no time for such indulgences now. In a matter of seconds, the rain had become a downpour, soaking her fur and already forming puddles and rivulets on the sand, and Grimya set to gnawing the rope that bound her forelegs. Her pulse raced and she knew that she must work quickly. The chances were that the young priestess might be too ashamed of her fear to confess her dereliction to any of her peers; but on the other hand, she might run straight to someone more courageous, who would come to see what was to do.

The rope was quite heavy, but it was also old, and nothing made from vegetable matter lasted long in this foul climate. The rain saturating the fibers made the work easier, and in less than a minute, Grimya's teeth had bitten through enough strands and the rope fell apart. She paused for breath and to lap gratefully at the downpour, then twisted her head around and set to work on her hind legs. She nipped herself twice in her haste, but at last the second rope also came free.

Elated, Grimya sprang to her feet—then staggered and fell over as her numbed limbs refused to support her. For another minute she lay panting and helpless, dreading that at any moment someone would discover her. But the priestesses had other preoccupations; no one came, and at last she felt she could trust her legs.

She scrambled to her feet. The sky overhead was now so black that it had blotted out all light; the downpour had extinguished the torches by the lake, and only the frequent but short-lived flashes of lightning illuminated the scene. Grimya gave silent thanks for the storm, for the darkness and rain would hide her from view as she ran for the safety of the forest. Soaked through now, her fur plastered to her body, she stared through the veils of falling water until a triple fork of lightning overhead showed her that the way was clear; then she dashed toward the trees. As the newest roar of thunder faded, a wailing cry went up from the priestesses by the lakeside, and for an instant Grimya thought she had been discovered; but the cries were answered only by the renewed rattling of the sistrums, and she realized that this was simply a part of the ceremonies, made more frenetic by the storm. She raced on, and moments later, involuntarily uttering a bark of sheer relief, she plunged into the wet blackness of the forest undergrowth.

The sounds of the drums and sistrums were still fitfully audible between thunderclaps as Grimya pushed through the dense vegetation. She was making for the far side of the lake; though there was no logical reason for it, instinct seemed to be pulling her in that direction, and besides, it would take her as far as possible from Uluye and her women, while still enabling her to keep the citadel in view. The downpour was lessened by the dense foliage overhead, and the lightning, now almost continuous, showed her the easiest path. She had almost reached the lake's farthest edge when something new shimmered in the periphery of her senses. She slowed and hesitated, unsure of what it was that her consciousness had picked up.

And then, in her mind, she felt the soft, tentative telepathic call.

Grimya . . . ? Grimya, where are you? Can you hear me?

"Indigo!" Grimya barked aloud in uncontrollable excitement. She broke into a run, wriggling through the crowding, sodden bushes toward the source of the call. Indigo was close; she was here, by the lakeside. Her instinct *had* been true—

The wolf emerged from cover into a blinding wall of rain. For a moment she could see nothing at all, until lightning lit the surface of the lake, a churning silver glitter only yards away. Grimya blinked, trying to shake water from her eyes. Then there came another titanic flash, and she saw the soaked, dazed-looking figure that sprawled at the water's edge.

"Indigo!" Grimya's cry was lost in the thunder as she ran to Indigo and, ignoring the last smears of the ash and charcoal mask that the lake and the rain hadn't washed away, licked her face in joy and relief. Too excited to speak coherently, she lapsed into telepathic speech. *Where have you been, where have you been? What's happened to you?*

Indigo hugged her tightly. She was still too stunned to speak and could hardly believe that she was truly back in the mortal world. Fighting her way upward through the dark water, her skull pounding and lights flashing before her eyes, she'd known that she could hold out for only a few more seconds before she'd be forced to open her mouth and try to breathe. Then, just before the pressure grew too great to bear, her head had broken from swirling darkness into the mayhem of the storm; with a great, rasping inhalation, she'd swallowed air and felt rain beating down on her face, and as the pounding and the lights began to loose their hold on her, she'd somehow found the wit to flounder to the bank, and had dragged herself out of the lake to lie coughing and choking on the shore with the lightning flashing around her and thunder roaring in her ears.

She was still giddy now, and her throat felt as though it had been rasped raw; but the relentless physical reality of the storm was driving out her disorientation, and she was grateful for it. Immortal or not, she didn't care to speculate on what might have happened if she hadn't reached the surface when she did. But she was back now. She was safe. And there was so much to be told.

Grimya had calmed a little but was still brimming with questions. *Where have you come from, Indigo?* she asked. *I have been trying to make contact, but I couldn't find you, I couldn't hear you!*

"Wait a few moments, dearest; let me get my breath." Another bawl of thunder eclipsed Indigo's words, and she rubbed the wolf's fur. For another minute or more, they sat hunched together against the downpour. The lightning was a little less frequent now, though the rain fell as hard as ever, and as her reeling senses began to settle into more rational order, Indigo thought, Goddess, where to begin? There was so much to say, so many confusing threads to unravel. But then she remembered the first thing, the starkest of all, and her fingers clenched in Grimya's ruff.

"Grimya, there's something you must know. Shalune and Inuss—they're dead."

Thunder grumbled again, and the wolf's eyes grew troubled. *I know.*

Indigo stared at her. "You *know*?"

Yes. Grimya paused, then added unhappily, *Their bodies were washed up on the shore during the night. The priestesses say they will become* hushu. *But Indigo, there's more. Yima—*

"I know about Yima; I know what she tried to do. Shalune told me the whole story."

But she's been captured! Indigo, they're going to kill her, and it is my fault!

"Your fault?" Then, as Grimya started to explain, Indigo held up both hands. "No, Grimya; wait, wait. We *must* piece this together from the beginning, or we'll make the confusion even worse.''

There may not be time. Yima and her man are to die at sunset, and the ceremonies have already begun!

Indigo looked quickly across the lake, but the ziggurat on the far shore was invisible in the pouring gloom. In a brief lull, the sound of the women's chanting drifted faintly over the water above the hiss of the rain, and for the first time, her mind registered its significance.

"How long until twilight?" she asked tensely.

I don't know; the storm makes it impossible to tell. I think we must have two hours or more until dark comes. But if we're to do anything—

"No," Indigo interrupted her again. "There *is* time. Let's get into the forest, under cover, and then we must piece both of our stories together. It's vital that we each have the whole picture.''

They got to their feet and stumbled through the deluge to the trees. There, sheltered by a spreading, huge-leaved giant, they both recounted their stories, and the whole ugly tale emerged. Grimya told of her discovery that another candidate had been substituted for Yima, and of how, fearing for Indigo's safety, she had in desperation gone to Uluye for help. She recounted the story of Yima and Tiam's capture, and Uluye's decree that they should be executed to appease the Ancestral Lady.

She is ready to kill her own daughter, the wolf said miserably. *I don't understand that, Indigo—I don't understand how she can do such a dreadful thing!*

"Oh, but I do," Indigo replied grimly. "And that's a part of my story. You see, I've learned the nature of the demon we're seeking, and it's not the creature who calls herself the Ancestral Lady.''

It is not?

"No. In fact, the Ancestral Lady is in thrall to this demon, Grimya; and so are Uluye and all of her women, and the Dark Islers who owe them fealty.''

And she told the wolf of her experiences in the Ancestral

Lady's realm. Grimya listened wide-eyed, not interrupting, and when finally Indigo finished, the wolf whined softly.

"The d-demon is *fear*?" This time she spoke aloud, and there was grave concern in her voice. "But how can we fight that, Indigo? Fear has no body; it isn't a *thing* that can be c . . . aptured and killed. All the others—the Charchad and the s-serpent-eater, even the demon of Bruhome—they were *things*, and we could s-*see* them and face them."

"I know. But I think it can be defeated, Grimya, although I realize now that we'll have to use very different weapons from any we've used before." Indigo looked into the she-wolf's worried eyes. "Do you remember what you said to me some while ago, about the ways in which I've changed since we began journeying together?"

"I th . . . *ink* so."

"You asked me that day if I believed I still had my shape-changing powers. Well, I know the answer now. I discovered it by chance when the Ancestral Lady tried to use those three images against me: Nemesis, the Emissary and my own wolf self. When I banished the wolf image, when I took it from her grasp, I knew then that although it was part of me and always will be, I could no longer use it." She smiled sadly. "It was as you said: the cub outgrows its games when it no longer needs them for learning. I don't need to become the wolf to overcome this demon. I believe I've learned how to call on other powers now."

Grimya looked uncertain. "Other p-powers?"

Indigo nodded. "I'm not sure that I can explain to you; I'm not even sure that I can explain to myself. I just . . . *feel* it, Grimya. Something has changed; something very fundamental." She glanced up at the sky, then suppressed a shiver that coursed through her despite the suffocating heat. "That day, you also said you felt that Nemesis might be afraid of me now. That isn't true; at least not in the way I think you meant it then; but I believe, Grimya, I *believe*, that I no longer have any reason to fear Nemesis. It has no real power over me; only the power that I've been foolish enough to let it usurp."

Grimya shook her head. "I don't under-stand."

"No." Indigo saw the futility of trying to express what she felt in words that would make any sense. Words couldn't communicate it; the feeling—the conviction—was too formless. Yet it *was* a conviction, and in attempting to challenge and overcome her, the Ancestral Lady had, however unwittingly, done her a great service. If she could only hold on to what she had learned, hold on to it and use it, then this demon might be defeated and Yima and Tiam's lives saved.

If, she thought. That was the imponderable. She had yet to put her own power to the test, and there was so little time. But the skeleton of a strategy was already taking form in her mind, and with Grimya's help, she believed that she could prepare quickly enough for what she must do. Poor Grimya; the wolf blamed herself entirely for Yima's predicament, and felt her guilt and shame so deeply. She'd move mountains and forests, if she could, to put right what she thought was a betrayal.

Indigo turned to the wolf again. "Grimya—do you know how many of the priestesses are still in the citadel?"

"I don't kn . . . *know.* Very few, I think. Most are with Uluye on the sh-shore."

"Would it be possible for us to reach the caves without being seen? Could you find a route?"

Grimya considered for a few moments before replying, "Yess, I can do it. And the storm will make it easier." She blinked. "Wh-what are you planning, Indigo? Will it help Yima?"

Indigo hesitated. Then: "I can't be sure, Grimya. It's a gamble. But, yes . . . if it works, I hope that Yima and Tiam will be free by morning."

The rain was slackening when they emerged from the trees, though it was still heavy. Lightning flashes were intermittent now, and the thunder less deafening; the storm was passing as quickly as it had come, and Grimya was anxious to make haste before they lost the advantage of its cover. With no route into the citadel other than the broad, open stairway, it took time and the greatest care to reach their goal, and Grimya sneaked to the ziggurat to reconnoiter, while Indigo waited at the forest's edge for the signal to follow.

Despite the storm, the ceremonies at the lakeside had continued unchecked, and the crowd of onlookers had swelled to what seemed a vast throng. People stood sodden and forlorn, rank upon rank, silent, frightened, their numbers stretching back into the forest as far as the wolf's eyes could see. In the arena, a large coterie of priestesses formed a semicircle around Uluye, who presided over them like a grim statue on the oracle's rock, ignoring the water beating down on her as she watched the progress of the rites. Still the grisly wooden frames were unoccupied, but the atmosphere had an ominous quality, which the storm had done nothing to lessen.

Some of the women, Grimya saw, were about to begin a circuit of the lake. This ritual would be very different from their customary nightly procession, for they carried offerings of food, ornaments, clothing—offerings perhaps brought by the villagers—to cast into the water in an attempt to appease their angry goddess. A shrill, bloodcurdling song of praise was sung before the women set off, and while the crowd's attention was focused on this, Grimya called out telepathically to Indigo.

Come now, but quickly! The rain has almost stopped, and I can see the sky growing lighter. Run to the stairwell—I am waiting for you there.

In her dark robe, Indigo was almost invisible as she came in a crouching run from the forest. She joined Grimya, and as she paused to get her breath, they both looked uneasily at the nightmarish scene on the shore.

They haven't brought Yima and her man down from the citadel yet, Grimya communicated. *I don't know where they are being kept, but they must be guarded. We shall have to take great care.*

All the same, I don't think we dare wait, Indigo said. *They may not be brought out until the last moment.*

Grimya peered up at the stairway rising above them. *There is no sign of anyone up there at present. If we must go, I think we should go now. The first flights of steps will be the most dangerous. If we can reach the first cave level, it will be much easier to hide.*

Then let's go now, while their attention's diverted.

They left their hiding place. Indigo allowed herself one quick glance back; then, as Grimya called that the way was clear, she turned to the staircase and started to climb, moving as quickly as she dared on the wet and slippery surface. The rain had almost ceased now, and as Grimya had warned, the sky was lightening in the west as the stormclouds began to clear. Aware that within a matter of minutes, they would be all too clearly visible from below, they gained the first ledge and climbed the second and then the third flights. As she set foot on the fourth staircase, Indigo was beginning to think that they might, after all, reach the upper levels without encountering anyone, when Grimya suddenly communicated a frantic warning.

Indigo! Lie down, quickly!

Instinct propelled Indigo before her conscious mind could react, and she threw herself flat on the stairs, where the parapet was high enough to shield her from view. Grimya, belly to the stone, crawled back and peered cautiously out from the parapet's end—then uttered a tiny, involuntary whimper.

Moments later, the small procession came into view, and Indigo drew in a sharp breath. Four priestesses with spears in their hands, and faces as hard as the rock of the ziggurat, strode along the ledge below them and turned onto the staircase they had just climbed. In their midst, two figures dressed only in short, sacklike garments and hung about with fetishes, shuffled with an air of hopeless defeat, their heads bowed and their feet dragging. Though she had never seen him before, Indigo knew that the young man must be Tiam. His left cheek sported an ugly, spreading bruise, and the eye above it was so swollen that it was closed to a slit. Yima's face was hidden behind the curtain of her unbound hair, but Indigo could hear her rapid, shallow breathing as the two captives, clutching each other's hands, passed by with their escort.

The party descended the stairs; the last Indigo saw of them was the priestesses' spear tips glinting in the gloomy, reflected light from the sky. As they dropped out of sight, Grimya communicated urgently, *This means we have very little time left. Whatever we mean to do, we must do it quickly!*

Indigo glanced speculatively at the staircase and the tiers of ledges above them. Now that the prisoners had been taken down to the arena, she thought it unlikely that anyone else would be left in the citadel; even those with no part to play in the ceremonies, the very elderly and the very young, would be among the watching crowd.

They started up the stairs, more quickly now, but still with a cautious eye for any movement above them, and she said: *Grimya, I need to go to our quarters to make ready, and then I want you to go to the temple on the summit.*

Me? To the temple? Grimya's mental voice sounded puzzled.

Yes. I think I know how we can best contrive what we need to do, and your help will be vital.

And, quickly, she explained the plan that was taking form in her mind. Grimya wasn't entirely happy with the thought that it meant her leaving Indigo's side, even for a moment. If something should go wrong, she said, she wanted to be with her friend, to protect her. But she gave way, albeit reluctantly, and they hastened on until they reached the uppermost ledge. While the wolf waited outside to keep watch, Indigo ducked through the curtain that hung over the entrance to the oracle's cave. No lamps were burning, but the light outside was growing stronger and she could see well enough to find what she needed. First, a rapid change of clothes, from the sodden black robe into the oracle's ceremonial garments. Then the oracle's crown, which to Indigo's relief still stood in its niche at the back of the cave. She'd feared that Uluye

might have removed it, but it seemed that the High
Priestess still respected the taboo against entering the
cave when the oracle was not in residence.

Then . . . Indigo paused, looking at her crossbow, which
lay among the baggage she'd brought with her when she first
arrived at the citadel, and which she hadn't touched since.
No; she wouldn't take it. Although she would feel a great
deal more secure with it in her hands, it was too worldly a
thing, too mundane; it would detract from the image of
unearthly power that she must rely on now. Her knife,
though, was another matter, for it was small enough to be
hidden. At least she'd have one physical weapon if things
went wrong. . . .

She was tying the knife in its sheath firmly to her sash
when she heard Grimya's mental voice call to her from the
ledge outside.

*Indigo, the sky is almost clear and I can see the sun. It
will set very soon. We must hurry, or we'll be too late!*

There was anguish in Grimya's tone, and Indigo swore
softly. She needed more time in which to gather her wits
and prepare herself. The plan was so haphazard, her
skills so untried . . . even another hour might have made
all the difference. But there was nothing she could do
about it. Prepared or not, she *had* to make the attempt,
and she couldn't afford to consider the possibility of failure.

She tucked the oracle's crown under one arm and left the
cave. The light outside startled her; the great mass of stormclouds was rapidly receding into the east, and the orange-
red globe of the sun hung low over the trees in a lurid sky.
The ziggurat walls shone fierily, and light flooded the arena
below. Looking no bigger than ants from this distance, the
priestesses were moving on the sand, long shadows spearing
out from their hurrying figures. They were relighting the
torches—the fluttering flames seemed pale and insignificant
under the brilliant sun—and a large group were gathered
around the oracle's rock, on which a single figure stood

motionless, presiding over the scene with a brooding and watchful air. Faintly, the drone of the women's chanting, emphasized by a muffled thud of drums, drifted up on the still air.

Indigo felt her stomach contract in queasy trepidation, and she looked at Grimya. "I'm ready. Quickly—go on to the temple, and I'll make my way back to the arena."

"Be c-careful," Grimya urged her. "Now that the light is good again, if anyone sh . . . ould look up—"

"I know, dear one, and I'll take the greatest care. But I think they have other preoccupations. I'll be safe enough."

She watched the wolf lope away along the ledge toward the last flight of stairs that led to the ziggurat's summit, then turned and hastened in the other direction.

The quiet after the racket of the storm was eerie; even the sounds of the rituals continuing far below seemed unable to impinge on the huge stillness that gripped the world. Yet, despite the clean-washed atmosphere, Indigo felt that there wasn't enough air in the world to make breathing possible. She made her way down the first three flights of stairs without incident, then paused at the top of the fourth flight to send a quick message to Grimya on the summit. The wolf assured her that all was well; satisfied, Indigo started down the steps—

And stopped halfway down, as from nowhere came an attack of near-panic. She couldn't do this—it wouldn't work. It was impossible, she hadn't the power—

Yes, you have! She forced the savage denial into her mind and snatched at the panic, grasped it, crushed it. The demon was trying to feed on her weakness; she must *not* give way! She steadied herself, looked down at the crowds massed below her, and quickly hurried on.

Luck—or perhaps something more than luck—was with her, for she reached the foot of the last staircase safely and ducked under the stairwell, thankful to be safe at last from the gaze of anyone who might glance toward the ziggurat.

The panic was still there, still trying to snare her, but she willed her breathing to slow to a regular rhythm, and willed her hands to be steady as she raised the oracle's crown and set it carefully on her head. Strangely, it seemed less heavy than it had on previous occasions. Then she sought Grimya's presence in her mind.

Are you ready?

Yes, came the reply. *I am ready. I wait only for you to give the word.*

Indigo looked up at the sky and thrust the last of her doubts away. Though she had no logic to support the conviction, she believed that she could achieve what she had set out to do. She had learned several valuable lessons in the Ancestral Lady's realm, and one of them was the folly of underestimating her own power. She closed her eyes, focused her will. In her mind she visualized the Ancestral Lady's bone-white face, within its shrouding frame of black hair, and her eyes, blacker than night, blacker than the deep of space, with their silver corona glimmering cold and ghostly. The image came to her with startling ease, almost as if her consciousness had been anticipating this moment, like a player waiting in the wings for a cue. Indigo smiled to herself, and in her mind, silently, she spoke.

Well, Lady, this is the greatest test of all. Her words were not a direct address to the Mistress of the Dead, nor did she believe that the Lady was truly listening; at least, not yet. But the link forged in the dark underworld still remained—and now Indigo drew on the power latent in that world, calling it to herself, forming it, shaping it, focusing it. In her mind, shadows crowded and crawled, and against a background of soft, sibilant hissing, a choir of thin voices whispered, *"we are her. she is us . . . we are her. she is us . . ."* In her mind, she reached out toward them—and felt her fingers touch the glittering, electric force of raw power.

Now, Grimya! she called silently. *Now!*

On the ziggurat's summit, at the edge of the towering

cliff, Grimya felt the hackles rise from the nape of her neck to the base of her spine as excitement and anticipation and a sense of furious determination rose within her. Silhouetted against the sky, she lifted her head, drew breath—

And the challenging, ululating howl of a wolf rang out shatteringly across the arena far below.

·CHAPTER·XXI·

Five hundred faces turned upward in shock, and Uluye snapped out of her semitrance with a jolt that shook her from head to foot and almost pitched her off the rock where she stood. Her minions tried to help her restore her balance, but Uluye savagely shook them off. As the last echoes of the wolf's howl died away, she turned, crouching like a cornered cat, and stared up at the ziggurat where Grimya stood poised, a silhouette against the bright sky.

What was this? What did it mean? Uluye stared fixedly at the wolf's distant shape, her mind racing as she struggled to understand and interpret what she saw. She was still dazed; the ritual had been close to its climax, and she had almost completed her achievement of the waking trance in which her love for and dedication to the Ancestral Lady eclipsed all else; then as the final, triumphant moment approached, her spell had been shattered. *Why?* Uluye screamed silently in her mind. *Why, Lady? What are you telling me that I don't understand?*

There was total silence in the arena now. The ceremony had collapsed into chaos; the drums and sistrums had stopped as the women wielding them stared open-mouthed and terrified at the vision on the ziggurat. Everyone, priestesses and onlookers alike, waited. Then suddenly, from the direction of the ziggurat, a new voice cried out.

"Uluye! In the Ancestral Lady's name, I command you to stop this murderous insanity!"

Uluye hissed in shock and spun to face the stairs at the ziggurat's foot. The stone knife dropped from her grasp as she suddenly lost all control of her fingers, and she stared in stunned disbelief at the figure that had emerged from the shadow of the staircase and was now walking slowly across the sand toward her.

"No . . ." The High Priestess's voice cracked on the word as hysteria clutched at her. "No—it isn't possible! *You are dead!*"

"I am alive." Beneath the towering crown of the oracle, Indigo's lips smiled, though her eyes were cold and still. "I have been to the Ancestral Lady's realm, Uluye, and I have returned."

The group of priestesses clustered around the rock at Uluye's feet shrank back, whimpering. Indigo stopped five paces from the rock, and Uluye stared down at her. To either side, the throng of onlookers were starting to murmur. Few could see for themselves what had disrupted the ceremony; of those who could see, none understood, and their uncertainty was rapidly giving rise to agitation and fear.

Uluye ignored them. Her entire consciousness was focused on Indigo, and a chaotic mayhem of clashing emotions tumbled through her brain. Her jaw worked; her voice, when finally it came, was a savage hiss.

"What *are* you?"

Indigo suddenly saw through the mask of the High Priestess's face to the confused, frightened and unhappy woman beneath. Truly, Uluye *was* a servant of her goddess; and both, in turn, were enslaved to another power that neither of them even dared acknowledge, let alone try to control and overcome. Pity filled Indigo: pity, and a fierce renewal of her vow that this demon's reign should come to an end.

She said, "I am one who has come to reveal to you the *true* face and the *true* will of your goddess."

Uluye's hard, dark eyes narrowed. "That is a blasphemous lie!" she spat. "You are not our oracle. Our oracle betrayed us, and the Ancestral Lady claimed her soul!" She licked bone-dry lips and seemed to be trying to swallow something that threatened to choke her. "I ask you again, I *demand*—what manner of evil and unholy demon are you? Are you the *hushu* that the false oracle became when the Lady cast her soulless corpse out of her realm? Or are you Indigo's vengeful ghost, seeking to wreak more havoc?" She pointed a threatening finger. *"I will have an answer!"*

Indigo gazed steadily back at her. "No, Uluye, I am neither *hushu* nor ghost nor demon. I *am* Indigo." She stepped forward, and as Uluye's acolytes scattered from her path, she held up one hand. "Touch me. My flesh is warm; I am human, and as alive as you!"

Uluye didn't flinch, as her women had done, but her mouth curled in a sneer. "Touch you, and be infected by the spell of the undead? You must think me a child, demon!"

Indigo smiled coldly. "I don't think you a child, Uluye. But I think you are afraid." She reached out a little farther, and this time Uluye couldn't control the reflex that made her shrink back. "What are you afraid of? Demons and *hushu*? No, I don't think so. I think you fear the consequences of daring to acknowledge the truth you see with your own eyes."

"Truth?" Uluye spat venomously.

"Yes, truth! That I have returned, living and breathing and unscathed, from the Ancestral Lady's realm. Your goddess didn't kill me, or punish me for the blasphemy of which you so righteously accuse me. She didn't take vengeance, Uluye—she doesn't possess that power over me, for I will not allow her to take it!"

Before Uluye could react, Indigo turned from the rock

and walked to the center of the arena. The sun, swollen and crimson, was touching the treetops now, and the lake looked like a vast pool of blood. The women on the arena drew back quickly, so that when Indigo turned again to face the High Priestess, her figure, alone on the sand, looked stark and dramatic against the spectacular backdrop.

"You claim to love the Ancestral Lady." Indigo's voice carried clearly to the crowd; ranks of silent faces stared back at her, and she felt sickened by the terror she saw in their eyes. "But what manner of love is it that drives you to murder your own child in her name?"

She turned to look at the ugly outlines of the two wooden frames at the lake's edge. From here, the helpless forms of Yima and Tiam were no more than indistinct silhouettes, but Indigo's sharply heightened senses could feel their misery and despair as tangibly as Grimya might catch scent on a breeze. Anger gripped her, and she grasped hold of it.

"What crimes have Yima and Tiam committed, Uluye?" she demanded furiously. "Have they broken your laws? Have they stolen, or cheated, or murdered? No! Their only sin was to defy your will—not the Ancestral Lady's will; *yours*!"

Uluye's face twisted in outrage, and she drew herself up to her full height. Her whole frame trembled with rising wrath, and her voice rang shrilly as she flung out one accusing arm to point in the direction of the torchlit square, where Shalune and Inuss still lay. "With her own hand, the Ancestral Lady executed those miserable conspirators, and she has sent their bodies back to us to be given to the *hushu*. Her will is clear, demon! And the punishment for flouting it is destruction!"

"No!" Indigo retaliated. "You claim to be her High Priestess, you claim to know her will, but you are *wrong*. The Ancestral Lady didn't kill Shalune and Inuss—you did, Uluye. *You* did!"

Uluye stared down at Indigo, and for a moment—for just a moment—her virulence wavered and a hint of uncertainty showed on her face. Then her mouth and jaw hardened into a brutal line once more, and she hissed dangerously.

"You *dare* to claim—"

Indigo interrupted hotly. "Yes, I dare! You caused their deaths, as surely as if you'd plunged a knife into their hearts. Do you know what killed them, Uluye? Do you? I'll tell you. It was a demon, and that demon is called *fear*! The same demon that you, and your mother before you—yes, I've heard the stories about that monstrous woman—and all of the High Priestesses who have reigned here for centuries past, wielded as a weapon against their own followers. You rule by fear, Uluye; it has become your watchword. Yet you, and the Ancestral Lady in whose name you rule, are slaves to a fear far greater than that which you seek to strike into your people's hearts.

"You and she are afraid of losing your place in the world. You are afraid that a day may come when your followers no longer love you. And you want to be loved; you want to be respected; you want to be *revered*. But what *true* reverence can there be for a cruel goddess and her harsh and unyielding High Priestess? What *real* love can your people have for a woman who is ready to slay her own daughter, or for a deity who demands such a monstrous sacrifice to be made in her name? Oh, they respect you, Uluye. Perhaps they admire your strength and your faith. But do they love you? Or are they simply too terrified to admit the truth: that you, and the Ancestral Lady, are nothing better than tyrants who hold them in miserable thrall?"

For perhaps five seconds there was stunned silence. Then, barely audible at first, but increasing rapidly from a murmuring to a muttering to a muted roar, voices began to rise from the crowd like a gale approaching through the forest. Uluye stood as motionless as a statue while the noise swelled around her, and her sharp ears caught individual words bobbing like flotsam on a tide. *Uluye . . . the goddess . . . oracle . . . hushu . . . sacrifice. . . .*

With a violent movement, she spun around to face the throng. She flung her arms wide in a commanding gesture, and the women near the rock at her feet drew back in shock as they felt the current of psychic energy that suddenly surged from her. Then her voice shrieked above the babble as she howled for silence, and instantly five hundred voices fell quiet and five hundred faces turned to stare at her in stunned awe. Ribcage heaving, legs trembling beneath her robe, Uluye scanned the crowd with a fearsome, glittering gaze. For the moment, she had them under control; they were more afraid of her than they were of Indigo, or of the thing that Indigo had become. She must hold them, keep her grip on them, for if she was weak, or showed a moment's uncertainty or indecision, she would be lost.

And you, Uluye, what are you afraid of . . . ? Suddenly her heart lurched so hard that she nearly choked as, unbidden, her memory conjured the image of her daughter as she was led down from the citadel and past the rock where her mother, her judge and executioner, stood watching. *My only child . . . she didn't look up as she went by; she didn't once look at me. . . .*

A surge of violent fury erupted in her mind and crushed the momentary emotion out of existence. She would not be swayed; she would *not* doubt! The Lady had exacted her just vengeance on Shalune and Inuss for their crimes, and now Yima and her lover must pay the same penalty. Anything else was unthinkable. *I am the High Priestess*, Uluye thought ferociously. *I cannot be mistaken—I cannot!*

Her voice rang out over the heads of the crowd. "Hear me! I, Uluye, the chosen servant of the Ancestral Lady, speak to you in her sacred name, and I denounce this false oracle who stands before me. The Lady's will is clear, and her will is paramount! Hear me now, and be warned that I shall call the Lady's wrath upon any who *dare* to defy her!"

She dropped to a crouch and snatched a spear from the hand of one of her acolytes below, then jerked upright once more. The light of the dying sun made the spear tip glitter like fire as Uluye raised it high above her head.

"I am the Lady's chosen!" she shouted, and the crowd

cried out in response, though their cries were nervous and uncertain. "I am the High Priestess, and spiritual daughter of the Mistress of the Dead! And I curse this demon who prowls among us as the *hushu* prowl in the night. She seeks to turn you from the Lady's service, and one faithless heart is all she craves; just one heart in which to sow her poisoned seed!" Her voice rose to a venomous scream. *"Is there one such heart among you?"*

"No!" the watchers cried. "No, Uluye, no!"

"Be sure of that!" Uluye exhorted them in a threatening and murderous hiss. "Be sure of it; for if there is anyone among you, man, woman or child, who does not keep faith, I shall curse that one, and I shall devour that one's soul, and I shall name that one *hushu* even as I name this vile demon! *Do you hear me?*"

"We hear, Uluye! We hear!"

Fired by their leader's wild tirade, three of the priestesses nearest to Uluye had snatched up drum and sistrums, and now they began to rattle out a harsh, staccato rhythm. Their voices rose shrilly in a chant that others swiftly took up, and they formed a line to either side of the rock where Uluye stood, their bodies swaying and their feet stamping. Quivering with the knowledge of her ascendancy, Uluye turned about. With the spear still gripped in her hand, she sprang down from the rock and, beckoning to two of her women to follow, stalked slowly and menacingly toward Indigo, who still stood alone and defiant on the sand.

"Now," she said, savagely but so softly that only her quarry and the two attendants could hear, "I shall show you the meaning of fear, oracle!" She snapped her fingers at the women. "Take her!"

As the two started forward, Indigo could see from their eyes that they were afraid of her; but their terror of Uluye was greater still, and they dared not disobey the order. She didn't resist as they caught hold of her arms—that, too, disconcerted them—but as they pinned her, a voice sounded silently in her mind.

Indigo! It was Grimya. The moment Indigo had made her

presence known to the crowd, the wolf had left the temple
and streaked down from the ziggurat to wait and watch at
the foot of the stairs. *Indigo, be careful! She is dangerous—*

No, Grimya, wait! Indigo sent back the swift message as
she sensed that the wolf was about to come running to her
aid. *Stay where you are!* It was vital that Grimya shouldn't
intervene now. She must cope with this alone.

Uluye was advancing, the spear now poised to strike directly at Indigo's heart. She was only seven paces away;
six; five. . . . Indigo felt her muscles tensing, but she forced
herself to show no outward sign of the tension, and her gaze
stayed fixed unwaveringly, calmly, on Uluye's face.

This is what you wanted, isn't it, madam? Contempt gave
the unspoken words extra emphasis as she thought of the
Ancestral Lady hiding in her dark realm. *A confrontation
with your High Priestess, a trial to see whose will is the
stronger. How far will you go in testing Uluye's faith and
my courage? How far, before I prove to you that your worshipers' fear of you can be overcome?* Still the Mistress of
the Dead refused to answer her, but Indigo thought she felt
the faintest of stirrings somewhere deep down in her consciousness, the sense of something listening, waiting. . . .

Uluye took another pace forward, then stopped. The spear
was only inches from Indigo's heart now, but Indigo didn't
so much as glance at it. Strange . . . she didn't know what
would happen if Uluye did strike. She had no doubt that the
spear would pierce her, but what then? What if her heart
was split, or if she bled and the bleeding couldn't be
stanched? She couldn't answer those questions; all she knew
was that no matter what might befall her, she would not
die. She wasn't *willing* to die—and besides, she felt certain
that it wouldn't come to that.

Uluye was looking into her eyes, and a cold smile curved
the High Priestess's lips. "Are you afraid now, oracle; now
that the moment approaches when your soul is to be con-
signed to destruction?"

Indigo said: "No."

"Then you are a greater fool than I believed." But Uluye's eyes suddenly belied the smile; that was the sign that Indigo had been waiting for, the first brief flicker of wavering confidence. "Do you not know what it is to be *hushu*?" Uluye continued. "Can you not imagine what life in death will be like for you, when you walk the forest each night, howling with a hunger and a thirst that can never be assuaged? Do you know what it is to lose your soul, yet to know that you will never truly die?"

The spear in her hand trembled suddenly, briefly; and Indigo knew then that Uluye was desperate.

"Oh, yes." She spoke softly. "I can imagine that, for I have seen far worse, and I have faced far worse. The *hushu* hold no terrors for me. I feel only pity for them. Don't you, Uluye? Don't you pity Shalune and Inuss?" She paused, just long enough to see and be sure of the sudden, fearful tensing of the muscles in the High Priestess's face, then added with terrible gentleness, "Don't you pity Yima?"

For a moment she thought it would be as she'd prayed it might, for Uluye's eyes grew wide with shock as, perhaps for the first time, true understanding of what she had done to her daughter broke through the barriers she had created in her mind and hit her like a hammer blow. Desperately, the High Priestess's roiling consciousness reached out for help, for guidance: *Lady, could it be true? Have I been wrong?*

And before Indigo's inner vision, a silver corona flared about eyes blacker than the deeps of space, and in her skull she heard the Ancestral Lady's laughter.

Uluye shrieked. She flung her head back so that the great feathered headdress fell awry, and raised the spear high in both hands.

"*Demon!*" Her eyes were mad with terror and loathing. "Demon! I send you to the *hushu*, I curse you, I damn you to eternity!"

The spear came flashing down, a searing death strike to Indigo's heart—and Grimya burst from behind the line of chanting women, a gray streak hurtling across the sand, leaping, flinging herself with a maniacal snarl at Uluye's throat. The spear flew spinning from the High Priestess's hand as she went down under the wolf's onslaught, and Grimya's fury crashed into Indigo's head like a breaking wave: *kill, I will kill, I will kill—*

"Grimya, *no!*" Wrenching her arms free from her captors' grasp, Indigo rushed at the wolf and tried to grab the scruff of her neck. "Don't do it, *don't kill her!*" Somehow she managed to batter the command through the red rage that was Grimya's consciousness, and they fell rolling together onto the sand, with Uluye sprawled three feet away.

As she struggled shakily to her knees, one hand still gripping Grimya's fur, Indigo had the impression that she and the wolf and Uluye had suddenly become the only protagonists in a bizarre ritual whose rules none of them truly comprehended. Or, perhaps more apposite, actors in a play that hadn't yet been written. She had expected that the other priestesses would come to the aid of their leader, but they had not; instead, they had shrunk back, forming a tight, frightened semicircle at a prudent distance. However afraid they might be of their High Priestess, they were now more terrified by far of the oracle and her companion.

Uluye began to move. Grimya bared her fangs and snarled again, but Indigo shook her. "*No*, Grimya! Leave her." And to Uluye: "You know she has the power of human speech and understanding. She will obey me."

Uluye got to her feet. Grimya had torn the towering headdress to shreds in her efforts to find the Priestess's throat, and with an unsteady hand, Uluye pushed the remnants to the back of her skull, where they clung amid the oiled tangles of her hair. Her right ear, arm and shoulder were bleeding, but she either didn't know or didn't care.

Indigo, too, stood upright, watching her adversary intently. She had miscalculated, and that was a mistake she couldn't afford to repeat. The next few minutes, she thought, would be vital.

"Uluye," she said, "I am not your enemy." Uluye made a choked, vicious sound at the back of her throat, and Indigo shook her head. "You must believe it; you have the evi-

dence.'' She indicated the wolf. Grimya was calmer now,
though the moment Indigo released her, she had placed herself like a sentinel between the two women, her stance tense
and protective.

''Grimya could have killed you just now. She would have,
had I not called her off. But I *did* call her off. Would an
enemy have spared you, Uluye?'' She smiled thinly, ironi-
cally. ''Would you have spared me if our positions had been
reversed?''

She saw the answer to that in Uluye's eyes, the glitter of
angry and bitter resentment. But the deadly moment had
passed. She must speak now, Indigo thought, before Uluye's
pride regained the upper hand and the advantage was lost.

''Madam.'' She used the formal mode with which she
had addressed the Ancestral Lady, at the same time making
the ritualized gesture that was a sign of deep respect between equals. She saw Uluye's eyes narrow in wary surprise. ''I am not your oracle. I never have been. The
Ancestral Lady attempted to take control of my mind and
use me, just as she controls and uses you and your priestesses, and all of the people who pay her fealty. She didn't
succeed, because she couldn't compel me to fear her. She
tried . . .'' Her eyes grew suddenly introverted, and she
stared down at the sand beneath her feet. ''Sweet Earth
Mother, she tried . . . but she failed, because I discovered
that I had no good reason to be afraid of her.''

Indigo looked up again. ''That, Uluye, is your greatest
mistake, and your greatest burden. You love your goddess;
I know that, I've seen it. But your love has become warped
and distorted by your terror of her—terror that drives you
to sacrifice your own daughter's life in a desperate bid to
prove your faith. What manner of evil must infect a deity
who could exact such a price? The Ancestral Lady isn't
evil—you are her priestess; you must know that better than
I do. So how can you think, how can you believe even for
a moment, that the true test of your love for her demands
that you should kill Yima?''

There was a sudden, violent shifting deep down in her

mind. Something was stirring, something alien, something that emanated from beyond her consciousness . . . and overlaid on it she heard Grimya's soft and troubled mental voice: *Indigo . . . the sun is setting. . . .*

Indigo turned her head. Behind her, above the lake, above the trees that crowded to the water's edge, all that remained of the sun was a thin arc of furious fire. The entire sky was turning to gold and orange and scarlet; shafts of light radiated across the firmament, and when she looked back, she saw that a huge, soft wing of darkness was moving in from the east.

"Uluye," she said, her voice urgent now, "I ask you again, and I beg you to search your heart before you answer. Do you truly believe that only your daughter's death will satisfy your goddess now?"

Uluye looked at the sky. Then she looked toward the lakeshore and the two frames, and again her tongue touched her lips. Lastly her gaze moved to the torchlit square and the two forlorn bodies that lay together between the protecting rows of amulets and offerings. There was a long, long pause. Behind them, the priestesses were still leading their rhythmic chant, but the singing and the thump and rattle of their instruments had taken on a note of hollow desperation. The chanting had lost its meaning and had become nothing more than a device to boost confidence and pacify their congregation. But they didn't stop. They dared not.

Suddenly, shockingly, Uluye's voice cracked through the chant, echoing harshly across the arena. "I will listen to no more!" She made a savage, negating gesture. "*I* know the Lady's will! I am her High Priestess; I have looked upon her face and received her blessing from her own hand. You will not usurp my power from me, Indigo; nor will you sway me from the duty with which the Lady has charged me!"

"I don't want to usurp your power, Uluye," Indigo argued desperately. "I'm not your rival or your enemy; I'm trying to *help* you!"

"No." Uluye's tone was contemptuous. "I want none of your help. I *need* none of your help. You are not one of the Ancestral Lady's own; you understand nothing. *I* understand. I love her—I am *hers*, heart and body and soul. And what she demands of me, I shall give, for there is no price too great to pay in her sacred service."

They stared at each other, and Indigo knew then that there was nothing more she could say. No words, no reason, would convince Uluye. The priestess's conviction was too strong, her fear too great.

Indigo felt again the stirring deep in her mind, and a sense of shadowy amusement, and on its heels came bitter anger. *Very well,* she thought. *You believe that you have won. We shall see, Lady—we shall see!*

It was, she knew, a perilous and possibly lethal gamble, and if it failed, Yima would pay with her life. But Indigo dared not dwell on that. The risk had to be run. It was her only hope now.

She dropped one hand to her sash and drew out her knife.

"Very well, Uluye," she said quietly. "You're right; I can't sway you. So I concede." She held the knife out, hilt-first. "I offer you this as a token of my capitulation. Take it, and do what you must."

As she spoke, the last livid edge of the sun sank behind the trees. There was a huge, massed intake of breath from the crowd, audible even above the drums and the chanting, and the long, gaunt shadows on the arena merged suddenly to form a pall of gloom. The torches sprang into renewed brilliance as the sky's gory light began to die, and the first pinpoints of stars appeared in the east.

Uluye stepped forward. She took the knife, and for an instant Indigo felt a glimmer of her emotions as, her face unreadable in the torchlight, the High Priestess made a small and perhaps faintly sardonic bow to show that she both acknowledged and accepted the significance of the gift. Then, abruptly, the old, remote arrogance was back, and she turned to her women and made a sharp, canceling gesture.

Their chants ceased, and with a last toneless rattle, the sistrums fell silent. The crowd took some seconds to follow the women's lead, but at last, complete quiet gripped the arena. The atmosphere grew tense and stifling as Uluye began to walk, slowly and with controlled deliberation, across the sand toward the wooden frames. As she drew level with them, Indigo thought she faltered, but the hesitation was so brief that it was impossible to be sure. Then, her shoulders set firmly and her head proudly erect, she stopped at the very edge of the lake and stood motionless.

Grimya, at Indigo's side, watched the High Priestess anxiously. *She is dedicating herself to the Ancestral Lady,* she said. *She is speaking to her in her mind, I think, and asking her blessing. Indigo, what are we to do?*

We must take the chance, Indigo replied. She was trying to quell the thick pounding of her pulse, with little success. *There's nothing else we can say or do to influence her. Our only hope now lies with Uluye herself.*

She probed deeper into her consciousness again, searching for the dark, mocking presence. Oh, yes; the Ancestral Lady was there; still listening, still waiting. Indigo's heart thumped out of rhythm with sick disgust, and she sent a savage message to the dark goddess: *well might you be afraid of being abandoned, madam! You deserve nothing less!*

Uluye had completed her private dedication. As she turned from the shore and took the five paces that would bring her to the first frame, she felt the Ancestral Lady's benediction filling her. She was ready; she had asked for the blessing and the blessing had been given. She had been tempted to stray from her proper path, but she had overcome the temptation, and now the power was in her; she was a cup, a chalice, a vessel brimming with the heady dark wine of the Lady's will.

She reached the first frame. She stood before it, an avatar, an avenger, an executioner, and she raised Indigo's knife high above her head so that the torchlight flashed on the blade as though anticipating the bright slick of blood. There was no ritual to accompany this; it was a stark deed, a solemn deed, and must be done swiftly and in reverent silence.

Uluye tensed the muscles of her arm, summoning the physical and psychic power. Her grip tightened on the hilt. She was ready, this was the moment—

She looked down at Yima's face; a stark mask of light and shadow, beaded with the sweat of terror and the day's heat, looked back at her in silent, hopeless grief.

Suddenly Uluye was paralyzed. She tried to tear her gaze away, but she couldn't move, couldn't even blink. She had steeled herself to see a final appeal in Yima's eyes, to turn a deaf ear to her pleas for mercy. But there *were* no pleas, there *was* no appeal; not even the last glimmering of hope for which she had prepared herself. There was only the sorrow of a child who knew, beyond all doubt, that the one who through all her life had been her sole nurturer and protector had abandoned her utterly.

Still upraised, still clutching the knife in a ferocious grip, Uluye's hands began to shake. She struggled to stop the reflex, but she couldn't do it, and now it was spreading to her arms, to her body, to her legs, shattering the paralysis, driving it out and bringing a wave of uncontrollable panic rolling in its wake.

No! she thought: *No! I must! I must! She has sinned; the punishment has been decreed! I must do the Lady's will! I must!*

And crashing in on her brain came the black despair of certainty. *I can't do it! Lady, strike me down and devour my soul and consign me to the* hushu *if you will, but I can't kill my own beloved child!*

·CHAPTER·XXII·

"Uluye!"

The sound of her own name snapped the High Priestess back to earth, and she stumbled, dropping the knife. As her mind slammed painfully out of its paralysis and into the real world, she saw Indigo, with Grimya at her side, running toward her.

"No!" Uluye shouted hysterically, flinging up both hands, palms outward, to fend Indigo off. "Keep back, don't dare to come *near* me! This is *your* doing, *yours*! You have poisoned me, you have infected my mind and made me an unfit vessel, and now the Lady denies me her strength and her power!"

"Uluye, stop this!" Indigo reached her, took hold of her upper arms and shook her so violently that Uluye's jaw chattered. "*Listen* to me! This has nothing to do with the Ancestral Lady. It's your will, Uluye, *yours*, that denies you the strength to kill Yima."

Uluye stared back at her wildly, and Indigo realized that her words weren't getting through. It was like hurling stones against a solid wall; she simply couldn't break down the barrier and reach the priestess.

Oh, but the Ancestral Lady was laughing now! Indigo could feel the Lady's mirth like a worm eating through her, and suddenly her self-control snapped. She pushed Uluye away, turned and ran back across the arena. Where the sand had been churned by their earlier scuffle, the oracle's crown lay forlorn and discarded. Loathing the thing for what it symbolized, Indigo snatched it up and strode to the lake-shore again. Ignoring Uluye, who still stood rigid but help-less, she ran into the shallows of the lake and held up the crown.

"Here, you craven bitch!" she yelled, her voice cracking with rage and loathing. "Here's the precious symbol of your tyranny and your cowardice! Take it back, you monstrosity, you serpent's spawn, you *murderess*! You're so afraid, aren't you, that you haven't even the courage to show your face; instead, you hide behind your human puppets like a weak-ling child behind its mother's skirts. Here, weakling; here, child—take this, and play your games with it, and I wish you *oblivion*!"

She hurled the crown with all her strength out into the lake. It hit the water with a dull splash and sank. Seconds later a procession of small, sluggish ripples lapped the shore at Indigo's feet. She stared down at them, her lungs heaving and her breath rasping as the storm of fury slowly subsided to a cold, hard core. Then at last she turned and waded out of the water.

Uluye hadn't moved. Her body was rigid as an oak; only her jaw hung slack with shock. Her eyes were blank; she couldn't assimilate what Indigo had done, couldn't bring herself to believe what she had seen and heard. Across the gulf of the arena, the women were staring in silence, as stunned as their leader and as incapable of reacting. Indigo ignored them and strode to where her knife lay in the sand. She picked it up, walked back to the frames.

Yima was staring at her in fearful amazement, but the girl said nothing and made not the smallest movement. She looked the picture of abject helplessness, and Indigo's sympathy for her was suddenly tinged with a faint edge of disgust. Yima was so passive, so weak. Did she believe, somewhere in her heart, that she had earned death?

She thrust the thought down and stepped up to the frame. The knife blade sliced through the ropes at Yima's wrists, ankles and waist. Once, because her hands were shaking with anger, Indigo nicked the girl's flesh, but Yima only continued to stare at her, limp and unmoving, and when the last bonds fell away, Indigo had to shake her and snap her name before, fearfully, the captive at last crept to freedom.

As Yima crouched on the sand, rubbing life back into her arms, Indigo paused briefly to seek in her mind for a reaction from the Ancestral Lady. There was nothing. The presence had gone. She turned to Tiam.

Tiam, at least, had no doubts about his salvation. The instant he was free, he scrambled clear of the frame and ran to Yima's side, pulling her to her feet. Holding her in a close, protective embrace, he turned to Indigo.

"Lady Oracle, how can we ever thank you for our deliverance?" His voice was breathless with emotion. "Your name will live in our hearts for—"

Indigo cut short the flow of words. "There isn't time for that, Tiam, and I don't want it. This isn't over yet by any means. Get Yima away, as far away as possible, *now*." And as he hesitated, "Do it, Tiam. For the Earth Mother's sake, go while there's still some glimmer of a chance for you!"

Her words, or the urgency of her tone, got through to him, and with a quick nod of assent, Tiam started to lead Yima away. The priestesses stared at them as they crossed the arena, but no one made a move to stop them, and for a few moments Indigo almost believed that the crazy ploy would work and that they would simply leave the scene and melt away into the forest without a hand being raised against them. But she'd reckoned without Uluye. The women, who in any case were all trained to take their cue from her, might be too stunned to make the smallest move, but suddenly the High Priestess's voice rang out to break the silence.

"You mindless fools, what do you think you're doing? Stop them!"

Her cry broke the hiatus, and suddenly there was a babble of voices and a surge forward as the priestesses awoke to what was happening. Tiam saw them and began to run, pulling Yima with him. Uluye started after them across the sand; others hastened to intercept them.

Then, from the far side of the arena, came a shrill scream of unfettered terror.

Quarry and pursuers alike came to a chaotic halt and heads turned wildly, looking for the source of the dreadful cry. Then another shriek went up, and a third, and a man's howl of fear—and suddenly there was pandemonium as a whole section of the crowd saw the dim shapes that were emerging from the forest.

Six of them . . . eight . . . ten . . . a dozen . . . shambling, shuffling, their heads wagging mindlessly and their arms reaching out, the *hushu* closed in on the throng. Indigo saw Uluye cast a horrified glance over her shoulder and knew, even before she too turned her head, that more of the horrors were coming at them from behind. They advanced in a slow but steady line, and her stomach turned over with fearful nausea as she realized that the monstrosities were moving in formation, as though some grim intelligence had taken hold of their dead brains and was coordinating them into a single, hideous entity, with one common purpose.

Around her, the scene was erupting into mayhem as more and more of the onlookers realized what was afoot. The air shuddered with screams and yells, and panicking masses of people ran in every direction, even those who didn't yet know the cause of the terror fighting and flailing against their neighbors to get away. Indigo saw a woman and two children trampled as the mass of humanity closest to the arena, and therefore to the danger, strove to push its way through to the crowd's edge and flee. One man, insane with terror, snatched a torch from its tall pole and slashed the blazing brand into the face of anyone in his path.

Still the *hushu* came on—but as the first and more fortunate of the throng burst from the press and fled away into the forest, Indigo realized suddenly that the ghouls had no interest in them. Indeed, she could see now that the huge, swaying mass was breaking up as more and more people got away from the arena. The *hushu* were ignoring them; she even glimpsed one of the horrors crash to the ground as a panic-stricken mob barreled past it into the trees, and none of its fellows so much as paused, although the running figures were within easy reach. And suddenly Indigo realized why. . . .

As though a huge hand had slapped her face, her mind jolted into clear, harsh reason. At her side, Grimya, infected by the mass horror, was barking and snarling furiously, her hackles bristling and her eyes feral; Indigo whirled and dropped to a crouch, grabbing her muzzle and shouting into her face. "Grimya! Grimya, listen to me! This is the Ancestral Lady's doing—we must find Uluye!"

The arena was now like a scene from a nightmare. The last glimmer of light in the sky had gone, and the only illumination was from the cold stars and the few torches that hadn't either been taken as weapons or knocked from their poles and trampled out, so that it was all but impossible to recognize man from woman, or human being from living corpse, in the shadowy chaos. But the cries of the villagers were diminishing as more of them made their escape. Only a few stragglers remained now—and thirty or forty others, unconscious or dead, who lay prone on the sand or in the undergrowth at the forest's edge.

Priestesses were milling everywhere, some wailing and crying, others making at least some attempt to gather both their wits and their friends, and at last Indigo glimpsed Uluye's tall figure near the lake. She was trying to rally her women around her, and her voice, raw and hoarse, cut through the clash of noise.

"Uluye!" Indigo started to forge through the crowd toward her, and as she approached, she saw with a shock that the first of the *hushu* were only yards away. With Grimya snapping at ankles and flying skirts to clear their path, she reached the High Priestess and grabbed hold of her arm.

Uluye spun around. For a moment she seemed not to recognize Indigo; then, as though her arrival had acted as a catalyst, Uluye jerked her arm free and covered her face with her hands.

"What have I done?" she moaned. "Lady, forgive me; *what have I brought upon us?*"

"You've done nothing!" Indigo shouted. "This isn't your fault, Uluye. It's the Ancestral Lady's; it's her attempt to cow us and break us."

Uluye shook her head, the ropes of her hair flying wildly. "We're lost!" she cried. "They will kill us all. This is the Lady's judgment on me!"

"No! It isn't you she wants vengeance on, it's me. Uluye, listen, *listen*! There must be a way to destroy the *hushu*. How can it be done? Tell me!" *Earth Mother,* she thought, *she's beyond reach, she's helpless*. Then, in the midst of frantic despair, Indigo saw again in her mind the silver-haloed eyes, and heard in her head the echoes of triumphant laughter. . . .

"Oh, you *demon*!" She screamed the words at the full pitch of her lungs and saw Uluye start in shock. But Uluye didn't matter now. This, Indigo thought, this was between herself and the Ancestral Lady. And she would not be bested!

She broke through the circle of terrified women around the High Priestess. As she burst clear, she saw before her, not fifteen feet away, the unhallowed square where the bodies of Shalune and Inuss still awaited their gruesome final fate. Even in the throes of panic, no one had dared to touch the four brands that burned there, and beyond their smoking glare, Indigo saw the grim figures of the *hushu*, still approaching, still moving with an air of dire, mindless purpose. The two ranks were closing on the arena, drawing in like a net surrounding a shoal of fish.

The last of the villagers had escaped now and were gone, but the priestesses were trapped, and their terror was rising as they milled about and herded into a tight crowd on the sand. Indigo knew, though, that the *hushu* were no more interested in them than they had been in the fleeing onlookers. She herself was their goal, the target on which the eyes of this army of the undead were so unwaveringly fixed. And this, she knew, was the final test.

Grimya! she communicated urgently. *The spear that Uluye used when she tried to kill me—find it and bring it to me, quickly!*

As the wolf raced away, Indigo's mind roiled; she could feel a massive surge of energy rising in her, and she took hold of it with all of her strength. *Power—yes, Lady, I have power, and it's greater than yours, because the demon called fear no longer holds me!*

She ran forward, ran to the square and cut the nearest of the torches free from its pole. The first of the *hushu* were no more than five paces from her now, so close that she could see every detail of their ruined faces and decaying bodies. They hesitated as they saw the torch in her hand, then came on.

Indigo's eyes turned black, and around them an ice-cold silver corona flared into life. *Silver for Nemesis—my own dark twin, but it no longer holds me in its thrall. I don't fear you or your legions, Mistress of the Dead!*

The power came to life in her, and the torch in her hand exploded into a towering column of silver fire. Thin, whistling sounds of alarm or anger came from the throats of the *hushu*, and Indigo spun around.

Uluye stood alone in front of the wailing, praying mass of her women, her figure stark in the brilliance from the brand that Indigo held.

"Uluye!" Indigo's voice seared through the babble. "Help me now! Help me to kill the *hushu*!"

Uluye couldn't tear her gaze from the burning stars that Indigo's eyes had become. "I can't!" she cried hoarsely. "They can't be killed, it's impossible!"

Indigo shook her head. "They *can* die! You only believe

it's impossible, because you've always been too afraid to try!''

Grimya came running back to her side, dragging the spear with her; with a quick movement, Indigo bent to grasp the haft. ''Help me, Uluye!'' she exhorted again. ''Use the strength and the power your goddess gave you, and end your people's thrall and the *hushu*'s miserable existence!''

She turned again, raising the torch in one hand and the spear in the other. Two steps from her, dead eyes stared back with a hollow glare as the silver light was flung full on the body of the advancing ghoul. The *hushu* raised its arms jerkily as though to embrace her, and its half-rotted jaw dropped open in a ghastly parody of a welcoming smile. Indigo took aim and thrust the spear straight at the misshapen head, plunging it through the brittle cranium and deep into the skull.

The *hushu* shrieked. It was an awful, yet piteous, sound, like the scream of a small animal. For one instant it seemed that a spark of human intelligence returned to the *hushu*'s nacreous eyes as the twisted brain inside the skull, the seat and source of its life within death, was cloven, and in the look was understanding, gratitude and joy. Then slowly, almost gently, the body of the ghoul folded and collapsed to lie still and silent on the ground.

With a convulsive jerk, Indigo pulled the spear free and turned again to Uluye and her women.

''Now do you see?'' she called to them. ''They *can* die! Help me, Uluye. Rally your women, take your spears and your machetes and free yourselves from fear of the *hushu*. In the name of your own goddess, give them peace!''

Uluye stared at her, transfixed. The priestesses' prayers and pleas had subsided into shocked silence, but as Indigo and their leader continued to gaze at each other, a muttering, a whispering, arose gradually from their huddled ranks.

''She killed it . . . she slew the *hushu*. Power . . . power . . . an avatar, a true avatar. She can kill them. . . .''

Behind her, Indigo knew, the *hushu* had halted. The Ancestral Lady was waiting; waiting to see what her servants would do, which way they would turn, whether they would find the courage within themselves to do as Indigo urged them. Indigo held Uluye's gaze. She dared do nothing now; the High Priestess must make the first move.

At last, trembling, Uluye did move. She reached out behind her, her fingers splaying in a gesture to her followers. A woman ran forward, carrying a spear; Uluye took it. Still watching Indigo as though mesmerized, she began to walk forward. Indigo stepped aside as she approached, and Uluye stopped before another of the now motionless *hushu*. Her jaw clenched; she struck—and again there was the whistling cry, the moment of release, before the ghoul dropped limply to the ground.

Shaking, Uluye turned to Indigo. Her face bore a look of wonder, and her eyes glowed with the light of revelation. "You have come among us . . . ." she whispered; then, before Indigo could react, she turned to the assembled priestesses, raising the stained spear high above her head.

"The Lady is with us!" she yelled. "She has shown us the truth and shown us the way; she blesses us! Lady—oh Lady, you are our beloved goddess!" And she fell to one knee and, arms outspread, made the ritual gesture of the cult's deepest obeisance; the obeisance of a priestess to her deity.

Indigo was stunned. And as the High Priestess's palms touched the ground, a titanic voice boomed shatteringly out across the arena.

"NO! I AM YOUR GODDESS! TRAITORS AND BLASPHEMERS, *I AM YOUR GODDESS!*"

The surface of the lake had turned to silver. Rising from it like smoke from a forest fire, a dark mist boiled and seethed. Shapes writhed in the mist, unnameable, hideous, and at its heart, above the lake's center, a huge black column wavered like the lethal head of a tornado.

The priestesses cried out, cowering and groveling, and Uluye looked in horror and confusion at Indigo. The transformation, and the show of power, had convinced her that Indigo *was* the Ancestral Lady, or at the very least, her avatar, and that the goddess had been speaking and acting through her. Now, though, she realized her mistake and began to shudder, backing away from Indigo; and as she did so, the giant voice spoke again, shaking the air.

"IS THIS THE WAY YOU SHOW YOUR LOVE FOR ME? DO YOU *DARE* TO TURN YOUR FACES AND GIVE FEALTY TO ANOTHER? AH, MY VENGEANCE UPON YOU SHALL BE DIRE—DIRE AND EVERLASTING!"

Uluye covered her head with her arms as though to ward off a rain of blows and started to scream. As she collapsed to the ground and her women fell to their knees, wailing, Indigo turned and ran to the lake's edge. Her voice was puny in the wake of the Ancestral Lady's vast wrath, but she yelled with all her strength, gesturing violently toward the swaying column.

"No! You fool, you blind, frightened fool! They don't worship me; they worship *you*! They haven't turned from you—they believed I *was* you!"

The reply dinned in her ears. "YOU ARE LYING, ORACLE! YOU SOUGHT TO TAKE MY PLACE AND WREST THEM FROM MY GRASP!"

"I did no such thing!" Indigo threw a swift glance over her shoulder and saw that Uluye was getting to her feet. The High Priestess began to stumble toward the other women, and Indigo realized what she intended to do. It was mad, it was insane—and it was shattering proof that Uluye truly loved her goddess and would continue to love her, no matter what horrors the Ancestral Lady might inflict on all of them.

Indigo turned again to the lake, and shouted, "Don't you see them? Don't you see what your High Priestess is doing, don't you *understand*? They don't want to turn their faces from you! Listen to them!"

Unsteadily, struggling to find a true tone, Uluye had begun to sing. It was a song Indigo had come to know well during her time in the citadel: a hymn of praise to the Lady, a promise of obedience and a declaration of love. One by one, the women began to join in as her example gave them confidence—or as desperation drove them—and the hymn rose quaveringly on the air.

"Do you hear them?" Indigo cried.

"I HEAR THEM. BUT IT IS TOO LATE. MY ANGER MUST BE APPEASED, AND MY SERVANTS MUST PAY THE PRICE. THEY SHALL DO PENANCE FOR THEIR DEFIANCE, AND THEY SHALL LEARN TO FEAR ME!"

"But they have done you no wrong!" Indigo screamed back. "What crime have they committed? What sin?"

"MY HIGH PRIESTESS HAS FAILED IN HER DUTY. HER CHILD TURNED HER FACE FROM MY SERVICE, YET ULUYE DID NOT EXACT THE PUNISHMENT THAT I DECREED FOR HER. THE FAILURE OF ONE IS THE FAILURE OF ALL."

Suddenly the silver light on the lake's surface blazed dazzlingly, and the Ancestral Lady's huge voice took on a new and doubly ominous note. "ULUYE. SILENCE YOUR WOMEN AND FACE ME."

The chant collapsed into chaos before lapsing into a dreadful silence. Shuffling, shambling, with no more will than a *hushu*, Uluye took three paces forward; then her nerve failed, and she sank to her knees on the sand.

"YOU HAVE DONE WRONG, ULUYE," the voice intoned cruelly. "I MADE MY WILL KNOWN TO YOU, BUT YOU DID NOT OBEY ME. YET THE PRICE MUST STILL BE PAID. WHO WILL PAY IT NOW? WILL YOU TAKE THE PENANCE UPON YOUR OWN SHOULDERS, OR SHALL I SEND *HUSHU* TO REND YOUR WOMEN'S BODIES, AND NIGHTMARES TO PLAGUE THEIR MINDS? MY JUSTICE IS SURE, AND YOU CANNOT ESCAPE IT. CHOOSE, ULUYE. YOU KNOW IN YOUR HEART WHAT THE PAYMENT IS TO BE. *CHOOSE*."

For several seconds Uluye stayed utterly still. Then, unsteadily but unflinchingly, she rose slowly to her feet.

"Sweet Lady." Her voice was barely more than a whis-

per, but it carried chillingly in the sudden stillness that
gripped the arena. "I stand alone before you. I am your
servant, but I have failed in your service. Mine is the fault,
and mine is the just and rightful punishment. I am not fit
to ask your mercy; I am not worthy to hope for your for-
giveness. I only pray that my penance may serve for us all,
and that my sisters may live in hope of profiting from the
knowledge of my fate, to earn once again your love, which
is the fount of our existence."

And silently, urgently, in Indigo's mind, Grimya cried
out, *Indigo! She has a knife!*

With a huge mental jolt, Indigo's mind snapped back to
reality, and she realized to her horror that she herself had
momentarily become ensnared in the Ancestral Lady's web,
mesmerized by the supernatural voice, caught up in the confrontation between the goddess and her High Priestess. Only
now did she realize what Uluye meant to do—and at the
same instant, she knew that no words she could utter would
sway the Ancestral Lady now. She had lost. Fear, the demon fear, had conquered.

No, she thought, *no! It can't be! I can't fail, there's another way, a greater power—*

In her mind, a hollow voice was laughing. In her inner
vision, eyes like coals wreathed in silver flame glared with
ice and fire. And a hundred, a thousand, ten thousand voices
cried out to her: *"we are her . . . she is us. help her . . .
help us, Indigo—Indigo—"*

*Indigo. Indigo, Anghara, Nemesis, wolf, emissary, ava-
tar, goddess.* Suddenly she seemed to be in five places at
once: she was Indigo, watching in horror as Uluye raised
the knife high in both hands; she was Grimya, transfixed
and helpless; she was Uluye, gazing up with dread at the
blade she held above her own head, yet too consumed with
the desire to please her goddess to stay her hand; and, too,
she was back in the dark underworld, with the dead clam-
oring around her; and she was the Ancestral Lady herself,
a whirling pillar of smoke, a voice from a silver lake, a tiny,
wizened creature cowering in the dark and too afraid to

show herself lest she lose her grip on the devotion of her
human followers. All these things she was, and more. And
the fear that imprisoned each of them was a writhing worm
beneath her feet.

She looked deep within her heart, within her soul, and
she understood. She had learned a greater lesson in the underworld than the Ancestral Lady knew; greater even than
she herself had known until this moment. She needed no
avatar to show her the way, or to mediate between her own
soul and the true power that lay behind life and death, the
power that was the love encompassing them both. She *was*
an avatar. She was the Earth Mother's child, and if the Ancestral Lady's being held the spark of godhood, so did her
own being. She was sister to the Ancestral Lady, as to a
thousand thousand others like her. But while the Mistress
of the Dead feared for her place in the scheme of things,
the entity who was called Indigo had accepted and embraced it. That was the difference between them. And of
the two, she was the stronger now.

Indigo reached out to the angry, mocking, terrified image
in her mind, and she took control of it. Her eyes snapped
open, and they were eyes like coals, wreathed in silver
flame, glaring with ice and fire. She looked across the arena
to where Uluye stood alone.

The knife blade hung above the High Priestess's heart.
Uluye gazed on the world for what she believed was the last
time; then her eyes closed and her words echoed to the
citadel and the forest as she cried out, proudly and strongly:
"For my Lady's sake, I am glad to die!"

And from the place where Indigo had stood, a new voice
spoke.

"CEASE." It was as gentle, yet as powerful, as a calm
sea, and it filled the arena, filled the minds of all who heard
it, like liquid light. Above the lake, the black column shuddered as though a gale had struck it. On the arena, a host
of dark, frightened eyes turned. . . .

The figure that stood on the sand was not Indigo—or if
it was, then Indigo was no longer wholly human, but some-

thing far, far greater. A golden aura burned around her, as if the sun had just risen from darkness at her back. A cloak of sky and earth and water and fire flowed from her shoulders, and her hair was a shimmering cascade of all those colors and more, flowing, merging, *living*. Only her face was unchanged. And her eyes—

Her eyes were the black eyes of the Ancestral Lady, and the milky golden eyes of the emissary who had set her on her quest, and the silver eyes of Nemesis, and the amber eyes of a wolf, and the blue-violet eyes of a woman who had known love and seen death, and who, after half a century of wandering, still strove to understand. Uluye's knife fell from her fingers. The priestesses, as one, sank to their knees.

And from the misty tower of darkness that hung over the heart of the lake came a thin, fearful wailing, like the cry of a child waking in the night and finding itself alone.

The being that was Indigo turned. Behind her, in the ritual square, three torches still guttered, though now their light was a pale reflection of the light that blazed around her. Beyond them, the *hushu* waited. Indigo felt their ruined minds, their pain, their misery, the hope that still clung like smoke lingering when all else had burned away; and she pitied them.

She raised her hands. "GO," she said. "YOU CAN BE AT PEACE NOW."

In her head, a voice, pleading, despairing: *no, no, no, they are mine, you cannot—*

WHAT NEED DO YOU HAVE OF SUCH PITIFUL SLAVES? RELEASE THEM, LET THEM COME TO YOU AT LAST, AND WELCOME THEM.

There was a sigh, as soft as a summer breeze across the great southern tundra. One by one, as the power, as the freedom, flowed to them from Indigo and from the dark goddess whose will she held within her own, the *hushu* dropped to the ground. Indigo felt the bittersweet moment as their hunger and their thirst were finally slaked and their broken minds departed from the mortal shell, and she smiled for them and wanted to laugh for them as she felt them merge with something that perhaps might be named *eternity*. Then, as the aura about her blazed anew, she turned and looked back at Uluye and her women.

The High Priestess was weeping. She didn't truly understand; Indigo knew that even as she began to walk toward Uluye's sobbing figure. What she saw before her was what she had longed, had *ached* to see: the pivot of her life, the touchstone of her existence. Indigo drew closer, and Uluye, as her women had done before her, sank to her knees in the sand.

"Sweet Lady . . ." Her voice cracked with emotion. "You have shown mercy to the damned. Will you not show mercy to us, who love you more than life? We are yours, Lady, and we want nothing more than to serve you."

In Indigo's mind there came an agonized cry: *They are leaving me! I am lost, I am lost!*

NO. Indigo turned toward the lake and saw that the great column of darkness was breaking apart. The surface of the water boiled, the silver mirror shattering, and she felt a surge of pain and fear as, like her High Priestess, the Ancestral Lady wept.

NO, MADAM. And suddenly the water was still again. *I HAVE NO WISH TO STEAL FROM YOU YOUR RIGHTFUL PLACE IN THIS WORLD. MY ONLY DESIRE IS TO DESTROY THE DEMON THAT HAS BOUND YOU.*

The lake shimmered; Indigo felt a great shudder run through her, and a piteous voice echoed in her mind. *If that were only true. . . .*

IT IS TRUE, she said. *THEY LOVE YOU. LOOK INTO ULUYE'S HEART AND ACCEPT WHAT YOU FIND THERE. DON'T FEAR HER, LADY. DON'T FEAR THAT SHE AND HER KINDRED WILL TURN AWAY AND FORGET YOU. THEY ARE YOURS. DO THEY NOT DESERVE TO HAVE YOUR LOVE, AS YOU HAVE THEIRS?*

A chill breeze danced across the lake and set tiny ripples in motion. *I love them. Yes, I love them. But how can a mother hope to hold her children?*

The being that was Indigo, human and animal and goddess, smiled with ineffable sadness. *OH, LADY, A MOTHER DOES NOT NEED TO HOLD HER CHILDREN, FOR THEY WILL ALWAYS COME BACK, AND THEY WILL ALWAYS TURN TO HER AT LAST. YOU ARE THE GUARDIAN AND KEEPER OF THEIR SOULS, AND YOUR PLACE IS AN HONORED PLACE AMONG THE AVATARS OF SHE WHO IS MOTHER OF US ALL. BREAK THE SHACKLES THAT YOUR FEAR HAS CREATED; CAST THEM OFF, AND COME TO THOSE WHO LOVE YOU. COME TO THEM, MISTRESS OF THE DEAD. GRANT THEM THEIR HEART'S DESIRE, AND SHOW THEM WHAT YOU TRULY ARE!*

She felt it, she felt the power, the love, the comradeship, the *oneness*, and her voice, blending with a thousand voices, rang out across the night.

"IN THE EARTH MOTHER'S NAME, I ASK YOU, ANCESTRAL LADY, TO SHOW YOURSELF TO YOUR CHILDREN!"

The column of darkness, the tornado at the lake's heart, flickered—and vanished. For a moment the silver mirror of the surface was utterly still; then a slow march of ripples began to flow outward from the center. They lapped at the edge of the lake with a tiny, gentle sound, one after another after another. And at their source, something rose from beneath the water.

The black boat came slowly toward the shore, sculled by the figure who stood in the stern, cowled in mist and darkness. Uluye, kneeling on the sand, watched in breathless silence as it drew closer. Tears still stained her cheeks, but her eyes were like a child's eyes, wondering and enthralled, and her hands clenched and unclenched spasmodically, as though she longed to reach out to the approaching vision, but didn't dare.

The boat grounded, and the Ancestral Lady shipped her oar. She didn't move.

"MADAM." The voice that had once been Indigo's voice spoke softly. "WILL YOU NOT COME TO US?"

The Ancestral Lady's head was bowed, and her reply came small and sad to Indigo's mind from beneath the shrouding dark hair. *To show myself as I truly am? Ah, sister, you are cruel!*

Indigo didn't answer at once, but her shining figure walked forward to the lake's edge and halted before the boat's prow. Still the dark form in the stern didn't move, and at last, silently, Indigo spoke again.

LADY, LOOK AT ME.

Slowly the Ancestral Lady raised her head. Through the cascade of black hair, the face of a tiny, wizened old woman with filmy eyes gazed back at Indigo with intense misery. The sunken mouth trembled, and the Lady said: *This is what I am. This is what fear has made me. You showed me the truth, sister, but in doing so, you have made me unworthy of my people's love.*

Indigo felt a warm surge of sympathy, and with it a sudden deep sense of fellowship. At the heart of the greater mind with which her own mind had blended, power moved like a great tide, and she held out a shimmering hand.

NO, she said gently. *YOU ARE WORTHY. COME, AND TAKE WHAT IS RIGHTLY YOURS.*

The Ancestral Lady took a step toward her and, uncertainly, reached out. In the moment before their fingers touched, she saw another face mirrored in Indigo's face, other eyes that were black and silver and gold and brown and blue and green, changing and changing, yet always filled with light. Then the contact was made. . . .

Indigo felt the shock, fire and ice together, a shudder like an earthquake that began in the depths of her being and flowed through her and from her to the dark figure in the boat. For a shattering instant, they became one, and suddenly Indigo knew what it was to be mistress of the underworld, Mistress of the Dead, guardian of souls; and a thousand thousand voices rang in her mind: *we are her, she is us, we are one, free, free, free—*

She gave of herself, gave of the power within her. Light erupted from the Ancestral Lady's figure: a shining, silver aura that lit the arena, lit the night, with the brilliance of a rising full moon. The Mistress of the Dead raised her head, and her black lips laughed with joy, and her white and beautiful face was the timeless face of a goddess; and her eyes, like dark stars, but filled with life, turned their gaze upon her worshipers, and she cried out, spreading her arms wide as though to embrace them all:

"MY CHILDREN!"

Indigo saw Uluye and her women rising, but even as they gained their feet, even as they rushed forward to meet their beloved Lady, a huge darkness seemed to implode on her. The world spun; vision and sound faded, swelled, faded again, as Indigo's senses reeled; and the power was leaving her, streaming from her, collapsing—

She heard Grimya's mental voice in her head—*Indigo! Indigo!*—and felt the wolf's presence racing toward her. Her legs wouldn't support her; she spun, feeling nothing, helpless, her last strength fleeing.

And in the moment before she fell in a dead faint to the ground, she heard Yima's quavering voice, like a bird's cry in the imploding dark: "Mother? Oh, Mother!"

·CHAPTER·XXIII·

She had been conscious during that last hour on the sand, but in a remote and separated way, as though she were watching events from a vast distance in time as well as in space. She could still remember the women's singing; she heard it in her dreams, a silver thread running through the mists of sleep. In her dreams, too, she often relived the moment of the Ancestral Lady's departure, as the shining figure sculled its boat out into the lake once more while the priestesses chanted a final ecstasy of praise.

At their goddess's command, they had extinguished the torches and cast aside the amulets in the square of the *hushu*, and had solemnly lifted up the bodies of Shalune and Inuss and carried them to the boat where it rocked beside the shore. Then they had sung another song that was both a dirge for the dead women and a hymn of thanksgiving that the sins of Shalune and Inuss—that had been no sins at all— were forgiven and that the two were no longer condemned to roam the forests as hungering *hushu*, but would serve the Ancestral Lady in her realm.

No more retribution; no more *hushu*; no more ghouls and

dark spirits to plague the living. The Ancestral Lady's boat had sunk down into the lake, into the world below the lake, and she was gone from her worshipers' sight; but her promise had remained. The demon fear was conquered: the vengeful terrors of the night would be no more.

And Indigo wished bitterly with all her heart that the promise had been kept.

She shifted her position, pushing aside some of the offerings that were heaped inside her cave and turning it into some kind of treasure house. Food and clothing, ornaments, fetishes, carvings, implements . . . gifts from grateful priestesses and wide-eyed, wonder-struck villagers; gifts that half their donors couldn't afford but which they must, *must* make to the light-skinned stranger who had become their oracle and who had had the power to summon the Ancestral Lady from her dark realm to bless her people. Gifts for one who, in their eyes, was little less than a goddess herself; gifts for one they revered. And already the borderline between reverence and fear was beginning to blur.

It hadn't taken long before the first signs began to show. They had carried her back to her cave, and there she had slept for three days, her mind, body and soul exhausted by the events of that momentous night. She had wakened at last to find that she was a heroine, but more, *far* more than that. Though they agreed obediently with her when she told them that she was not an oracle, and not the Ancestral Lady's chosen avatar, she knew that their acquiescence went no deeper than words and gestures intended only to please her. In their hearts it was not so, could never be so, and for Indigo, that had been the first indication that, though they had learned to love her, they also feared her.

Then there was Uluye. Uluye could not change. Oh, she and Yima had been reconciled, and Uluye had given her blessing to Yima and Tiam, the blessing that the Ancestral Lady had sanctioned and sanctified, but already she was seeking out a new candidate to take on her mantle in years to come, another girl to be taken and nurtured and trained to her mold; and she would rule her new protégée's life as she had ruled the life of her daughter. And the nightly lake-side ritual . . . that, too, had been at Uluye's behest. At first it had been her decision to continue the nightly patrol-ling of the lake, with its torches and chanting and the rattling of sistrums, simply as a mark of reverence to the Lady, an expression of the cult's gratitude. So they had sung, and they had danced, and they had made the offerings.

But the nature of the offerings was taking on a sinister tinge. Charms against this or that were beginning to be cast to the lake among the simpler gifts of food; and twice in the last seven days, humble delegations had come from nearby villages, and there had been whispered consulta-tions, and on the nights following their visits, new hex am-ulets had joined the offerings given to the Ancestral Lady. Slowly, insidiously, the old ways were beginning to reassert themselves.

Indigo had tried to warn them, but she knew already that her efforts were doomed to failure. They listened to her; oh, they *listened* to her; but they didn't truly *hear*, for to them, she was not quite mortal, not quite human, and there-fore not quite real.

She could have changed matters. All she needed to do was don the oracle's feathered cloak again and take her place on the oracle's chair in the temple on the ziggurat summit. Then they would have listened, and they would have obeyed her every word. She could have usurped Uluye's power, set herself above the highest of High Priestesses, *ruled*. And that, Indigo knew, would have been the worst choice of all.

The curtain over the cave's door shuddered suddenly, and Grimya came in. Only one small lamp was alight in its wall niche, and in the dim glow, the wolf's eyes shone like em-bers.

"I think they are all as-leep now," she said softly. "The night ritual is over, and there has been no movement below for some time." She paused. "Are you rrready?"

"Yes." Indigo climbed to her feet and gathered up the packs that lay close by her side. It felt strange to be wearing

her old clothes again instead of the robes that she'd grown
accustomed to during her stay here; they felt strange and
unfamiliar. She looked around at the cave, at the piled gifts,
and felt a painful blend of sadness and bitterness well within
her.

Still, she thought, *there is so much fear. The demon might
have died within me, but for them, it is still alive. I think it
always will be . . . and I'm so sorry that there was no more
I could do.*

She'd take nothing from among the offerings; not even
one small souvenir. In fact, she had something to leave behind, a gift for the Ancestral Lady. What the dark goddess
would make of it, she didn't know, but perhaps it would
serve her in her turn. And it was of no use to Indigo now.
It had played its part in her life, but its time was done.

She wondered what the women would think when they
found her gone. Would they guess at the truth, or would
they believe that the oracle and her companion had been
spirited away, called perhaps to the greater service of the
Ancestral Lady? In a way, she hoped so, for it might ensure
that they would forget her all the sooner.

She blew out the lamp. The cave sank into darkness, and
Indigo and Grimya stepped out onto the ledge. The night
was clear and fine; stars glittered in the velvet sky, and the
half-moon was just beginning to rise above the trees' dark
silhouettes. The lake below was still, like a great pewter
shield cast down and abandoned in the forest by some careless warrior. The citadel and the arena were silent. Somewhere a bird chattered with a sound like mad human
laughter.

Indigo put one hand to her throat and grasped the thong
that held the lodestone in its bag around her neck. The old
leather was brittle with age; it snapped easily, and she held
the bag in her hand. She didn't want to look at the stone,
not even for one last time. She didn't want to see what it
would tell her, for her mind was made up and nothing would
sway her now.

She threw stone and bag and thong together out and away

in the direction of the lake. They spun, turning, turning, just visible in the moonlight and starlight—and then a tiny glitter broke the lake's smoothness momentarily as they struck the water far below.

This is my own small offering to you, madam, she thought. *Accept it as a token of my gratitude, for you showed me that the thing I feared above all else had no foundation. Fenran is alive, and I believe I can find him. Nothing else matters to me now, and I thank you for setting me on this path.*

There was no answering stirring in her mind, as she had known there could not be. The link was broken. Yet, Indigo thought, something of the Ancestral Lady would always live within her from now on, a legacy of the avatar within her own being, the avatar that had awakened here and that had known, briefly, what it was to be a goddess.

She looked down at Grimya and felt the warm, loving surge of the wolf's mind as she gazed back. Grimya understood what lay behind this last gesture, and wherever Indigo led, she would follow. Indigo couldn't find the words, or even the thoughts, to express what she felt, but she bent briefly to stroke the top of Grimya's head.

Then she shouldered her packs, and as quietly as two cloud shadows passing across the face of the moon, they moved together toward the stairs and toward the forest that waited for them beyond the sleeping citadel.

FANTASY BY
LOUISE COOPER

☐	53401-8 NEMESIS: INDIGO #1	$3.95
☐	50246-9 INFERNO: INDIGO #2	$3.95
☐	50667-7 INFANTA: INDIGO #3.	$4.95
☐	50798-3 NOCTURNE: INDIGO #4	$4.95
☐	53392-5 THE INITIATE	$2.95
☐	53397-6 MIRAGE	$3.95

FANTASY BESTSELLERS
FROM TOR

☐	55852-9	ARIOSTO	$3.95
☐	55853-7	*Chelsea Quinn Yarbro*	Canada $4.95
☐	53671-1	THE DOOR INTO FIRE	$2.95
☐	53672-X	*Diane Duane*	Canada $3.50
☐	53673-8	THE DOOR INTO SHADOW	$2.95
☐	53674-6	*Diane Duane*	Canada $3.50
☐	55750-6	ECHOES OF VALOR	$2.95
☐	55751-4	*edited by Karl Edward Wagner*	Canada $3.95
☐	51181-6	THE EYE OF THE WORLD	$5.95
☐		*Robert Jordan*	Canada $6.95
☐	53388-7	THE HIDDEN TEMPLE	$3.95
☐	53389-5	*Catherine Cooke*	Canada $4.95
☐	55446-9	MOONSINGER'S FRIENDS	$3.50
☐	55447-7	*edited by Susan Shwartz*	Canada $4.50
☐	55515-5	THE SHATTERED HORSE	$3.95
☐	55516-3	*S.P. Somtow*	Canada $4.95
☐	50249-3	SISTER LIGHT, SISTER DARK	$3.95
☐	50250-7	*Jane Yolen*	Canada $4.95
☐	54348-3	SWORDSPOINT	$3.95
☐	54349-1	*Ellen Kushner*	Canada $4.95
☐	53293-7	THE VAMPIRE TAPESTRY	$2.95
☐	53294-5	*Suzie McKee Charnas*	Canada $3.95

Buy them at your local bookstore or use this handy coupon:
Clip and mail this page with your order.

Publishers Book and Audio Mailing Service
P.O. Box 120159, Staten Island, NY 10312-0004

Please send me the book(s) I have checked above. I am enclosing $ _____
(Please add $1.25 for the first book, and $.25 for each additional book to cover postage and handling.
Send check or money order only—no CODs.)

Name _____

Address _____

City _____ State/Zip _____

Please allow six weeks for delivery. Prices subject to change without notice.

MORE BESTSELLING
FANTASY FROM TOR

☐ ☐	50556-5	THE BEWITCHMENTS OF LOVE AND HATE *Storm Constantine*	$4.95 Canada $5.95
☐ ☐	50554-9	THE ENCHANTMENTS OF FLESH AND SPIRIT *Storm Constantine*	$3.95 Canada $4.95
☐ ☐	54600-8	THE FLAME KEY *Robert E. Vardeman*	$2.95 Canada $3.95
☐ ☐	54606-7	KEY OF ICE AND STEEL *Robert E. Vardeman*	$3.50 Canada $4.50
☐ ☐	53239-2	SCHIMMELHORN'S GOLD *Reginald Bretnor*	$ 2.95 Canada $ 3.75
☐ ☐	54602-4	THE SKELETON LORD'S KEY *Robert E. Vardeman*	$2.95 Canada $3.95
☐ ☐	55825-1	SNOW WHITE AND ROSE RED *Patricia C. Wrede*	$3.95 Canada $4.95
☐ ☐	55350-0	THE SWORDSWOMAN *Jessica Amanda Salmonson*	$3.50 Canada $4.50
☐ ☐	54402-1	THE UNICORN DILEMMA *John Lee*	$3.95 Canada $4.95
☐ ☐	54400-5	THE UNICORN QUEST *John Lee*	$2.95 Canada $3.50
☐ ☐	50907-2	WHITE JENNA *Jane Yolen*	$3.95 Canada $4.95

Buy them at your local bookstore or use this handy coupon:
Clip and mail this page with your order.

Publishers Book and Audio Mailing Service
P.O. Box 120159, Staten Island, NY 10312-0004

Please send me the book(s) I have checked above. I am enclosing $ _____
(please add $1.25 for the first book, and $.25 for each additional book to cover postage and handling.
Send check or money order only—no CODs).

Name _____
Address _____
City _____ State/Zip _____
Please allow six weeks for delivery. Prices subject to change without notice.